Under A Montana Sky

Published by A Witch and a Woodsman LLC

First edition

ISBN: 979-8-9902635-2-9(ebook), 979-8-9902635-0-5(Paperback), 979-8-9902635-1-2(Hardback)

Library of Congress Cataloging-in-Publication data is available

Cover art by Rae ane Jules Studios

Interior art by Misti Flick

Editing by Misti Flick

UNDER A MONTANA SKY

Ivy M. Young

For Donald, the man who claimed me as his second wild daughter. You told me I could achieve anything that I set my mind to. From letting me write when I should have been working, to making it a point to ask me about my old rodeo days and friends to refresh my memory. Everything you did for me always made my days brighter than I think you will ever know they did. We miss you more every day, but we know you're keeping our Cleo company waiting for us.

"So, have you killed anyone new yet?"

RIP Dad

To Pam, who became so close to us you were a grandmother to Sammy in more ways than one. You'll never understand just how much we all miss you. But you'd be so happy to know your daughter has been welcomed among us. She's riding horses, and learning so fast, we're all extremely proud of her.

RIP

Playlist

The full playlist is UaMS by Harley Quinn Fones on Spotify.

Some Girls Do- Sawyer Brown

Black- Dierks Bentley

Rest in Peace- Taylor Austin Dye

The Way I Do- Madeleine Kelson

You are my Sunshine- Johnny Cash

Choctaw County Affair- Carrie Underwood

Thousand Miles from Nowhere- Dwight Yoakam

Little Sister- Dwight Yoakam

Amarillo by Morning- George Strait

That Girl is a Cowboy-Garth Brooks

Beaches of Cheyenne- Garth Brooks

Fire Away- Chris Stapleton

Merry Go Round- The JaneDear Girls

She Keeps Me Warm- Mary Lambert

Jolene but it's gay- Reinaeiry

Hey Cowboy- Autumn Brooke

Enjoy the silence- Lacuna Coil

She Keeps Up- Nickleback

I fell in love with the Devil- Avril Lavigne

Save Yourself- My Darkest Days

Bleed- Elliot Greer

<u>CONTENT WARNINGS AND TRIGGERS</u>

Abuse: child, emotional, physical, mental, verbal both past and present
Violence: scenes of physical harm to another, fights, stalking, trauma, representation of PTSD, panic attacks, injuries to animals, destruction of property, attempted rape, etc.,
Murder: both past and present
Drug use: marijuana, cocaine, cigarettes, alcohol

There are also numerous kinks in these works, from easy spanking to forms of breath play.

***PLEASE NOTE: The drinking age was lowered from 21 to 19 by the 1971 Legislature with the change going into effect on July 1, 1971. The new Montana Constitution lowered the state drinking age to 18 when it went into effect on July 1, 1973

<u>This also contains slow burn romances as well as age gap romances!</u>

Prologue

Aviston Montana, The Wildwood Ranch; Christmas 1967.

From where he sat on the couch with his best friend and mentor, Bandy, Grant had a full view of his living room and those in it. On the floor, enraptured by the new Rudolph show airing, sat his adopted son, Eddie, with Bandy's two granddaughters. He was crunching through the communal bowl of popcorn with a half-asleep Dacey using his lap for a pillow, his free hand toying with her blonde hair, finger combing it smooth. She and her older sister, Josie, were the ones who had chosen the show; Dacey's twelve-year-old voice out ruled them all at her insistence they had to, no matter what. All day her friends had been talking about their family traditions for Christmas and how they all planned to watch it together. Her blue eyes had promised retribution to anyone who dared argue against the idea.

Josie was curled sideways on the overstuffed chair, legs tucked up on one side of Eddie's head, her chin resting on his other shoulder. It almost appeared cat like the way she was draped over him, relaxed and carefree.

Grant chuckled when Dacey made a weak attempt to throw a bite of popcorn into Eddie's mouth, missing it by a wide berth and knocking Josie in the forehead. Her sister attempted to retaliate, throwing her own piece at the prone figure sprawled out over the thick blue carpet. Ever the protector, Eddie caught it, tossing it in his mouth to chew pointedly in her direction.

Though Eddie was four years older than Josie at twenty-two, a number of people assumed them to be fraternal twins with how they acted around each other. From snarky, playful fights, to the way they'd grown up almost inseparable. It helped that she stood almost the same height, just six inches shorter at five eight.

But she sported the same blonde hair, blue eyes, and freckles sprinkled across her nose and cheeks Dacey did, and growing more into the pear-shaped figure of her mother. Eddie was not. Standing a few inches over six feet, his auburn hair shadowed hazel eyes that stalked their prey, missing little. They fought over everything, from horse training all the way to who would run errands. When it came down to it, Dacey was the only thing they would both do whatever it took for. The show resumed, forcing the pair to quiet down, settling in once more to watch.

Grant's brown eyes drifted away from them to the crackling fire in the hearth, where his wife, Vanessa, was reading like she was the only one in the room. The fire's glow backlit her black hair, darkening its shade to an impenetrable depth.

Beside him, Bandy rose with a suppressed groan when the next commercial flashed on with a catchy little jingle. "Girls, I believe it's time to go. It's getting late, and we have an early morning ahead of us." At his words, Dacey let out a plaintive whine.

"Pawpaw, the show isn't over! We've never seen it before, and I really like it!"

"No, it isn't, but you are both falling asleep where you sit. No matter how much you tell me you really like it, you can't deny you're tired."

Knowing a protest was coming, he raised a hand to stop it. "Dacey Mae, come on now." His stern voice contrasted with his soft expression.

She pouted but remained silent, hugging Eddie until he made her squeal when he pinched the tip of her nose. He bent to whisper something in her ear that earned a laugh and an enthusiastic nod, a mischievous grin breaking out across her face. Josie wandered past them, ignoring their antics, carrying her mug to the kitchen sink, rinsing what was left down the drain. Dacey joined her, tapping out the remnants of salt and unpopped kernels into the trash from the popcorn bowl before adding beside the mug. The older men moved to the archway that separated the two rooms, watching the kids shuffle around. They worked on gathering coats, boots, and gloves, all while murmuring back and forth.

Grant frowned, glancing out the large bay windows that overlooked his ranch. "You're welcome to use the bunkhouse. That snow is deep and I'd rather the three of you be safe. Ain't worth trying to drive home in it." Bandy was his oldest friend in the world, closer to a father figure than anything. The older rancher was pushing seventy-five, kind face lined in wrinkles from years of laughing and working in the sun. He'd taught Grant everything he knew about ranch life, always ready with a kind word. The thought of losing him or the girls to a snowstorm made his stomach churn.

"I appreciate the offer. I know the girls will as well," Bandy replied.

"They'll be even happier in the morning to help with the horses. If Dacey has her way, she'll talk me out of half the herd." They laughed, Grant shaking his head. "But if that's the worst she does, then I think I can handle it. Just wish you'd move in, you're here every day as it is."

"Don't think I haven't thought of it, of course I have. But you know my home is the one I grew up in, I can't just let it go even if it's for a valid reason. Maybe one of these days the girls can move here, but that is my house and it always will be," Bandy explained.

"I get it, I do. If that's how you feel about it then why not ask them to? It'd save you a lot of headache in the mornings to get them here before the bus, if nothing else."

The older man fished a toothpick from the band of his Stetson, chewing the tip in thought. "Maybe. Dacey would be happier than Josie. Hell, if she could she'd move right into Eddie's place before ever considering living next door. I'll talk to them later, get back to you."

"No rush, none at all. Just figured all I can do is put the offer out there so you're aware it's an option."

"You'll regret it when you're missing stock to a tiny monster," Bandy teased, lips curving up around his toothpick.

"She'll talk you out of more than just stock," Eddie cut in, having made his way over to join the older men from where he had been sitting. He had only caught the last part of the conversation, but hope spread a warmth through him. When Bandy gave him a questioning look, he just shrugged, nodding to where Dacey leaned on the fridge under a black Stetson much too large for her. The men laughed harder, Grant clapping a hand on Eddie's shoulder.

"Make sure they get to the bunkhouse for me. And Bandy, be sure this one makes it in his, please."

"You got it. See you in the morning." Reaching over, Bandy patted Grant's arm.

"See you then."

Chapter 1

Blue Bedroom

Six Years Later

Waking up with a jerk, Grant lay where he was, the dream fading into softly worn memories pressing against the black canvas of his bedroom ceiling. His heart ached, tapping out a painful staccato against his ribs. What had caused him to dream of that night? It had been three years since he had last thought of them, with another three dealing with his own personal hell.

Thinking back on the dream, Grant remembered how the true nightmare unfolded the day after it had taken place. It still haunted both Eddie and himself when they allowed the memories to wash over them. Bandy had indeed taken the girls to the bunkhouse instead of trying to drive home in the deep snow. But the next morning, only the girls had gotten up.

From there, the very ground seemed to give way in an endless drop that had only stopped recently. Even then, Grant would swear it was just a temporary pause in the fall. As he lay there, the alarm blared to life with an unwanted cry, startling him into a sitting position. Reaching out, he slapped it off with a deep sigh and begrudgingly peeled himself out of the warm covers, forcing himself to get ready for another busy day.

Why were the memories pushed into the back of his mind for no reason? Or had he done it to spare himself the madness of not knowing where they were, what was happening?

The thoughts carried him to his dresser, where a forgotten picture was tucked away in the corner of its mirror. He avoided looking at himself, at the gray that started streaking his dark hair with stress, pretending it wasn't helped along with his mid-forties age. Reaching up, he touched the corner of the worn polaroid. In it, Bandy offered the camera his usual smirk, one hand on Josie's shoulder, her grin bright. The other was on Dacey's trying to keep her in place. Beside Dacey, Eddie had one hand buried in her blonde locks to ruffle them, knowing how much it riled her up. He laughed down at her while she glared up at him. Grant himself was laughing loudly beside Eddie, one hand stretched across them to ask Josie for help getting her sister in line.

They had taken a second, "proper" one, but this was the one he had kept; this was the true side of their motley family Now, who the hell knew where the girls were?? It had caused Eddie to become withdrawn, quiet, and short-fused, always ready to snap. Grant's ex-wife, Vanessa, wasn't in the picture to ruin it either, another reason he preferred it. Ever since signing the divorce papers six months prior, she was out of their lives as well.

That was one thing he was thankful for, more than anything else. After Bandy passed, she seemed hell-bent on driving Grant to the edge of sanity with endless ridiculous needs and demands for the ranch, hell-bent on making it more extravagant than necessary. When she realized that none of them were going to be met, she opted instead to try taking everything from him in the divorce. Again, she failed miserably, slinking off with her tail tucked between her legs. At least she was gone for the time being. The woman had a horrible habit of showing up like some demonic pop-up book from hell.

Shaking away the intrusive thoughts, he began getting dressed, forcing his mind on to more important matters at hand. There was livestock to feed, new calves to tag, and bulls to load for the rodeo out of town that weekend. His list of things to do was never ending, it seemed, despite their best efforts. From dawn until dusk, he and Eddie did the best they could to keep on top of that list, yet at the end of the day, there was always something new. Finishing up his normal morning routine, he made his way down the stairs to the kitchen.

When he snapped on the light, a dark, fluffy blur scurried in from the living room, wagging his tail before going to sit in front of the garage. Reaching down to rub the furry head, he made sure to scratch the Aussies' favorite spot behind his ears and down his neck. "Good morning, Ace. You ready to help get chores done, boy?" A sharp bark answered his question, Ace spinning two quick circles in place before resuming his post at the door. Chuckling, Grant opened it, letting his dog into the garage. Reaching the large bay door and hauling it open, he followed, careful not to disturb any of the clutter. Ace raced out, barks filling the chilly, misty morning air as he raced toward Eddie's bunkhouse.

Across the dew-soaked yard, the light from Eddie's bunkhouse cast ghostly shadows on the porch before spilling onto the lawn. Occasionally, his shadowed outline would break the light, letting Grant know that the man hadn't just left the light on, trying to fool him into thinking he was up.

Leaving the confines of the garage to head toward Eddie's, he looked out over the few round pens within sight. The largest held the bulls that were to be loaded on the large, sleek black trailer waiting across the gravel drive. They were only vague shapes where they lay bedded down in the hay they'd pulled from the round feeder. He watched them before continuing across the damp grass toward his main destination. The younger cowboy must have heard him on the old boards because by the time he reached the top of the steps, Eddie was already opening the door for him.

"I didn't think we had to leave already; I know I got up early enough to have a cup of coffee." The grouchy man ran a freckled hand through his tousled, auburn hair, stepping aside to let Grant in.

"You did, but I figured that if we got everything done in time we could stop at The Pit for breakfast."

"Sounds good to me. I ain't hungry anyway. Let me finish getting ready, then I'll pull the truck up to the loading chute and feed the horses."

"Alright, just try not to take the gate out this time." Grant teased, smirking at the dark look Eddie shot him.

"We both know it was an accident. If Whistle hadn't tried to use me as a springboard to get out the window, I never would've gone back too far," Eddie countered, crossing his arms.

"Sure, blame the poor dog for your bad driving. I'm going to run down to the pond pasture to check on the cows there while you get everything going; once I'm done, I'll be back up to run feed into the bunks."

"Deal."

Grant knew the way he received a single word for an answer was the sign Eddie wanted to be left alone. Even having raised him all twenty-eight years on the ranch, the younger man was never much of a morning person. Leaving Eddie to it, he nodded at the sight of Ace waiting for him at the bottom of the steps, patting his head when he reached it. “Let’s go get the queen, shall we?” Ace made a soft noise, leaping up to race toward the horses. Grant followed him, boots making a soft, soothing crunch when he reached the gravel drive that led to the barn.

Hauling the big white doors open, a chorus of whinnies greeted him while heads poked over their respective stalls. Heading to where the only mare was bedded down, Grant offered a gentle smile when her head popped over the half door. Reaching into the burlap bag hanging beside her stall, he fished out a small handful of dried apple treats, offering them out. “Good morning, beautiful. Are we going to have a good day today?” he asked her, massaging the tiny white star on her forehead. The perlino whiffled them up greedily, ignoring him when he slipped in to groom her.

He continued talking under his breath about anything that came to mind, from chores that needed done, to his hopes of sales on Sunday. She flicked an ear back toward him, not even turning her head from her hay when he left for the saddle. Returning with everything he needed, he had to soothe her when she sidestepped the blanket, ears pinned. “Easy, Lady, you’ll be fine. Come on now.”

After a couple of moments of being forced to work her around the stall so she would stand still again, she let him tack her, sliding the bridle over her head, cinching the girth in place around her middle. She held her breath the first time, forcing him to adjust her bridle until she let it out, darting back to finish the job. He praised her as he worked, rubbing all the best spots before leading her down the main aisle of the barn toward the door. Her hooves sounded out a calming beat, shoes clicking over the stones while she sashayed after her owner.

There were few others in the barn, the three breeding stallions Eddie had penned up the night before to keep them out of trouble. Every one of them did their best attempts at reaching the mare as she passed, snorting and stretching their necks out to lip at her. Lady pinned her ears, snapping her teeth once at a stallion when he got too close for her care. The buckskin jerked back, head bobbing as he side-eyed Lady, nervously shifting further back in his stall. Grant patted her, offering another bite of apple treat that she gobbled up. Satisfied she wasn't going to throw him clear across the yard, Grant mounted her, trotting in a couple of circles to work her out before aiming toward the pastures. Her smooth gait ate the ground in perfect strides, switching lead under his unseen directions. Nudging the mare into a smooth canter, he chuckled when Ace raced from wherever he had hidden in the barn to join in the ride, eager to face any adventure that may await them.

As they passed by the bunkhouses, Eddie stepped out, tugging on his hat. Grant raised a brief hand to him in greeting. Eddie's Aussie, Whistle, left her owner to join in the jaunt across the farm, her tiny voice making her namesake clear. The two dogs raced ahead, intent on chasing trails only they could smell. Lady paid them no mind, choosing instead to focus on the dark shapes looming up in front of them just past a latched gate. To her, they were as dangerous as any wild animal they could have come across, and Grant could feel her beginning to tense under his legs.

"Easy now girl, you're alright," he assured her, patting her as one shape wandered over to reveal itself as a cow. The cow greeted them with a low call, it's calf staying close to, peeking around her side to watch them curiously. Lady snorted hard, head bobbing up and down before settling under a firmer hand on the reins. "There we go, stubborn mule." An ear flicked back toward him at his words as though she truly understood what he was saying, a hard snort escaping.

The cow was at the gate, searching for a treat or bucket of feed, neither of which Grant had on him at the moment. He offered her head a light scratch in apology before turning Lady toward the rest of the herd. For a while, he milled about them, counting the newborn calves, checking for any signs of illness and dismounting to tag any new ones that had been born the night before. Time was lost to him in the fields where, during warm months, the animals and insects of the land sang a symphony only he could hear.

Around him, the cows paid him little mind, used to this from years of handling. A couple of calves put up small fights, tiny hooves flailing in the strong grasp keeping them in place. It was nothing to hold them, his attention focused on keeping the mothers from running him over at their cries. Lady kept herself between them, back hoof lifted, ready to launch at any who came too close for her liking. Grant knew the problems would come up later once he went into the heifers' pasture at the South Pond. That lot was the breeding stock of his bucking bulls, which were more than nasty on their first calf. Rank and deadly were the two best descriptions anyone could have given them.

Satisfied the herd was going to be alright until they returned, Grant mounted Lady, turning her toward the barns. Her ears went up, eager for the food she knew was going to be waiting, along with the knowledge she was done working. He had to hold her back a few times to keep her from taking off at a dead run but when they reached the well-beaten path they both knew by heart, he let her open up. Stretching out, her stride covered the ground so fast he questioned if they had retired her too soon from barrel racing to become a broodmare. Hearing them leave, the dogs reemerged from the brambles, doing their best to keep up. They streaked under the fence in twin blurs, Ace in the lead. The wind crept under the band of Grant's hat, doing its best to rip it off. One hand shifted the reins further up her neck while the other reached up to hold it in place. He laughed, the sound torn into ribbons that scattered behind them.

The outskirts of the ranch came into view, Lady slowing to a canter, then a smooth trot. Drawing close, he could hear Eddie coaxing the bulls from the pen they had spent the night in toward the loading chutes. They weren't moving quickly, ignoring the slaps to their rumps and the poke of a stick, choosing to remain in their comfortable piles of hay. Whistle broke away, wriggling under the fence to get Badlands up with a few well-placed nips, letting out her meanest snarls, trying to seem more intimidating. Once Badlands, the biggest bull in the lot, was on his feet heading toward the trailer, the rest heaved themselves up and fell in line. Eddie was muttering praises to them as they did, offering words of encouragement when needed. With luck, only a few would return home Sunday afternoon.

While the bulls were normally calm and well-mannered, Grant knew later at the rodeo they would become some of the meanest creatures on earth; worked into a whirlwind of fury by noises, smells, and nature itself. They had all earned their ranks among the world's best bulls, but it was moments like this Grant was more proud of. Moments where they did as asked with no dangerous consequences on the line, no one in the pathway to get trampled.

Eddie closed the trailer door once they finished loading up. "That's all of them. Do you plan on bringing any of the broncs?"

"No, not this time. They won't need them until next weekend." Grant dismounted, leading Lady past the chute and trailer. "I'll get her settled in for the day and get everything I need done up here. Make sure you have everything you need. Once we leave, we aren't going to be coming back until Sunday."

"Need any help?"

"I'm just going to get feed in the bunks for the weaned calves. Did you get them the round bale last night?" Grant lit a cigarette, offering out his pack and lighter.

Accepting, Eddie lit one, taking a deep drag. "Yeah, but you don't need to feed them, I took care of it already. Also filled up the water troughs, cleaned the stalls for the studs, and got her majesty all set. There were a few other things I got done while you were down with the cows to save time."

"Thank you. Go ahead and toss your stuff in the trailer, please. I put my bag in last night to be sure that I don't forget anything, which means something is bound to be left behind." They both laughed, earning an annoyed look from Lady. "While you're doing that, I'll get her put up, then meet you here." Grant offered a nod, watching Eddie hustle across the yard to his bunkhouse with Whistle close on his heels.

Grant didn't wait to watch him go, choosing instead to lead Lady into the barn. Hooking her to the cross ties she stood patiently, one back hoof cocked in comfort. He made quick work of her tack, starting at the bridle, working his way back to the saddle and pad. When everything was off, he hauled the set toward the small room near the main doors. While tucking them on the designated racks, a few sets of old tack tucked away in the corner caught his eye, coated in a thick layer of dust.

One was a child's saddle, lovingly placed on the rack, while the other was slightly larger, its saddle pad resting beneath it. The girls' old tack. He swallowed against the choking hold the past threatened to place on him, turning his back on the corner. Breathing in through his nose and out through his mouth, he finished placing his items where they belonged.

Controlling the urge to slam the tack room door, he returned to Lady, grooming her out. "Do you miss them? Do you even remember them?" The questions slipped out, whispered into a welcoming ear. She flicked it forward and back, heaving a deep sigh in response. "Should have known you don't care, it ain't food related is it?" Grant teased, rubbing circles on her forehead. She pushed back against the touch, bobbing her head in an attempt to gain more contact, causing him to take a small step back. Lost in his thoughts, he unclipped her, guiding her down the cluttered cobblestone alley. When he nearly tripped over a stray piece of baling twine, he forced himself back to the present moment, shoving the past to the recesses of his mind.

Normally, he would have turned Lady out with the rest of the mares for the weekend, but she was just going in season, making her meaner than ever. If he let her out with them, he risked serious injury to either party from them battling over who was in charge. When Lady reached the gate to the largest stall with an attached outdoor paddock, Whiskey poked his head over his door. Stretching his neck out, he lipped a bit, whickering at her. She squealed, throwing her head up high while taking a step to the side, attempting to kick out.

"Hey! Knock it off now, he's just trying to do his job," Grant assured her, tugging the lead rope. Paying no attention to him, her head snaked out, teeth clicking dangerously close to Whiskey's soft muzzle. "Lady! That is enough!" Forcing her to back up a few paces, Grant waited until she calmed before letting the pressure off. "There, ya got your brain back in place. Now, come on."

Guiding her out, he tugged off the halter, slapping her rump when she trotted past. Dropping to her knees with a low groan, she rolled around scratching itches from the saddle. Finished, she surged to her feet, shaking the dirt off with a hard snort, heaving a harder sigh. "You know, I'd have been pissed if I'd just bathed you."

Leaving her, he wandered back in the barn, rubbing Whiskey's nose when he chanced another peek. "Be more careful next time, alright, buddy? Can't have you slowing this weekend down with a vet trip." One last soft stroke ran down the stud's nose, making the large eyes half close. "Proud of you, big boy."

Walking to the double doors, he shoved them wider to allow the gentle breeze in. Grant watched a few stray pieces of hay drift past his boots, tumbling out to join what had escaped the pens. Leaving the barn, the gentle crunch of gravel alerted Eddie to his approach, leaned on the truck smoking a freshly lit cigarette as he waited.

"Lady just tried to rip poor, old Whiskey's face off. Seems like her love interest in him was rather short-lived." Grant told him, amusement coloring his tone.

Eddie shook his head. "You'd think he'd know she has the attention span of a dead gnat. Once she's done, she's done. But he can't help it any more than any other man with a woman like Lady."

"That's the problem, he'd have to think. Load up Slick, we need to get on the road." Climbing into the cab of the truck, he rolled his window down, Eddie flipping on the radio. "I turned her out into the back paddock until she's done being in season this go around. Also didn't wanna risk her jumping into one of the other pastures, cause knowin' our luck she'd end up with some of the colts. Unless she's determined, I'm not worried about her being out there all weekend, everything was full. Wade and his kids will be by this evening anyway to keep up on chores and keep an eye on things."

"Jack's in there, that's why everything was full. Good thing those two get along otherwise we'd be coming home to one dead horse and a rabid Lady."

"He must have been hiding in the lean to 'cause I didn't see him."

"Can't blame him when you see that beast coming. Poor guy doesn't understand that Lady likes him more than the rest."

"Because he's the only gelding around. Jack couldn't care less if she was in season or not; that and I'm pretty sure he's in love with Tink. The rest are studs, weanlings, and a bunch of other pissy ass mares." That earned a laugh.

"Too much estrogen running around for her highness' liking. Poor crabby bitch just has to learn that she's not the only queen around here. Would help if someone didn't spoil her as much as he did."

Grant shrugged. "Lady deserves it considering she's thrown some of our best stock and earned us a decent amount of money."

"Don't trash talk the other mares! They've earned plenty of money when we put them in the circuit or breed. You just favor her because she only likes you." Eddie pointed out.

"My favoring her is no different from you favoring them."

"They don't try to rip my face off for fun."

Grant grinned, offering a shrug. "She's smart, knows where her food comes from."

"Whatever." By now, Eddie was grinning as well. It wasn't often he was easy to tease, and Grant found himself resisting the urge to point it out. Chances were, if he said anything, the moment would be ruined. Rather than risk drawing up the brooding man Eddie had grown into over the years, Grant kept quiet, watching him.

Pulling into the parking lot of The Pit, Grant switched off the engine, the truck shaking faintly as the bulls shifted into more comfortable positions. Eddie peeked in the side, checking on them to be sure that they were okay. They ignored him, choosing instead to doze in the warm beams of sunlight filtering in. Satisfied with what he found, Eddie motioned for Grant to follow, leading the way into the small diner.

Chapter 2

This Cowboy's Hat

The scent of coffee mingled with breakfast cooking on the large griddle hidden away in the kitchen. Bacon grease blended into waffle and pancake batter so thick Eddie nearly tasted it in the back of his throat. Grant inhaled deeply, soaking it all in with an appreciative sigh, his body relaxing. When the bell tied to the door chimed, alerting her, the waitress glanced toward it, waving them to a booth to the left. Grant offered her a wave, leading the way. Halfway to their seats, Grant caught Eddie, stopping him at the table where Kent was sitting with Kyle and Lane. All three of their neighbors sat up straighter at their approach, exchanging greetings.

"How's it going boys? Why don't you pull up a chair?" Kent offered, whistling at Erica to gain her attention, waving toward two chairs near them that were unoccupied. The waitress simply shrugged, heading toward the food counter to tuck the tickets up on its rack. Grant drug the seats up, settling in next to Kyle, launching into a chat about grain prices while Eddie plopped down next to Lane.

"You two headed up to Grandfork rodeo?" Lane asked, leaning back in his chair, sipping his coffee.

"Yeah, Grant's going to see how the latest bulls do and if he's going to sell them off and try again, or if they're up to his standards and keep them."

"You and I both know that not a single one of them will live up to their grandaddy in his eyes, but at least he keeps trying. It doesn't hurt for him to keep some of the best ones to make profits off of bloodlines. Hell, I remember back when you were just a pup and the only one on the ranch was that goofy fucker with maybe a mare or two. Pretty proud of how far y'all have come, but don't tell him that."

Opening his mouth to reply, Eddie was interrupted by Erica, their waitress and daughter of the owner. Her hair was twisted up by a pen, pink flush across her cheeks. She used her notepad to swat his feet off the chair with a stern look. He dropped them to the floor, hands up in surrender when the pad was raised once again. "Thank you. Now then, gents, what do you want to drink?"

"Coffee, black." Eddie reached out, ignoring the thin, impossible to remove layer of grease soaked deep into the old, chipped formica top to grab the sugar container. "And just the French toast."

Grant glanced away from Kyle. "Coffee and the meat lover's omelet please." She gave a nod, scribbling their orders down, and turning on a heel. Dodging customers, she headed to grab the coffee pot and two cups. Pausing at the window, she tucked the slip up among the others that hung there.

"You ever going to try to ride again? I know you can't do any rough stock, but what about team roping or roping on your own?" Lane broke Eddie's gaze away from Erica as she wandered back to pour their coffee.

Grant offered her a gentle smile in thanks, Eddie giving a curt nod, pulling his cup closer.

"Nah, much as I want to, I do enough roping on the ranch with Grant. Besides, the stock we enter earns more than I ever could hope to." Even though he still dreamed of winning buckles, those days were behind him.

"That and you know Doc said you shouldn't risk it." Grant chimed in, having been listening with only half an ear. Eddie shot him a scowl, which earned him a simple shrug in reply. "Just stating the obvious. You got lucky this time, and they were able to keep your spine together. Next time they might not even manage that." He took a drink of his coffee. "On the ranch is one thing, we know Jack isn't going to dump you on your ass for no reason. Trying to rope with one of the others, who are made for it, comes with too many risks."

"I'm well aware." The answer was ground out through gritted teeth, Eddie leveling a glare at his coffee. Pouring in sugar, he stirred harder than necessary, the muscle in his jaw working.

"You know, if you want extra work, that's a little more exciting than the normal stuff you have going on, I have a couple of pastures down south that I need to bring back closer to home. You can tag along with me for a weekend, see some new sights. Mountains are better for them anyway now that summer is getting closer." Kyle offered, leaning around Grant to talk with Eddie.

"I would, but Grant keeps me busy enough without trying to pile more on my plate."

"You still ain't settled on a new hired hand?" Lane pressed, rolling his eyes. "I get it, Grant, I do, but you and Eddie are going to die out on that ranch trying to do it all alone. That place ain't built for only two people to be working on anymore. Two were fine when you started it, not now."

"Look boys, when I want your help and opinions, I'll ask for them. I haven't, so don't offer them. I know where you and half this town sit on my situation, and I kindly ask you to butt right on out." Grant pointed out, twisting his napkin into a tightly woven mess. Eddie knew the two men had a point, but he wasn't going to get in the middle of it. They were just trying, in their way, to help them out. They knew what Wildwood meant to him, but Grant was stubborn, refusing help at every turn unless he had a way to pay the person back.

Erica reappeared with their food, breaking up the tension as she set plates down in front of their respective owners. She offered the table a smile while topping up their coffee. "I happened to hear talk of needing hired hands, gentlemen?"

"Erica, the day Kyle is a gentleman is a day that cattle move around with no assistance." Eddie deadpanned, cutting a piece of French toast. The remark was rewarded with a rather rude hand gesture from across the table as Erica giggled.

"You just keep on out of it, hun." Grant patted her arm gently. "Got enough on your plate with this place without worrying about me getting a hired hand."

"Well, either way around it, Brody was in here yesterday with the Wheeler twins looking for work. Just something you should keep in mind if you ask me. Now then, I'll let you get back to eating." Leaving them, she began checking on the other tables in the cafe.

"You know, Brody wouldn't be a terrible choice, Grant. Kid's quiet, well mannered, but he's not afraid to take someone to the woodshed if they piss him off. He's kinda a big kid." Kyle hedged, shoving his empty plate to the side. "And those twins are a handful in and of themselves, but I've used them a couple of times and, believe me, they have some damn good ideas when there's an issue. Just have to get used to their wild antics outside of work."

"I don't mind Brody, does a good job with his farrier work." Eddie offered around a mouthful of French toast. The comment left half the table stunned silent; they all knew Eddie hardly got along with anyone anymore. Half the time, they were pretty sure he was rather close to biting someone if it came down to it. His demeanor reminded them he had once been an open, lighthearted young man always ready to do anything for anyone. Yet not one of them dared to question why he had changed so much. Between the tiny blonde shadow always beside him missing for years, coupled with the wreck off of a bull, none could fault him. While it had been Grant who raised him, the trio at the table were behind him every step to encourage and teach where their friend was unsure.

"I'll think about it if it gets you to shut up and let me enjoy my food in peace." Grant relented, stabbing a bite of omelet harder than necessary.

"The only reason I'm dropping it for now is I gotta get back to my place so I can be there tonight." Lane tossed down his tip with a crooked grin. "Otherwise, I wouldn't let it go no matter what." Standing, he gave a nod to the others before heading out the door while they called their goodbyes. Kyle wasn't too far behind Lane, bidding the others a farewell, Kent hot on his heels with comments about needing to stop at the feed store.

For a while, the two remaining men at the table were quiet, enjoying their meals and dull chatter around them. Grant broke the silence. "You think we need someone else around the ranch?"

"Much of a pain in the ass the whole thing is, I do. There's only so much fence that I can fix in a day before something else takes priority. I can't keep up with bookwork while trying to keep up with breeding schedules. Besides, that other bunkhouse needs someone in it to keep it from going to junk." The admission hurt more than Eddie wanted it to. A lump formed in his throat, making swallowing impossible. Shoving away the last few bites of food, he fought the sudden urge to throw up.

Grant heaved a hard sigh, sitting back in his chair and lighting a smoke. "Alright, after this weekend, I'll start trying to see who wants to help us. But they ain't touching that bunkhouse. It's been empty six years, and it'll stay empty so long as I'm alive or the rightful owners come home. They can figure out their own lodging."

His words eased the twists in Eddie's stomach. Drumming his fingers on the tabletop, he sighed. "Might as well hire all three, at least that way they can occupy each other and leave me the hell alone. I'm better left to do my own thing without having someone under my feet needing to be told what to do." Eddie warned. "If those twins are what's promised, they could be a good investment. What if something happens to one of us and it's down to just them? Two of us can't keep up anymore. Five would be best." He swallowed the last of his coffee with a grimace at the cold liquid, wishing he had allowed Erica to keep topping it off every time she passed by.

"Fair enough. Erica!" The girl made her way over, setting the check down.

"Need something else, Grant?"

"Yeah, sweetheart, can you let Brody know that he can come by anytime Monday? Bring the twins and I'll see what I can do for work."

If Erica was surprised, she hid it well as she accepted the payment. "Sure thing Grant, I'll make sure they know. Do you need anything else?"

"Thank you. No, if you'll excuse us, gotta get back on the road. Have a good day, Erica." Rising from his chair, Grant led the way out of the diner. Eddie offered a small wave to the girl as he followed, dropping his hat back on his head. Reaching the truck, Grant checked on the cattle and, once he was sure they were calm, hopped into the cab. Eddie had propped his feet up on the dash, lighting a cigarette with a quick peek at Grant from the corner of his eye as a heavy silence settled upon them.

"Just spit it out, no sense in staring at me like this." Annoyance was clear in Grant's words.

"Not much to spit out, really. I'm just surprised that you finally gave in; my back and I thank you."

Grant gave a noncommittal grunt and shrug, staring intently out of the windshield. Eddie could tell it was going to be a long ride, so he pulled his hat over his eyes to take a nap. With the way the morning had started, he knew he was going to need all the rest he could get on the way up to their destination. Grandfork wasn't far, but any time spent not dwelling in the pressing silence was good enough for him.

Chapter 3

How 'Bout Them Cowgirls

Chewing on a toothpick to keep from shifting around, Dacey heaved a sigh from what seemed like her very soul. Leaning on the door, she tried hard to focus on the world flashing by instead of turning to stare at her sister. Catching a wayward strand of windblown hair to shove it back under the worn-out black Stetson, the courage for her to take the chance was finally summoned. Licking her lips, she tried to keep her voice steady when she spoke, still not daring to glance at Josie. "You know, we're already this close? Why can't we just drive on down after?"

Josie narrowed her eyes at the road ahead of her. "Because you know for a fact that if we did that, then the trouble following us would latch onto them faster than a snake bite. I'm not about to be the cause for them to lose everything on account of us appearing on the property."

"That's assuming the trouble will find us. You gotta admit, Josie, we would be a lot safer there than the way we're going. Or have an actual bed at least." Dacey hedged, spitting the toothpick out the window to opt for a stick of Big Red gum. Fishing the pack out of the cluttered cup holder, she shrugged. "Even if it wasn't for long, it would be nice to see them and let them know we aren't dead as a doornail." Finding the gum among the half-empty peanut packets, change, and receipts, she ripped it open and shoved the red stick in her mouth. "It's like ever since Dad took us, they've been dead to us. Wonder if they think that of us?" It was a dirty blow to play but at that point, Dacey was desperate to try anything to see the two men she spoke of.

"We aren't going and that's final." Reaching across to the dash in front of the steering wheel, Josie grabbed a pink cigarette, punching in the dash lighter with her other hand. Satisfied it was on, she drummed her fingers on the leather under them, trying to keep from chewing the butt of the smoke. "What would we say, Dace? 'Hey, sorry to show up out of the blue, but we're kinda tired of sleeping in horse trailers and the cab of the truck. Can we move back into the old bunkhouse? And while y'all are at it, we're on the verge of starving because all the winnings go to keeping gas in the truck and food for the horses.' Yeah, Dace, that's gonna be a great welcome back." Rolling her eyes, she grabbed the lighter as it popped out, pressed the red-hot end to her smoke and took a deep drag. Releasing it in slow increments, she held the rest of it for a few moments before it came out in a rapid exhale. "Look, I know our situation is shitty, no matter how we look at it. But invading them when we're running from problems isn't fair or right."

"We both know that they'd take care of the trouble with no issues."

"Well, we ain't gonna use them like that, are we? Think that's any better?"

"Fine! I just miss them a lot and I know you do as well, so why do we keep lying to ourselves when we know that, no matter what baggage we have, they wouldn't care?"

"Because I'm more responsible than that! And how the hell do you know they wouldn't care? Been making late-night phone calls I don't know about? A lot can happen in six years, Dacey, a lot you don't know about, just like they don't. Why is this so hard to sink into your head? What, you think we can start trying to play *The Brady Bunch* as if my ex isn't hunting us like a prize elk to mount on his wall? What if they aren't even there? Huh? Gonna get your hopes up just to fall flat on your face again?"

Dacey's glare could melt steel in the arctic as she huffed, throwing herself back against the seat. "I'll just be glad when we get to where we're going. I'm sure we can both agree we need to stretch our legs and take a bit of a break away from this talk. I don't like fighting with you, but right now I want to just choke you. I'll settle for trying not to break anything and be a good little girl." Grinding her teeth, she took a deep breath. "Besides, I'm running low on soda and we both know that's a tragedy."

Josie knew that it was her little sister's way of apologizing as best she could without coming right out to say it. "Sounds like a plan to me. Pretty sure Buckshot could use a good workout before tonight anyway after this drive."

"Cash is going to try eating someone if he doesn't get a nice hard run in." A wicked grin crossed freckled cheeks. "That is… if I don't want him to eat someone."

"You keep that Hellspawn under control. I'd rather we didn't get kicked out of the circuit this close to finals. Just a few more rodeos, then we'll be scot free to go anywhere and do anything we please. Barring, of course, that you keep Cash from becoming unhinged the rest of the way."

"Don't talk crap about my sweet baby boy! He is a pure gentleman when I'm with him."

"Only when you're around! The other day he tried to take a chunk out of the farrier's face when you went to go get a soda."

"Then he shouldn't have been talking smack."

"Dacey, he was trying to get Cash to pick his feet up like he needed!"

"So you say." Laughter bubbled up, spilling out as Dacey reached for her Dr. Pepper. Josie cracked, her own giggles joining in, shaking her head. They both knew it was a losing argument, but one that always broke the tension. "But in all seriousness," she took a deep swig, "he's been a prick ever since Cheyenne. Remember when that stupid bitch tried her best to claim that he belonged to her and I was lying about which stall he had been stuck in? Guess he assumed I was gonna let her take him or something. You'd think the dummy would realize that he's not about to go anywhere without me."

"Who knows what Hellspawn thinks about other than food and fighting?" Josie sighed

"Is there any reason that's his official nickname?" Dacey asked wryly.

"Fits, doesn't it?" Josie smirked. "Got a bit of a ring to it if you ask me, and I like it, so it's what I'm gonna keep calling him."

"Whatever." Ripping open a package of honey roasted peanuts picked up at the last gas station, Dacey poured them into her soda. "Think Lisa is going to be at this one?"

"I doubt it. After the last outburst she had in the arena with me in front of the judges, she won't crawl out of her hole until next year. She's going to find an entirely different circuit to run in, if she's smart."

Dacey chuckled, swirling the peanuts around in thought. "Think they'll be there?"

"You keep your head down and out of their way if they are." Once more, the authoritative tone was back, Josie leveling her sister with a hard look. "I mean it, Dacey. You can't go doing something stupid just because you think you know better than I do. What are you going to do when Eddie shows up with a kid on his hip? Or, Grant refuses to have anything to do with us?"

"You said it, not me."

Knuckles turned white in their grip on the steering wheel. "I'm serious! We cannot have them around us!"

"Okay! Okay, I get it. Just get us there before you have a heart attack behind the wheel and kill everyone, geezus." Dacey let it drop a few minutes, reaching up to shove another loose strand of hair under the hatband. Blowing a few bubbles, she leaned to the dash for an old, worn out salebarn card covered in scribbles. The name had long since been rubbed away from use, only the occasional red letter left behind. Clicking it open, she doodled a small smiley amongst the latest budget. "Why are you so against it, anyway? What if Seth wasn't stalking us? Would you change your mind?"

"Not in the least, Dace." Josie's voice softened. "What we've gone through is something that they wouldn't understand. And I'm not about to force them into a corner like it's just all water under the bridge."

"It is at this point, considering that he's the only loose end that won't go away. He's like a rash from hell on the ass: downright infuriating," Dacey muttered, slouching against the worn fabric behind her.

Josie slowed at their exit, humming a low acknowledgment while monitoring the signs that pointed the way toward the arena. A line of trucks and trailers were already waiting outside of the gates when they pulled up to find the parking lot. Josie lit another cigarette, staring out the window absentmindedly as they crept along. Dacey finished her soda, sucking on a couple of leftover peanuts, and tapped along to the radio on the outer part of her door.

Horses and riders streamed past them, some in groups, while others were alone. Every once in a while, it would just be families or stock contractors that joined the rush of bodies headed toward the arena and barns. It felt like it took forever before they were signed in and given stall numbers, along with a sheet of paper listing times and events. Finding an empty space toward the middle of the field dedicated for competitors, Josie parked the truck.

Hopping out to stretch while popping her back with a small yawn, she rose up to the tips of her toes. "Finally!" The air hung heavy with the scent of animals, freshly cut grass and greasy vendor food.

Dacey shook her head at the sound of a hoof crashing against the trailer door. "Look you! Knock that shit off. I'll get you out in a second," she scolded, rapping her knuckles on the side. "While I'm getting these two into their stalls, can you grab us something to eat?"

"Yeah, just make sure that you keep a sharp eye out, Khloe." The fake name made Dacey wrinkle her nose, but she kept her mouth shut. While she unhooked the latch keeping the trailer door closed, Josie left to find the concession stand. Cash greeted her with another swift kick to the wall behind him, ears pinned flat against his skull as she made her way in.

"Don't look at me in that tone, or I'll make you shut your face." Dacey warned. She reached up to release the knot of the lead rope holding Buckshot in place. "You first, girl. Come on, let's get you settled in." The buckskin mare backed out easily, waiting as Dacey finally released Cash. The bay stallion backed out quickly, snorting hard and looking around the area they had stopped in. Breathing hard, as though he had already run the arena, nostrils flared wide, he pawed at the ground. Dacey grabbed Buckshot's lead rope again. "I said knock it off!" Swatting his nose, she leveled a glare at him. "I will let the next blonde-headed moron brave enough to try to take you get away with it!" She warned, popping the lead rope, forcing him into backing up a few paces.

Cash whickered, shaking his head with each step he took. When she stopped, he did as well, dropping his head to rub it hard against her. "You done?" He snorted, lipping at her shoulder. "Good."

He let her guide them to the barn that was going to house them for the night. "Now, you both know there's no stupid stuff allowed but, of course, I have to remind you; if you act out and cost us this chance at the finals, I'm not saying that a glue factory will be on the list, but I'm not saying that it isn't either." Hell would freeze over before she ever sold Cash off, but he didn't need to know that.

Checking the stalls over, Dacey rolled her eyes. "Lazy asses in charge couldn't even put the straw down beforehand so we didn't have to do everything?" Looking around, she spotted the pile at the end of the alleyway where other riders were getting bales.

"Stay here, don't eat or try to kill anyone," Dacey warned, pulling Cash's face level with hers as she spoke. When she was sure he understood, a quick kiss was dropped to the end of his nose before she let go, walking out. Closing the door behind her and locking it to head down the alley, the blood in her veins ran cold while a ringing invaded her ears.

Chapter 4

Biscuits

"Well, I'll be damned if it isn't one of the very people I've been looking for."

The voice crept up her spine, freezing the air in her lungs as she turned to face the speaker. Chances were slim to none Seth wouldn't do anything with an audience, but it didn't ease the terror that flooded her system. "I figured after everything that happened last weekend with Lisa, the two of you would be here so I took a chance and lucky me!" He kept edging closer with a smirk that only appeared friendly to those who didn't know him. It was the smirk he wore when Josie had been laying in a hospital bed after he had gotten through with her trying to escape the first time.

Dacey swallowed hard against a dry throat, standing to her full height. Fighting off the tremors that threatened to overcome her, she met his gaze dead on. "You get any closer to me or my sister, and I'll make sure you never leave this barn. Now, get out of my way. I have horses to bed down." Shoving her way roughly past him as a trio of bronc riders drew level with them, she rushed down to the safety of the straw pile. A few of the people there gave her odd looks while she struggled to take a steadying breath. Her stomach churned, bile scalding the back of her throat. Her instincts cried for her to run, to hunt Josie down. She couldn't, not without risking Seth following in the shadows right to his goal. They had assumed they were safe, but the joke, as always, was on them.

"You okay?" A slender brunette approached her, honest worry on her face.

"Yeah, just a little car sick, happens all the time. It hit harder than I thought it would, but I'll be okay." Dacey tried a reassuring smile, almost positive that it came out a grimace. The brunette didn't seem to buy into her lie, brown eyes studying her closer, but instead of pushing, she shrugged and grabbed a bale of straw.

"I'm Riley. If you change your mind and need help, I'm down in number sixteen." With that, she turned to walk back up the alley. Dacey watched her go, waiting only a beat before grabbing her bale and rushing to catch up. Seth had taken to leaning on a gate close to where she had left him, flashing a smile her way. She offered back a quick, rude gesture.

Falling into step with Riley, Dacey took a chance to bump their shoulders. "See that guy over there? The one that looks like someone shoved something up his ass, but he's too embarrassed to admit it?" Riley snickered as Dacey spoke. "He's stalking me and my sister. Anyway, could you lend me a hand with that? I ain't got a lot of cash, but anything to make him go away, I'm up for."

Riley was quite for a moment, and Dacey wondered if she had asked too much. She allowed the other time to mull her words over, shifting from one foot to the other. A devilish look slowly crept over Riley's features, a lock of wayward hair falling into her eyes. "Don't you worry, I have the perfect idea. How about we bed the horses down first, and we can go from there."

"Thank you." Nerves flooded Dacey's veins at trusting a perfect stranger, but she knew she didn't have many choices. If left alone, the only thing keeping her safe was Cash, and he would be useless if Seth had his cronies. The only choice was to stick to someone, despite the fact they just met. Even with others milling around, she ran the risk of him dragging her off under their noses the first chance that came up. With her hands tied, she was forced to trail after Riley. Head up, back straight, Dacey refused to let him see the fear his very presence brought. Seth's eyes bore into her back, following them to their respective stalls. Noting their numbers, he pushed off the wall, walking away without another word, letting the crowd swallow him up.

Stopping first at Riley's horse, Dacey helped with getting her set up, scattering the flakes of straw over the floor. Riley worked at the feed and water buckets, tethering them up against the wall in the proper places. Unsettled by the quiet pressing in on them, Riley cleared her throat. "You know, I gave you my name but you never offered yours. Of course, we've been a little distracted, so that's my fault for rushing ahead as always. This is Ariats Lost Silver Bullet, but we just call her Silver." Riley patted her mare proudly, offering a bite of carrot that was gobbled up.

"Oh, I'm Khloe," Dacey lied, offering her hand. "My older sister is Nicole, she's around here somewhere getting us a bite to eat."

"You're lucky you have an older sister, I was stuck with all brothers.

Speaking of which, Rider and Rusty are here too! They do the team roping, and some of the rough stock depending on the selection."

Dacey couldn't help the snort. "Sorry, that's rude of me. But your parents were bored trying to think up names, weren't they?" There was something in the back of her mind, tugging at her to pay attention. Why was this all sounding so familiar?

"Mom said by the time she knew what she was having, she didn't have a whole lotta of time to be original. Some are family names anyway, so she and dad just went with it."

"All valid reasons." Finishing up with Silver, Dacey chanced a glance toward where Seth had been, startled not to see him there. She began noting the sheer number of riders that were steadily filing in, wondering if that was what had run him off or her rather chatty new companion. How many of them were his goons? Trying to keep that thought shoved down, Dacey led the way toward Buckshot. "Okay so, I'll take care of this ding dong if you don't mind working with her alone? Buckshot is Nicole's and about as safe as you can expect a mare to be. Cash, however, does not like people he doesn't know, or anything with a pulse to be honest, so I can't trust anyone other than myself or my sister."

"Nah, I get it. We have some that only my brothers can handle. There's a mare we shipped only my dad managed, she turned out great with her new owner, but I'm just tryin' to...well, at least you warned me. Thank you for not assuming that he would behave for someone else. I've had that happen and gotten kicked hard enough that it put me out of the running," Riley blurted.

"You were set up? That's pretty shitty even for the girls around here, but I can see that happening." Dacey flicked Cash's nose as he whiffled at her hair. Hanging the buckets up, she hunted down the loaned hay net to add it beside them. "I'm not a dirty cheater. I like a good healthy competition that isn't set up for me to win when I shouldn't." It was for those reasons Dacey had no issue flattening the competition in the right way. Opening the stall door, coaxing Cash to take a step back to prevent him following her out, she spotted Josie returning.

Noting Riley in Buckshot's stall, her sister frowned, holding up the food. "Khloe, I didn't know we were going to be expecting company, I only got us something to eat." She offered a smile, but Dacey could see how the handles of the plastic bag crinkled in her clenched fists, shoulders pulled up toward her ears.

Reaching out, she took the cold styrofoam cup before Josie's nails poked holes into it. While she wouldn't kill her sister over spilled Dr. Pepper, she might cry. "Riley's here to help us with a problem that showed up. Figured it wouldn't hurt to have someone on our side finally instead of always getting raked over the coals." She took a long, deep drink of the soda, ending it with an exaggerated sigh of bliss. Josie's jaw muscle flexed, keeping words locked tight behind her teeth.

Riley watched them nervously, glancing down the alley to see if the culprit was still milling around. He wasn't, though she had made sure to get a good look at him earlier. "Would you be more comfortable talking about this somewhere less crowded? There's a lot of people showing up, and I know my brothers won't mind if we use the trailer to talk." She offered, hoping not to piss the older sister off further.

Josie eyed her, trying to gauge if the newcomer was someone to be trusted or if it was an elaborate trap. Biting her lower lip in thought, she shrugged, holding the bag of food toward Dacey. "Isn't like there's a lot of choices, but we have to make this quick considering we need to get the horses ready. I will warn you, if this is a trap, you won't wake up tomorrow."

Dacey paused in her acceptance, eyeing her sister with a startled look. Josie was always the calm one, the softer of the two when it came down to matters of violence. She'd never been thrown out of school for fighting, never gotten into half the trouble Dacey had. To hear her threaten Riley so easily was a testament of how close she was to the end of her patience. "If it'd been a trap she woulda already tossed me to him. Unless she's the best actress in this place."

"I still don't care. We have too much at stake this weekend, too many blind corners to deal with. The last thing we need is to waltz into a trap pell-mell. She turns her back on us, or tricks us, then I'm gonna beat her ass." Josie crossed her arms, feet planted in the deep sawdust.

"Deal."Josie popped the lid off the plastic container holding her sandwich. Wrinkling her nose at it, she picked off a thick slice of tomato. "I said none of this mushy junk." She complained, using the tips of her fingers to pass it over onto Dacey's cheeseburger.

"It's like someone knows I love them." Her sister teased, tucking it under the bun with the other slice. Taking a massive bite, she gave a taunting hum of enjoyment. Josie flicked a pickle at her, eyes narrowed. Devouring the burger as quickly as she could without choking, Dacey offered out a few of her fries to Riley. Why couldn't she put her finger on what it was about the other girl? Even Josie kept casting her the occasional look, brows furrowed in frustration.

"So, are y'all from around here? I'm not too terribly far from here." Riley piped up, trying to break the ice. "Just south of here, a super tiny town called Aviston, born and raised there." Dacey inhaled her mouthful of soda at the name, doubling over in a coughing fit, trying to clear it from her lungs. She rested her hands on her knees, gripping the worn fabric of her jeans for comfort. Josie was at her side in a second, pounding her back, doing her best to help the only way she knew how.

Panicking a bit, Riley helplessly gripped her forearms, swaying back and forth. "Is she okay?"

A weak nod was offered, Dacey rising, still clearing her throat. "I'm okay." Her voice was rough despite the assurance. "Just tried to breathe and drink." She refused to admit the truth hit her harder than Cash could ever throw her. Riley and her family owned land to the south of Wildwood, and once was a classmate of Dacey's. They hadn't been friends, hadn't talked other than in passing, both ran in different circles that never met. Chances were high neither of them would be recognized, but part of Dacey worried. Waving off Josie's concerned look with the barest shake of her head, she plastered on a fake smile. "Well, now that I've tried to drown myself on dry land, how about we saddle up to save time?"

"Sounds like a plan. Are you sure you're okay?" Riley pressed.

"Yup, good as gold," Dacey lied.

Separating to their respective stalls, they worked in silence, keeping a close eye on those wandering past. Dacey tacked Cash faster than the others, walking him in tight circles in a weak attempt at burning off his excess energy. When Josie held the door open, he tossed his head before dropping it to the ground with a few crow hops. His third one earned a quick warning tug on the reins, Dacey gritting her teeth.

Gaining control, she forced him to walk out to the alley, ready for anything he tried. Riley mounted Silver, eyes running down his body rather curiously. "How old is he?"

Dacey slapped her boot with her quirt in warning to remind Cash who was in charge. The stallion pranced in place a little longer, giving in to lower his head with a huff, calming down and standing still. "He's four, going on moronic. I've had him a year now after I found him in a kill pen, which should have been my first hint." She sighed, shaking her head. "But I love him to bits, and he's won us every entry, so I guess I can't complain a whole hell of a lot."

"Did he have any papers?" The trio walked out the double doors, Josie and Dacey trailing behind keeping sharp eyes out in between the trailers in case the trouble found them before they could come up with a solution.

"Nope. Wouldn't matter anyway, mean as he is if you ask me. I'm not sure it's a good idea to breed him, no matter how much I have considered it. It depends on the mare and her temperament for me to be convinced, though. Can't fault Cash for his behavior, it's well-earned, but that don't mean his offspring won't run this hot." Dacey rubbed the warm neck under her hand with a fond smile. "He'd throw some gorgeous babies, we can all agree on that."

"Think hard on it, 'cause if he keeps winning like you say he does, then you're gonna be getting a lot of offers. Considering today, I better be at the top of the list. I'm extremely picky about who I breed this queen to but he's already on my radar from body condition alone. Temperament can always be worked out once we know the foal better," Riley answered. A long, sleek, black trailer came into view with a large, bright, sterling silver brand prominent on the living quarters; a lazy bar rested over top of a capital W, just above *Lazy Bar Wheeler Ranch* in smaller letters.

Dismounting, Riley tied Silver to the side of it, rubbing at her nose while the sisters tethered their horses. Satisfied they hadn't been followed, and they were secure, the trio made their way into the spacious living quarters where the scent of cedar and pine wrapped around them. All the furnishings were the same black and chrome boasted on the outside, dark hardwood flooring under their boots. A queen sized mattress was to their right on the gooseneck, while the left housed a leather couch, appliances, and a door to what could only be a bathroom. Directly in front of them, a closet housed enough clothes some were forced to hang beside it on a second rack.

Closing the door, Josie leaned on it, studying the two younger women with a look of pure annoyance. "Look, I'll be blunt; I don't like the fact you had the gall to get someone else roped into this. Since I couldn't risk causing a massive scene in the barn bawlin' your ass out, spit it out, what the hell are you doing?" Josie barked out at Dacey.

Riley held up her hands to placate the brewing argument. "It was my nosing around that got us into this predicament! She was in a bind with this creep, so I offered some help so she wouldn't end up on the back of a milk carton." Her voice wavered, pitching higher at the end, hands shaking.

"What do you mean 'creep'? And who the hell helps someone they don't know?"

"Hey! I'd love for you to grill this poor soul to bits, but we have plans to make!" Dacey snapped, hands on her hips, eyes narrowed. "So, let's focus on what matters, okay? Which means get your tantrum over with and move on from trying to play 'big dog' in the park. We need her and whatever help offered right now, since you wouldn't let us find the ones who wouldn't have minded. I'm sick of being alone in this fight!" Her eyes bore into Josie's, the two nose to nose, neither of them backing down until Riley gave a light cough.

"Fine, but don't think this is over once we're alone. I'm going to chew your ass out." Josie sat down, tapping her booted foot, leg bouncing.

"Whatever gets you to pay attention. Ready?"

Chapter 5

Fastest Girl in Town

Taking a deep drag off his cigarette, Eddie held the smoke a while before letting it drift from his lungs to mix with the dust in the air. Sometimes, the small cloud would drift across his line of sight, laying a haze over the world. His hand rose to push the brim of his worn black Stetson back up a freckled brow to see better. After all, this was what had kept him plastered to the fence of the arena for the past ten minutes.

The country song filling the stadium was cut off, and while Eddie couldn't complain, he was rather annoyed at the loss of a good song. "Up next, we have Miss. Khloe Von Bokel on Cash from Underneath the Mattress. I will say this folks, this girl wasn't built on a Monday! God was having a good day when he made her; it must have been a Friday. Now, this young lady here has taken home every buckle in the breakaway calf roping since she and this wild pony showed up at the start of this year's circuit. I know everyone here is wondering: can they do it again?" The audience gave a loud cheer of encouragement to the words rolling over them.

When the roar died down, the announcer began explaining in detail what was going on. “Calf keeps leaning back on the push man and when they do it isn’t a good sign. They can’t get him up to turn him out properly, which means we have to wait until he does for these two to get their chance at their run. So, now he’s switching it up and what he keeps doing is he keeps running his head up. That’s not any better than pushing back because if he keeps it up, Hercules himself couldn’t get that steer out right, no matter how hard he tried. Those horns would hit that chute wrong and will cause him to veer the wrong way instead of going straight out. Folks, this calf is just determined that it ain’t going to be run today, but our men in that chute aren’t giving up. And there we go, he’s finally up ready to be shipped out. And we are off! Look at the reach on those little bitty horns!” The stadium roared to life.

“There you have it folks, I don’t believe it! A flat 1.8 seconds! I believe that is a new arena record!” The crowd cheered as the announcer shouted the time once again in astonishment.

The clown couldn’t help cutting in. “Let’s give thanks to not just the participants and the livestock haulers, but we need to give a great big thank you to the one that matters most in this event.”

Playing along, the announcer didn’t miss a beat. “Oh? Who’s that?”

“The calf pusher outer guy! Do you think he needs a degree in calf pushy outy?” They continued to blather on, but Eddie tuned them out. The young girl certainly had caught his attention and not because she was top of the ranks from nowhere.

The bay stallion she rode was what had first captured Eddie’s eye earlier that afternoon. At first, Eddie had assumed him to be a new horse for the bronc riders, considering his foul temperament. He had been snorting and bucking, charging around a training pen like some wild mustang freshly caught with low throated bellows. Making his way closer to study the creature, his notions stamped out like one of his finished smokes.

A slip of a girl made her way into the pen, talking low and gentle to ease the mad dash. Like a switch flipping, his head went down, and the bucking stopped, as if he had never been going berserk. He nuzzled at her before lipping up whatever treat she offered with a whicker of thanks, butting against her hand in search of more. Eddie watched in disbelief when she mounted him with ease.

Fascinated, he lurked against the small set of bleachers most of the afternoon, smoking and watching the pair as they worked. They were a flawless team, going through different patterns and routines with a few minor problems. She handled each well, putting Cash back in his place every time. In the middle of their workout, a tall, skinny cowboy in a tanned Stetson wandered from his perch against barn doors, sauntering lazily toward the pair. As fast as the horse had been calmed, he changed back into a wild thing quick enough to leave Eddie breathless.

His ears pinned flat against his skull, deadly hooves pawed the sawdust below them. He half-reared, front legs lashing out in the girl's loose hold on the reins. When he landed, she dismounted, arms crossed tightly over her chest, glaring at the newcomer. Moving closer, he muttered something Eddie couldn't hear from his position no matter how he strained his ears. Eddie noted how her voice rose, a sharp edge in it the man had lacked. Whatever answer snapped back wasn't what the man wanted to hear and, risking the rage of the horse, he delivered a resounding backhand to a freckled cheek. The girl staggered back, bracing herself on the now fully frenzied stallion that shoved his way in between them. That was enough for the man to back up hastily, hands up in a defensive position, before whirling to face the doors he had come in.

Eddie knew a big mistake when he saw one; rule number one of any horse worker was never to turn your back on a mad one. He couldn't blame the animal. A spark of rage burned to life low in his stomach. What kind of man hit a woman over a comment? His palms itched, begging him to return the blow for her.

Lightning quick, the bay lunged, sending his owner sprawling to the sawdust floor with an undignified shout of "Cash!" as he sank teeth into offending flesh. The guy screamed, jerking his arm away, sending blood pouring to the ground. Cursing loudly, he stumbled back to the gate and jumped it, letting out a strangled groan as he landed. Clambering to his feet, he faced the pen.

"You'll regret that! You and that fuckin mule of yours!" The words echoed around the barn even as the one who shouted them vanished from sight to seek help for his now profusely bleeding arm.

Fists clenched in utter rage, it took all the self-control that Eddie had in him not to follow the asshole out and show him just how it felt to be cold cocked out of the blue. But he didn't. He remained hidden in the shadows, watching to be sure the girl was okay.

Rubbing her cheek with one hand and the smarting pain in her ass with the other, the blonde sighed. "Thanks, Cash. We better get the hell out of dodge before he comes back with his cronies." Her words were meant only for the horse, but Eddie caught them. Part of him wanted to ease her pain with a hand of his own, the rest of him wanted to leave his mark on her round ass. A pair of riders appeared in the door, one trotting over quickly.

"You okay? We saw Seth leaving." Helping dust herself off, Eddie watched the newcomer hug the shorter girl.

"Yeah, I'm fine." She held a hand up. "Don't even start. I knew the risks of practicing alone, okay? But we know this knuckle head doesn't play well with others." Mounting her horse, she led the way back out of the barn, filling them in on what had happened.

A roar filled the arena, dragging Eddie back to reality. People cheered, hooting in reply to the announcer shouting a time and score for a new rider. Cursing himself, Eddie stamped out the now almost finished cigarette in a rush, taking off after her retreating back to take a chance and make his move.

Scanning the pens where most of the riders were milling around waiting for their events proved fruitless, but when he went to the training barn, it proved more successful. Her tanned arms were hugging a dark neck, laughing while she nuzzled him in return. Stepping back, one hand offered the horse a handful of some colorful treats, catching his nose to lift it up for a kiss. "That's my good, smart boy!" She was full of glee, and rightfully so.

Their moment was short-lived as a breeze through open doors sent an unfamiliar scent to the horse and the brown head shot up. Dark liquid eyes turned to face the man who now had his lanky frame draped on the gate, a single snort of warning given as a freckled face peeked out from under the neck between them.

"You're a fantastic roper, with a damn fine horse." Eddie said casually, stepping out into the bright lights. His gaze raked her from head to toe now that he was able to get a good look. She wasn't tall, but her legs were long, clad in jeans that hugged sweet hips and an ass that begged to be marked by teeth. With a wider waist and truly lovely tits, she was enough to make any man want to take a second look.

"Thanks." Her curt reply was punctuated with a turned back, focus returning to Cash.

"You're new here, aren't you?" He wasn't about to be dismissed so easily. From across the pen, she gave him an annoyed look. She wasn't used to being bothered while she took care of her horse.

"Not really. I've been riding and roping for years, my sister is the can chaser. We've both been in the circuit off and on when we can this year. What's it to you, Cowboy?" A hand rested on one hip, studying him carefully, having gained her full attention. The reply earned a lazy quirk of his lips. He couldn't help but admire her fire.

"Just tryin' to make small talk is all, Darlin'. Besides, that horse is something else, that's for sure. He up for a stud fee?"

"That's putting it mildly." It was delivered with a snort. "But no, he isn't up for leasing out. Cash hates anything that moves aside from me and my sister, which is about how I feel. So, is there anything else you want to bother me with?"

"Got a name?" Eddie wasn't sure if she'd cough it up, but figured asking couldn't hurt. Besides, it gave a reason to continue pestering her despite attempts to be rid of him. He wasn't one to give up easily once he set his sights on something. It was why, even after his wreck, he continued pushing to new goals. When he moved closer and she didn't protest, he took it as a good sign. With each step, she studied him intently like a hawk would a mouse, unaware she was the mouse.

"None of your business if you can't pay attention to the announcer. Cash!" The quipped answer was unhelpful, but at his name, Cash froze, no longer trying to creep closer to the stranger. Dacey laid a hand on his neck, stepping forward to keep in between them. An unreadable expression crossed her face, eyes taking him in from head to toe. He was attractive, she would give him that. Tall, slightly lanky despite the slide of muscles under his pearl-snap shirt. His hat cast his face into shadows, only allowing a brief glimpse of a smattering of freckles along a sharp, clean-shaven jaw. He carried himself with the grace of a lethal hunter, steps slow and sure. Her bottom lip was drawn between her teeth, creases between her eyebrows. The man gave her another lazy grin, wolfish enough it earned a tinge of color on high cheeks.

Promising.

"Do you expect me to buy that?" He gave a small head tilt, a smile widening dangerously. He motioned to the ever closing distance between them.

Despite the low timber of his voice, she snorted, breaking whatever spell seemed to have befallen her. Rolling her eyes in his direction, she took a step back to Cash. "Just here to flirt with me, Cowboy? Or did you have a real reason to hunt me down?"

Her words coaxed a dark chuckle from him, and he caught how she swallowed at the sound. "And if I am? If there was no other reason?"

"Then I say don't. I won't be here much longer; besides, I ain't looking for a quick fling in a stall." The annoyance that colored her words threw Eddie for a loop. Was she annoyed at him, or was it something else crawling under her skin?

"Well, why not? Rodeo next weekend isn't far from here, so why leave when you're doing so good?" He faked confusion, dodging her remark about a quickie in a stall. Another tiny step, moving him closer and causing another blush, fueling the creature rising in him. His mind was becoming a dark playground other ways he could make her flush and make that smart mouth work.

She broke their locked gaze, subconsciously shivering. “My sister and I are… moving soon.”

He knew she was lying, just by the way she had hesitated and studied the horse like he was the only one in the barn suddenly. “Shame, hate to see a pretty little thing like you go, especially since I still don’t even have a real name. Come on, Darlin’ just give me that at least.” While he spoke, Eddie could feel a familiar, haunting ache rise in him. The tremble in his hand showed as he reached out to touch her finally while he spoke.

Damn it all! Why now? Why did the crushing need for the powder hit him now, of all times?

He cursed it, temper flaring up and lighting a deep burning rage that had been kept tamped down this whole day. It was helped along as she sidestepped the touch and he let his hand fall empty back down to his side. “How old are you, anyway? Twelve? Thirteen? I shouldn’t be caught talking to kids.” The words came out with a harsh snap, and he swallowed down a curse, mentally chewing himself out as anger flashed across her face, causing her to step closer to Cash.

“I’m eighteen, thank you very little.” She spat back, crossing her arms. Sure, it was a rather fresh eighteen. Her birthday had been two months before, but he didn’t need to know that.

“Old enough for a drink then? Let me make up for that sudden outburst?” Of all the places that he needed to get to, the bar was top of the list. His brow was arched, causing the smirk to be teased out again. Besides, he didn’t care about her age, even if it was ten years younger than his twenty-eight. She blanched but recovered quick enough to fire back a smirk that mirrored the wicked one aimed at her.

"I'm a little young for that, don't you think? Sorry to ruin your great plans."

"You think that matters to me? Besides, come on, the legal drinking age here in Montana right now is eighteen, you and I both know that." Fuck, while Eddie loved the banter they were having, his trembles would become visible to her soon. It was taking all he had to keep a hand from scrubbing at his nose.

"My sister is riding soon. And how do I know that you're going to bring me back? There's been a lot of talk of serial killers moving around these last few months." Every paper they could scrounge up, she devoured. Josie had called her morbid, but she couldn't help it. Something about the way these killers lured young women fascinated her. Maybe, if she studied their tactics enough, it would keep the two of them safe on the road.

Eddie lit up like a sunrise at her words. She was as good as his now if she went to the bar with him. There was no promise, and damn sure no trust, but Eddie knew he couldn't just take off with her and never come back. "Guess we'll see, won't we? Gotta learn to live on the wild side."

"Let me get Cash put up and we can see then? Maybe I will 'learn to live' as you say." Was she backing out? Leading him on? He didn't like that, not one bit, and it pissed him off, yet he held his tongue. If he was going to get what he wanted, it was best to play along and keep his head on straight, at least for now.

"I'll give you my name if it means you come with me. Goes both ways, doesn't it?" The challenge hung between them like poorly placed bait. Should he take it?

Cornflower blue eyes rolled to the ceiling, paired with a heavy sigh. "If you have to know my name, it's..." She stalled a moment, toying with a piece of her saddle. What could it hurt? She'd just told him they wouldn't be in town after Sunday's rodeo ended. Taking a deep breath, mouth opening before a third voice broke into their conversation.

"Eddie!"

The pair spun around, eyes landing on Eddie's foster father. Walking over, Grant caught how Eddie hastily stepped back from the girl beside him and frowned.

"Hey, Grant! What brings you this way? Thought you were watching the rest of the rodeo before we headed to the hotel?" Was it obvious Eddie wanted the other gone? Could Grant read his face? Eddie wished to get the girl and go; fix the shake that was now growing impossible to hide and feel the soaring high the powder always gave him. Whatever Grant was going to say was forgotten in his haste to jump the fence separating them. The blonde had hit the ground hard in a dead faint. Her horse went wild, front hooves lashing out dangerously close to Grant's face as he bellowed a deep throated challenge.

"Whoa! Hey now! I won't hurt her. Come on, now." Grant tried soothing, sidestepping to keep the horse focused on him. In an unspoken tag team effort they used on the bulls, Eddie lunged forward to grab the girl out of the danger zone. She weighed almost nothing, but was still almost too much for Eddie as he hauled her up and over the fence.

The horse was a four-legged dragon at this point, bellowing his anger with every rear at Grant. It was nothing for the older man to roll under the fence to Eddie's side once he was sure both were safe from harm. He made it in the nick of time as two powerful back hooves slammed into the wood just inches from his head. Another round was delivered before the horse threw his head up and squealed, charging around the pen. Eddie couldn't focus on him at the moment, turning instead to the one who had caused the commotion.

The girl was limp, head rolling back as Eddie hoisted her up into a sitting position. "What the hell happened, Grant?" He tapped softly on her cheek, concerned at how pale it was under the freckles when just moments ago it had been full of life.

"No idea, but we need to get her up and to the medical tent if she doesn't come 'round here soon." Their debate was cut short as another person made their way into the barn to investigate the racket the stallion was causing.

"Cash? What's..." The woman shrieked, breaking into a sprint to cross the barn. "Dacey! What the hell have you done to her?" Hitting her knees, the newcomer slid to her sister's side, ignoring the two men who both had become pale where they sat.

Had their ears misheard? Was it simply wishful thinking?

Josie slapped away Eddie's hands as she tugged her sister to her. "Dacey! Come on, what happened to you? Wake up, please, wake up." Terror sunk its deadly claws into her throat, choking her to the point Josie could only pant for air.

Grant shot Eddie a stunned look from where he sat on the dirt floor, heedless to the stallion that had calmed some. Instead of rearing and bucking, the beast had taken to tossing his head with quick snorts and low throated bellows. Their eyes locked, twin looks of astonishment on their faces as the woman tried to rouse her sister.

"Josie?" Grant whispered, almost cracking on the last syllable. Emerald eyes flashed up to meet the brown ones, her mouth dropping open. She tried to form words, just a few, before she was hit with a wave of disbelief. Almost unable to breathe, she forced herself to bend at the waist, head between her knees, scrambling to process. The world spun in a dizzying, nausea-fueled whirlwind while her heart thundered in her ears so loud she couldn't hear anything over it.

"Damn it!" Eddie cursed, lifting Dacey in an easy hold, moving out of the way. Grant moved to Josie, unsure of how to help her. From where he had settled Dacey on a stack of hay to get her off the ground, Eddie turned to face him. "Grant, there's no fucking way, absolutely none! How could they…" He trailed off for a second, studying her.

No matter how he tried, his brain worked furiously to string more coherent sentences. The young woman in front of him bore little resemblance to the little girl physically ripped from his arms. How had he not noticed it before? Cornflower blue eyes, blonde hair in twin braids down her back, it should have all clicked sooner. "Ghosts don't come back from the dead."

"I get it, I do," Grant assured, looking between the sisters he had dreamed of that morning. "It's like I'm living in a nightmare I can't wake up from. I know they're here, but…" He couldn't figure out what to say. Nothing was adding up or making the least bit of sense while the two men stared down at the prone bodies before them, hypnotized. He rubbed at Josie's back, murmuring to her under his breath in hopes she would drag herself back to the present. If she didn't, he knew he would be forced to find her more qualified help.

In the distance, seemingly from miles away underwater rather than just a barn wall, came the voice of the announcer. "He could have gotten an inflight movie or some frequent flier miles with that one, but either way, I think he might have spurred himself right outta the saddle! That is one thing you can't do folks, the way he sits on his spurs is like sitting on the eject button, as we all just saw." The laughter that followed the words roused the two men from their daze.

"So, do we move them or leave them here till they come around on their own?" Eddie wasn't keen on the latter; he had already seen Dacey get slapped around once by a man he didn't know.

"Not like we can exactly get Cujo there out of the pen and not get our faces ripped off our body," Grant drawled, raising an eyebrow at the stallion still pacing back and forth only feet away. "I quite like my face where it is." Neither of them had to choose as a soft groan slipped from Dacey, her blue eyes forcing themselves open. For a moment she lay there, staring up unseeing at the roof before she shot up, falling from the hay back into a firm embrace. Eddie held her tightly, easing her to the ground to make sure she didn't trip herself up trying to run.

"Cash!" At his name, the horse snorted, wheeling around to let rear hooves land a solid kick at the wood separating them.

"Dacey! Hey, come on, calm down." Eddie soothed, hands moving to cup her cheeks, forcing her to look at him. She struggled, attempting to slap him away, although she was unsure of where she would go. "Look at me." He commanded, his finger under her chin jerking the wild eyes back to him. Something clicked within her, terror ebbing away as her eyes searched his.

"Eddie?"

He placed a steadying hand on her shoulder, nodding once in confirmation. Hazel eyes gazed deeply into blue, searching for any signs of her fainting again. When they found none, he jerked her forward in a bone-crushing hug, burying his face in the crook of her shoulder. Stunned, she sat there a moment before returning it, tears welling up, her body trembling in its fight to keep them from spilling out. He inhaled deeply, drawing the scent of horses mingled with wild honeysuckle in like it was the only thing keeping him alive. Dacey swallowed thickly in her fight against the tears, finally winning over them to turn her head toward Cash. She refused to let go of the man holding her, instead calling out softly from where she finally was feeling true safety for the first time in years.

"Easy buddy, it's okay. I'm alright, I promise." Her words soothed Cash, almost seeming to draw a slight bobbing nod from him. Eddie drew back, allowing one hand to trail his fingers down her cheek to confirm she was real. Satisfied, he pulled her back to him, noting the way her body easily fit to his.

"How's it going over there?" He called to Grant, noting Dacey hardly turned her head from where it rested on his shoulder to peek over it. Her breath ghosted along his neck, warmth soaking to his very core.

Alive! She was alive and in his arms.

Clearing his throat, he shifted them both to allow her a better view of her sister and Grant.

"It's going about as well as you think." Grant replied, ready to call it and seek the help they needed.

"Josie!" Dacey's voice was soft when she called her sister's name. When she pushed away from Eddie, he fought the urge to pull her back to him. Wherever her mind had wandered, it was on a bat out of hell speed back to the situation at hand. Her head snapped toward Dacey, as she tried and failed to lunge to her feet.

"Dacey! Thank heaven, Dacey!" Her voice was rough, lungs still pleading for more air than she could give them. Grant caught her in a light hold to prevent her from hurting herself.

"Welcome back to the world of the living," he joked weakly, offering her a slight smile. She wavered again in his grasp for a few moments, jerking back as though stung once it all sank in. Terror welled up within her, hands slapping away those that held her in place like they burned.

"Dacey?!"

"I'm okay, I'm okay!" Rushing over, she slid to a halt, just shy of landing on her. "Josie!" Linking their hands, she waved them a little, noting how Josie was shaking hard enough to rattle bones. The panic was clear in her gaze as she kept looking over her sister's shoulder, nearly breaking Dacey's heart. "Focus, you're okay and so am I. Inhale." She guided her sister in a count of four through her nose, letting out a count of six through her mouth. "Exhale. There you go. Come on, look at me, nowhere else. Again, inhale, and exhale." The men could only watch as Dacey eased her sister out of the panic attack. By that point, both were trembling to the point their teeth chattered, but Dacey refused to let them get the best of her. She clenched her jaw as Josie let them consume her.

Eddie took a step forward slowly, unsure of what to do, looking back and forth from the girls to Grant. "Someone tell me what the hell's going on?"

Before anyone could say a word, an unfamiliar voice cut in. "Excuse me, but I'd rather the two of you get away from my fiancé." Seth drawled as he sauntered in. His arm was heavily bandaged, and Eddie realized this was the loser from earlier who had threatened Dacey and her horse. His vision nearly went red at the very idea of this piss-poor excuse of a wannabe cowboy getting near the two girls after that. Eddie tried to remain calm as he possibly could while everything within him screamed to deal with this man on his own.

Chapter 6

I See Red

Dacey whirled around, rage consuming her as she stood to her full height in front of Josie, hell bent on protecting her. She was acutely aware of the way the attack slammed into her sister with full force, though there was nothing she could do about it. "Go fuck yourself, Seth! You didn't learn earlier today that you're not going to manage anything here? She hasn't been your 'fiancé' since you put her in the hospital!" Josie clung weakly to her sister, trying to keep her in place, shaking so much it spilled over to Dacey's arms. In his pen, Cash started up again, charging back and forth in an attempt at getting to the man on the other side.

Eddie stepped between everyone, crossing his arms, an unreadable expression on his face as Dacey allowed herself to be drawn back once more to help her sister. Grant knew that body language well; the man had drawn himself up to his full height, hat pushed up just a little to allow Eddie to see better, arms crossed almost lazily as his hands gripped his biceps. Fury. Pure, unfiltered fury was building up in him, though outwardly he seemed bored by the whole situation. "I suggest you move along while you can, 'cause if she says you're full of shit then, buddy, you best believe I ain't about to put up with whatever lies you're spewing."

Seth frowned at the somewhat jovial tone the stranger was speaking in, almost as if he were an errant child needing coaxing to return to his parents. "The hell did you just try and tell me?" he spat, trailing a gaze over the other man in disgust.

"You heard me. Now move on along before you find out I ain't in the mood for this shit. Go on, get on outta here." A faint smirk curled the corner of Eddie's mouth as he talked, but it never reached his eyes. All he could feel was the steady shake in his limbs merging with hatred that he hadn't felt in so long, it was almost shocking. Blood pounded in his ears until it was a deafening roar he couldn't hear over. His heart hammered against his ribcage in ever faster increments, his breathing becoming shallow pants. Yet he stood there stock still, easily containing it all. It had been a while since his last physical fight, but that didn't mean Eddie wasn't about to see just how hard he needed to throw a human body into a fence to break it.

Grant broke the tension swelling between them, stepping in the middle, hands held up in a mild attempt at keeping Eddie in place. He wasn't stupid. He had seen the younger man in more than one bar fight, and knew better than to try holding him back. It would have been easier to capture lightning in a jar than stop Eddie once he had his mind set on beating someone's ass. "Two on one ain't very fair, but let's be honest, shall we? Eddie ain't gonna need my help to turn you inside out.

"Even if he did, I'm pretty sure a retired Green Beret should be something that you should take more seriously." It was all said as if Grant was simply talking about a day's work ahead of them, moving to cross his arms over his chest instead of having them held out.

Grinding his teeth, hands clenched in fists, Seth snorted with a shake of his head. "I ain't about to just leave after all the hell I've been through trying to find them. So, keep barking all you want. It ain't going to work; they come with me even if I have to drag that youngest bitch by her hair kicking and screaming. Although, that's nothing less than what she deserves at this point." Seth pointed a finger at Dacey. "I've done it before, I'll do it again."

Dacey snapped at the threat, jerking away from Josie to lunge at Seth with a cry of indignation. Eddie caught her easily, arms wrapping around her in an unbreakable hold. She kicked out, still struggling to reach Seth, spitting a litany of curses toward him. "Come on now, knock it off. I got this, you gotta trust me." Eddie assured her, gripping her harder as she continued to thrash against him.

"You touch me anymore, Eddie, and I'll knock you on your ass. Let me go!"

"As you wish." The powerful arms that kept her pinned against a firm chest let go suddenly, dropping her to her ass in the dirt with an undignified yelp. Rage clamored through his body, refusing to leave much room for rational thought. Even though it had been Dacey he dropped, Eddie didn't seem phased as he kept his eyes pinned on Seth. The blonde scrambled up to her feet, face flushed. Her chest heaved as her fists clenched so tightly at her sides that her knuckles went stark white.

"We'll discuss who is dropping who later on. Right now, you keep out of my fight." She tried to argue, not even flinching when a hand landed softly on her shoulder from behind.

"Dacey, come on now kiddo, let Eddie be." Grant tried to soothe, sounding so much like her grandfather Dacey found herself with more than just tears of anger welling up in her eyes. He tugged at her, earning a single step back from Eddie's side. Still, the other man never once broke the staring contest he was in.

Knowing she wasn't going to get anywhere with Eddie at the moment, Dacey let Grant help her back over to where Josie was huddled against the hay bales, wheezing. A guilty look flashed over her features as Dacey knelt, receiving a pat on the top of her head as she took her sister's hands.

"Let them have their pissing contest. Trust me when I say that Eddie is a lot meaner than he looks now. I've bailed him out of the local jail plenty of times to know that for a fact." More times than Grant wanted to admit, and it was always with the other person coming out worse for wear. Their local sheriff, Dean, had once threatened to buy a cell just for Eddie if he kept it up.

Seth moved closer to the girls, attempting to ignore Eddie, who watched as Seth stood to his full height, chest puffed out like a banty rooster, hoping it would intimidate the other. "Now, you see, I've tried nicely to explain why what you're doing is a very bad idea. Yet your dumb ass just keeps walking closer." Eddie gave a humorless laugh as he spoke, uncrossing his arms, head tilting in a mockingly curious manner.

With every step, Seth walked into deeper danger. "Shut the fuck up. I'm not here to have a bitch session with you or the old man." Grant made a noise of protest at being called old. "I'm here for those two and they're–" He couldn't finish the sentence. Dacey streaked past both men in a flurry of blonde pigtails and an enraged cry. Her fist connected as hard as it could with Seth's jaw, snapping his head roughly to the side. He dropped unconscious to the ground in a crumpled heap.

Standing over him panting, the adrenaline flooding her system ran dry, forcing her to sink to the ground beside him. Trying her best to catch the breath that seemed determined to allude her, and cradling the hand she had struck Seth with, Dacey smothered a quiet, angry sob. A scream of pure fury erupted from her, along with another swing landing square on his nose, breaking it. A knuckle split wide at the contact, painting both hands in her blood when she pulled it back, holding it to her heaving chest.

"That was stupid, but I guess you're gonna do what you want, aren't you?" Eddie was shaking as his fist unclenched. He had been ready to strike, to shut the other man up, but found himself a little at a loss at the sudden shift in the situation. "Well then," He stepped over the prone figure, spitting on it. Reaching down, he lifted Dacey like a rag doll to keep her from continuing the blows. She snarled and spat like a wild animal, trying to land a few more even as he hauled her away. Walking over to the soft hay pile Josie sat near, Eddie dropped her. "You two have some serious explaining to do. For now, you need to let me fix that hand. Josie, do we need to get you medical attention?" The concern was genuine. Josie bent in half against Dacey, teeth chattering, body quaking.

It was enough to snap Dacey out of her blind need for violence. Turning on her heel, her hands reached out, resting on Josie's cheeks, forcing their eyes to lock. "Come on now, focus on me. It's okay, he's down for the count. You need to breathe or else I will be forced to call someone in to help, okay? I know that neither of us wants that, so work with me, Josie." She soothed, starting the steady breathing pattern from earlier.

Words so soft neither Eddie nor Grant could hear them were whispered to Josie, some earning weak laughs while others earned stronger and stronger nods. The men allowed them time to collect themselves, neither sure of what else to do without causing another spiral. Once she was sure that she could remain on her feet without assistance, Josie allowed herself to be helped up, Dacey ready to catch her at a moment's notice. Grant held out a hand to Josie, drawing her to him in a protective hold, whispering into her ear.

Offering a nod of thanks, Dacey left the trio, walking to the pen where Cash waited impatiently, pacing the length of it. Eddie followed her, leaving Grant to guide Josie toward the doors and peace of mind. Josie glanced back at Eddie, face pale, but he didn't miss the warning look cut toward him. *"I will deal with you myself,"* it screamed out. He ignored it, moving toward Dacey, who had caught Cash to check him over. Eddie watched one hand stroke along a warm flank, his own gaze checking her over.

She hadn't expected the crash after the emotions that ravaged her. Her body trembled hard enough it rattled her teeth, the edges of her vision darkening until it seemed she was looking through a tube.

He was beside her in an instant, guiding her once more to the ground, forcing her head between her knees. "There you go, breathe, just focus on my voice." Cash snapped his teeth dangerously close to Eddie's ear, earning a hard swat in return. "Fuck off, Cujo, you know she needs me." Rubbing her back, he settled next to her. "You know, I ain't exactly keen to keep ending up on the ground."

Dacey managed a weak snort, focusing on regaining control. Sitting up, she allowed him to pull her back against him, resting his chin on the top of her head. "Follow my breathing." He spoke softly, his chest expanding in a larger inhale. Doing as instructed, eyes closed, her body fully relaxed into his. They remained curled together for a few moments, unwilling or unable to stand. Eventually, Eddie drew back. "How come you're as thin as you are? Don't lie either, I know there's a reason."

The noise made was inhuman, hands shoving him down on his ass while she rose to her feet. "Don't start on me. Now isn't the time or place for this conversation to happen. Later, okay? We need to get moving to check on Josie, and Cash is tired of being good." It was like the stallion understood the words, teeth clicking so close to the back of Eddie's neck he felt the brush of velvety lips.

"Noted." Standing, he dusted off stray bits of hay and dirt that now painted his jeans. Dacey took Cash's reins in one hand, the other scratching behind his ears. "Cujo, I've warned you once, so this is your final warning cause this ain't baseball; there's no three strikes and you're out with me. You get two and then you're glue." Walking toward the gate, he opened it, motioning for them to go first. She mounted, not trusting her legs to carry her all the way back to the stalls. Cash sidestepped Eddie's hand when he reached to touch her leg.

"Do you think he took her to the medical tent or to her stall?"

"That depends. If she got worse between the time they left us and getting to the horses, then he would bring her to the tent. Otherwise, he'll take her straight back, so we don't have to struggle looking for them." Eddie lit a smoke, exhaling a quick smoke ring. "Either way, we gotta put him up first. Know where her horse is?"

"Buckshot's with Riley. They were waiting for their event soon. I don't even…what time is it? She has to be worried sick." Her heart rate kicked up again, mouth drying. "Shit. This could get a little complicated."

"Now what the hell did you do?" Pinching the bridge of his nose, Eddie counted backward from ten.

"Do you remember the Wheeler family? Riley was in my year at school, but always in different classes. They live to the south of you. We ran into each other earlier. She started helping Josie and I figure out a plan to deal with the moron you saw earlier."

He had to restrain from cursing out loud. "I wish I'd never asked. Just come on, which way are we heading?"

They were quiet for the rest of the walk back, Dacey starting plenty of sentences she never spoke. Her mind was so tangled, a dull ache began forming behind her eyes. It throbbed with every step Cash took, bounced between thoughts. What now? Was Josie going to make them run? Could she stay and fight for their freedom?

Eddie watched the way her eyes grew distant, seeing nothing in front of them. Reaching up, he rested a hand on her knee. "I'll remind you of your own statement, shall I? We can talk about all of this in greater detail later." She was spared from having to answer as Josie and Grant came into view, her sister wearing holes in the floor of Buckshots stall. Drawing closer, they caught the tail end of what appeared to have been a deep discussion.

Chapter 7Something Bad About to Happen

Grant spotted them coming, waving for them to deal with Cash. Dacey nodded, dismounting. Eddie joined her in the stallions stall, leaning against the wall to watch.

"Why are you sorry? You didn't do anything." Grant asked, brow furrowed.

"That's the whole point, isn't it? I did nothing! Let him get in my head, let Dacey put herself in danger again, ruined my plans of keeping you two out of this mess we're in." She was babbling, hands waving, voice creeping higher the longer she went. Beside them, Dacey flinched away from the words thrown so carelessly. Cash shifted, shying away from sudden, harder curry strokes. Eddie pulled his brim down. Josie sniffed hard, hand scrubbing over her face. "I'm sorry I let everything go to hell in a handbasket, Grant. I swear I didn't want this dumped on you. We were trying so hard to avoid this, to keep you out of it."

The words stung. Dacey and Eddie shared a glance, both wondering what he would say. "Josie, let's get out of here so we can talk somewhere a little safer, please? I understand you have a lot you want to say right now, and we will, I promise, but this isn't the time or place. Come on, let's focus on the horses. Where's yours?"

She chewed her lower lip, looking at Dacey rubbing Cash's nose, offering the headstall out for Eddie to hang up. "Buckshot is with a friend up near the gates, though by now they should be heading back. I was supposed to run, but when Dacey never showed up to help me get ready, I came looking for her. I need to go get her."

"Eddie!" Grant called. "I'm leaving you with Dacey to tend the horses. When you're done with that, meet us at the truck." Eddie offered a nod, accepting the saddle to set it on its stand. "There we go, come on. Please?"

Josie caved, letting his arm drop around her shoulders. Part of her wanted to break away from the warm touch, run to Dacey, and haul her to the truck. To just run away from it all and start over. She fought it down, casting one last look over her shoulder. Dacey was shutting the stall door, offering Eddie an exasperated sigh when Cash nipped at him. An exhausted laugh slipped from her lips. Those two were going to be worse than ever if she let them continue being together, but for the moment, she needed to focus on the man walking beside her. It was going to be a long night, that much she knew for certain, and Josie wasn't looking forward to it.

They walked in silence, her mind racing so quick it could have won the round she had missed. What could she say to them? Why was it she wasn't good at making up stories on the spot, yet Dacey could weave a tale from nothing? Try as she might, when they reached his truck, she was speechless and unsure of how to respond. Grant opened the tailgate for her, offering a out a hand to help her up.

"Go ahead, take a seat. We can wait for them." He assured her, leaning against the steel frame. All Josie could do was nod, climbing up inside, wishing it was acceptable to curl into a ball as she silently begged Dacey to hurry. Instead, she let her legs dangle, looking at him.

"Are you sure? I know you've got questions. And even though I'd rather lie through my teeth answering, I can't."

"You never were good at it." Grant agreed, lips turning up at the corners. Josie offered a rude gesture, sticking her tongue out. "What? You weren't! If you couldn't look the person in the eye, then you were shifting around in place so much you could have started a fire."

She gave a nonchalant shrug, neither confirming nor denying his statement. He joined her on the tailgate, listening to the sounds of life around them. Settling in, Josie moved to lean on the fender, legs stretched out. "Guess we just wait, then?"

"We wait."

Back at the barn, Dacey finished brushing out Cash, tucking her grooming kit beside her tack. Worry bit into her bones, making her look up every time someone walked past. Joining Eddie, she took a deep breath. "I think we need to go find Riley. Chances are nothing happened, but she should have been here by now."

Eddie pushed away from the wall he had been resting against, eyes keeping track of each person walking by. "If you want, we can." Luck must have been listening in on their conversation, stepping in for the first time that day. Riley rounded the far corner with the horses, talking softly to them. Dacey's breath rushed from her lungs. Moving to them, she took the reins of Buckshot.

"There you are, Khloe! When Nicole didn't show up to run, I came to find you and no one was here, so–Oh. Who is he?" Riley stopped dead in her tracks, a slow grin spreading across her face. "I'm Riley Wheeler. A pleasure to meet you." She offered a hand to him, standing up straight. Dacey ignored the pair, guiding the mare into her respective housing for the night.

"Eddie." He shook Riley's hand, hardly paying attention when she smiled at him. His eyes tracked Dacey as she began unsaddling a gorgeous buckskin mare. Jerking himself back in line, he moved to the small garbage can tucked between the stalls. Both horses' names were on it, and he popped the top.

"Nice to meet you, Eddie." She turned back to her friend. "Khloe, you scared me half to death when neither of you showed up for the barrels! I didn't know what to do. When her chance to ride was coming up, I panicked and told them she had gotten sick and couldn't ride." She babbled, unaware of the tension radiating off the other girl. "I didn't know what else to do. I hope that was okay?"

"Thanks, Riley. What you did was a good move. If you don't mind, I'll fill you in tomorrow. It's been a long, bad evening." Dacey tried to turn the girl away, heaving Josie's saddle onto its stand.

"How many scoops?" Eddie called.

"Two each. Right now, I want nothing more than a bar, dance floor, and drink, in that order." Dacey said, hanging the headstall up. Accepting the bucket offered out, she tossed Eddie the hay net.

Riley noted how they moved in a perfect routine, as though it was something they did all the time. "Can we still talk there? Sometimes after a hard day, a good, cold, yellow jacket helps." She hinted, leaning on the stall door. Dacey mulled over her words, stepping out of Eddie's way for him to hang up the net.

Humming in thought, she moved to Cash's stall, battling him back. He pawed the sawdust under his hooves, growing leery of all the people around, his nostrils flared. "I'm not the only one who can make the choice. While I'm all for it, he's one of the others." She motioned to Eddie, who was now filling Cash's feed and water buckets safely outside of the stall.

"Will it convince them if I offer to buy the entire night?" Riley offered. Eddie turned to her, passing the items to Dacey without even looking at where she stood. Once again, Riley marveled at the smooth, almost flawless duo.

Eddie leaned on the door, watching Dacey, eyes running over her as he tried to focus on the conversation at hand. "I asked her earlier today if she wanted a drink with me."

"I'll tag along if you don't mind! My brothers are going to be at the Lone Star, anyway. We can all get to know each other better and fill them in on what's going on. I mean, if the plan is still going to be the same? This way, we can kill two birds with one stone." Riley offered. Eddie frowned at the suggestion, shaking his head just a bit when Dacey looked his way in silent question.

"I'm not sure that's where we're going. Eddie and I have to meet up with Nicole and a family friend at their truck." Dacey tried to hedge, unsure of how to tell Riley the extra company wasn't a good idea any longer. Her throat tightened at the lie, stomach dropping. Here she was, given the chance to make a real friend, and she was ruining it.

"Not a problem. I'm sure Nicole will understand." Riley grinned, draping an arm around Dacey's shoulders. "Once I explain that's where they are, she'll agree. If not, then you can drop me off with them."

"I mean, I guess." Dacey caved, shooting Eddie an apologetic look that earned an unsympathetic shrug in return.

"Perfect!" Riley bounded away from her, falling into step with Eddie, smiling up at him. "So, what are you entered in this weekend?" She asked him, toying with the end of one brunette braid. Dacey mocked a gag behind her back, hand at her throat.

Eddie's gaze flicked between the two, a corner of his mouth quirking up. Amused at the other's reaction, he spoke to Riley. "Nothing, we brought some of the bulls they're bucking." Glancing down at her, Eddie almost rolled his eyes at her obvious attempts to flirt. His mind was far too preoccupied to even begin to think about anything she was offering at the moment, but he filed it away. Maybe later he would get a chance to look into it once he had a few drinks in him and the truth from the girls. Riley was oblivious to his lack of interest. "You didn't enter anything? You can't tell me with that build you aren't a rider of some sort," she hedged.

"I used to ride thorough stock, but those days are long behind me.

Ain't got time to deal with riding when you're running the stock." He didn't feel the need to tell her the complete truth about why he no longer rode.

Trailing behind them, Dacey watched Riley gravitate toward Eddie as though he were the only person in the barn. Exhaustion teased the edges of her mind, toying with her even though she knew they had a long evening ahead of them. Josie had to be feeling worse; she always crashed out after a panic attack, and it made Dacey worry. What if she passed out before anyone could even talk about anything? If that were the case, Dacey knew it would be up to her to make sure everything was under control for the rest of the night. Longing for a piece of gum to chew in order not to bite her lower lip in half, she was jerked from her musings when hands caught her shoulders. Head snapping up, she met Eddie's gaze as he held her in place to keep her from walking straight into him.

"You in there? Or are you off in left field picking flowers?" he teased, ignoring the way Riley pouted a little at their contact.

Dacey pulled away with a scoff. "Don't you worry about me." Marching past him, she lit up at seeing Josie. Sprinting the rest of the distance between them, she caught the hands reaching out. Her eyes raked over her sister, making sure everything was in place. "You okay?"

"Just tired, ready to get this over with. What's with the tag-a-long?" Josie whispered back, chin pointing at Riley, where she leaned on the bed of the truck, talking with Grant.

"I tried to get her to stay, sticking to the original plan. She decided to expedite us meeting her brothers from tomorrow morning to tonight," Dacey whispered. "It can't be helped, but maybe this can work in our favor?"

Eddie broke away from the others, moving closer to the sisters as they talked quietly amongst themselves. "Y'all think it's a good idea to tangle her up in this?" he asked, leaning on the cab, blocking their view of the girl in question.

"Not like we have much of a choice now, do we? You can thank Dacey for dragging her into the middle of it without permission." Josie sighed. Dacey offered her a rude gesture in return, earning a laugh. "I'm just telling him the truth. We already agreed to meet her brothers, and honestly, I vaguely remember the Wheeler twins if I try hard enough. They were a nightmare growing up when we had to help them."

Dacey frowned, trying to draw memories up of the family in question. "I don't remember them at all, but I wasn't a very popular kid in school. If I try hard enough, I remember Riley, but she was one of those not exactly popular but not an outcast types. Everyone liked her across the board, I think?"

"What are you three over there conspiring about?" Grant cut in, earning a guilty look from both women while Eddie pushed away from the truck.

"Nothing. What's the plan?" he asked, fishing a cigarette out of his shirt pocket.

Josie held her hand out, hiding her surprise when he lit it and passed it over. Grant followed suit, lighting one of his own. Dacey wrinkled her nose, shaking her head.

"Miss ma'am, you wonder why you have asthma worse than you did growing up." Dacey snarked. A small cloud of smoke was blown into her face, and her eyes narrowed.

"I'll choose what kills me, thank you very little," Josie snapped back.

"Ladies! Enough please?" They ducked their heads, chastised. "Thank you. Okay, so, where is this Lone Star bar?" Grant asked, taking a deep drag.

"If you don't mind, I'll just ride with you so I can give directions. My brothers can take me back to our hotel room once it's all done. Khloe and Nicole need to talk to them anyway, so I figure it works out." Riley pipped up, taking a step forward to gain attention.

Eddie made a face behind Riley's back that earned a half grin from Grant. "That sounds good to me." His agreement had Eddie rolling his eyes hard enough Grant feared one would fall out, causing him to stifle a laugh. Eddie wasn't one to just allow others to tag along when it came down to it, but there were too many questions to just it let go. If this is what it was going to take to get his answers, then he was more than willing to play along. Patting the roof, he looked at the group. "Load up slick. Riley, you're gonna sit in front with me. The girls can ride in the bed, cause there's no reason to bring both trucks." He glanced at Josie for confirmation.

"I agree. We'll be fine in the back. Not like it's the first time I've had to sit back there, and it won't be the last." Using the tire as a step, she gave an experimental bounce before hauling herself over the side. Dacey scurried up with Josie, settling on a wheel fender and tugging her hat off. Staring down at the worn black fabric, she idly wondered if the previous owner had even registered it during all the chaos. Josie watched her, pulling her hat off to keep it from blowing away. "You alright Dace?" She kept her voice low. Grant started the truck, his voice muffled by the glass while he talked to Riley and Eddie.

"Peachy. Think we still need the original plan now? Seems like with Grant and Eddie here, they aren't likely to mess with us anymore, are they?"

"Seth would've gotten into a knock down drag out with Eddie if you hadn't just taken a cheap shot." Anything else she could have said became tucked away for later as Grant slowly pulled out into the parking lot and began picking up speed. Dacey shifted to hold on better as the truck rumbled down the road toward their destination. Josie watched her, trying to gauge if her younger sister was shaken as she was or taking it all in stride.

Inside the cab, Riley tried to sit as close to Eddie as possible without being rude. "So, what's your ranch's name? Anything I'd know?"

"It ain't my ranch, it's Grant's. I just work on it."

"You grew up on it, live on it, and pretty much own it in all but name until I'm gone." Grant cut in, having been listening keenly to make sure Eddie didn't get too harsh. "It's Wildwood, down in Aviston. Nothing fancy, but your family has been living behind us for generations."

Riley's eyes went wide, and she nearly swooned. "Nothing fancy?!" Her face grew redder by the second. "You turn out almost *all* the bucking stock for so many circuits! There is a literal *waiting list* to breed to your stock! You *own* the top bull in the nation for the third *year* in a row."

Grant shrugged at her outburst. "There are waiting lines for a lot of breeders. Doesn't mean a whole lot."

"*Are you kidding me?!*" The men winced at her screech.

"If you're gonna go all giddy and groupie on us, get lost. We ain't got time for this shit." Eddie snapped, pressing himself closer to the door. Riley shot a dark look back at him, unfazed.

"I've been trying to get my mare in with your studs for over two, going on three, years, and I'm still waiting. I think I have the right to be excited." She drawled at him with her arms crossed over her chest. The blush from earlier was gone, replaced by an unreadable, almost bored, expression. Eddie ground his teeth, jaw locked, to keep from snarling a retort; they still needed Riley to be sure everything went smoothly.

Chapter 7

Neon Moon

Lost in thought, Josie was forced to make a quick grab along the truck bed to keep from face planting when Grant pulled to a stop at the bar. The parking lot was crowded, noise spilling out of the open door in a cloud of smoke that twisted around the ankles of those clustered close to it, shouting to one another. Neon lights flickered in the fading light, their hum adding another layer to the sounds pouring from the bar. She wrinkled her nose at the boisterous laughter and shouting that fought to be heard over the live band set up somewhere deep inside. All she wanted was the quiet bliss of a warm shower.

Standing, she watched Eddie climb out of the cab, annoyance on his face as he fought the urge to slam the door in Riley's face. Dacey joined Josie, bracing herself on the edge of the bed to vault over. He caught her, settling her closer to him than Josie cared for.

Riley seemed frustrated as well, waiting for Grant and Josie to climb out of the truck. "My brothers are in there somewhere. No idea where, though," Riley confessed, glancing at the door.

“Only way to look for them is to head in. Come on, then.” Grant gestured for Josie to go before him.

“Want to help me search up by the bar?” Riley offered with a grin aimed at Eddie. Dacey snorted, moving to catch up with her sister. Eddie controlled himself in order to keep from clenching a fist. The need for a drink and the powder were thrumming through his veins hard enough his knees shook in time with his hands. Well controlled movements carried him through the door with ease.

“You’re a big girl. Find them on your own, besides the girls need them more than I do.” Waving her off, he tried to slip into the crowd without drawing too much attention to himself. Striding across the dance floor to cut over to the corner where pool tables were tucked away among dart boards, he scanned the crowd.

The tables were crowded with games in full flow, but he didn’t mind waiting. Instead, Eddie stood in line for a drink, scanning those around him for a certain type of man he knew had to be around there somewhere; one that kept off to the corners and seemed to be out of place as they lounged around like they owned the place.

Shuffling forward step by step, he finally reached the bartender. She leaned forward to hear him over the music as he shouted his order at her, the singer hitting a high note at that moment. He didn’t have to wait long. A yellow papered bottle pressed into his hand within seconds of the name. Taking a satisfied pull from it, Eddie made his way toward the corner booth where a stranger sat.

As he drew closer, a woman stepped between them, resting a hip on the tabletop, eyeing him. “Can I help you?” Heavily painted eyes fluttered at him as she rested a hand on his chest.

“Fuck, I hope so, baby doll. But I’m more interested in what your boss can help me with at the moment." He kept his voice hardly audible. She understood, sliding into the booth beside the man. He was scruffy, at best in Eddie's opinion. A ragged, worn-out hat sagged down over eyes that appeared haunted, dark circles under them creating more shadows than the low light dropping over him. A day or more of growth covered his jawline down his throat, leading to a threadbare shirt missing the top button, sweat stains blooming from the underarms. If it wouldn't cause issues, Eddie would have curled his lip in disgust. Was this what he was going to end up as one day? A slob of a human that catered to the lowest of them all? Shaking away the troublesome thoughts, he rested his palms on a greasy, scarred wood tabletop.

"What do you need?" The dealer leaned back against the booth seat, one arm dropping down around the shoulders of the woman.

"Coke, if you got it, time, if she does."

A slow smirk curled the edge of the dealer's mouth. He gave a jerk of his chin toward the woman. "She's extra."

"Fine by me." Whatever it took to sate both hungers clawing at his nerves.

"What's fine with you?" Dacey's voice broke through the little world they had built around themselves. Eddie whirled around in anger, glaring down at her as the woman in the booth laughed.

"Looks like you got a tagalong there, honey. Seems you don't need my services after all." Turning away in clear dismissal, the woman focused solely on the dealer. Eddie had to control himself from punching something at the sight of Dacey crossing her arms with a look of boredom. Gritting his teeth, fists clenched so tight they turned white at the knuckles, he rounded on her. The sheer *need* unfurling in his gut was raw and pure as it consumed him, and here this whelp was ruining it.

“What the hell do you want? Why are you even over here?”

“Riley found her brothers, and they sent me to look for you like some kind of dog.”

“I’m a goddamn adult, Dacey. I don’t need a babysitter huntin’ me down. This ain’t even my problem! Get your ass out of here and quit fuckin’ my night up.”

Her gaze narrowed at him, arms uncrossing to rest on her hips. “An ‘adult’ you say?” She raked her eyes over his body, then flicked them toward the booth before aiming them back at him. “Cute, could have fooled me, but oh well.” Turning on her heel, she made her way around the outer edge of the dance floor. Something snapped deep within him, his vision tunneling as a roaring filled his ears.

Stalking after her, Eddie pushed people out of his way without a care if they were offended or not. He wasn’t sure exactly what was driving him forward in order to catch up to her, but the creature clawing his throat in an acidic burn wanted nothing but answers to sate it. Who was she to think she could talk to him that way? His jaw ached from clenching it so hard he should have feared teeth cracking. Catching up with her, Eddie grabbed her upper arm, whirling her around to face him.

“The hell you think you’re doing?” Dacey jerked her arm fruitlessly in an attempt to make him let go. His grip was solid, tight enough she should have winced, but she looked more annoyed than anything as she tugged again.

Eddie used that momentum against her. Jerking her back flat against his chest, he lowered his head in order to be heard over the music. Lips brushing against the shell of her ear, he could feel her shiver while he spoke. “You don’t get to fuck my night up, Darlin’, and then just assume you can waltz on away; that ain’t how it works with me.”

Dacey felt her pulse kick up a notch at the teeth grazing the skin of her ear in a light nip as he spoke. Swallowing hard against her drying throat, she dug deep to keep hold of her courage. "Since you're not my keeper, I think I'm capable of doing as I please." She turned her head a little to meet the hazel gaze boring into her in a blaze of clear fury. "Now, I gotta go meet up with the rest of our group so, if you don't mind," she tried to jerk away without any luck, "Let me go before I resort to measures you really don't want me to use."

His grip on her arm relaxed enough to slide down to her hips, gripping them in an equally painful hold. "Try me and see what happens. I had some pretty good plans set up for tonight before you came back in, like some sort of bad haunting I didn't want. Now you're gonna fix those plans. Seems only fair, doesn't it?"

"Not in the least bit."

Pushing her back toward the back bar, Eddie kept his grip tight. "Oh, I think it is. They can manage just fine without us for a little bit. You're gonna keep me company while I get a drink and keep from tossing you out the door for ruining said plans." Dacey shot him a glare, trying to dig her heels in to stop their progress. "Walk, Darlin'. My temper's almost gone, and I can't tell you the last time I had a hit. You're pushin' a bear that will bite." His mind was a hurricane of thoughts; dark and twisted in their search for the powder and a warm body to bury himself in. To forget the world around him even for a brief moment. Nothing was making sense anymore. It was flashing past at a warped speed and all he could do was cling to the ride. The girls falling back into their lives, the moron man-child that followed like the desperate dog he was, and withdrawal creeping up made his insides turn.

"Look, I would *love* nothing more than to get a drink with you," she snarked, gripping his hands to gain his attention, “But if you had a set of eyes in your head that worked, then you’d see the man I knocked out just came in through a back door.” Pressing harder against him, she missed Eddie stopping mid-step, almost knocking them both over.

Turning her sharply around to keep her from being spotted, Eddie took a moment to sort out what to do next. His grip on Dacey loosened even as his temper continued to climb. First her, then that waste of space and air? What was going to happen next? Part of him didn’t doubt a herd of bulls would rush the place if it came down to it.

Shaking his head to clear the dark thoughts brewing, he took a deep breath. “Alright, we won’t deal with that particular issue right now. While I don’t mind a good bar fight once in a while, if I get into one now, Grant will kill us both and leave us to rot here in the bar. He ain’t a fan of fighting, even if it is someone who deserves to get his shit kicked.” Dacey hummed an agreement, burying her face into his chest for a brief moment. Teeth clenched, hands resuming the bruising grip on her hips to quell the shake, Eddie slowly let out another breath. “Come on, let’s try getting to Grant and Josie before I end up picking that fight to burn off all my steam.”

“No.” She cast a hasty glance around them, brain scrambling to form a semi useful plan. Linking their fingers, she drew him out onto the dance floor in a more secluded section couples had taken over. “Follow my lead.” Spinning to wrap her arms around his neck, Dacey shifted until her body was flush against his. Eddie kept a firm grip on her hips, trying to find the beat. Dacey found it first, her body moving in time to the song pumping out of the speakers. He followed her lead, spinning her every now and then as the others did, his mind easing its frantic downward spiral. “Remember when you taught me how to dance?”

Eddie almost missed the words, a broken laugh escaping him. "Unfortunately, I do very well. Pretty sure I still have broken toes from that." Her laugh warmed something in him, and he pulled her closer. It had been far too long since he had heard it and now that he had, all he could focus on was finding another way to coax it from her. "But it seems like you've improved." It wasn't a lie. The way she was moving her body made him almost groan.

Dacey's shoulder rose and fell in a quick shrug. "I wasn't that bad! I've always loved to dance; I just didn't know how to be with a partner." She reminded him.

"Oh, I know, trust me, I know."

Eddie had just settled down for the evening after supper in the main house, bare feet propped up on the coffee table as the TV screen came to life. Just as he was taking a swig of soda, Dacey burst in, causing him to choke on the little he managed to swallow. She didn't say anything as he coughed, just waited for him to be done.

"What the hell, brat? Any particular reason you come bursting in like the damn world's on fire?" he asked, looking past her to see if anyone had tagged along. It took him a moment before he realized she had tears in her eyes, and her hands balled into fists at her sides.

"Josie told me I can't go to the Follies this weekend because I can't dance with someone else. She said that the dancing is only for people who know how to have a partner and that no one will ask me and if they do, they'll make fun of me." She began to sob harder, anything else she may have said was lost to the fresh wave of tears.

Sitting up, Eddie looked to his ceiling as though it were going to offer up the answers for him. When none came, he offered her a light pat on the back.

"Oh, come on now, that ain't true. She's just being petty. Anyone can go, and anyone can dance whenever they want." He tried to assure her.

"No they can't! Josie told me that most dances take two people and if I want to dance instead of playing with the other kids, I have to learn, but she won't teach me." Dacey was worked up to the point her little chest was heaving hard enough that it made Eddie wonder if he needed to hunt down an inhaler for her. Josie was the one who always needed one, but at that moment, he wouldn't have doubted if Dacey might.

"Dace, look at me." He set his hands firmly on her shoulders to gain her undivided attention. At only eight years old, she was more of a handful than half the kids that Josie drug home with her at the end of a school day. Making her focus took more patience than he wanted to admit. "When's Josie ever told you something that wasn't just plain mean lately? Your sister is just at that age, okay? She wants to impress her friends, and she thinks bullying you'll get her that attention. There are plenty of dances you know that they'll play there, okay?"

He earned a small nod with a hiccup, thankful she had started to calm. "But what about the ones I can't do alone? Josie said she won't ever teach me and, if she doesn't, then who will? How am I going to learn when she and her friends just laugh at me and kick me out of the room? I want to learn too!"

Gritting his teeth to keep the scathing comment contained, he stood. "I'll just have to teach you then, won't I? Ain't got anything else to do, anyway." The sun hadn't fully set, so the worst of his night hadn't even started. What was the harm in teaching her if she wanted to learn?

Dacey lit up at his words, bounding up from the couch to hug him hard. "Thank you, Eddie!" She giggled as he rolled his eyes, hand offering a playful tap to the top of her head.

"Don't thank me yet. I might still kick you out if this goes south," he

warned, wandering over to turn the TV off so he could fire up the record player. Choosing one most likely to be played at the Follies, he waved her over. "Alright, now pay close attention because I ain't gonna have you here all night, understand?" He couldn't, not anymore, since it had all started against his will. As much as he wanted to use her as a shield, Eddie wouldn't risk it. Shifting her until her toes were on his, he took a few steps to the beat, watching her watch their feet. Her little brow was scrunched in concentration, and he couldn't help the laugh that escaped him. "You keep makin' that face it's gonna stick," He teased. Dacey stuck her tongue out at him, resuming her determined focus on the floor to memorize the movements.

It didn't start out well. Dacey stepped on his toes more than he cared to keep count of. But, as time passed, she caught on quickly until she didn't even need to look down. Pride filled him when they made it an entire song without her slipping up. "There you go brat, that's all for tonight. I'm gonna be limping enough tomorrow without trying to teach you the next one. We got all week, okay?" She pouted at his words, arms folded over her chest.

"I don't wanna go back to the bunkhouse. It ain't fair, Eddie. Why can't I stay here? I always used to stay!" She refused the bottle of soda he held out.

"Because little ladies need to be in bed for school in the morning."

"I ain't a lady. You tell me that all the time."

"Well, maybe you can start to be one tonight."

"Fat chance."

"Clearly."

One song bled into another, and soon three had passed when Eddie was drawn from the memory to Dacey touching his cheek. He didn't say anything, just drew her closer to whisper in her ear. "Waltz across Texas, with you by my side."

It earned a broken smile as she rested her cheek on his shoulder. "I haven't danced to that in years. Never wanted or needed to, even when the chances would arise." Stepping away from him, Dacey worried her bottom lip between her teeth for a second. "Look, I'm not going to pretend I didn't know what you were doing with a hooker over there, but get whatever it is you need. You look like you're going to go feral on the entire bar at the drop of a hat, and I'd really rather not have to lie to Grant more than I already am. If you do, I'll trade a single secret of my own."

It was a weak offer, but Eddie thought it over for a moment. From the moment she had appeared in his life earlier that day, she had been more than resistant. To know she was willing to offer even a crumb of truth up to him was too hard to resist. Nodding, he looked back to where Seth was trying to talk a thin blonde into a dance as her friends studied him with an air of distrust.

Dacey tracked his line of sight with a small frown. "I'll get his attention. He can't do shit here to us, not without making an ass of himself. While he's happy to do that when others aren't around, he won't with this many people. After all, Seth has to maintain his image of 'Mr. Big Shot Oil Man's Son' or whatever bullshit he assumes of himself."

Letting her go, Eddie eyed Dacey as she took a step away from him. The loss of her body warmth made him notice the light sheen of sweat cooling on his skin. A shiver racked him, earning a quick glance from her that he waved away. "What do you gain out of this? I ain't fuckin' stupid." His guard rose once more.

"Nothing you need to worry about now, just go get your garbage before I change my mind." Stepping forward, Dacey sauntered toward the bar as if there were no one else in the place. Eddie watched her, eyes drawn down her body toward her ass to watch it as she walked away. A feeling of mild dread crept up his spine, one he was never sure to act upon or not when it flared. He stood back, letting her wander right into the lion's den without so much as lifting a finger to protect her. Maybe that was why it was bubbling up. Shaking it off, he moved in the opposite direction back to the dealer. Skirting around the cluster of people she had wandered into, he made a quick pause at the corner booth again.

Dropping a small stack of cash, more than he needed to pay, down on the tabletop, he watched the man lean forward with a nod of approval, taking it in hand. "You still want both orders for this, or just one?" The dealer asked.

"Just one, quick as possible." Eddie had to force himself to keep from drumming his fingers on the tabletop as he waited. A small baggie, small enough to fit in his palm, slid across old beer stains mingling with the crumbs of whatever food they had eaten. It was a quarter of the way full, almost half. Taking it and shoving it in his back pocket, he tipped his hat in thanks before turning to hunt Dacey down. It was taking all of his willpower not to do a line of the stuff right there and he knew that wouldn't be a bright idea in the open of the bar. The least he could do was take a quick jaunt to the bathroom to do it.

Chapter 8

Burn it to the Ground

"Where are they? Surely, Dacey isn't having this much trouble finding him?" Josie stood on tiptoe, trying her best to look over the sea of people.

Grant leaned back on the bar, sipping his beer while Riley peeled the label off a soda he had gotten her with a rather put off face. "Chances are, Eddie isn't willing to come with her and she doesn't know that once that boy plants his feet that there ain't a thing on this planet that can make him change his mind. I should've been the one to look for him knowing that." Reaching into his shirt pocket, he pulled out a pack of smokes and offered one to Josie, attempting to calm her down. She took it, still casting the occasional anxious glance over the crowd as he lit it for her.

Exhaling the smoke, she took a seat with her beer bottle for a moment, spinning it and peeling the label off. "I just worry. There's no way that…well regardless, one of us should have gone with her. She's just a kid."

"She's eighteen, from what she told me, the same age as me. And, honestly, I ain't a kid," Riley quipped, throwing down the shreds of label onto the bar with more force than necessary. "You can't always mother hen someone and then wonder why she took off on her own at the first chance. Let her breathe."

"I didn't ask for your two cents, so butt out. The only reason you're even here with us is because of my sister." Josie hissed, crushing her smoke out. "You don't have the faintest idea of what we've been through, or why I worry, so shut it while you can."

Blue eyes narrowed as a sarcastic smirk curled one pale pink lip. "Do you ever stop and think about what *she* wants when it comes down to it? Because last I knew she was the one who asked for help and if you really knew *anything* about this world, then you know that rodeo helps those in it, even if you don't know each other well. Or maybe you're jealous of the fact she came to someone else?"

Josie wheeled to face her, ready to put her in her place, but was cut short as shouts reached the trio from across the bar. Grant couldn't help shooting an exasperated glance at Josie as they tried their best to make their way quickly across the dance floor. A small crowd was gathered around what seemed to be a rather large brawl in the center. Josie let out what seemed to be a halfhearted groan when she spotted a head of blonde hair backed against the taller auburn-haired male. What surprised her more were two brown-haired men that seemed to be helping them.

Riley couldn't help the disbelieving laugh that escaped her at the sight. Catching Josie's arm in one hand, she pointed with the other. "Looks like my brothers were up for helping, even though we never got to talk to them." She gave a weak smile to try easing Josie's fear.

Seth was failing to hold his ground against Eddie as the older man grabbed a beer bottle from the last remaining table, throwing it as a distraction. When Seth ducked, one of the brothers darted in, landing a sharp blow to his jaw hard enough even he swore when Seth hit the floor dazed.

Dacey was keeping the upper hand on the only other woman in the fight, one Josie recognized as Eva, Seth's younger sister. Eva took a low shot at Dacey, trying her best to land a hit. Easily dodging it, Dacey stepped back to be flush against Eddie's back once more when a badly dyed red head leapt from the crowd to tackle Eva. Dacey let out a bark of laughter at the two when they began wrestling on the floor, exchanging blows. They rolled among broken tables, shattered bottles, and splatters of blood, heedless of those around them. Before Dacey could really enjoy the sight, a massive mountain of a man forced his way into the crowd.

Josie grabbed Grant's hand, hauling him through the throng of onlookers toward her sister, just as Eddie grabbed Dacey to help force her out the other way. Across the crowd, when he glanced up to see if there were any other people going to jump him, Eddie caught Grant's eye. A hard nod was given in return to the jerk of a chin Grant offered toward the door. Riley was pushing her way toward her brothers, shouting out their names and gesturing toward the same door the others were disappearing through. They waved toward her, one scooping her up to swing over a shoulder so easily it was as though she weighed nothing to him.

It took a few chaotic moments while the group tried to sort out where the others were going. Finally, they found themselves grouped both on and around Grant's truck. One of Riley's brothers had a piece of his ripped shirt pressed to his bleeding nose, a rather self-satisfied grin on his face. The other brother rubbed at his sore hand, cursing under his breath, gauging if it was broken. Once he was sure they would be left well enough alone, Grant took a seat on the top of the cab and let out an ear-piercing whistle. Every head close by whipped around to look at him, even a few he hadn't the faintest inclination to pay acknowledgement, and he couldn't hide his smile.

"Well, that was rather interesting, wasn't it?" he dead panned, crossing his arms. Josie let out a watery laugh, drawing a rather irritated Dacey close to her side. "I think what all of us are wondering, more than anything, is what the hell just happened?"

The four who had been in the fight looked to each other, trying to gauge who would offer the story up. Finally, Dacey broke away from Josie to slip across the truck bed. Sitting by Eddie, she slapped his hand away from where it pressed against a cut on his chin, trying to keep blood from further staining his shirt. "Seth showed up and saw me." It was all she seemed to be willing to offer as she assessed the wound. Motioning toward the brother that had already torn his shirt, he ripped another strip off, passing it to her. Eddie hissed faintly as she applied pressure, eyes narrowing when she slapped his hand away once more.

Grant gave her a frown when it was clear she wouldn't continue willingly. "You know that's not enough. Tell us everything, please, from the point of meeting Riley until now. Seems only fair, doesn't it? Considering these two helped you out."

She fought the urge to roll her eyes before launching into the day's events, Riley and Josie adding their own parts when prompted. Eddie gave a subtle squeeze of her leg in warning as she reached the point in the bar. Tapping her knee against his, both missed how Riley caught the moves. “I was trying to get to Eddie as he got a drink when Seth saw me and started running his mouth like he always does.” Dacey lied. “So, when his buddies and Eva showed up, I panicked, trying to figure out how to get Eddie and make it back. But once they realized what I was doing, Seth pointed him out to those two idiots he calls friends, and one took a cheap shot at Eddie.” She waved a hand toward the cut on the man’s freckled cheek. “They all tried to jump him at once, which is bullshit, so I started helping when these two came in.”

The brothers gave slight waves from where they sat on the tailgate, the one who had injured his hand sitting up taller. “I’m Rusty. This is my twin, Rider, and that slip of a girl is our little sister, Riley. Seems like we beat you to the point, didn’t we, sis?” He taunted with a wink.

Rider patted her back as she leveled Rusty with a glare. “I’m just glad we could be there tonight. But seriously, seems like this Seth loser can’t understand. He ain’t gonna win any fight he picks, so why keep trying?”

“Because he can’t stand the thought of not getting his way. Gets even worse when it comes to things that he thinks belong to him,” Josie piped up, fishing one of her pink cigarettes from the top pocket of her shirt. Lighting it, she took a deep drag, her gaze drifting to the stars above before slowly exhaling toward them. “Thinks he owns me, so he won’t give up on getting me back.” They watched her, none of them sure what to say or do as they waited. She licked her lips, taking a few more drags for courage. Dacey pressed her knee harder to Eddie’s, unaware of doing so as she waited anxiously for her sister to talk. He shifted until they touched from the hips down, arm dropping behind her on the truck bed.

Grant leaned forward from his perch, resting his elbows on his knees. When it was clear Josie wasn't going to offer up any more information, he turned his gaze to Dacey. She toyed with the end of a braided pigtail, trying to form the words. "Long story short, he thought he was going to marry her. Turns out, he ain't, so now he's throwing a tantrum and is here to force her, regardless if she wants to or not." Dropping her hair, she sat back and shrugged. "I'm not going to say a whole lot more, so there's no reason to keep staring at me like I'm going to do a trick."

The twins shared a look between them in silent communication. Rusty shook his head while Rider heaved a heavy sigh. "I get the feeling that before we showed up tonight, the four of you already knew each other? Reason being, y'all talk freely, and most folks don't do that with complete strangers. I get it, I do. I'm glad we were able to help you tonight, at least." He took his Stetson off to scrub at the top of his head for a moment. "I assume our sister is with you for a reason?"

"Khloe approached me earlier in need of help," Riley offered up. Dacey bit her lip before shaking her head.

"Fuck it, my name isn't Khloe, and hers ain't Nicole. We were hoping fake names would keep him from finding us. Guess that joke's on us now, isn't it? Either way, Riley was there earlier today when he showed up like some possessed puppet. I didn't know what else to do and I'm sick of running from this nut job. All we have to do is make it through this weekend, then we can pack up and hit the road again."

Eddie whipped his head to look at her. "Excuse me? Hit the road again?"

"I agree with Eddie. We aren't going to let that happen," Grant said. Josie swallowed, looking down at the bed of the truck as a silence fell over them. Faint music drifted across the parking lot, intermingled with the sounds of laughter or shouting.

Dacey stood, moving away from Eddie to tap her sister on the shoulder. The two shared a moment of silent conversation that left the others lost. Finally, Josie nodded. "You guys don't have to help us, but this could go a lot faster if you did." Her words were aimed toward the Wheeler siblings, the cherry on her cigarette bouncing as she spoke.

The brothers shifted where they sat on the tailgate, each leaning on the opposite side of the bed. They glanced from each other to their sister and back as the trio debated on what to say to the proposition. Riley chewed her lower lip faintly as she prayed they would help, knowing there was nothing she could do if they didn't. Rusty sat up first and turned to face the group. "We'll help, but there's a small price to it."

Eddie scoffed. "'Course there is. What do you want?"

"Don't act like we told you we're going to kick your dog or something. We just want breeding rights to one of your bulls at no charge. We know who you both are, world renowned Grant Sawyer and Eddie Malone from the Wildwood Ranch just north of us. Trust me, Rider and I will do pretty much anything to get a cow in with Ultimate Recall. His list, and cost, are something we wouldn't be able to wait for, but he is by far our favorite. We have a heifer out of Rock a Billy that we think would be perfect for him."

Grant couldn't help but throw his head back with a laugh. "You boys got yourself a deal, and if all goes well this weekend, I'll even let you have a cow in with a different bull of your choice." He held his hand out, waiting for the young man to shake it.

Rider grinned, tapping Riley on the shoulder. "How about she gets her mare in with one of your studs?" She lit up, standing to face Grant.

"Silver is the most important mare to me, and to know that I could get her in even just a little while with either Hemingway's Whiskey or Straight Moonshine is more than a dream come true. Rumor has it, Gentleman Jack isn't up for breeding anymore." Riley bemoaned. At her words, Eddie's face closed off, the man slipping off the bed of the truck to the door. Lighting a cigarette, he leaned against warm metal. Dacey watched him, the others continuing to talk.

He caught her curious look, shaking his head the faintest bit, earning a frown. She could tell something about the conversation got to him, made him withdraw. When he narrowed his eyes and pointedly looked at the others, she rolled hers at him, noting his fingers twitch on his forearm.

"Deal. Even if it doesn't go as we hope for the rest of this weekend, I'll still let you get them in. Sometime this week, drop them off and we can take care of the rest."

"You got it. So, what is the plan, anyway?" Rider questioned, shifting a bit in place. Riley let out a hard yawn before anyone could say anything, and Grant couldn't help but laugh again at her embarrassed look.

"How about we worry about it over breakfast in the morning? Meet us at the Knotty Pine Inn at about seven and we can talk plans then."

Nodding, they all stood and stretched respective knots out as they did. Riley reached over, grabbing Dacey's hand. "Before I go, can I ask you something alone?"

Dacey raised an eyebrow, but gave a half nod of consent to be led over to the side of the brother's truck, away from the rest. "What's up?" Leaning on it, she crossed her arms.

"Are you and Eddie a couple?"

A bark of laughter bubbled up before she could stop it, earning a startled look from Riley. “Are we what? Seriously? I haven’t seen him in six years, Riley. He’s not the man he was when I was twelve, and I’m far from that little, naive girl.” Shaking her head, Dacey shoved off the truck. “Is that all?”

“Yeah! Just making sure I wasn’t going to cause a couple’s quarrel or something.” Grinning, Riley took off to gather her brothers without giving Dacey a chance to say anything. Something inside of her hissed at the thought of Riley pawing on Eddie. Shoving it back into whatever corner of her mind it had come from, she reminded herself of what she had just told Riley. Eddie *wasn’t* the young adult she had been physically ripped away from that day, kicking and screaming until her lungs ached.

Hell, she wasn’t sure *who* he was at this point, or if she even wanted to know what type of man he was. The same creature that had hissed seemed to calm at the idea of getting to know who Eddie was now. Slamming the mental lid hard on its face, she shook her head. From what she had gathered, they all were vastly different people from who they had been six years prior. But she couldn’t help feeling a pull toward him.

“You gonna sit here fuckin’ pouting all night, or are you gonna get your ass in the truck?”

Speak of the devil and he would show.

Eddie stood in front of her, black Stetson tilted back to see her better. His shadowed eyes dragged over her, making a shiver creep up her spine. She fought to stand her ground, ignoring the flight response he always seemed to trigger.

“Fuck you, Cowboy.” She shoved past him, catching him off guard, causing him to stumble a step back. Making her way to the back of Grant’s truck, she frowned when Eddie climbed in behind her instead of taking his normal shotgun seat. Josie offered a halfhearted shrug from where she perched on the wheel fender, settling in while Grant started the truck. Dacey shifted, moving away from Eddie as far as the truck bed would allow. Trying to get comfortable on the warm steel, she couldn't help the flare of irritation when he plopped down beside her, jerking the hat from her head. A rather indignant sound erupted from her throat as he held the hat up, inspecting it closer.

"You really kept this? How the hell did you manage that one?" He offered it back, smirking as she snatched it, preventing the wind from taking it.

"Who says it's yours?"

"My initials are in the band. I put them there if I lost it riding." She blanched, gripping it tighter as he continued. "I can't believe you held onto it this whole time. Hell, it's about to disintegrate any minute."

Dacey glared at him as he mocked her hat. "Shut up. One, I kept it because I thought the owner was still a decent person and two, it isn't like I can afford a new one every time I turn around."

Their banter continued, Josie straining to hear over the wind as Eddie leaned in to talk almost directly into Dacey's ear. Something nagged at her as she watched them, annoyed he sat shoulder to shoulder with her. Josie remembered how the two had been thick as thieves before it all fell apart. Dacey trailed Eddie like a shadow from the time she could walk, and he had always been as overly protective of her as Josie was.

At one time, a small six-year-old Dacey had yelled at their grandpa for over an hour because he had firmly told her she would never be allowed to ride broncos like Eddie. Eddie had laughed at that, swooping in to lift her high over his head as she squealed until he held her close to him, whispering in the tiny shell of her ear. Whatever he said soothed the rage. Dacey giggled and returned the hug just as hard. It was always Dacey who had hidden away in his bunkhouse after terrible wrecks, reading to him, or playing cards games to keep him company. Toward the bitter end, there were rare times Eddie drove her off, an unexplained rage falling over him. When it did, he wouldn't let anyone near him, no matter how hard Dacey begged and pleaded to let her in.

Vanessa had scoffed at those times, an ugly sneer on her face aimed at the broken-hearted little girl. "Children shouldn't be playing with adults." She had snapped at the quiet tears slipping down Dacey's cheeks. "You're always in his way and slowing him down." Those comments earned more than a few retaliations from all three of them; with dead mice on her pillows, grease in her boots or gloves being their top favorites.

But now, something about him made Josie want to take Dacey and run so far, they would never find them. Was it because of all they had been through and she was simply too cautious? Or was it perhaps because he now seemed to emit a predator-like aura? Something so feral it made Josie's throat dry and her heart rate kick up a notch. Maybe it was because Dacey had suddenly shifted her attention to him, and she felt a little left out? She couldn't blame her sister for wanting to talk to someone other than her, but the sudden distance stung. Josie felt the smallest stab of jealousy at the idea. She and Eddie had started out close until life drove a wedge between them. She watched them, wondering if they would slip back into that same old routine after years apart.

It could have also been the plain and simple fact Dacey had grown up in worse ways than she should have, and it had changed her almost beyond recognition to everyone around her but Josie. The older woman felt compelled to protect her, no matter what the cost may be.

Jerked out of her thoughts as Grant parked the truck, she frowned up at the neon lights of the motel. They didn't have a room, just planned on crashing in their truck bed that night. Grant caught her look, and the way Dacey didn't move to stand, even when Eddie offered her a hand. "Are you ladies going to just sit there staring all night, or are we going to get some sleep?" Grant asked, leaning his crossed arms on the bed of the truck.

"Kinda hard to sleep when our bed is back in the parking lot of the arena," Dacey deadpanned, ignoring the hand inches from her face. Grant sighed, shaking his head.

"You can't possibly think that we're going to toss you out on your asses and head back to the barn. It won't kill Eddie to give his room up to you. I am sure we'd rather know you're safe and get a good night's rest." He shot Eddie a look as he opened his mouth to protest.

Josie climbed to her feet, Dacey following suit to hop over the side gracefully. Josie allowed Grant to offer her a hand down from the tailgate, nodding her thanks. He shot a pointed look at Eddie as he did, making sure he would go along with it.

Eddie looked like he'd swallowed something foul as he fished the key to his room from the front pocket of his jeans and tossed it carelessly to Josie. "What the fuck ever! Just don't cost me my deposit." A deep, tired sigh escaped Grant.

"Enough, please. We're all tired and overwhelmed by today's events. Just head to bed and we will see each other in the morning."

"Thank you, Grant." Josie managed.

The older man gave them each a gentle pat on the back, turning to head down the row of doors toward his room. Eddie caught Dacey's eye, giving the barest jerk of his chin toward the sign that pointed out the pool area.

"Later." He mouthed before following Grant. Josie turned around to be sure Dacey was following, so all she could do was nod at them both, hoping her sister assumed it was only for her. They walked in silence to their room, Josie trying to figure out how to bring up the day's events to Dacey.

As she closed the door behind her, Dacey held up both hands pleadingly. "Not right now. Just get a shower and we can worry about all this shit later. It's late, we have an early morning, and we're both exhausted. Please Josie, don't make me keep talking." Josie studied her for a moment, letting a heavy sigh escape and her shoulders drop.

"Alright, tonight I'll let it go. But don't think for a second that we *aren't* going to talk about it." Looking around the small, tidy room, she shrugged. "I don't know how much good a shower is going to do me, considering we have to wear this again tomorrow, but I know I need one. Beats sleeping filthy. I'll try to hurry so you can have one too." she offered.

Dacey shifted from one foot to the other, shrugging in agreement. "I'm going to see if they have a working vending machine to get a soda. Want anything?"

"For you not to go out there alone, but I know you will. I'm okay though, thanks, Dace." Josie made her way to the bathroom, shutting the door as Dacey hurried out. She waited until her little sister had gone before the hot, stinging tears she had been battling overflowed.

Why? Why could they never be safe anymore? What was she going to do once the morning came? The questions just kept coming as she tried to gain control.

Turning the water on to let it warm up, she grasped a semblance of control. Crying wasn't going to do either of them any good, even if she wished it would. Testing the weak spray, she found it hot enough for her liking. Climbing in, she lifted her face to it, trying to wash away all traces of her tears. She didn't want Dacey to worry about her or ask any more questions than she was forcing on herself. How could she answer any of them, anyway?

Closing her eyes, she tried to relax, to let the warmth of the water cleanse away the worst of her thoughts and the dirt on her skin. They would get through this, they always did. Having the men back in their lives was unexpected, however. While part of Josie longed to stay, feeling safe for once, a distinct part of her hated putting them through the dangers she and Dacey faced. Neither of them seemed bothered, not even when the panic attack set in at the sight of Seth in person. They helped without question, without a second thought. But how long would that last? Would it last? As more questions crashed down over her mind, Josie felt fresh tears well up, causing her to curse both herself and the tears. She felt her chest heave as her body finally allowed her to cry after years of trying to suppress her emotions.

Reaching out, she cranked up the hot water until it was nearly scalding her skin. It pierced through the chill, settled bone deep, and seared away the terror attempting to latch back on. Josie settled on the floor of the grimy tub, head buried in her knees, with water cascading on her, and gave in.

Chapter 9

Save Yourself

Dacey toyed with the cold soda, pacing along the pool's edge, waiting for Eddie to show up. Chances were he wouldn't, and it had simply been a way for him to annoy her even further. Giving up, she was getting ready to head back to the room when he slipped through the gate.

Striding over, he threw himself down in one of the cheap plastic chairs with a slight groan, while fishing around in his upper pocket. When his full weight landed, it gave a warning creak in a quiet threat to break at the abusive use. Finding the baggie of powder, he dipped a little onto his finger before snorting it. Dacey froze, taking a half step back as she watched him repeat the process before he lit a cigarette. "Grant know you do that shit?"

Eddie sent her a dark look, leaning forward in the chair. "No, and he better not find out from you, or I'll fucking teach you a lesson you won't like." His voice was low, the threat clear. She wrinkled her nose at him, sitting on the opposite side of the table.

"Why am I out here, Eddie?" Popping the top of her soda, she took a deep drink. When she went to set it down, he grabbed it from her and took a large drink against her protest.

"Because I deserve answers, considering you know a few secrets of mine. Only fair, isn't it? Remember the deal at the bar?"

She paled under her freckles, turning away from him to stare at the sign announcing the name of the inn and that there were no vacancies. Trying to come up with a good excuse not to tell him anything, she couldn't come up with any, not even a good lie. He had a point. "One question for one secret. No more, no less."

"No, no, Darlin'. I hate to break it to you, but you know two things about me no one else does. So, I get two out of you." He smirked as he leaned back in the chair. "First of all, I know it'll take too long to tell me everything, and that wouldn't count as a single secret, so I'll go easy on you." He tilted his head back to look up at the stars above them, closing his eyes for a moment. The coke rushed through him, making him feel like he could do whatever the hell he pleased. Instead, he blew the smoke out hard and met the narrow blue gaze across from him. Fuck, she had grown up so damn good-looking. All he wanted was to bury his hands in her braids and yank them out, claim that pouting mouth with his, and–No. He crushed the thoughts like a bug before they could invade further.

"What?" she quipped, crossing her arms over her chest, having noticed the look on his face.

"You don't want to know, believe me." A dark smirk crossed his features, causing a blush to creep up her neck.

"Then ask me the questions before Josie comes looking for me." She snapped.

Anger flared up; he rose from his seat like a tiger creeping from the shadows over its prey. Her throat bobbed, swallowing hard, but held her ground as he loomed over her.

"Watch that mouth, I ain't in the best of moods tonight, so you're flirting with fire," Eddie warned, reaching out to jerk on a pigtail. She flinched at the hand, causing him to stop just shy of touching. "Found my first question. What the hell did that piece of shit do to you?"

"Which one?" It came out before she could stop it, and Dacey wished more than anything to pull the words back as Eddie's eyes darkened in rage. If anything was going to get her killed before her time, it was going to be her mouth.

"The fuck you mean, '*which one*'?"

"Does that count as your second question?" she asked weakly.

He made an inhuman noise low in his throat, slamming his hands down on either side of her. The plastic handles of her chair gave a plaintive whine at the abuse, threatening to crack. Dacey flinched away, but Eddie caught how her eyes held a glint of warning. She wouldn't lie down and take a beating easily from anyone. "Tell me who fucking did what to you. Make it short and sweet, Darlin' so we don't waste all night."

She wanted to run; her heart pounded so hard it felt like it was trying to force a hole to escape. Yet she managed to keep their gazes locked as she answered. "Dad." The word was hardly above a whisper, and Eddie drew back a bit.

"Keep talking."

"You said keep it short and sweet. He happened, Eddie, to me and Josie. He screwed us both up so much I don't think we will ever be ourselves. Do you think Josie has panic attacks for fun? He tossed her to Seth like an unwanted doll, but I couldn't just be thrown away, not right then. So, he turned on me instead." Throwing her hands up in exasperation, Dacey tried to find the right words. "It was a joy to him, ruining everything I ever understood. I was *twelve*, when they ripped me away from you, away from home and comfort and safety. And he thought that was the best thing in the world. He loved to throw it in my face almost daily."

Eddie kicked the chair next to them halfway across the deck. Letting out a string of curses so loud, a small voice in the back of her mind feared he'd draw attention to them. Dacey jerked away, worried he would do something to her in his fit. Was this that powder? Or something else?

Stalking back over, he towered over her, Dacey braced herself, only to be surprised when a calloused hand gently caught her chin, tilting it up so she could look at him better. The soft touch nearly broke down her walls until he spoke. "He hit you?"

Dacey let out a mirthless laugh. "What the hell do you think? Hit us, made us feel two feet tall, everything short of the worst thing a father would do to his own daughter. He's the reason that Seth thinks he owns Josie! Seth's dad is a huge oil man down south and was friends with our dad. The two hung out constantly, and dad offered Josie up trying to gain status and wealth from the match." Bitterness and anger flashed across her face as she crossed her arms. Trying to calm down, she continued. "She wasn't his first choice, of course. Dad wanted me out more than he did, the one who kept that pathetic excuse of a house up and going. But I was way too much for that family, and Seth's dad told ours no. Told him point blank he'd kill me before allowing me to be his daughter-in-law. Even when Seth put Josie in the hospital, our dad told her it was too bad and that she was going to marry that monster. Seth's dad isn't any better; he just paid off the staff to keep it all hush hush. They played it off like she was in a riding accident, then put her horse down. But none of it matters now. What matters is we escaped."

"Your dad up here with Seth?" Eddie paced, chewing the end of his finished smoke. Dacey sat back in her chair, trying her best to calm down, watching. His thoughts raced with ways to make the man beg for a mercy that wouldn't be noticeable. He'd make that waste of space cry just as the girls had at his hands; make him suffer so much death would be a welcome embrace.

"Can't be when he's six feet under." That stopped him in his tracks.

"What?"

"That your second question?"

"Quit fucking trying to be cute."

She sighed. "You heard me, he's dead. That's how Josie and I got away. Seth had us both pretty much on lockdown after it happened, but we slipped out one night. Got him good and drunk, used a couple of sleeping pills, and hit the road. Turns out he wasn't going to take no for an answer."

Eddie resumed his pacing. "So, Seth's here to drag you back to that hell thinking you're just going to go? That even with our help he's going to get his way?"

"Yup." She replied, popping the p. Taking a swallow of her soda to keep from offering more than Eddie deserved, she shrugged. "Wants her as his beating toy. Look, I can't tell you everything he did to her, because it isn't my story to tell. Just know he didn't hold back. She was pretty fucked up to the point he almost killed her. He's never faced consequences; if he wants to do it, he does." Hazel eyes turned to burn into her as she stood up.

“Where do you think you’re going?”

“To sleep. Like you need to.” She offered a trembling hand. Was it because she was actually scared of him? Or because of everything she was being forced to remember? Watching him stare at it, something assured her that the fear wasn’t due to him. He took it, jerking her to him in order to bury his face in her hair and breathe deeply. She clung to him, letting the tears fall. Would he even remember this in the morning? What did he care for her now, anyway?

“I got you, Darlin’, and believe me when I swear he isn’t going to touch you or your sister again.” His hands slipped up her back, unbraiding her hair and raking his fingers through it. It was smooth; slipping through his grasp, the scent of wild honeysuckle and horses assaulted his senses, twisted together with the faintest hint of his own cologne from their earlier contact. Tightening his grip, he let her cry against his chest where she had so many times before. “You have no idea how badly I’ve missed you, Dacey.” He whispered into the warm locks. The words were strangled as he fought his own tears.

She gave a watery laugh. “You sure have a funny way of showing it, asshole.” Drawing back a little, she looked up at him. One hand reached up to swipe a tear off his freckled cheek. Eddie almost never cried, but Dacey remembered each time. As a child, she had carefully crawled into his lap to wipe them away.

“I’m a different person now, not one you should be close to anymore.” He warned her, cheek pressing harder into her hand. Something in her ached, a dull throb that couldn’t be ignored. Seeming to remember where they were, Eddie stepped away. Her hand fell back to her side, cheeks burning as though he had slapped her.

Hell had the perfect spot already picked out for him. It was dangerous to let her get close to him again, stupid even. No matter how much he wanted her there by his side, he had to think about what was best for her. To him, it was easy to throw his life away to be sure hers would flourish. She deserved nothing less. But to ask the same of her seemed an insult to them both. Why would he allow her to waste her time on someone so damaged? He wasn't stupid. He knew he was a selfish bastard, and that was what drove him.

Dacey clenched her jaw, biting her tongue to keep from speaking up. Regaining control of her temper, she went to shove past him, but he caught her. "My last question; why did you keep my hat? Really?"

The question took her off guard and it was a moment before she met his stare dead on. "Because it was the only hope and piece of my life that reminded me, I may have a chance at living. It reminded me there was someone, somewhere, who once loved me without question, who wasn't my sister." The red on her cheeks crept up her ears as she continued. "Living where we did, how we did, I kept that hat to keep the hope alive, I'd find that person again. I never did. I found someone I don't know." With that, she pulled away, turning to walk back to her room.

This time, Eddie let her go. The words surprised him, and he found himself moving to follow her. Stopping as quickly as he started, he watched her slip off down the walkway. She wasn't wrong on most accounts, but he refused to admit he did still love her. The love had changed, shifted to something he never would have guessed was possible, yet it was there. It wasn't just the simple love of an older brother keeping his favorite person alive, it was a love he wasn't sure he himself understood just yet.

Chapter 10

Tonight, the Heartache's on Me

"Fuck." Eddie exhaled, running a hand through his hair. Getting his wits back about him, he made his way to the room he shared with Grant. It wouldn't do him any good to dwell on their conversation if he wanted to sleep that night. Grant was seated in the chair at the desk, smoking the day's last cigarette while watching the grainy TV. He looked at Eddie as he walked in, watching him toss his hat down on the desk next to the other.

"Something wrong?" Grant asked, propping his feet up on the desk.

"Too much to list. So how are we doing this? Why are we doing this?" Eddie sat down heavily on the edge of the bed. Burying his face in his hands, he resisted the urge to scream in frustration.

Grant set the bottle of beer he had down hard on the desk, feet hitting the floor with an audible thump. "I'm only going to say this once, so pay very close attention." Grant's tone left no room for argument. "Do not ever question why we are helping those girls. They're family, and we owe them this much. I don't know what possessed you to ask why we are doing it."

Eddie lifted his head, ready to snap back, but caught himself. "I didn't mean it like that. It came out wrong. It isn't why we are doing this; it's why do I feel we are doing this for different reasons than the ones you just said? It's like we just feel the need to play heroes for them, not actually help them."

His words seemed to catch Grant off guard. Scratching at his salt and pepper stubble, he mulled over his answer. "Because they're strangers to us now. They aren't the girls they were, they're both young women. Anything we do right now is going to feel hollow, no matter how hard we work at it. It isn't easy to explain, slick, and I'm sorry. What you're feeling is how I am too, believe me. It's like seeing a pup along the road; you know you need to stop and get it somewhere, but that somewhere ain't home. But now, with these ladies, that pup is coming home. Make sense?"

Eddie rose to his feet, opening his travel bag to dig a pair of fresh boxers out. "Much sense as you can make. I'm grabbing a shower, you need to take the bed for tonight."

"Why do I need to take the bed? I don't mind sleeping on the floor."

Eddie's lip curled in disgust. The floor appeared to have once been shag, thick and deep in all its putrid green glory. Now, it was so trampled and filthy there was a permanent flat path of travel he would bet money on hadn't seen a vacuum since it was laid. "At that point, why not just sleep in the tub? That floor ain't worth sleeping on for a dog, let alone a person. I planned on just sleeping in the chair."

"Won't be good on your back."

"Or yours, so deal with it. Once I'm out of the shower, we can sort this out."

Grant turned back to the television, picking his beer up to swallow down what was left. "Don't come crying to me tomorrow when you can't hardly walk."

"I didn't plan on it. If it were you sleeping on it, you wouldn't be able to get off of it at all. Look, if it comes down to it, I can crash in the truck cab or its bed. Either way, I ain't worried about it, so you don't need to be. Just take the stupid bed before I light the fucker on fire to end any further argument about who's sleeping where." It earned a laugh from Grant as he waved Eddie toward the bathroom, chuckling to himself.

In the room next door, Dacey slipped in, quiet, head low as her mind continuously ran over the events that had transpired. Josie didn't say anything to her, just sat against the worn-out headboard watching a show with unseeing eyes. It was like she was in a whole different world.

As Dacey moved about the room, tossing her hat down and kicking her boots off, Josie looked at her. Arms crossed over her bare chest, it took a few more moments before she broke the silence. "Dacey, I know I said we would talk in the morning, but before you get your ass in the shower, what in the *hell* do you think you're doing?" She hissed, her eyes narrowing, freezing Dacey in her tracks.

"Excuse me?"

A hand waved at Dacey, who had the decency to swallow the lump in her throat, eyes finding a rather interesting spot on the wall. It looked like dried blood, and she forced herself to turn back to Josie. "Do you realize you smell like you've rolled all over, Eddie? Seriously? What the hell were you doing out there with him? You told me you were going to get a soda! Now you come back to the room reeking of him, looking like you ran a mile. I'm not stupid, Dacey. I see the way he's been looking at you tonight, and I don't like it. Stay away from him. He's a grown man and you're a kid! The hell are you thinking? We have enough going on in our lives without you messing around like this!"

Dacey bristled at the words. "Excuse me?! A *kid*? I'm eighteen! I'm a legal adult now, and I stopped being a kid a long ass time ago! How dare you think you get to tell me what to do anymore? You're my sister, Josie, not our mother!"

Josie's cheeks flushed at the words. "I'm aware I'm not our mother! But that doesn't mean I'm not responsible for you! It's funny how now you're an adult who can make her own choices since he showed up, yet just yesterday you and I wouldn't have had anything even close to this argument. Have you lost all common sense?" Josie hadn't realized she was shouting until someone pounded on the door. They tensed up, sharing a terrified look before Josie snuck to the window. She relaxed as another knock came. "It's just Grant." Rushing to grab her shirt and pants, she got dressed, calling for him to wait a moment. Opening the door, she offered him a small, embarrassed smile.

"Everything okay? Eddie and I heard yelling." He peered past her to where Dacey stood in the middle of the room. "We were worried."

"Yeah! Sorry we were, just um, sort of arguing." Josie admitted, glancing to where Eddie leaned on the wall by the door. She shot him a look of annoyance. He raised a brow at her, offering a sarcastic smirk. "But thank you."

"Didn't you wear that earlier today?" Eddie asked, jerking his chin toward her outfit. "It doesn't make sense to take a shower, then put the same shit back on."

"Well, Captain Obvious, you two put a pin in the plans of us going back to where all of our stuff is." Josie drawled. Eddie pushed away from the wall to respond, but Grant held up a hand to him.

"Please, please just stop." Grant barked, shaking his head at Eddie. "Josie, come to our room for a moment. I have my bag in there, you can sleep in some of my things." He offered. She bit her lip, gaze sliding to Eddie, but he was looking past her to Dacey. He jerked his head toward their room and Dacey shoved past her sister to follow him. Josie made a mild noise of protest, jaw dropping. Grant shot her a confused look, earning a sigh in return.

"Don't ask." She murmured, following her sister. When she got to the room, Eddie was handing over a shirt and boxers to Dacey, who accepted them with a smile. Grant made his way to his bag, digging around for a shirt to offer Josie. She took it, pressing it to her chest. "Thank you both. Now, good night." She stalked out, grabbing Dacey to drag along. Her sister slapped away the offending hand with a huff, blazing past Josie. Grant waited until their door was closed before turning to face Eddie head on.

"What did you do?" Grant leaned on the door, arms folded over his chest. Eddie let out a bark of sarcastic laughter.

"What did *I* do? Why the hell do you assume it's my fault?" Grant shot him a look of disbelief. "I didn't do a damn thing. I just talked to Dacey when I ran into her getting a soda. That's it. If Josie wants to get her panties in a twist, that's on her, not me."

"Josie's trying to keep an eye on her sister."

Something in Eddie snarled at the insinuation. "You think I give a fuck? You really want to sit there acting like I didn't spend most of that girl's life trying to keep her safe, and protect her, too? What about you

Grant? You want to stand there and tell me I can't have anything to do with her? Did you forget what she used to mean to me? To you? Both of them! I loved them, Grant, loved them like they were my own little sisters. Don't you dare stand there telling me what I can and cannot do with them when I have just as much right to worry and care about Dacey as Josie does." Eddie seethed. His eyes burned as he raged, hands gesturing. "But realize this Grant, you made that perfectly clear to me earlier when you were getting on my case when I asked why we were even doing this. You can't just sit there pretending like you are going to run this show, but then turn around and make me out to be the bad guy."

Forcing his way past Grant, he stalked out into the night, slamming the door behind him. Chances were, the inn would make a comment on it in the morning, but Eddie couldn't care. Long legs carried him out to the truck, where he climbed up into the bed. Lighting a cigarette, he lay down on the warm steel to watch the stars make their journey across the sky.

The morning was going to royally suck.

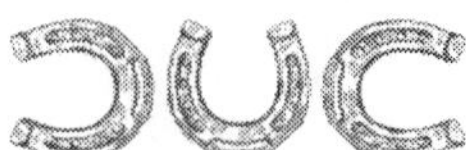

The echo of the door slamming resounded in Grant's ears as he continued to stare at it long after Eddie had disappeared. Scrubbing a hand over his face, he stifled a groan at a gentle knock on the door.

"Grant?" Josie called.

He opened the door, exhaustion weighing heavily on him. "Yes, Josie?"

She bit her lip, shifting from one bare foot to the other. "I wanted to be sure you were okay. I'm sorry if my sister and I have already caused issues between the two of you." Her gaze shifted toward the parking lot she had watched Eddie cross. She cared a little about him, and felt bad the arguments happening were centered on him, but deep down, Josie knew she would always choose Dacey before Grant or Eddie.

He waved away her concern. "Eddie and I have been having problems lately, and I don't understand why. Seems like both of us are running into issues, aren't we?" He joked. Their latest argument was just a drop in the sea of fights the two had found themselves in the past year. Grant had more than once wondered why it felt like his entire life was slipping away faster each year, yet he never would give up on it.

Josie nodded in agreement with a soft hum. Shifting her weight from foot to foot, she took a tiny step into the room. "Do you want to talk about it? I know it's late, but if you're like me after everything that's happened, there's no way you can just lie down and go to sleep."

Grant nodded, patting the space beside him on the worn-out mattress. Josie joined him, the springs giving a light wail in protest at the added weight. Her knee bounced, mind scrambling, thinking of what to say. He took pity on her and broke the silence himself. "Seems like everything hasn't just gone to hell in a handbasket. It took the damn red-eye flight."

She laughed at that, erasing the tension building between them. "With my hellcat of a sister as the pilot."

"Eddie wouldn't be the copilot; you and I both know that. The day that man doesn't take charge when I'm not around is the day that I'm six feet under."

"Ain't that the truth!" Her laughter slowed to the occasional giggle until it was gone. Rubbing at the faded bedspread, she let her eyes wander around the dingy room. The walls were yellowed with years of smoke, a thin layer of dust coating the tops of ruffled, outdated curtains.

The desk sagged in the middle, bending in on itself in such a tired way, she found herself yawning. Covering her mouth, she dropped her gaze to the carpet, riddled with cigarette burns and more than one mysterious stain. Wrinkling her nose, trying her best not to think of what they could be, she flopped back to stare at the ceiling. A wide, dark stain crept across the tiles from the top of the window, from water damage she guessed. "Why is everything so complicated now? I don't understand. Even now that we somehow found our way back, nothing went the way I pictured it."

"Did you envision it often? Keep in mind, Josie, none of us expected any of this to ever happen; you two were gone for what seemed like would be forever. Maybe it was your subconscious guiding you up to where you would have a slim chance of salvation. You came up here knowing we could be here in the back of your mind without realizing it. What your subconscious didn't bank on was that Eddie and I bicker worse than you and Dacey do now." He lit a cigarette, offering it out to her.

Josie accepted with trembling fingers. Inhaling deeply, she held the smoke until her lungs burned before letting it out in a harsh rush. It drifted away in hazy patterns, the gray cloud stark against the orangish glow of the lightbulb.

"You never fail to call me out, even now. No matter how I fought with myself, the pull to come back was stronger than my common sense. Dacey knew, I think, what I was doing. She and I even argued about it on the way here this morning that we shouldn't get near either one of you. But here I sit. I drove my baggage all the way here just to spill it in your lap like I never grew up." She mused, curling her toes into the gritty, worn-out carpet.

"You missed home. Everyone always longs for home when life gets rough. That's normal Josie." Grant patted her leg. "You're only human, sis, don't beat yourself up for having those feelings."

Josie sat up, resting her head on his shoulder, eyes staring toward the door. "It still isn't fair to you, Grant. Much as I hate to admit it, I never should have brought this on Eddie, either. Growing up, I watched him go to war for Dacey over so much less. Why did I think this would be any different? That he would just go along with anything I said?" She reached past him, grabbing the remote. Making a face at the greasy feeling of it, she turned the small TV off. The static of dead air annoyed her, putting her teeth on edge. "This has to be hands down one of the stupidest things that I've ever done in my life."

Her fingers curled around what was left of the smoke until it snapped in two, dropping the cherry onto the carpet. It smoldered among the cheap fibers, adding another dark hole for another dark night. She yelped, leaping to her feet, scrambling to find something close to put it out. Grant was faster, snatching his discarded boot up, pounding out the tiny flame that had taken life. They sat there a moment, staring fixated at the little hole. Josie broke first, strained laughter breaking free until she was bent double holding her stomach. Grant's chuckle started slowly, building until it was a full, deep belly laugh. It echoed around the room, bouncing between them in a rising tide.

When their neighbor pounded against the wall, Josie looked at Grant with tears in her eyes. Clapping her hands over her mouth, she broke into a fit of smothered giggles, leaning on him for support. His own joined hers, body shaking, a snort slipping out. It was the last straw for her, and she let out another loud laugh at his startled face.

Another round of pounding came, forcing them to regain some

composure. Josie wiped at her eyes, hiccuping. It was a wonder a fist hadn't come through the thin wall, considering how hard the person was beating on it. Clearing her throat, she took a deep breath. "I haven't laughed like that in a while." She breathed, flopping back against the mattress. "I needed that."

"I agree with you. I don't remember the last time I did that." Grant caught his breath, the occasional chuckle escaping.

He chanced a glance toward the clock beside the bed, bemoaning the late hour. Josie caught his change in expression, rising to her feet with a small quirk of her lips.

"I'll let you get to bed. I'm sorry again about everything." She slipped out of his room before Grant could say a word in response.

Waiting to hear her door shut, Grant moved to check his. He didn't lock it in case Eddie chose to come back. It wasn't likely, but he could at least make the effort to assure him he was always welcome back. Settling back down in the bed, he stared up at the ceiling, wondering how the next day would play out.

Chapter 11

Dear Sister

Grant wanted to shoot the alarm when it wailed to life beside the bed. It grated on his ears with its shriek, and he slapped it harder than needed to shut it up. His eyes felt like someone had poured sand in them. Blinking hard, trying to gain some form of consciousness, he scrubbed at them. They burned more than they had in over a year, and he cursed himself to the very sun and back for staying up until two that morning, trying to get everyone settled down. Through the thin walls, he heard a female voice cursing something fierce as the girls woke up to their alarm.

It brought a weak smile to his face, hearing them clattering around and getting ready. They were home where they belonged. They weren't dead somewhere; he wasn't going to spend nights wondering if he would ever see them again. Motivated by the thought, he got ready to leave his room. Snatching his hat off of the desk, he paused, studying the black one next to it on the desktop.

Eddie was nowhere to be seen, even though Grant had left the door unlocked. Slipping his wallet into his back pocket, and the keys to his truck in the front, he grabbed it. Stepping out of the dim room into the warm, bright sunlight, he squinted, searching. Nothing in the parking lot stirred, save for a stray tabby cat that crept along the vine covered office building. It paused as he moved, watching him before sprinting off. Coming up empty-handed, he resigned himself to worring later once he knew the girls were ready. They only had a half an hour before they were due to meet with the Wheeler family, and he wanted them ready and waiting in the restaurant the inn offered.

Dacey jerked the door open when he knocked, a look of annoyance plastered over her tired features. "Unless you have caffeine of any kind, please fuck off." She drawled, leaning on the door. Grant laughed, ignoring how she narrowed her eyes at him. "Do I amuse you?" She groused, head resting on the wooden frame.

"We'll get you coffee at the restaurant, scouts honor. Are you and Josie ready?"

"Princess is taking ten years in the bathroom." Dacey moved to let him come into the room, flopping back down on the bed. "Man, if I didn't have so much hanging on today's ride, I would say fuck it all and just–not." She bemoaned. Josie appeared out of the bathroom, hair in a single long blonde braid down her back.

"We both have a lot on the line with today's rides, but you don't see me pissing and moaning." Josie ground out, throwing the towel she had been drying her hands off with onto a corner of the chipped sink. It slipped off, earning a quick kick into a corner. She'd deal with it tonight. Turning back to Dacey, she rested her hands on her hips. "I'm exhausted too, so get over it. You did this to yourself with your little meeting last night." She reminded her, sitting on the edge of the bed, pulling her boots on.

Dacey raised a single finger from her spot across from her sister on the full-size mattress.

"How very mature of you. Come on, sit up so I can get that rats' nest under control." Josie offered. Grant took a seat on the one flimsy chair the room contained, watching them go about what seemed to be a normal routine for them: Dacey yawned and muttered things better left away from good company while Josie scolded her, fingers nimble as she worked on braiding her sister's hair.

Once her sister was done, she tapped the brush on a shoulder to give Dacey permission to move. Leaning down, Dacey pulled her boots on, Josie standing to grab their hats. Offering the ragged looking one to Dacey, Josie tugged hers on.

"Ready?" Grant asked, standing. His question earned matching looks of exhaustion, but they joined him at the door.

"Much as we can be," Josie replied, leading the way from the room. The trio paused, allowing their eyes to adjust.

"Where's Eddie?" Dacey asked, looking around the empty stretch of doors on either side of them. Josie lit one of her cigarettes and tried to locate the man in question.

"I have no idea. He took off last night after we got into it." He left it there, walking off without looking back. The sisters shared a quick glance, rushing after him.

Making their way across the parking lot, Josie broke the pressing quiet. "Does he do this often?"

"More than I'd like to admit. I don't know what's going on, but ever since…" he trailed off, looking back at them. "Well, ever since you two were taken away. But since the wreck, it just got worse. Disappears for a night, but comes back in the morning like a tomcat on the prowl. I've had to bail him out of jail once or twice, but since Dean's taken over the sheriff's position, we don't have to worry about that." The color seemed to leech from their faces, and Grant caught it. A frown marred his features, a hand gesturing toward them. "Don't even start. This isn't your fault. Dacey, you were twelve and Josie, you were only sixteen. Need I remind you that your father had every legal right to pull you away after the funeral? What happened will never, ever be your fault, so don't start trying to assume any sort of blame. Whatever road it he went down, Eddie did so choice."

"And I'll ask you to stop fuckin' talking about it while you're ahead, Grant. They don't need to know my business." Eddie's voice was dripping ice as he approached the trio. Grant had the grace to look a little guilty as the lanky cowboy reached them, looking like he'd been drug backwards through a bush. Holding the hat out, Grant didn't flinch when Eddie snatched it away, pulling it on.

"Where were you?" Dacey asked, ignoring the pissed look Eddie shot her.

"Where I slept." He snapped back. She rolled her eyes at him as he drew level with them.

"Whatever, Cowboy."

Grant exchanged a nervous look with Josie as the two went back and forth. She offered a slight raise of her shoulders in reply to his unspoken questions. Whatever pissing match her sister picked with Eddie, she was going to deal with it alone.

Clearing his throat to gain their attention, Grant led the way to the door of the restaurant. Josie caught up to him, leaving Dacey behind to their muffled argument. "I hope they don't do this all day, I'm already sick of fighting with Dacey. I don't want to be dealing with that as well." She confessed.

"You and me both, Josie. I think it's just the sudden surprise of you two showing up and then everything that went down. Things will be back to normal by tonight." He tried to assure her. She lifted a hand up, biting a nail in thought.

"I know you say none of this is our fault, but it seems like—"

"Drop it," Grant interjected, reaching out to tug her hand away from her mouth. "Do not start that bullshit again right now. At least not before I've had coffee. Deal?"

Josie nodded, looking over her shoulder to where Dacey and Eddie were locked in a personal conversation. Debating on if she should interfere or not, she chose instead to continue forward. The smell of pancakes, coffee and bacon tickled her nose, causing her to inhale deeply, drawing their fragrance into her lungs. A soft moan escaped her as she took another.

"You gonna faint on me at the smell of breakfast?" Grant teased, flagging down a waitress.

"We haven't been in a diner since we hit the road. Most of the time it's just cheap gas station food or a terrible burger from some hole in the wall fast food place. This is like walking into heaven." Josie admitted. She turned, glancing back out the glass door. "Think we need to get them?"

"No, let them have their moment."

When Dacey moved to follow Grant and Josie, Eddie caught her by the arm, holding her back as they drew farther and farther ahead. "Let me go." She hissed, tugging against his hold.

"No can do, you're gonna have to wait." He caught Josie looking back at them, only to be ushered along by Grant to prevent her from doubling back.

Dacey shook his hand off her arm, crossing them over her chest to study him. "What do you want that is so important we can't even have food first?" She demanded. He didn't say a word in reply to the bait. Instead, he snatched the ragged hat off of her head so fast she had no time to stop him. Anger rose within her, but before she could do anything about it, he dropped his new hat on her head. Like the old one, it was a bit too big, nearly falling over her eyes when it landed. Standing there stunned, Dacey reached up, touching the butter soft black suede. Eddie watched, waiting for her to do something. When she bit her lip, ducking her head down to hide her face, he knew she wouldn't say anything.

"I think we both agree this one needs to be retired. I'll get a new one today from a vendor set up around the arena." He put the old one on to keep it safe as he spoke. Finally, Dacey looked up to offer a shy smile at him, nodding.

"Just make sure I get that back when we get to where we're going?" It wasn't a question, more like a kindly worded order. Reaching out, he rested a hand on her shoulder.

"You'll get it back once you get home, Darlin', so be sure that's where you aim to be at the end of this weekend."

"Not sure I can call it home after all this time, can I?"

"It never stopped being your home just because you were gone." Turning on his heel, he headed toward the door. She jogged to catch up, linking their arms with a bright smile on her face.

"Thanks, Cowboy."

"Whatever."

If Dacey hadn't been looking at him, she would have missed the lighting fast smile he gave.

Opening the door, he held it open for her to slip in. Grant gave him a curious look when they made their way to the table. Eddie shook him off, waving away the question in the warm brown eyes. Pulling the chair out for Dacey, he helped her settle before sinking into his seat. Spending the night in the truck's bed had seemed like a brilliant idea at the time, but now his body was paying a heavy price. Every bone in his body tried to protest, one knee making a pointed crack as it bent. Hiding a wince, he grabbed the sticky, laminated menu to use as a shield from the rest of the table. Josie was whispering to Dacey across the table, tapping her chin with the spoon in thought. Whatever she had said earned an annoyed glare, and Dacey snatched her own menu off the table to browse it.

Just as their waitress was making her way back to the table, an ear-splitting shout rocked the dining area, causing people to turn around in search of the source. "Dacey!" Riley was the first through the door, barreling across the room with a bright grin on her face. Bounding up to the table, she slid to a halt just in time to keep from slamming into it. Her brothers trailed after her watching her take the free seat on Eddie's right side. The man looked like he wanted to speak up, but remained silent. The twins reached the table, settling themselves down with nods of greeting. Rider had taken up a seat on Dacey's left, the last chair on their side of the table, while Rusty sat directly across from him. Josie was face to face with her sister and Grant finished the table off at the head, a chair between him and Josie.

When she was sure they were ready and no one else was going to burst in, the waitress made her way over for their drinks, handing menus to the fresh faces. The rambunctious trio refused to lower the volume of their chatter, unaware of the various exhausted states their companions were in.

Rider was the first to address them. He leaned back in his chair, one hand draped on the corner of Dacey's closest to him, crossing his long legs. "How was your night?" he asked, switching the toothpick tucked in the corner of his mouth from one side to the other. He was completely at ease, like the rest of the diner didn't exist.

"Could have been a lot better, I assure you. How are you this awake?" Dacey groused, rubbing her temples, eyeing their coffees being brought over. She accepted the sugar container he offered with a grateful nod, pouring a generous dose into the dark liquid.

Eddie chewed the inside of his lip hard enough he tasted the metallic blood on his tongue as he fought to keep from slapping Rider's hand away. When Dacey finished with the sugar, she slid it down the table to him, fingers brushing his with a nod toward his cup.

"Well, honey, that's just the life of a cowboy, isn't it? Up with the sun to get the work done." Rider answered, a crooked smile aimed her way.

"I don't have to be full of fuckin' energy to do it. I can be up with the sun and still drag ass to do what needs done." She countered, cradling her mug. Blowing across the top, she chanced a sip, nose wrinkling a little. Eddie hid the amusement at the sight of her scrunched features, flagging the waitress down.

"I ain't energetic. I'm always this way no matter what time of day or night it is. Why be miserable when you can make the most out of life?" Rider toyed with his spoon, glancing at the waitress as she appeared.

"She forgot to ask for milk, hun. Any chance she can have a glass for her coffee?" Eddie spoke up, earning a grateful look from Dacey.

"Sure thing, love, anything else right now?" The woman asked.

"No, but thank you."

She offered him a nod, then headed toward the kitchen. Rider watched her walk away before he turned to Eddie. "How did you know Dacey wanted milk?" He was curious, leaning back in his chair to look at Eddie behind Dacey.

"I pay attention, that's how," was all Eddie would offer him, a faint smirk on his face. Her knee tapped his under the table in thanks, earning one back. Their silent communication was cut short when Eddie shifted to make room for the arm that appeared between them holding the milk.

"Thank you." Dacey smiled, taking the milk to pour in her cup. Rider watched her, memorizing the amount she added.

Grant cleared his throat to gain everyone's attention. "Boys, I was thinking last night you guys are from Lazy Bar Wheeler Ranch, correct? Not the Wheeler family from Beaver Creek Ranch?" Grant asked, pouring sugar in his coffee.

"You got it. Your southernmost pasture borders one of our smallest that we use for hunting more than anything. I've seen you both out there now and then when we go to keep the paths cleared down. Isn't that where your heifers are?" Rusty sat forward to face Grant.

"I was talking yesterday with Erica about hiring Brody and maybe you two," Grant explained, rubbing the back of his neck. "I need the help, and Eddie had already agreed he doesn't mind you three around so long as you pull your weight."

Riley's eyes widened, "Are you serious?" She breathed, leaning forward almost on the table. Rider jerked her back into her chair.

"You have manners. Now use 'em." He warned. She had the decency to blush, dropping her gaze to the table. "Anyway, we can discuss that later if that's okay? While my brother and I are both looking forward to an opportunity like that, I believe there are more pressing matters at hand."

Their waitress appeared once more to take down orders and make sure their coffees were full. There was a small argument at the table as she questioned who would be paying, taking a step back at the playful shouting match that ensued between Rider and Grant. While they bickered, she wrote down what the rest asked for. When Eddie asked for extra bacon on the side, Dacey schooled her features into a look of innocence.

"Nice try, but there ain't no way I forgot if I had something on my plate you didn't, you'd eat half of mine instead of your own." He pointed his fork at her. "You were the one who chose the cheesecake stuffed French toast, no one ever said you couldn't get bacon."

She cracked, giggling into her coffee mug. "I have no idea what you're talking about."

"Like hell."

Once the waitress was back at the kitchen window, the bill debate settled, and everyone was once again sipping coffee, Rider broke the question on their minds. "How much are we allowed to know, and how much are we not allowed to know?"

All eyes turned to the sisters and Josie let out a small sigh. "There's more that you can't know than there is that you can." She admitted as Dacey slowly and steadily shredded her napkin. Grant reached across the table to offer Josie a soft pat on her hand in encouragement. She was pale, chest rising and falling in short pants, trying to remain calm throughout the talk. It would do no one any good if she was consumed with a panic attack. Dacey was clenching her jaw, refusing to speak until Eddie knocked his knee against hers under the table, making her look at him. He didn't speak, he didn't need to. She could see in his face what he wanted to say. The barest of nods was offered in return, her hands dropping what was left of the napkin.

"Why don't you just tell us what you can?" Grant hedged. Josie licked her lips, straightening her posture. This was her family, and potential friends. If she and Dacey couldn't trust them now, when could they? Taking a deep breath, she let it out slowly.

"You all know who Seth is and why he's here. We told you guys that last night. To make an endless story short, Dacey and I have been on the run since we escaped him this past February. For a while, we thought that we had tricked and lost him." She took a drink, hoping the warm coffee would offer courage. Her knee began to bounce, the uneven pattern knocking into the table every once in a while. Riley watched her, chewing her lower lip, wishing for a way to help. "We never stayed more than a weekend anywhere, or even within the same circuit, just chose random rodeos wherever we could. No rhyme, no reason, no trail. No pattern meant there was no trial to follow, or so we assumed. Somehow, last month he found us. Either we have the worst streak of luck, or we weren't as careful as we thought. Now, no matter what we do, we can't shake him. He's always one step ahead of us." She gripped her coffee mug like a lifeline as she spoke.

Eddie sat back in his chair, a hollow laugh escaping. "So, essentially, you two brought a stalker along with you." Grant glared at him as he continued on, heedless of the warning look. "And you want what from us? Have you ever thought that once he found out what to look for, he'd always know how to find you?"

Josie's look could have melted steel at that moment. "Nothing. You can go fuck yourself, Eddie, if you think I want anything from you right now. If it comes down to it, Dacey and I will pack up and hit the road to settle this on our own. We've managed this far without your help." His question gave her pause as she mulled it over. "But no, I hadn't thought of that. It makes more sense than just being lucky all the time. He's capable of coming across as this good looking, friendly man when he needs to be."

Eddie leaned forward, one finger pointed toward her, a warning clear in his eyes. "You may not, but if you think for even a second that I'm about to lose Dacey again, you have lost what little mind you have left. Not a damn chance." A hand on his knee did little to cool the fire building within him. If anything, the weight of it spurred him on to fight for Dacey. "We gotta get rid of Seth to figure out who the rat may be. Once we do, we can go from there. You're not leaving, and that's final."

Rider cut in, raising his hands in a gesture of placation. "Can someone *please* fill in the gaps here? Even with the headline version of it? Maybe that can keep another argument from starting. None of us can do anything if we keep squabbling back and forth like little kids." The table was quiet for a few minutes, giving them all a chance to calm down.

Riley tapped her fork on her palm as her gaze flicked between Eddie, Josie, and Dacey. Unable to take the quiet tension any further, she blurted the first thing that came to mind. "How do y'all know each other so well?"

Dacey waited a beat, debating on if she should answer it or not. “Josie and I were raised at Wildwood. Grant, our father, and Eddie’s dad, were Green Berets in World War II, in the same unit. That’s how they met. The three got pretty close, as one is prone to do when your life is on the line. Once the war was over, they came back here together to settle down. Eddie’s dad was obviously the first to have a kid of the trio, but…” Dacey trailed off to look at the man in question. A white-knuckle grip on his coffee mug had the porcelain screaming under the pressure, but he gave her the faintest of nods to continue. Swallowing a large mouthful of coffee, she pressed on. “His mom split. Eddie was only two when she walked out.”

Grant felt his stomach churn, the coffee he’d been drinking threatening to come back up. His hands grew damp, wishing he could ignore the story being recounted. He knew it needed to be told, knew it was only fair to let them know. It was one less thing for Seth to use against the girls in the long run. He wanted to stand up and walk out, to take them and leave without looking back, but knew that it would be pointless to run; no matter how they tried to shake him, he was always in the shadows.

Dacey took another gulp of her coffee before plowing on. “She was the first. His dad went south mentally after and turned to the bottle. That’s how Grant ended up with Eddie as his own kid and how they know each other so well. Our dad stuck around, watching one buddy drink himself to death while the other raised the son he wanted more than anything. Before you ask how Grant got Eddie instead of our dad, trust me, ours tried his best, but neither of them ever told us what happened between them or why it never worked out. I’d suggest you don’t ask. That’s between those three, if Eddie even knows. Instead, the year Eddie's dad died, our dad had a girl." Dacey gestured to her sister, who looked like she wanted to throw her soul up on the table.

Eddie cut into her story; eyes haunted. "Ain't a reason to hide it from you anymore. Now's a good time as any to tell you a lot." He chanced a glance at Grant, the man trembling so hard what little cold coffee remained spilled over the rim. Their eyes met, but Eddie caught the way his foster father resigned himself to the tale ahead.

"It seems like no father does anything right anymore in today's world. Dad never was home, wanted nothing to do with me, just worked his ass off. Only wanted me around as a way to let his frustrations out at the end of a long day. Now, I don't remember any of this and, if I do, it's buried so deep I never will, no matter what I try. Everything you hear, Grant told me at sixteen." He paused his story long enough for their waitress to come by, refilling their cups. She rushed through the process, sensing the way the atmosphere had thickened to the point of suffocating.

Taking the empty milk glass, she sat another down in its place, scurrying off toward a different table. They took the break, unsure if they had made the right choice in telling the story. Dacey's hand stayed on Eddie's thigh, her gentle touch the only thing that kept him from losing it. Josie kept her mouth shut, watching her sister take the sugar container from him, pouring it in herself. Riley had since switched from nervous tapping to leg bouncing, wishing she had kept closer to her brothers.

When he knew it wouldn't do any good to continue dragging it out, Eddie plowed on. "The drink got its claws into him, turning him into something no one recognized. One night was worse than any of the others; and I don't remember any of it. Luck, fate, something must have taken pity on me because Grant came by to visit and saw me lying there in a puddle of my blood. Grant rushed me to the ER, hoping I made the short drive. Once I was checked in, he went back and taught dad a lesson; albeit, Grant didn't beat the bastard as badly as he did me, but Grant made his point clear. Once I was out of the hospital, Grant had me pack a bag." He mumbled, lighting a cigarette to take a deep drag of smoke, staring into the depths of nothing to avoid the eyes around the table watching his clear admission.

It was Grant's turn to look like he was going to throw up, but he remained strong. Riley attempted to take Eddie's hand under the table. He pulled it away, curling it into a loose hold on his spoon to swirl his drink. She bit her lip, dropping her gaze from him to her feet, embarrassed.

The table remained quiet for a few minutes, letting his story sink in. Josie couldn't help the small bubble of guilt that welled up. She knew Eddie had a rough childhood before she was born, but she hadn't known it was that traumatic. How had he always been so loving, so happy to see her and Dacey with that behind him? Maybe it was the cause of his attitude now? Either way, she wasn't sure if it was a topic she wanted to broach at any point with him after today.

Rusty gave a low cough, clearing his throat. "Holy fuck." He breathed, resting his head on the back of his chair. Looking around at the others, he drummed his fingers on the tabletop. "Are we going in together on therapy bills? Cause after this, we're gonna have to."

Rider snorted, breaking up the heavy cloud settling over their table. Riley threw a balled up napkin at him, reaching up and pinching the bridge of her nose. Josie choked a bit on her coffee, clearing her throat to cover the broken laugh that escaped. It triggered a snort from Dacey, who in turn caused Eddie to chuckle a little under his breath. Grant pinched the bridge of his nose, closing his eyes. Knocking his knuckles on the tabletop, he gained their attention back. “Alright, alright. While I am all for, and appreciate the break in the horror, I think it’s time to get back on the nightmare wagon. The sooner we get this over with, the better.” He assured them. Gesturing to Dacey, he encouraged her to continue.

What little courage she had left was failing her, so Dacey picked up the threads of the story. “Our dad didn’t care much for Josie. He kept trying for a boy, and our mom refused to believe the worst of him, no matter how hard her friends tried to point out the warning signs. Then, I was born. Dad lost it. All he wanted was a boy to carry on the family name. When I was born, he hit the bottle as hard as Eddie’s dad did. They became mean together. Our grandpa wasn’t about to just let him raise us like that; not when his daughter was dying. We don’t know what mom had, but within a year of me being born she was gone.” Her voice was steady, almost monotone as she spoke, while her gaze was a thousand miles away.

“Dad went off the rails when mom died and all he had was two girls and a father-in-law that wanted nothing more than to kill him, so he split. Never heard a word out of him for eleven years and we all liked it that way. Grandpa, Grant, and Eddie were the ones who raised Josie and I that whole time. The only woman in our lives was Grant’s wife, Vanessa. I don’t think she counts, however, because she hated all of us since we weren’t her real kids. Then, six years ago on Christmas night, Grandpa passed away.” Her voice started to waiver and break, tears threatening.

Eddie broke out of his mental nightmare, snaking an arm around her shoulders. His hand rubbed at her back, while half the table lit cigarettes to calm nerves on edge. Out of her normal, pink ones, Josie had to bum one from Grant, taking it with a hand shaking so hard he ended up lighting it for her. They paused long enough to let the waitress set down plates of steaming food that none of them wanted anymore. She topped up their coffees and, with one last check, made her way to a different table. They stared at the food, unsure or unable to even think of eating.

Finally, Rusty inhaled and took a bite of egg. "Let's get this down, because we all know that we need food to get through today. Take a moment, eat, and once we are done, if you feel up to it, we can continue?" He offered. Dacey gave him a grateful look that had Eddie scowling into his eggs.

"Thanks, I agree. We do need to eat something." They all needed a break from the heavy conversation. Eddie seemed to be pushing his food around more than eating it, while Josie seemed intent on drinking more coffee than actual food. Dacey raised an eyebrow at her, taking a pointed bite of her French toast. In retaliation, Josie threw a bite of her own toast at her, earning a laugh as Dacey ducked. It broke the tension that had enveloped the table, causing the Wheeler family to join in on the laughter.

They made quick work of the food, only Eddie seeming not to want more than a bite or two of anything. His stomach turned and he couldn't figure out if it was the lack of sleep or the conversation they were having. Either way, he finished a few pieces of bacon, nothing more. Shoving the rest toward Dacey for her to finish, he waved away her concerned look.

She leaned closer, whispering in his ear, "It's a lot more fun having to steal it from you. Are you sure you're done?" Neither was aware of

Josie's intent stare pinned on them.

"Positive. I can't think of eating a lot right now." He took a tiny bite of toast to pacify her. "Just finish it for me."

Poking at the bacon, Dacey began munching her way through it, talking between Rider and Rusty about not much of anything. Conversation flowed easier the longer the group ate, until they were all involved in some debate or another. Making sure that everyone was done, Dacey sat back in her chair with a soft sigh. "That's better. Instead of continuing this story, does anybody want to try figuring out how to get rid of Seth and his lackeys?"

Grant looked around at the people that were coming in to fill the tables that surrounded them. "Legally, I'm not sure there's a lot we can do." He kept his voice lowered to be sure only those at the table could hear him. "Stalkin's about the only thing, maybe?"

"I have no idea about laws, and I sort of wish I did," Rusty admitted, toying with the spoon sticking out of his mug. "Is there any way we can scare him off? Maybe sheer numbers would work?"

Josie let out a snort. "Hasn't worked so far. I know chances are he has four of his own; Eva is his younger sister and she's just as mean and entitled as he is. The other possibilities are Ben Anderson, Cole Fields, and Layton Green." She ticked their names off on her hand while speaking, pausing to think if there could have been anyone else. Coming up empty-handed, she continued. "Those four have always been thick as hair on a dog's back. Cole was trying his damnedest to get with Dacey, but Eva got jealous. She didn't stick around, just long enough to throw his attraction off Dacey so she could feel superior to her, I guess."

Dacey pretended to vomit at the idea, causing Riley to laugh. Her brothers wore matching grins as they watched the blonde give a full body shudder. "If it ever came down to it, I would have rather jumped off the roof than sleep with him. He tried to get anything that had a pulse." Wrinkling her nose in disgust, she leaned forward, grabbing the last slice of bacon on Eddie's plate. "His dog looked better than he ever did, anyway."

Narrowing his eyes, Eddie kept her distracted with one hand, pretending to reach for her chin as the other shot out to grab her coffee mug. She gave an indignant half shout, trying to snatch it back. "Problems?" He held it out to Riley, who took it from him, setting it down by her mug.

"You both suck. But I needed to lay off, anyway. Keep drinking it and I'm going to be out running Cash today." Shrugging, she settled back in her chair. "What about a good enough ass beating that he can't come back?"

Josie frowned hard at Dacey. "That's called assault, remember? I'd rather not go to jail."

"Oh yeah, I forgot only those with money can beat someone half to death and still get off scot free," Dacey muttered bitterly. "Good to know that's how this works."

Eddie looked like he could have flipped the table across the room, locking his jaw to keep from saying anything. A small plan formed in his mind, one he wasn't going to be sharing with anyone, at any time, if he could help it. Grant watched him from across the table, wondering what was going on inside the twisted mind. The conversation flowed around them both, solutions offered and tossed out. Each idea was closer to an actual plan, but none of them were sticking.

"Can we let the ones running the show know what's going on and have them removed from the property?" Riley asked.

"We risk being thrown out for bringing drama with that. Dacey and I tried that at the very first one he showed up at, and they threw us all out for 'disrupting family safe sports', as the asshole said," Josie explained. A general outrage rose from the Wheeler family at her words, causing her to raise a hand up to keep them from getting too loud.

Exhaustion threatened to overtake Grant, and he scrubbed a hand over tired eyes. Nothing would stick, no matter how hard they threw it, and he knew he would have to step in. While Dean wasn't someone he wanted to drag into the mess, he knew he'd have to. Tossing his napkin down across his plate, he broke up the chatter. "We ain't getting anywhere with this, and we need to get going. I have bulls to check on and feed, while you lot have horses that need tending to. Let's get the day on a roll. Just be sure that neither of you goes anywhere alone, okay? Once the animals are cared for, we can meet back up as a group." Grant stood up, Eddie following his lead. Riley was on her feet after them, glancing between her brothers and the two older men.

"Can I ride with you?" She asked with a smile up at Grant. "That way, I can ride with Dacey and Josie."

Eddie wanted to admit he'd rather walk across town to the arena than ride with the brunette again, but kept quiet around her brothers. Dacey's face gave away nothing, turning her back on Eddie to talk to Joise, rising in sync from the table. They headed toward the truck, Rider and Rusty close behind them, interjecting in their conversation.

"Maybe I can help you with your bulls today?" Riley asked, looking up at Eddie, offering a slow smile. Annoyance flashed through him, his gaze running over her. Taking another quick look at Dacey, he was surprised to find her eyes ablaze with anger toward the other girl. A wicked smile spread across Eddie's face as he offered Riley his arm.

"Why sure you can. Could always use a little extra help with them." His actions earned a startled look from Grant at the sudden switch flip. The pair led the way from the restaurant toward the trucks.

Dacey slowed up to fall into step with Rider. "I wouldn't mind helping you guys with your warm-ups if you want." she offered, peeking at him out of the corner of her eye. "Josie likes to work her patterns alone, but with everything going on, I know she can't. We can help the two of you and then swap?"

He seemed stunned for a second, staring at her like it was a trick. "I'd appreciate it, so long as Rusty is okay with it. We need an outsider to give us real feedback, not just tell us we'll be awesome, or scream at us." he gave a pointed look toward Riley that went ignored. Rusty smirked at Dacey when she snorted.

"You laugh, but it's true. Riley just sits on the fence and claims we are the best roping team out there. Not good in the way of constructive criticism." Rusty spoke up. "We could fall on our asses, and she'd still be like 'oh that was an incredible run!' like we didn't just break something."

Dacey cracked up. "I get it. Josie does the same thing to me when I'm trying to practice my break away. She gets even worse when I'm running poles or the plug race. Occasionally we team rope, but we end up shouting at each other more than anything." She admitted with a grimace.

Rider clapped a hand on her shoulder, nodding. "Sounds about right! Siblings, no matter how much you love them, fight like cats and dogs most days." Reaching the trucks, Rider dropped the tailgate of Grant's for her with a smile. Dacey took his hand, allowing him to help her up, settling down on the fender. Rider offered her a crooked smile, tapping the side of the truck. "See ya there." With that, he walked away to get in his truck with Rusty.

Dacey jumped a bit as the door to the truck slammed behind her. Turning, she pursed her lips at the back of Eddie's head. She had the nagging feeling it was going to be a rather long day.

Chapter 12

Little Red Rodeo

Half the day was over by the time Grant gave in to the annoyance simmering below his calm demeanor. Between the creeping heat within the barns of the rodeo, the lack of care others around them gave his animals as they handled them, and their tag along, he knew he needed to find the others.

The false, high laugh Riley kept giving Eddie wasn't helping, making him wish he could throw her in the bull pen and pretend that he had never seen her. Jaw aching from clenching it to keep from snapping, Grant forced himself to blow out a slow breath. Did he want to hire her brothers? If he did, Riley was bound to tag along, never leaving again. Eddie appeared annoyed by her as well. The thought of how Eddie's plan backfired on him earned a smile. Why he even changed his mind from trying to get rid of Riley to wanting her around was a mystery Grant didn't want to deal with.

Walking away from them with instructions to find him if they needed him, Grant relaxed. When he reached the main alley of the barn, he paused to consider his options. Oblivious to the stray bits of hay drifting past his feet, he lifted his face up, watching the birds above. A pair circled not far from where he stood, their small nest tucked into the corner of the roof. They took turns fluttering up to feed the tiny chicks poking their heads up.

People passed him, offering nods or smiles in turn, some leading horses, others in clusters talking about the night ahead of them. These were the times he missed home the most, when the noise pressed in on him from all sides. It was never ending, even in the hours where it was only contestants and the animals they use. Their aftershaves and perfumes blending together with feeds, hay, and manure overwhelmed him. But Grant would never pass up the chance to bring his own stock. Eddie had offered over the years, growing more capable each time. Yet he always turned the man down.

Startled out of his musings by a young girl rushing past clutching a container of buttered popcorn, he pulled out a cigarette. Josie. He needed to find Josie. Grant reasoned she would appreciate the break from the others, if this morning had been any indication. Reaching his decision, he meandered down the main alleyway of the training barn toward the warmup pens.

"Bum a smoke?" Turning to face Josie as she guided Buckshot up to him, he offered out the pack. She made the tiniest of faces at the brand. "You wouldn't think that strawberry smokes were all that great till you have to go back to plain. Wish I caught how I was low on them before getting here. I guess they'll do."

Grant laughed. "Such a tragedy. You could always quit instead of mocking my choice of a death trap. Where are the others?" It irked him that they let Seth's primary target wander off on her own.

"Why quit when I know it'd make me that much of a bigger bitch some days? Besides, I tried that once before about a year ago. Dacey ended up stealing an entire display of the kind I smoke. She threw every pack at me while telling me in no uncertain terms never to try again." Josie laughed at the memory, the bright sound filling a hole in Grant he hadn't realized had formed in his heart. Her laugh was faint, more worn, and husky from the cigarettes, but it was still perfect. Drawing the smoke deep into her lungs, she waved toward the doors. From atop Cash, Dacey returned it, nodding once to Grant. Behind them, Grant could see the twins seated on their horses like sentries, chatting.

Trotting over, Dacey raised one split rein in warning toward Cash's pinned ears. "Do it, and I will knock your teeth down your throat, buddy." He snorted, sidestepping once at the tone of her voice. When she was sure he was settled, she turned back toward her sister. "We were trying to find you." The words were snapped out, the hand on the reins fisting. Buckshot pinned her ears, squealing when his head snaked toward her.

Josie pulled her away, eyes narrowed. "I knew where Grant was. I was fine. You were busy with the poles when I left, figured it was best to leave you to it." She retorted.

"Ah, good. Cause I was gonna chew your ass about sticking together in groups." Grant interrupted the sisters, stopping the fight he knew would erupt. Dacey slouched in her saddle, head turned away. A large head nudged at him, insistent on getting the attention Buckshot thought she deserved for sitting still. Grant obliged her, scratching her forehead. She melted under the touch, closing big brown eyes with a snort.

Clearing her throat, Dacey glanced back at the twins. "Sorry, Grant.

We didn't know she took off on us until I went to ask a question."

"It's fine. Just don't do it again, understand?" His voice left no room for argument. She nodded, sitting to her full height in the saddle. "Good. Go on then, they're waitin' for ya."

She nodded once, turning Cash around. Nudging him into a quick lope, the trio disappeared through open barn doors. He watched them go, sunlight filtering down on dirt packed floors. Buckshot snorted, pushing against him harder for more rubs.

Josie shook her head with a laugh, patting her warm neck. "You're such a baby!" Turning back to Grant, she shifted in the saddle. It rasped a little, the worn leather protesting use. "What brought you to our end of the barn, anyway? Thought you were in with the bulls getting them taken care of?"

Grant made a face, earning another laugh from her. "Riley was kind enough to help us, so I needed a small break." Lifting his hand, he pinched his thumb and forefinger together for emphasis. "Thought I'd come watch you practice instead and be sure that you're okay."

"They had me run first, since I only do one event anymore." She offered a shrug, one hand moving to play with the black mane in front of her. "I wouldn't mind the company, but I was heading to get her back in her stall to find you. Seems this works out for us both." Josie beamed down at him.

"Anything in particular you wanna do?" Taking a step back to be sure his feet were out of Buckshots' range, he fell in line beside Josie.

"There's the vendor barn I want to check out. But just walk and talk, for the most part." Her hopeful tone made Grant pat her leg.

"That sounds like a plan. We can also swing by your truck to put your bags in mine."

She flushed, looking away to study the perked ears in front of her as though they held answers. "We don't have a lot to move from one to the other."

Grant didn't miss a beat, keeping her from further embarrassment. "I wouldn't think so, given the circumstances. Ain't nothing wrong with only a few things." He made a mental note to get them a few things at the vendors as they made their way to Buckshot's stall. Curiosity burned through him as they worked in sync to get the mare unsaddled and settled in. Neither had much to say, worried they may cross an invisible line.

Once Josie was satisfied with how Buckshot was situated, she closed the stall door. "Ready?"

"One question, if I may?"

She side eyed him, walking toward the exit. "Fire away, I guess."

He waved a hand back toward the stalls. "Okay, so I have a couple of questions. First of all, where did you find Cash?"

Unexpected laughter rang between them as Josie relaxed. "A sale last year, same as Buckshot. We convinced the dead beat if he let us back in the circuit, we could make him the money he bitched it took to keep us." She wrinkled her nose, eyes narrowed. "Never mind the fact he would rather let us starve naked than spend a cent on us. But he knew the buckles would impress the high shoulders he was trying to rub up on." Holding a hand out, she tapped the pack tucked away in his shirt pocket. Pulling two out and lighting them, he passed one over. "Cash was in a pen by himself with a sign saying slaughter on the gate. Dacey took a look at him and just walked in like there weren't people yelling for her not to. He charged her, and I was sure he was going to kill her; not going to lie, my heart was all I heard. But before he reached her, he slid to a halt like someone dropped a wall between them and he hit it. Instead, he started running around her, acting like he would rip her face off, yet still did nothing."

Pausing in her story, Josie glanced back at the barn they had left. "Dacey had lifesavers in her pocket that day. I can't remember why, she doesn't even like them, but she took them out and just kept ignoring his tantrums. Pretty sure that's why Cash didn't kill her. He was too confused about what the hell was going on." Grant could hear the resignation in her voice. Drawing the smoke deep into his lungs, he motioned for her to continue. "She held some out, almost bored, and he stopped. Just stood there breathing harder than I've ever seen. Then, bam. That asshole walked right up to her and took the treats. That was it. Game over, he was hers. Ever since she got him, she's worked long hours any day she can with him. He must know she saved him from death because their bond is crazy. He only tolerates me because he realized I'm part of the group now."

Grant watched her as she spoke with rising astonishment. Whistling, he shook his head. "Well, you answered every other question I had with that. Seems like they had some serious luck on their side that day, and not just making it out alive. From what I was hearing yesterday when she was under the alias, those two have become impossible to beat at break away. But, why do you only chase cans then? You used to love team roping."

"Cash is a powerhouse, I agree. He just wants Dacey proud, I think. I don't know what it is about that horse, but I swear he's smart and knows what's going on around him." She stepped into the vendor barn with a mild shrug. "Buckshot has been the best horse I've had since we lived with you. She's more talented than I ever could have hoped for. We put in the work and it shows. But when it comes to team rope, Cash is better off alone." Pausing by a stall, Josie eyed the shirts hanging there. Some were typical button downs while some were cotton t-shirts. She toyed with the short sleeves of a lilac colored button down before looking at Grant. "Most of the winnings go to the horses, gas, and whatever is left we use for us. Bet that was the next question?"

"I can't deny it, but in my defense…"

"You have none." She cut in.

He shot her an annoyed look before continuing, "In my defense, I can't help wondering because you're sleeping in the truck bed when that's more than a little dangerous, given the circumstances." She didn't look at him, instead focusing on the shirts. Grant noted each one she lingered on for longer than a moment or two, walking behind her to slide each off of their respective hangers. The pile he held grew, a few that weren't even for her dropped atop the rest.

Exhaling a little harder than she meant to, she tossed one back on the tabletop. "We do what we can. But what other options do we have? Dacey isn't known for her stellar temperament, and I can't begin to explain how I can't stand being bossed around by someone I don't even know. We're at this crossroads where we *need* money, but we can't work. We have nothing but some clothes, a truck that some days makes me wonder how much longer we will have it, and two horses we can't pay to board." It rushed out as she stared unseeing at a boot stand. "Dacey's always wanted to come back, but how can we do that to you? I didn't even want to come this close to your area for fear of exactly what happened."

An indignant noise escaped him as he caught her arm in a light hold, almost dropping the stack of clothes he had accumulated. He felt the way she stiffened and noted the panic that began to set in her eyes. Letting her go, he held his hands up. "That was my mistake, and I apologize. I know better, but I wasn't thinking."

Josie let out a shaky breath. "It's another reason I can't find steady work. After what Seth's put me through, I have panic attacks at the stupidest things if I don't catch it in time or have Dacey to talk me off the ledge." Closing her eyes, she counted to herself as her heart made a home for itself in her throat. Once she was sure she wouldn't suddenly burst into tears, she met his worried gaze. "I'm okay. I am. Come on, let's keep going. We can talk later, before I cause a scene by mistake." Catching sight of the shirts, she flushed. "What are those for?"

"Rags, what else? They're for you and Dacey, obviously, so don't try arguing." He offered cash toward the owner of the stand, ignoring Josie as her mouth dropped.

"Grant!"

"Josie?" He nodded his thanks as the clothes were bagged, slipping the handles over his arms.

"You can't just…"

"I can, and I will. Knock off telling me what I can and cannot do, understand me? You should remember that never sat well with me, and I do things just because I'm told not to."

She let it drop, choosing instead to keep wandering the stalls, pausing at a few that seemed to catch her attention. At one point, Josie clung to a pair of boots so long Grant feared he'd have to pry them from her. "Do you want them?" She jerked, dropping them back down in embarrassment.

"I'm fine. We can't afford them anyway, I'll be okay." Taking his arm, she guided him toward a different stall. Pausing, she took a step in a different direction when she spotted Eddie talking to the salesman of a black Stetson. Riley looked glued to his hip, trying on different styles and colors of hats, looking for one that was better than the others. Grant caught sight of them and hurried to follow Josie toward a stall selling engraved belts.

"I want to talk to him about what he's up to with her, but I can't when it boils down to it. Part of me feels like I need to warn the poor girl, while the other part of me knows it won't do a lick of good and she needs to learn the hard way so she stops coming around."

Josie cast him a curious look. "Hard way? I assume he already has a girlfriend that he somehow conned into dating him?"

Grant smothered a laugh to keep from drawing attention to them. "Not even close. Hasn't kept one since Bethanie about four years ago. It only lasted about six months and once she was out the door, he just went to one-night stands or random hookups. He's a grown man, ain't my place to tell him what he can and can't do. Besides, even if I could, he wouldn't listen to a word I had to say. As long as he doesn't knock someone up, I couldn't care less." Setting a belt down that had wild horses charging down the length of it, he picked up one that was simple scrollwork to study the details closer. Checking the price tag, he waited until Josie found one that caught her eye. "Hey, can you measure her? And add a little extra on for later?" He knew once they had steady meals, work, and a home, she would fill out a little better.

She flushed. "No! It's okay, really!" Even as she attempted a weak protest, the sales clerk made her way over with the measuring tape. Lifting Josie's arms away from her waist, she hummed to herself as she worked, nodding with each noted size.

"How come I never get free belts?" Eddie questioned, walking over to smirk at Josie. Sending him a withering look at the comment, she glanced over at Riley. The brunette was lifting the belt she had been hoping to get for Dacey if she and Buckshot won later that night. Trying to keep her mouth closed in order not to cause any issues, she turned her gaze to Grant.

"You don't get them because the last one I bought you ended up missing about six months after I got it," Grant countered, not even looking at Eddie. Instead, he kept his attention focused on making sure the belt for Josie was being cut to his standard, extra holes and all. Satisfied with the work, he gestured toward the belt Riley put down. "I need that one as well, please, a little smaller than this young lady. Seems like the kind Dacey would like, isn't it?" He asked.

Josie stammered, unable to form words. The woman moved to Riley, eyeing her up.

"Instead of smaller, I can make it her size and just add a few extra notches." She offered, measuring tape in place around Riley. The young woman kept silent, watching the stall owner work. Eddie never moved, a faint scowl on his face pinned to Grant's back. The older man wasn't phased, and didn't even bother turning around as he felt it bore into him.

When the seller stepped back, Grant pulled his wallet out. Watching him while biting her lip, Josie caved and caught his wrist. "I can't thank you enough for any of this." Her cheeks flared with heat when Grant offered her a gentle smile.

"What size boot does Dacey wear?" Eddie cut in, beating Grant to the belt that had been made for the woman.

"She's seven and a half. Only reason I remember is because there's no way I can fit hers since I wear an eight and a half." Josie looked at him. "Why?"

"Why the fuck does it matter? Just do what you're doing."

He strode off, Riley blinking toward his retreating back. "I, um, I hope it's okay I tag along to shop?" She asked.

"You can," Grant replied, bumping their shoulders. When she tensed a little, he made a mental note; it seemed all forms of contact were off the table. Stepping away, Grant could feel the gaze boring into his back from a few stalls over where Eddie selected two pairs of boots. Riley peeked over her shoulder toward the man in question.

"Are we going to wait for him?" She asked.

He grabbed the bag with their belts in it, making sure Josie put hers on right away. "He can catch up." Looking at Josie, he studied the belt. "Fit okay?" At her nod, he took a step away from the stall. "Then let's keep going, shall we? There're a couple of stalls I want to hit on the way back as well over on that side."

"I can't accept you spending more money on me," Josie tried to argue.

Grant crossed his arms. "Look, you can choose what you want on your own, or leave it up to me and my poor tastes. Either way, you need clothes and deserve a few extras." Leading them toward the next stall, he lifted a gaudy necklace in warning. Both women laughed at his display, Josie reaching out to slap it back down to the table.

"If that's what you think is a good choice, then you force my hand." Josie's smile was small, though it lit her eyes. "This one." She lifted a small, simple pendant where a horse was etched in silver.

"Oh, that's gorgeous." Riley breathed. Leaning past Josie, she lifted up a bracelet of twisted silver set with small blue stones. "Do you think Dacey would like this?"

Josie eyed it. "Not really. Dacey isn't big on gems." Rather, Josie selected a solid leather bracelet with wildflowers stamped on the surface. "This would be perfect, though. Or this one." She lifted a similarly sized band that boasted a forest scene with the silhouette of a stag in the center. While they hunted through the jewelry talking amongst themselves, Eddie made his way over carrying the boot boxes. Grant accepted them with a nod of thanks, opening each to look them over.

"You made some great choices. I think they'll like these." Shutting the lid on Josie's boots, he looked up. "Any chance you can go check on Dacey and bring her to the trucks? Figure once we get done here, we need to plan out how tonight is going to go. With everyone at different areas for their respective events, it's gonna get tricky to keep an eye on them."

"I ain't her fucking babysitter anymore, Grant. She's a big girl with big boys. She's fine." Eddie snapped. Riley's head jerked up, eyes widening a fraction at Eddie's tone. Glancing between the two men, ready for a shouting match, she took a step back toward Josie. Instead, the older man shrugged, continuing on to check the other stalls hawking their wares. Josie tagged along, falling into step with him after glancing over her shoulder to watch Eddie turn the opposite direction. He stalked off toward the barn she knew Dacey to be in, Riley keeping hot on his heels.

Chapter 13

What the Cowgirls Do

For a while, the two shopped and chatted, working their way toward the door that led out to the trailers. At the final stall, Grant grabbed three bags of kettle corn, tossing one at Josie for her to eat. She accepted, grateful for the midafternoon treat.

Halfway through the parking lot, they heard a ruckus heading their way, Dacey's voice carrying toward them above the others. Grant popped the door of his truck open, motioning for Josie to deposit their items. She dumped them in, keeping the popcorn. Tossing back a handful, she moved out of his way to jump in the bed. He followed her, dropping the tailgate. Taking a seat, he accepted the handful she offered out to him, waving it toward the group making their way over.

Rusty returned it, joining Grant. "Where's our goodies? Wasting away over here." He joked, finishing off a can of Coke.

Grant patted the space on his other side, motioning for Riley to join him. She did as asked, reaching behind him to snag a handful of Josie's popcorn, earning a hand slapping. "I see you earned a treat for being such a good girl." She teased, dodging a kick aimed at her. "Oh, come on! You were one shirt away from having a breakdown that someone was spending money on you!"

She was saved from having to respond when Dacey tapped her shoulder. "Can you unlock the rig for me?" A bag of cotton candy was held up in explanation.

Eddie shook his head. "You put that in there, it'll melt, and I ain't gonna eat a sugar brick later."

Dacey shrugged. "I need gum too. Besides, I never said I was gonna share it." She pointed out, stepping out of Josie's way. When it was just the two of them at the cab, she lifted her chin toward the others. "Riley said you got to spoil yourself a little," Dacey stated, voice low while digging around in the cupholder. Josie leaned on the frame, watching her.

"Grant spoiled both of us rotten if you ask me, and Eddie helped." She accepted the stick of gum her sister offered out. Dacey popped a piece into her mouth, hoping she could convince someone to stop at a gas station to restock. The twins had kept her supplied in soda and peanuts as the day passed, but gum was harder to come by. Josie caught the look on her face and kicked her foot. "We can stop on the way to the hotel, ain't no way these guys aren't out of smokes."

"Eddie just bought a pack off of a complete stranger because he was out this morning and had forgotten to ask amidst the chaos." Dacey's shoulder rapidly rose and fell. "But thank you." Josie wanted to say more, to thank her sister for what little calm she was offering. Instead, she linked their arms, guiding her back.

Grant took his place at the back of the bed, leaning against the cab. Folding his arms over his chest, his demeanor turned serious. "Tonight's going to be a little trickier now that we know we have unwanted company and everyone in varied events. So, boys, you are up first if my schedule is right, then Riley and Josie, then Dacey. Somewhere in there, I believe you two wanna try your hands at the rough stock?"

"We talked it over, but we agreed that we're going to pass on it. No reason to do it this weekend with everything going on," Rider spoke up. "But yeah, we're first up on this list."

"Josie rides before I do, so I can sit with her before her ride, but when I'm on deck, I can't keep an eye on her. Do you think you guys can come back under the guise of helping with the horses?" Riley asked.

"To hell with that. Why make them run halfway across the barn when I can be there with all of ya? Between me and Cujo, I'm pretty sure that it'll go just fine." Eddie blew a small cloud of smoke toward the ground.

Dacey blinked a few times, stunned at his relaxed manner of inserting himself into the fold. "You're going to be back there with us?" she asked, looking him over.

"Why not? You think that I'm about to let you go parading around alone back there? Were you born last night?"

Grant gave a sharp whistle, breaking up the brewing argument. "Okay! That settles it. Rider, Rusty, you boys focus on your rides. Eddie will have the ladies in hand until you're done with everything and can join him. I need to stick with the bulls as much as possible tonight, but if there's an emergency, you better find me, understand?" They all nodded the affirmative. "Perfect." He clapped his hands on his knees, standing to his full height. "Let's get this ball rolling."

Eddie caught Dacey's wrist when she moved to follow the others. Pinning him with a look of annoyance, it melted away when he offered out a small belt buckle. A horse's head was front and center, lifted in pride. "Thank you?"

"Pay close attention." He reached out and slipped a small pocketknife out that had appeared as a silver band behind the horse's head. "If I can't get to you, do not forget you have this. I don't care where you stick 'em, just stick 'em hard enough it counts. That ain't all." He pulled a bracelet from the same pocket the buckle had been in. Clasping it in place, he watched as she turned her wrist. It was one of the leather band ones, stamped in muted earth tones with pictures of hats and horseshoes with honeysuckle veins along the top.

She closed the blade, tucking it back where it belonged. Fighting tears, she reached out to hug him. "Thank you, Cowboy."

He planted a light kiss on the top of her hat. "As long as it keeps you safe, Darlin'."

The closer it got to the time to saddle up, the more nervous Dacey got. While it had been a lot of fun spending the day alone with the Wheeler twins, she couldn't help but wish just a little that she had Josie around. Josie would fix her braids, tell her she and Cash would win, and assure her that, no matter the outcome, she was proud of her. Chewing her lower lip, she wondered if she would find that kind of pep talk from Eddie. Dacey dismissed the thought with a hard snort. Chances were if she asked Eddie, she would be told to piss off and if she lost that she could always sell Cash for a better horse to win more.

As she finished getting leg wraps on Cash, familiar voices floated from Riley's stall door.

Trying to ignore the conversation and focus on the task, she wasn't expecting Eddie to poke his head over the door. "Are you fucking making those leg wraps yourself or just putting them on him?" He drawled. Cash pinned his ears, snaking his head forward, trying to land a bite.

Dacey tapped his shoulder in warning, keeping her voice low. "Shut up." Looking at Riley, Dacey was a bit surprised to see the obvious annoyance on Riley's face. She quirked a brow at the brunette in a silent question but received only a shake of her head in return. Letting it go, she figured if Riley wanted to talk to her about it, she would. Right then, they had more important things to focus on. A small part of Dacey felt bad. She knew chances were high Josie was going to clobber Riley at the barrels, while the rest of her filled with pride at the thought.

"Eddie, can you help me with Silver? It'll go faster if you do." Riley hedged, trying to draw the man away from where he leaned against Cash's stall door.

He glanced over at her, then back at Dacey. "Do you need help?" He asked.

Dacey rolled her eyes. "No, she does, though." Just before she turned her back, she caught the anger at the clear dismissal in his eyes. It didn't last long before she heard him join Riley. Last night, she had managed an impossible time to beat, leaving everyone expecting more. It drove her half crazy to know that most of the pressure she felt was her own fault. Every time she set a new goal or time, she always wanted to break it. Cash was a godsend for putting up with her always trying to push him harder.

Currently, her sister was focused on getting Buckshot to put her head down, muttering obscenities blended with threats of becoming a glue stick if she didn't. The mare tossed her head more, backing up until Josie had her in a corner. Dacey suppressed her laughter. At least when she told him, Cash would let his head down to be bridled. "Maybe you shouldn't use that bit like I told you the last time." She called out, faking innocence.

Sensing her anxiety, Cash dropped his nose into Dacey's hair, blowing into it as though he could blow away her problems. Laughing, Dacey hugged him, offering a few lifesavers he eagerly lipped up. "Thanks Cash. I know I don't need to worry, you always take us to the win. Faster than even those boring, old can chasers," she whispered to him. He butted against her in search of more sweet treats, crunching through them.

Josie's head popped over the top of the stall divider, hair a wild mess, hat nowhere to be seen. "If I don't use a bit, then she gets a worse attitude than she has now. Why don't you try coming in here if you think you can do it better?" Josie hissed.

Dacey gave Cash one last loving pat, partnered with a soft kiss on his nose. "I'll be right back," she assured him.

Slipping from one stall to the other, she assessed the mare backed into a corner. "Here, try this," Dacey offered out her extra bitless bridle. "I know you think this won't work, but all you can do is try."

Josie seemed to melt in on herself as she caved, taking the bridle with a face. "If this works, I won't ever doubt you again."

"Yeah right, tell me another! Look, we may have both graduated from Grant's old school of hard knocks as kids. But don't forget, Pawpaw had a hand in our teaching. I get it's hard to think back on those lessons, but you aren't listening to her like you should be. That's her problem. You have her, you just want to be boss." Dacey pointed out.

Josie approached Buckshot, talking soft and low to the mare, bridle held out. From the stall they worked together in getting Silver ready, Eddie and Riley peeked over the divider to see what would happen.

Eddie couldn't deny the small flood of pride he felt when his eyes shifted from Josie to Dacey; she was in the exact stance he knew he trained her in as a child. Her hands rested on her hips, left foot forward to step in, hat pushed up for better sight.

Reaching Buckshot, Josie started rubbing her nose and forehead, whispering under her breath. The mare dropped her head, lipping at her in search of the apple treats she usually received. When Josie got to her ears, Buckshot butted at her for more scratches, allowing Josie to slip the bridle over her. "Such a wonderful girl." Josie was almost faint with relief. Her mare was willing to work with her. Dacey broke first, body relaxing, offering them a bright smile.

"Well, she didn't eat your face over it!" Her teasing was met with a rude, if half-hearted, gesture.

Confident Josie had everything in hand, Dacey left the stall door open in order to head back to Cash. Riley whooped, clapping at the display, startling Eddie. Silver snapped her head up, ears pinned at the sudden racket. Eddie disappeared as well, moving back to the mare he was with. Finishing up, Dacey led Cash out into the alleyway to join Josie, freezing in her tracks at the sight in front of them. Back ridgid, she hid the frustration from her sister the best she could.

Riley had Eddie pinned to the wall opposite the one shared with Cash's stall, standing on tiptoe to kiss him like there was no one else around. His hat was in the dirt and Dacey knew that was going to cause a lot of trouble by itself. Making a half horrified, half gagging noise, Dacey kept going. What the hell was Riley doing? Did she think something like that would upset Dacey? Dacey had made it more than clear Eddie was free game. Josie tapped Dacey's upper thigh with her reins in a gentle display of assurance, head nodding away from the two.

The pair were nearly at the warmup pens when Eddie caught up to them, brushing the dirt off his hat, annoyance clear on his face.

Dacey stifled a laugh, mounting Cash. “Are you that bad of a kisser that you had to run?” she asked, voice low and fake sweet. Riley trotted past them, catching up with Josie, a bright grin plastered across her face as she pulled Silver level with Buckshot. The two fell into their own quiet conversation, Riley leading it as she chatted at a hundred miles an hour. Josie could only nod along with her and add the occasional comment.

“You’re lucky you’re already on Cujo, or I’d prove a fuckin’ point to you right now, Darlin’.” he snarled back. The laughter she was smothering broke free, causing his face to flush in anger. “Keep laughing and I’ll rip you off of him with those pigtails and find something better to do with that running mouth of yours.” Cash pinned his ears, head snaking out toward Eddie. Dacey drew him back easily. “I’ll fuckin’ thump you if you bite me.”

“Thump him and I will gut you like a buck,” Dacey warned from behind him, hand resting on her belt buckle. Eddie’s face was unreadable when he stepped up to rest a hand on her leg. Cash snorted his feelings out hard, ears still back in annoyance. “Don’t mind that big baby, Cash, he’s jealous of your beauty.” She assured him, rubbing his forehead. Her thigh burned, every nerve where his hand rested, feeling overly sensitive. Forcing herself to keep breathing like nothing was wrong, she tried not to shudder.

“Excuse me?” Eddie demanded.

“You heard me. Don’t be jealous of my baby because he’s prettier than you.” The desire building in her subsided. Rubbing Cash’s neck, she ignored the hand on her leg when a child on a pony blasted past, forcing Eddie closer against her. The little boy wasn't the only one. Plenty of the competition was buzzing in alleyways, in and out of stalls, and shouting to each other over the walls. It was a cacophony of noise she relished. At least here she couldn't get trapped in her own head. Steadying herself, she chanced a look down at the man who, even mad at her, was refusing to leave her side. His hand still rested on her leg, warm even through her jeans, ready to do anything in his power if something happened. Part of her longed to link their fingers, trace the callouses catching on the fabric. She took a deep breath, watching her sister in front of her.

Josie and Riley reached the warmup pen first, losing themselves in the chaos of other riders. They kept close together, Josie watching Dacey bypass the main pen where everyone else was, knowing Cash didn't like to be crowded. Riley watched them as well, brow furrowed as she eased Silver up to a light trot.

"Something on your mind?" Josie guided Buckshot to Riley. Her voice was calm, knowing the racket the other riders made would keep anyone from overhearing. Riley kept silent as they made a few rounds of the pen, dodging wild children and those pushing their horses harder than necessary.

"I kissed him, and he walked away." Her frustration leaked down the reins to Silver's mouth. The mare shook her head, fighting the bit. Easing up the firm grip she had, she sighed. "I don't get it? Dacey said they weren't a couple." Riley blurted out.

Josie almost toppled off her horse. "Well, I mean, we saw it happen. And she didn't lie, they aren't together and never will be as long as I'm around." Gritting her teeth, she pushed on. "Eddie is…well he's always been sort of standoff-like. Doesn't show his attention to someone like the rest of the world, so by doing that you threw him off his game. He also has this thing about control." Josie wished she had a cigarette. "Just back off of him a little and he might come around. Considering I'm giving you information that's years old, I can't promise you that'll work, either." She cautioned.

Riley shrugged. "I mean, I get that, I do. I'm just not used to it. I'm the one who makes all the moves because the guys around here have no clue what a woman is." They both laughed, Josie shaking her head. "How I missed him is beyond me, but I am surprised I did."

Buckshot sidestepped a loose horse, kicking at it when it passed. Regaining control, Josie licked her lips. "Well, I can't help much in the men department. Not my thing." Riley whipped her head to study her, surprised at the easy admission. Josie ignored her reaction, continuing. "Grant said Eddie never left the ranch much after the accident, and he spends weekends at a bar. Otherwise, he's a homebody. Chances are, when he was running circuits, he ran different ones than your family. The further away, the better. Not to mention, he's older by ten years."

Slowing Buckshot down, Josie smirked toward Riley as the mare easily spun a few circles, switching directions with ease. She then skirted side to side, sorting a calf that wasn't there under Josie's invisible instruction.

Riley cackled. "Show off!" Josie loped back to her, eyes bright and a smile on her face.

"She did so much better! I guess I have to cave and tell Dacey she was right. Buckshot works a lot better without a bit. Maybe I'll keep it to myself tonight." The two giggled before they resumed their warm-ups. Satisfied, they headed toward the gate in order to hunt down Dacey and Eddie.

Chapter 14

Hooked on an 8 Second Ride

After passing the main pen, Eddie wondered where they were headed until they reached a smaller, empty pen at the back of the barn. He opened the gate, allowing Dacey in with a glare at Cash. The stallion snorted in his face, blowing snot and spit across it. Eddie closed his eyes, counting back from ten to smother the urge to slap the rump before passing him. Cash was temperamental enough without risking Dacey by hitting him. Even though from the moment they had left her sister and Riley, she hadn't said a word to him. She seemed lost in her own thoughts, eyes unfocused, one hand on her thigh, the other loose on the reins, letting Cash guide them.

Eddie followed them into the pen, stopping next to her. "What's on your mind?"

Eyes flicking toward the roof, she chose her words with care. "Why are you so bent out of shape? You have her eating out of your palm, something most men would be crowin' over."

Eddie attempted to swat her, but Cash sidestepped him with ease.

One back hoof raised, head lowering in warning, he left no room for a second attempt. Not wanting to risk losing a hunk of flesh, Eddie settled for reaching into his pocket for a cigarette. "Wake up, Darlin', she did it because she thinks it'll make me change my mind." Letting the smoke calm his nerves, he left to lean on the fence. The old wood creaked in protest, but held firm. A pair of barn swallows fluttered in and out, building a nest above his head in the open rafters. He watched them, Dacey following his line of sight. There were more nests, some new, some old, scattered across the boards. She watched another pair hard at work making a home for themselves.

She licked her lips, breaking the silence. "And you have no interest in that?" Nudging Cash into a trot, she started their warm up.

"Why would I? I don't know her, and I'm happy with being alone. Besides, she couldn't handle me, no matter what she thinks." He took a deep drag on his smoke. Holding it until his lungs begged for fresh air, he released it in a harsh cloud.

Easing him up to a lope, Dacey thought over what Eddie had said. She hadn't stopped to think about how Riley would handle his mood swings. In the short time she had been back around him, he ran through them like they were water. Sensing her distraction, Cash broke into a gallop, charging around the pen. Squealing, she forced herself to focus on him instead of Eddie. If she let him get too out of hand, he would run Eddie over without a second thought. As they warmed up, Eddie never left his spot, watching them as he smoked off and on. When Cash no longer tried testing her and responded to each que, Dacey called it good.

Walking Cash toward him, she picked up the dropped threads of their conversation. "Why would being in a committed relationship be such a horrible thing?" She studied him from head to toe, curious. "I thought everyone was looking for their better half in some way or another?"

"I assure you it ain't for everyone. I've been through enough without a woman moving into my life, bossing me around like I ain't got a mind of my own. Some of my buddies have already been married and divorced within a year and they were in happy relationships with no issues before that ring." He opened the gate, motioning her through it. "Seems like something just flipped in one mind or another. I do have some friends that are married, and I know they'd lay down and die for each other. But if Riley's under the impression I'm the one for her, then she's in for a rude awakening. I'll make it clear that I ain't 'the one' or whatever garbage she's thinking, but I ain't going to pass up a chance to have some fun, either."

Dacey wrinkled her nose. "You'd really do that? Is that even dating?"

"Nope, I don't date. Got too much to do without a woman whining.. Just hook ups, and if that won't be good enough for her, then she knows to keep going. She's a grown woman, just like you, but also, she's young and dumb, like most people your age." He raised a hand at the argument he could see her building. "I said most, not all. Keep in mind, I am well aware of the fact you and Josie had to grow up much faster than was fair to either of you. But so did I. It can cause issues with the mind falling back to when it thought things were safe. You wanna be a kid again, let others run your life because you didn't have that when you needed it most." His fist clenched at his side, a soft ache in his chest. "It makes you irrational, naïve, and unable to see the real world the way you need to. No, it's not all the time, but I've screwed myself over more than once doing that in the past." He paused, looking up at her.

"I never said that you didn't understand. I just don't understand you."

"Not yet, but in time, you'll learn." He patted her boot, chuckling at the kick aimed his way.

Grinning, she rolled her eyes. "Whatever. Walk us to the arena? I need to get my number and make sure this knucklehead here doesn't get any ideas." It was a hesitant request, considering he was likely to blow her off. Theconversation weighed heavily on her, setting her mind on an endless spiral of questions she wanted to ask, but knew she couldn't.

He gave a jaw cracking yawn, languidly stretching. "I guess, ain't like I have shit to do anywhere else, and I'm not allowed to leave you, anyway. But I'm pretty sure I pissed off the others."

"I'm not worried about them. Josie isn't mad at you, I can promise you that much. She's going to be way more focused on working Buckshot with new tack, with no real time to learn it together as a team. She always underestimates that mare, and it drives me up the damn wall. If she'd listen, pay attention, and let the horse tell her what she wants, they'd have the same bond me and Cash do. It's been so long since we've been on horses, I think part of her has forgotten those things."

Eddie's lips twitched a little, though he schooled his features. "Oh? You sure it ain't her way of gaining control of something?"

Dacey felt guilt creep up on her. "No," she whispered, "I didn't think of it like that." Clearing her throat from the lump that formed, she looked down at Eddie. "Probably should back off of her a little, huh?"

"Probably." They walked in silence toward the tables that housed the sign-in sheets.

Giving in, Dacey looked down at him, changing topics back to their previous conversation. "You worried this'll complicate things?"

"Why should I be? Sounds more like you are."

"I ain't the one that has to worry about them, considering that Grant's hiring her brothers? Chances are, you're going to be the one wishing you'd given up and in just for a little while to keep the peace." She countered.

"I couldn't give a fuck less. Those boys don't scare me even when they're together. If they want this job and the deals we made bad enough, they'll keep their mouths shut and let us handle this on our own," he snapped.

Dacey hummed, waiting only a beat before asking the next question bothering her. "Where's my hat?" The brand new one on his head made it clear the old one was somewhere, and she vowed to make him cry like a baby if he had thrown it away.

Eddie snorted, reaching up to touch the new black Stetson. "You're worried about that raggedy ass old thing?" When she shot him an unreadable look, he shook his head. "In the truck where it belongs."

Relief flooded her at the words and she eased the tight grip she had on the reins. "I expect it to be returned to me by the end of the night, then." He wasn't going to keep it, no matter what he thought.

"You ain't gonna wear it anymore. Why the hell do you think I gave you the new one?"

"No, stupid, I want it back for the memories." Did he think she was that ignorant? Gritting her teeth, she inhaled a deep breath before slowly letting it out.

"I'll leave it in your truck. Now, is anyone here worth your time? Anyone you need to look out for?" He asked, scanning the competitors as they waited in line to get numbers.

Dacey couldn't help herself. "Other than Seth?" Eddie shot her a warning look. Turning to take in the other riders around her, only a few stood out. "If I had to wager a…fuck me a running. Of course." The sight of a long, pin straight, blonde ponytail set her pulse pounding in her ears. Her nostrils flared, hands once again resuming the white knuckle-grip on the reins. "Of all the fucking places she has to be, it's here."

Eddie tried to figure out where she was sending the ugly glare to. When he came up short handed on which girl Dacey was trying to burn to a crisp with the glare she was giving, he tapped her knee. "Eddie to fucking Dacey. Are you in there?" She kicked at him, and it was only from sheer reflex he dodged it. "Knock that shit off. I can't beat your ass in public." He snapped, rapping his knuckle harder on her knee. She winced, but forced herself into some semblance of calm.

"Remember how growing up there was that one stupid, rich brat that I always got into trouble at school for knocking on her ass all the time? Or crying my eyes out if she got the rest of the class to shit talk me?" Dacey breathed slowly in through her nose to the count of six, releasing it to the count of four through pursed lips. One vivid memory stood out from the rest, one she cherished on nights when it seemed like they'd never get out of the hell they lived in.

The chill, autumn wind lifted the ends of her braids as a young Dacey sniffled, scrubbing a hand over her nose. Kicking a rock down the driveway, she ignored Josie waving toward the bus as it pulled away. Breaking into a run, eyes blurry with tears, she collided with something solid.

"Easy there, brat! What's the hurry?" Eddie steadied her, looking

her over. When it became clear she wasn't going to tell him, he guided her toward his bunkhouse. Josie continued past him, wandering into the barn where Grant and Bandy were cleaning stalls. Settling her on the porch swing, he went in, intent on grabbing them each a soda. Dropping her heavy school bag to the floor with an audible thump, he cringed, hoping there was nothing breakable in it. Rummaging around in his fridge, he pulled two out, popping the tops off the orange drinks. Rejoining her on the porch, he passed one to her, taking a pointed sip of his.

She toyed with the cold glass bottle, turning it in her hands, still fighting sniffles. Eddie didn't press her, knowing if he did, she would break down again. Dacey took a steadying breath, drinking half the soda in one go. Satisfied, she shifted to lean against him, melting into the warm hug he offered. "Aimee was being herself, mocking me, talking trash. But now Lizzy and Rachel won't talk to me! They told me I'm too much of an issue to be friends with because now Aimee has started in on them."

Eddie closed his eyes, jaw clenched. His grip on her tightened a bit, causing her to look at him. Feeling the weight of her gaze on him, he forced himself to relax. Standing up, he took her hand to help her off the swing. "Come on. I have an idea."

She cocked her head to the side, letting him drag her into the kitchen. "I don't feel like baking." While she usually liked to bake with him, Dacey wasn't in the mood to do anything at the moment.

Grabbing the truck keys, he spun them around his finger. "Who said anything about baking? Let's hit the road, okay?" Excitement filled Dacey as she followed him out to his pickup. Eddie opened the door for her, giving her a boost up onto the seat. The familiar scent of old smoke, tack, horses, and his aftershave wrapped around her close as any hug he had ever given. He slid into the driver's seat, turning the engine on and cranking the old heater to high. Waving at Bandy and Grant when they stepped out of the barn, he pulled down the driveway without a word.

"Eddie?"

"What's up?" Reaching into the cup holder, he found a crumpled pack of gum. Fishing a piece out, he handed it to her.

She accepted, bottom lip wobbling. "Why does she hate me so much? Why does everyone believe her?" Dacey felt fresh tears slip down her cheeks. He lit a smoke, mulling over her questions. Exhaling with a hard sigh, he reached over, tugging a pigtail.

"They hate you because you're a better cowgirl than they are. Jealous because you are smarter than they are, trust me, I've seen your grades since I'm trapped in reliving school with you." His words earned a weak giggle. "They're just plain mean ass girls with no other way to spin it. You ain't ever going to win them over, so why let them break you down like this?" He pointed the truck toward the south, stepping on the gas to get the heater running better.

"It still isn't fair. Who am I going to talk to tomorrow? Where will I eat lunch?" Dacey leaned back on the worn seat cover she and Josie had made when he got the truck.

He blew a thin stream of smoke out the cracked window. "Who cares? The ones that care won't let Aimee push them around. Only the ones who need a good thumping care what she thinks. You're going to be fine. You make new friends easily enough. Always have." He tapped a thumb on the steering wheel, reaching out to snap on the radio. For a while he simply drove, singing with her to every song that came on.

Finding a town, he knew was at least three over from theirs, he pulled over to the curb in front of a general store. "Come on, how about we do a little window shopping? Get your mind off it all?"

Dacey brightened, letting him help her out of the cab into the warm glow of windows filled with different Halloween decorations. "I'm okay with this! But I want some candy, please, before we leave?"

Pulling open the door to the store, he nodded. "You know, candy and some apple cider sound like just what you need."

Chapter 15

Them Bareback Horses

"Dacey! Are you having a stroke?" Eddie snapped his fingers in front of her face.

She jerked to attention. "Sorry! Sorry, anyway, remember?"

"Yeah, because I was always the one stuck watching you when you weren't allowed to go back. Ashley? Anna? A something or other? Maybe B? Bitchface?"

"Aimee. Aimee Rattermann." At the last name, Eddie ground his teeth. "Guess who wasn't here last night, but is tonight? Meaning that unless there is a judge here she hasn't bribed or slept with, I might as well just fucking give up. She's cheated at every event she's had the audacity to show up at. Not only that, she likes to screw with the other horses and it's only because Cash is such a monster that she hasn't done something to put him out of the running." Her breathing was shallow, hands shaking on the reins, causing Cash to snort. He pawed the sawdust under his hooves, side stepping. "I'd give anything to slap the piss out of her, but because you know her brother, I can't touch her. I wish the damn committee would throw her out, but yet again, they're either in his pocket or her bed." Her stomach rolled, bile crawling up the back of her throat in an unfiltered rage.

"Bet you anything I can make her quit riding, or at least get Grant to put his two cents in," Eddie offered, reaching up to rest a hand on her thigh. Looking back toward Aimee as she got her number, he clocked it for later use. Another girl, one he vaguely recognized, helped pin it to her back. "He's got more sway than he cares to admit, but he never uses it. Coming from him now, it'll have a lot more impact."

Dacey shook her head. "There's nothing you can do to her without bringing down the wrath of Zach on you, but it makes me feel better you even offered. As for Grant, I doubt that he would be interested in getting in the middle of this."

"Don't assume anything about Grant. He's quiet but he's the most dangerous shark in the water, just waiting to rip your leg off." Eddie warned, his own shark-like smile creeping across his features. "I know what I'm doing, too. You just wait and see." He promised.

Letting her leg go, the line shuffled forward. He waited until they were once more on their own, Dacey leaning down to allow him to pin the number to her back. Her silken hair flowed over his hands, teasing him with the scent of wild honeysuckle. All Eddie wanted to do was bury his face in her neck and inhale; try to envision an easier life with her there. Shaking himself hard, he stepped away as she looked at him over her shoulder.

"Something wrong?"

"Nope. Come on, you have a bit yet. We can stall him back here with the rest and I'll go find Grant. Are you sure you're going to be okay on your own?" The very thought almost made him change his mind. He knew he wasn't supposed to leave her alone, but he wanted to have a small hit before the chaos of the evening sank its jaws into him. Otherwise, he wouldn't be able to get one until the hotel room.

"Seth may be a moron, but not once has he tried anything with this many people around. One, it would show his true colors and he can't have that, and two, Cash has nearly ripped his arm off once before. I don't see him trying again anytime soon," she assured him.

They moved down the alley, locating the stall matching the number she had. Dismounting with his help, she tucked Cash away before standing on tiptoe, trying to find Josie. It was chaos all around them; horses, people, workers. They swarmed around each other, an ever-flowing river of motion. Giving up, she dropped back down, turning to him. "Find Grant, I'll wait here. Chances are, Josie will find me before I find her with this many people. If she doesn't, I know with this big brute I'll be okay. She's the one he has his sights on anyway, so she needs to be the focus of protection."

Eddie scoped out the crowd as well. Grant had already told him that once it started he was going to be with the bulls, talking to potential breeders and buyers. Eddie was more interested in making sure no one near Dacey posed a threat. When he came up empty-handed, he knew he needed to go. While he loved a good fight and was always itching for one, this wasn't the time or place. Besides that fact, Dacey wasn't his to protect, no matter what a small part of him kept trying. Caring about someone other than himself had only ended badly every time he tried it, so why bother? Why keep trying? "Alright, I'm gonna head out. Don't do anything too stupid, Darlin'."

She rolled her eyes, making him want to tug her pigtail. "I'm a big girl, I've been just fine this long." Sarcasm colored every word while Dacey wrinkled her nose. "Have to say I don't know why it matters so much to you all of a sudden. This whole time you've been so hot and cold it makes me wonder if you're on your period."

Reaching out, he jerked one of her pigtails, earning a squeal. "Shut it before I shut it for you." His eyes bore into her, warning clear. "Keep this shit up and I'll rescind the offer of getting Aimee off your back." He gave another hard pull, forcing her closer to him. Satisfaction filled him as she swallowed, but refused to back down. She glared back up at him, toe to toe, like he didn't tower over her. Smirking, he leaned down to whisper in her ear, "You don't want to test me, Darlin', I'll beat that ass until you can't sit." He warned her. Stepping back, he moved to open the door without a backward look.

Dacey watched him go, jaw on the floor, as Cash walked over to put his head against her. Instinctively, she rubbed along his jaw, watching until Eddie was swallowed by the crowd. "Cash, what in the hell are we getting ourselves into?" He bumped against her, searching for his favorite treat in lieu of an answer. Digging into her pocket, she offered out a couple of Life Savers toward him. They were eagerly lipped up to be crunched down like Cash hadn't been fed in days. "You know, I wonder if it was a better idea to just stay with the brothers at this rate." She mused aloud to him. The only response she received was being nudged for more treats in response. Laughter spilled out as she scratched his forehead. "Behave yourself tonight."

"Or what?" Dacey whirled to where Rider was leaning on the stall door, a bright smile on his face. Cash spun at the sudden intrusion; leg raised to kick. Patting him until he calmed, she turned him back toward the front of the stall. Satisfied he wasn't going to break a wall down,

Dacey let him go, moving to join her friend.

"You don't behave, and I promise Rusty will kick your ass from what I've seen." She countered.

"Rusty only wishes he could kick my ass, let's be honest. He's just all fluff when it comes down to it."

"Uh huh, sure. What brings you over here, anyway? And where's your better half?" She questioned, looking past him to the sea of people passing by them.

"He's back with the horses to make sure they don't get into trouble. Where's Josie?"

"No idea. I wanted to go find her, but figured that staying here would be my best bet because she can find me no matter where I am if she wants." Dacey admitted, fixing her hat. Rider watched, brow furrowing.

"How come your hat's so big? Didn't they fit you before they sold it to you?" Taking it off her head, he missed the way she locked her jaw.

"It wasn't originally mine to begin with." Fingers curled into a slight fist on the gate as he turned it over in his hands to inspect it.

"Tell you what, if we win tonight, I'll buy you one." He dropped the hat back on her head, smiling at her as he lifted the brim to meet her eyes. Dacey was stunned, speechless, mind trying to process the offer he had made so easily to her.

"You don't have to. This one works just fine," Dacey responded, ears turning red.

"It's almost two sizes too big for you, I don't mind. Besides, it sounds like that means you think we're gonna win tonight." Rider said with a smug grin.

"I'd be stupid not to know you will, or was that a completely different pair of twins I helped half the afternoon?"

"Fair point. Honestly, I do need to get going. We're one of the first up after the bare back." Slapping the door, he moved back a step or two, shooting her a wink. "See you after this is done Dacey." Like Eddie, he disappeared among the rest of the crowd. Dacey realized she was grinning as she watched him go, killing it the second she did.

"No, no, no, no." Shaking her head, she scrubbed a hand over her face. "What in the hell am I thinking? I'm sitting here grinning like a loon over a man I barely know, Cash. This isn't okay! First guy to flash a cute smile at me and I'm suddenly dumb as a box of rocks? I don't think so! Need to get a grip on myself." The pep talk didn't help as much as she hoped it would. The way he smiled at her hinted maybe it was normal to gain crushes on someone so fast.

Back in the town her father had kept them in, none of the men appealed to her. Either because she was too busy keeping them alive, or they were so deep with Seth and his father, she would have rather eaten mud than date the ones interested.

Sitting down in the stall's corner, she rested her head back against the warm wood. "What do I do Cash? Not like I can ask Josie about any of it. She'll treat me like I'm still five or something. 'Dacey you don't need to be focused on a guy right now. We have too much going on,' as if any of it matters, anyway."

Once again, he didn't answer. Instead, Cash opted to seem more interested in watching the other horses pass his stall. Once in a while, a mare would catch his attention and he would put a show on trying to gain her attention back. Some tried to answer him, but all were dragged away to their respective work. Heartbroken whinnies soon trailed their way toward the stall he held court in. Keeping a keen ear out, Dacey ignored them in favor of laughing off and on at the clown as he bantered back and forth with the announcer. During the bareback, she laughed harder, shaking her head at their antics.

"Now ladies, I know you're hoping one of these men land in your laps, but I assure you, throw them back to us! They're worse than stray dogs!" The announcer called as the crowd rippled with laughter of its own. During the break between the bareback riders and steer ropers, they amped up the jokes. Cash gave Dacey a clearly offended look as she filled his stall with her joyous noise.

"At least I don't put on makeup and work the night shift."

"Hey, I get paid to look stupid. You don't have an excuse."

"This is ugly you, not stupid you! But just so you're aware, you're the human version of menstrual cramps, cause at least I only see you every thirty days!"

"Well, you got a face that would make an onion cry, so I ain't complaining about the time between!"

Climbing to her feet, she worried her bottom lip between her teeth. She wanted to wait for Josie, but the team roping was rapidly approaching. She wanted to see the brothers in real action, not just during the practice they had earlier in the day. Weighing the options, she snuck out of the stall, Cash watching her go.

Chapter 16

A Little Less Talk

Josie picked at Buckshot's reins, rubbing them between her forefinger and thumb as her eyes hunted for her sister. "I don't understand why they have half of us on this side of the arena and half on the other. It's ridiculous!"

Riley leaned over, stopping her to spare the leather from being worn raw. "She's fine, she's with Eddie. I promise you, when we are done with everything we need to focus on, we can go and find her if she hasn't shown up to find us. Okay?"

Josie allowed her hands to be stilled, drawing in a deep lungful of dusty air. "Alright. That's all I can ask for, isn't it?"

"Yup. You don't want to ruin your chances tonight; you're at the top of the class and points both. If you back out now trying to be overbearing again, I'm pretty sure that she will beat you into oblivion." Riley pointed out.

"I don't understand why you feel the right to tell me how to feel about my sister." Josie jerked her hand away, tension settling into her shoulders.

"Because having Rider and Rusty as my older brothers, I've been in Dacey's place. I've been the one who's been crushed under misconstrued worry. Your need for control over her right now is because you have none, and you hate that. Wake up, Josie. The more you drown her in fear of the world getting her, the more you will just drag yourself down with her…and ruin your relationship." The words were spoken calmly, as though Riley were speaking to a cornered animal, but the undercurrent of warning rang clear in them.

They watched each other from across the small space, neither backing down. Silver sidestepped toward the far wall, breaking their contact as she tried to sneak over to a bucket someone had left. "You pig! There is nothing in it anyway!" Riley scolded, popping the reins.

The laughter the sight caused died in Josie's throat. Her attention was drawn away when she spotted Eddie talking with Grant, one hand waving in the direction he'd come from. Her heart kicked up in pace, her breath coming in shallow pants. The words Riley spoke were lost to the white noise filling her ears. Hard ground met the soles of her boots, heedless to the way the other resorted to half shouting her name and snapping her fingers. Grant's mouth moved in words she couldn't seem to grasp.

Drawing her hand back, she swung her full weight behind it at Eddie's face. She had been confident it would find its mark, only to be stunned when a grip so firm she felt the familiar needles of terror closed over her wrist. Her eyes located the opposing hand, following it up to

Grant's face. It didn't ease the panic attack building, nothing did until Riley was there, half shouting for everyone to calm down.

The brunette forced her way in between Eddie and Josie, her own voice raising back at him, her hands waving.

It was the familiar piercing whistle that snapped Josie back to a semblance of attention. Yet the world still seemed fuzzy, blurred at the edges. Grant's mouth moved, but nothing overcame the odd rushing noise in her ears, roaring like a train speeding toward her. Josie found herself being forced to the ground, head between her knees. Her fingers scrambled in search of purchase in the layer of dirt spread over the concrete to spare hooves. They dug their way in until the tips scraped the unforgiving rock, even then trying to continue. People passed them unaware of what was going on, as if the four had been shut into their own little world.

"Josie! Come on now, you need to focus, or you'll be useless right now. That isn't going to help anyone, understand me? You snap the fuck out of this right now, young lady, so we can focus." Grant's voice cracked over her sluggish mind like thunder over a meadow. "You get your head back in this game, Josie Rose Hempen or I'm gonna have to haul you to a hospital."

That word, that ugly little word, earned a weak jerk back, blue eyes locking onto brown. "Try, and I will pack up and leave without another question and I won't return." Her voice rasped harshly from a dry throat.

Backing away from her enough to not be fully in her face, Grant shook his head. "That ain't going to happen and you know it. Come on, talk to me, focus on me. Get you back to being steady on those feet before you end up eating that dirt you seem to enjoy digging in right now. How does Dacey do this?" He knew methods for the men he had been in combat with, but was well aware those methods weren't for everyone.

"It depends." Josie tried to collect the broken pieces of her mind into something that would function. "I think times like this she makes me do something, gives me a focus?"

Riley crouched down beside Grant, Josie's eyes flicking to her. "How about we go pet some ponies?" The weak joke coaxed the ghost of a smile on Josie's lips. "I know when I want to throat punch boys and cry on the floor, ponies are always the answer." She knew she was being stupid, being ridiculous, but Riley wasn't sure what other route to take. Being serious seemed to make Josie draw deeper into herself, pulling away both physically and mentally. Offering her hand out, she hauled Josie to her feet. Riley offered a nod toward the two men, jerking her chin toward the gate. They trailed behind the pair, halting just outside of the stall.

Buckshot moved to her owner, head knocking and rubbing against her chest in search of treats. Josie buried her hands in the mane before her, clutching at what she could feel was real and safe. Riley backed away to give them space, joining Grant and Eddie to watch for a moment. "Think this will work?"

"If it doesn't, then there are more medical staff running around this plot of land than there probably is at the local hospital," Eddie answered, crossing his arms to rest them atop the wood. "Why was she so worked up, anyway?"

"You, would be my guess. Considering she wasn't trying to swing for the fences at Grant. That hand was getting ready to be on a first name basis with your nose." Riley cast a sidelong look at him. "Why are you over here, anyway? Thought the whole point of us helping and keeping these two safe was for someone to be with them at all times? I'm here with her, but who has their ass parked with Dacey?"

"The fuckin' beast that she rides for starters. I was coming to find Grant in order to solve an issue that Dacey has dealt with since childhood, one I am sure you've had your fair share of trouble with as well." He snapped, offering his cigarette pack to Grant.

One was taken with a nod of thanks, Grant taking a hesitant step away from where Josie was talking to her mare. "Can I get right in the middle of this? How long does she have until she rides?" Grant asked.

"Soon, if our setup is correct. My brothers will get ready to do their run once this sorry lot is over, then it's us. I will worry about her, much as she can't stand me. But who or what the hell is Eddie even talking about?" Riley asked.

"Aimee Rattermann is here tonight, gracing us all with her presence. We saw her getting her number and Dacey lost it a little. Claimed there was no point in trying to ride in anything because of that entitled bitch. So, I came here looking for Grant after Dacey promised me, she wasn't going to flake out and go looking for trouble." Eddie explained.

"I will take care of Aimee, not only for them, but because girls like her are exactly why this sport is gaining a bad reputation, and talented riders drop out. While I am doing that, Eddie, I need you to head back and check on Dacey." Grant's tone left little room for argument, but Eddie still found it.

"Look, I can't hold her hand all night. I missed most of last night doing just that. There are events that I'd like to see, and it's bullshit that I'm here taking care of animals and kids like I don't have a free will." He snapped.

Grant gripped the bridge of his nose, reminding himself why a shouting match would do no one any good. "I understand that, I do. Yet you don't see me standing here pissin' and moanin' about it now, do you? No. I put my big boy pants on because I have problems to solve. I'd appreciate it if you did the same. If not for them, then out of respect for me. Please. Either stay with Josie or go check on Dacey."

Riley stepped forward, ready to duck any blows that could miss their intended target. "I can take care of them both. Josie isn't about to just skip out on us singing Kumbaya." One hand was waved at the blonde who was watching them intently; eyes clearer than before.

"I promise I'm not about to leave this stall any sooner than I have to. Eddie, I'd appreciate you watching her brothers for me. Let me know how they do." Josie hedged. "Considering Riley isn't going to be able to?"

He scoffed. "You know what? Forget it. How about I go get all of us something to eat for after the rides? After the crash you just had, we need to get something in you anyway before you bottom out and end up on your ass for different causes." The others sent him quizzical looks that went ignored. "If nothing else, I will get sodas and you a snack. But I swear if I bring you food and you bitch about what it is, I'll eat it in front of you."

Josie kept her composure. "Deal. Thank you, Eddie."

"Whatever. Riley, go check on Dacey and Cujo." With that, he was striding away from them toward the concession stand. They watched him go until he was lost in the throng of people.

"Alright, now that we have that settled, Riley, start looking for Dacey. If it comes down to it, she has Cash, so once her event is over, we can catch them at the gate. I have to get my ass in gear to deal with both Aimee and the bulls, so as soon as I am done, I'll look for you, okay?" Grant stepped away from the stall, keeping just his hands on the door.

Riley nodded, looking at Josie. "Are you sure you're okay?"

"Now, who's being an overprotective problem?" Josie snarked, lips quirked.

"Uh, huh. I'll be back, don't do anything stupid." She joined Grant outside of the stall, checking in on Silver. The mare was almost asleep, hind foot cocked with her head half to the floor. "Lazy bum. Wish I could just sleep wherever I am," Riley groused, shaking her head. Slapping the door one last time, she nodded at the other two people. "Wish me luck. Something tells me I'm gonna need it to find her."

Grant shook his head. "I doubt she went far, if she even left the stall to begin with."

Josie waved goodbye to them, settling down in the corner close to the gate. Riley stepped back, making sure Josie was no longer visible from the alley. Grant mirrored her, stepping to the left while she went right. When she was satisfied the blonde was hidden, she shot him a thumbs up. He returned it, tipping his hat at her. Turning his back on them, he left first.

Watching him go, she looked around her. "Where the hell would they even put her?" she asked herself, rocking up on the balls of her feet. A stray dog barreled past her, nipping at the horses as it passed. Its owner was hot on its heels, forcing Riley against the wall. "Jackasses," she muttered to herself, picking the alley to the left to follow. There were fewer people, making it easier to navigate. Humming to herself, Riley set out to find Dacey.

Chapter 17

Think Twice

Across the barn, Dacey darted in and out of the crowd, trying to keep to the wall until she reached the area for other riders to watch events. Climbing the few stairs to the benches, she perched on the edge of one. The few other girls waiting, who she assumed were either girlfriends or buckle bunnies, ignored her. They scooted down the metal seats further, allowing her to have a little more room. A few sipped beers, talking amongst themselves while waiting for the next run. Drumming her fingers on her thighs, Dacey resisted the urge to ask if they had an extra. Knowing her luck, one of them would recognize her.

Sitting up straighter, she looked around the stands. There were families clustered together, with siblings either squabbling over snacks, seats, or parent laps. Some parents trailed their kids, ready to catch them if they seemed even close to tripping or falling down. Part of her wondered if her life would have been different if she were in their shoes. Instead of learning how to help buckle Eddie's gear, she could have been smothering her hotdog in toppings. In place of heart pounding adrenaline from the moment he led her on her first barrel ride on a pony so slow he had to jog instead of run; would she be battling Josie for a cup of soda?

Taking a deep breath, she closed her eyes. Buttered popcorn, warm nacho cheese, funnel cakes, and corndogs perfumed the air. They did their best to beat back the underlying scents of livestock, sweat, and hay.

Clearing her throat, she turned her attention back to the cluster of cowboys and horses below her, searching for the twins. She spotted Rusty first as he smoothed a nose strip on his gelding's nose. Rider was talking to him, one hand patting his mare to calm her while she danced in place.

Above them, the announcer was in fine form, never missing a beat to heckle both the competitors and those helping. Even the livestock weren't spared from his playful commentary. "It's all the luck of the draw on these calves and it was just poor luck they drew a calf that can outrun Secretariat! No qualifying ride for them, unfortunately."

She groaned with the crowd as the first pair lost their chance at a check when the calf they had drawn blasted past them. They still waved to the crowd, patting each other on the back as they rode out after the calf on the opposite end of the arena.

Rider called something out to Rusty, and in perfect synchronicity, they mounted up, guiding their horses to their respective box on either side of the chute. When the brothers backed into place, she found herself eagerly leaning forward to keep from missing anything.

"Come on guys, you got this," she whispered to herself, tapping her hands on her lap as one leg bounced in place. Vaguely aware of someone sitting down next to her, she was too engrossed in the brothers as their calf ran down the chute. The person beside her shifted around a little, jostling into her faintly. Keeping her calm, she simply ignored them in favor of losing her temper as she normally would.

Calf ready, the brothers shared a look that had Dacey's whole body tense, shivering in anticipation of their ride. Just as Rider nodded, something pressed against her side, earning a sharp inhale through her teeth, gaze dropping away from them down to see what had happened. A knife rested against her, pressed hard enough to get her attention without drawing blood. Wide eyes followed the arm that held it up to the battered face of Seth as he shot her a deadly smile.

"Walk. Now." Despite the smile, his voice was pure venom. Standing, Dacey tried to remind herself to breathe as panic settled deep in her bones as they walked away from the bleachers toward the doors that led to the parking lot. Her mind raced, attempting to find ways of pulling her own knife to defend herself without being stabbed first. She tried to catch the eyes of those around her as they passed, but no one seemed to be paying attention to anything but the arena.

She was unaware Riley spotted them across the large alley. The brunette took off running to find her brothers, or Grant. Even Eddie, at that point, would have been perfect. Shoving people out of the way left and right, all Riley could think of was finding help. Dacey had seemed terrified as Seth frog marched her toward the doors. She knew if he got her out, then hope would be lost, no matter who she found. Giving up, she threw her head back and screamed the first name that came as hard and loud as her throat would allow. "Eddie!"

The barn fell silent only for a split second as people froze to look at her in disbelief at the action. But whoever was watching over her had chosen to answer her unspoken prayers. People parted in waves as if they weren't forced aside as Eddie stalked across the concrete floors toward Riley like no one else was in the barn.

"Do you know where she is?" He was pale under his freckles, but Riley could feel the rage-fueled adrenaline like it was a haze around him. Hazel eyes burned with hatred so startling she took a cautious step back, waving toward where they had vanished.

"Headed out those doors." She pointed to the double doors.

Eddie marched past. His long legs devoured the distance as fast as they could, short of running. "Get the others and a medic. I don't want you out here for this." He called over one shoulder and Riley nearly missed the words as they floated to her. He took off so fast she could hardly register it all.

"Fuck." she breathed, turning to run once more to the rest of the group. Shoving people left and right, Riley offered nothing more than rude gestures to anyone who complained. Her legs stretched to their full stride, muscles almost begging her to slow down. Her lungs added their voice in their plea for oxygen. Doing her best to ignore them, she reached the stall where Josie was just mounting up. Skidding to a halt, Riley almost fell face first to the ground, hands catching on the door to the stall.

"Get off, get off now." She panted, hands on her knees. "Eddie…Dacey." She could only wave toward the double doors. Her lungs ached so badly she feared fainting as she sucked down air in deep breaths. "Hurry up!"

Josie felt a light sweat break out as goosebumps prickled her flesh. The panic from earlier arose to crash over her like a tidal wave. "Dacey." She breathed, throwing herself from the saddle to rush to

Riley. "Where is my sister?!" Her voice was high pitched, sharp enough the younger woman flinched.

"We can't just go to her! Josie, we have to find Grant and a medical team! Eddie is heading to her. I promise you she is going to be okay. Just come on." Riley grabbed her by the wrist in a light hold, tugging her toward the area she prayed Grant would be. "We can't go in blind, okay? He's going to keep her safe." With every word that burned her tongue, Riley could only hope that she was right. Would Eddie make it in time? Were the others there and this would end in a losing fight? She hauled Josie behind her, feeling her attempt to dig her boots in, twisting her wrist to pull away. Riley spun to face her. "Josie! Look, I don't exactly like you, but I'm not about to let you run off and make matters worse! That defeats the purpose of all this! Come on! Let's get to the rest!" She snapped, attempting to keep her own rising fear at bay.

A familiar baritone spoke up from behind her, drowning her in relief. "Get the rest for what? Riley? Sis, what's up?" Never in her life had Riley ever felt such pure gratitude than in that moment when Rusty and Rider approached them.

"Put them up, put them up now." Riley gestured to the twins' horses. "Dacey is in trouble and Eddie needs backup, somewhere out the double doors over there. I have to get this one to Grant and find medical." Riley explained, feeling the shaking in Josie get so hard she feared the woman would rattle her own teeth out.

Her brothers ignored her, thrusting their reins in her face so fast the only choice she had was to drop Josie's wrist to catch them. They were heading off in a flurry of dirt and falling hats. Grinding her teeth, Riley turned to Josie, stuffing the strips of leather into her shaking hands. "Focus, come on Josie. You hear me, right?" She received a wooden nod in reply. “Good. Please get these two put up. They need to be taken care of and I promise you I’ll be back with Grant and help.” Another slow, grating nod was given in answer. “We got this.” Riley offered the hollow promise, grasping for anything real to offer.

Josie stepped into the larger stall the twins had been given, body moved on autopilot to perform the task. Riley watched her for a brief moment, making sure she wasn’t just trying to trick her. Satisfied, she turned, sprinting along the way toward the area where the rough stock were kept. She longed to scream again, twice as loud to release the emotions twisting her stomach to knots. Instead, she forced herself onward to her destination, hand pressing to the stitch in her side that formed. “Just hang on, Dacey.”

Chapter 18

Don't Blame Me

"Have you lost what little mind you had left in that caveman skull you call a head?" Dacey's mouth was going to get her killed one day, and she hoped that it wouldn't be tonight. She watched blind fury bubble up in his eyes, clenching his fist. While Seth was dangerous on a normal day, when Dacey got on his nerves, he got downright deadly. He also got stupid and less rational, something she hoped to use in her favor for at least this night.

He shoved her harder toward the trailers, intent on something she had no way to guess at, or wanted to. The further from the barn they got, the thicker the tension clogged the air until it was enough that Dacey was sure she could taste it. An icy finger of dread slipped down her spine, raising her hair on edge. She was isolated, and it was her fault. She had screwed up, thinking nothing was going to happen. No one had been looking for her. That it hadn't been the risk that it was. Tears welled up in her eyes, while her hands crept ever closer to the buckle she wore. Her jaw was locked, ready to risk it all to keep everyone else safe.

When they reached a trailer with the door open ajar, Dacey's plans changed. She gathered what little courage she had left, knowing that it was the last chance she would ever get to defend herself or make an escape attempt. Grabbing the trailer door as fast as she could, she swung it at him hard enough that her upper body continued with the momentum. Seth gave a strangled cry as it connected with him, causing him to stagger backward. He landed hard on his ass in the dirt with a strangled curse. The ghost of a smile flicked across her face, seeing him as he was, though she didn't linger to brag.

Her chance had come. It was now or never.

She ran as fast as she could. All she could hear was the way her blood rushed through her veins faster than a flash flood. She could feel how the earth seemed to rise to meet her feet. Panting, she tried to convince her throat to work, to scream, something other than rasp like sandpaper over wood.

Seth recovered quickly, gaining his feet to chase after her, heedless of the blood pouring from his re-broken nose. "Come on now, Dace, I just want to teach you a little lesson." He called toward her, the distance becoming smaller with each long stride he took. "Teach you that little bitches like you die screaming for getting on my bad side." The blade in his hand glinted in the floodlights around them. Its brief flashes of silver spurred her on faster.

A few tears she had refused to let fall broke free when Dacey slipped on the loose straw, attempting to round a trailer. She hit the ground knees first, the pain buried under relentless terror.

Scrambling to her feet, she found herself trapped between Seth and the unforgiving metal. Her stomach roiled in painful waves, vision tunneling down to him as he advanced on her step by step. She tried to figure out an escape route, eyes flicking between him and either side. The sun-warmed trailer refused to budge, no matter how hard she pushed against it. A tiny part of her began wondering if up was her only way out. A faint glance proved it would be a futile effort. He'd catch her before she could even get halfway. Balling up her fists, eyes clenching shut, she let out a scream that shattered the night like a pane of dropped glass.

With a snarl, Seth swung hard as he could at her; the knife grazed her ear and caused her to hiss in pain. She ducked the outstretched arm as it tried for another swipe on the backswing. A flare of hope rose in her as she escaped from being pinned between him and a trailer, but it was short-lived. He grabbed a braid, roughly jerking it as he wound it around his wrist. Dacey let out another scream that was cut short when a fist landed deep in her stomach. Eyes going wide, she struggled to breathe, mouth opening and closing to no avail. Seth laughed, letting her drop to the ground as his victim wheezed in a lungful of air. Before she could gain another breath, he kicked her hard enough to connect with bone.

"Not so full of yourself now, are you? Maybe you'll fuckin' think before you try to do that shit." He gloated, crouching down next to her. "You know, maybe I'll drag you into a trailer for some fun before this ends."

Dacey could do nothing but beg silently in her mind for air, holding what she assumed was a cracked rib from where his foot had connected. Damn him! Rage boiled up, filling her veins like poison as it rushed to thunder in her ears. Panting, she rolled to glare up at him, knowing it wouldn't be much longer before he either beat her half to death or stabbed her.

"I'm not full of myself, but you'll regret this soon." Her voice was hardly audible, using what little air she sucked in to spit the words at him. A sharp kick landed dead in her chest once more forcing the air out again. The pop she heard made stars burst across her closed eyelids as pain replaced rage. This was it. She was just going to let the darkness take her so she couldn't feel anymore.

Seth laughed, the sound breaking through the pounding that clogged her hearing. "Love seeing you like this, all broken and bloody. Such a pretty sight, if I'm honest." Seth taunted, lifting her head by the chin. "How about I tell you what I want to do, yeah?" She refused to open her eyes, just braced herself for the blows to come.

But nothing more came. Instead, she was faintly aware of another person shouting before it was answered by Seth's voice not far above her.

Eddie? Had he come looking for her when she hadn't come back?

A small part of her brain tried to sort out what to say, while the rest was screaming at her to just breathe. It was nearly impossible to do, the darkness sinking in more, but she needed to. Wheezing in a grateful, yet agonizing, breath of air, Dacey tried to get her vision to return. Her hearing returned first, bit by bit. When the darkness blinding her faded, she found herself staring at a sight she couldn't be more thankful for. Eddie had Seth pinned by the throat to the trailer he had cornered Dacey at. The knife Seth had been using lay abandoned on the ground as Eddie chose to use his fist to make a point. Each blow he landed on Seth's rapidly bluing face drew another line of blood.

"I warned you don't ever come near them again. I made Dacey a promise, and you broke that promise," Eddie spat, letting Seth fall into a heap at his feet. One boot buried itself into Seth's chest in a mockery of how he had treated Dacey. "You weren't ever supposed to touch her again, yet you had the gall to? Maybe I should cut a finger off?" Another kick was delivered to the prone body in front of him.

"Eddie." Pain shot through Dacey as she tried to speak. At first, his name came out as nothing more than a small squeak, making her grind her teeth. "Eddie." She tried again. He heard her, turning from Seth to drop to his knees beside her in a single motion.

"Shh, easy now, Dacey, easy. I got you." His voice wavered as he held his hands out. Unsure of the damage done to her, he dropped them to his sides. She offered a weak smile.

"Doesn't," she cursed the way her chest ached with each word, "seem like you're holding me very well, Cowboy." The metallic tang of blood was thick, coating her tongue, some of it spilling down the corner of her mouth.

He snorted out a trembling laugh, hands moving up to rest on her cheeks. "This better?" His thumb rubbed soothing circles. "Riley should be showing up soon with help. You just hold on, understand me? No going to sleep, no passing out."

"I'm not dying." She didn't think so, at least. "It just hurts so much."

Eddie wanted to kick Seth again, beat his face until there was nothing left of it. He wasn't able to respond when shouts echoed between the trailers. A medical team came into sight, with Riley just behind them, looking like she might faint when she spotted Dacey. When they reached the pair, Eddie scrambled to his feet to get out of their way, gesturing to her. "She needs care now. That thing," he spit on Seth as the other man groaned, "can wait."

"Sir, we have to ask you to please back up. We will handle them as needed." The medic explained, her team beginning their work. Annoyance flashed through him, as the adrenaline began fading out.

"He's the one who did that to her. He can wait." His words fell on deaf ears.

"Eddie!" Riley was crying. "I thought Grant, or my brothers, would have beaten me here! These clowns didn't seem to think I was being serious when I said someone was being attacked in the trailer lot." She managed to get out, hands on her knees. "Is she going to be okay?" Standing on her tiptoes in vain to get a look at Dacey, Riley shifted from one foot to the other. Her fingers tangled together, the whites of her eyes clear. They flicked from her friend on the ground to the man beside her.

"She's going to be fine, trust me. She's tougher than hell when she wants to be, and was talking to me when you showed up." The words were spoken to assure Riley just as much as himself while they watched the team's work.

When they moved apart, Dacey lay on a stretcher looking like she would pass out at any minute. Raw fear was clear in her eyes as they landed on him, and her hand stretched out. "Eddie, please." She was fighting tears, the sobs causing blinding pain. "I don't want to go alone."

"Sir, if you don't mind coming with us?" The same female medic that had spoken to him before drew him aside. "Only one." She stopped Riley in her tracks. "Sir, are you this young woman's legal guardian?"

"Dacey is eighteen. She doesn't have a guardian any longer. But her sister is here somewhere. We are trying to find her." Eddie supplied.

"I can't disclose much if you're not family or a guardian. You may pass along the message that we are going to get her to the hospital for x-rays and a few scans. I understand she is afraid, but we cannot allow you to come with her." The medic stood her ground, gesturing while she spoke.

The rage he had thought contained flared back up at her words. "Unless you fuckin' force me to stay behind, I am going with her." His words caused the medic to take a cautious step back.

"Sir, I really…"

"Eddie!" Josie nearly fell as she sprinted toward them, trailed closely by Grant and the twins. "Eddie! Where is she? What happened?"

Annoyed, the medic cut in before he could reply, stepping between them to gain her full attention. "Miss, may I ask who you are to this young lady?" Her arms were crossed as she addressed Josie.

"I'm her sister. What happened?"

"That, I am not sure, but if you want to come with us, you are welcome." She waved toward the barn where a couple of ambulances waited for any injured competitor. "There will be forms to fill out, naturally, but we can address those at the hospital. We need to get going, so she isn't waiting any longer for the scans." The woman spoke in an authoritative tone, tired of being interrupted.

Josie glanced over at Grant, doing her best to keep from crying. "Follow us?" She begged, shaking so hard her teeth clicked.

"Absolutely. Go on, Josie, we're gonna be right behind you." Grant assured her, giving a gentle push toward the medic. She didn't need any more encouragement to follow. Like Eddie, he wanted to climb in with Dacey, hold her other hand and assure her she was going to be okay.

Grant wanted to be there for them both, protect them and keep the staff in line. He waited until they were out of sight before turning to the four faces staring at him.

Eddie broke eye contact first, bending to snatch up the two black Stetsons that rested on the ground, brushing the dust off them.

One he placed back on his head, the other was clutched in a white knuckled grip to the point Grant was sure it would never regain its shape. Clearing his throat, Grant took charge of the situation. "I don't have a clue what happened, but you three are welcome to join us at the hospital after prize checks are handed out. And, if you can, please get their horses untacked and put away where they belong. Just whatever you do, do not push Cash too much. He can and will murder you if he thinks it's for the best. If he acts like he's going to do anything, you leave him tacked up, move on, we can worry about him later. Right now, there's nothing you can do but sit and wait with us, so be productive until then. Eddie, you are going to tell me everything on the way there, understand?" It wasn't a question as the former Green Beret training kicked in.

A nod was all he got in response from Eddie, the others headed to their truck, stepping hard on the tanned Stetson still on the ground. The twins moved to usher Riley in between them to guide her back toward the barn as they separated, none of them sure what to say as they walked.

Just as they reached the doors to part ways, Rider met Eddie's eyes. "It's going to be okay." He tried to assure the older man.

A snort was given at his words, Eddie continuing past him. Grant clapped a hand on his shoulder with a nod as he walked by. Unspoken worry hung over them all despite the light words; none of them dared to voice anything other than hope at that moment.

Chapter 19

Dancing on Broken Glass

Grant had to jog a few steps to catch up with Eddie. Falling into step with him, he glanced at the younger man. "What in the hell happened back there? Am I going to have to do a lot of talking to keep your ass out of trouble?"

Eddie's bruised hands curled into fists at his sides, relaxing a little at a time. "Right now, I couldn't care less if I killed that useless waste of space. I broke a fuckin' promise to Dacey, Grant, and she paid the price. Not only did my stupid ass leave her alone trying to find you and Josie, she didn't listen to me to stay put. Now look what the hell happened!" Reaching the truck, Eddie yanked his door open. The bags that had been piled on the floorboard were tossed into the middle seat carelessly. A muscle ticked in his jaw, eyes falling closed. Closing the door harder than he needed, he let his head rest against the seat.

"You need to care! We know she's going to be fine for you to yell at once she's out of the hospital. But you're not going to be there if I don't know what's going on and who I need to talk to before anyone else,"

Grant countered, slamming his door. "You need to tell me everything you know so we can reach the right people first."

Eddie lit a cigarette, taking a deep drag on it, trying to calm his nerves before he started. Grant took the one offered, rolling his window down to the early summer heat. Eddie rolled his down as well, blowing a steady stream of smoke out, mulling over the words. "I didn't know anything until Riley got my attention. Screamed the barn down right in the middle of everyone. You'll have to ask Dacey about anything before I showed up. What I can tell you is I found that jackass kicking the shit out of her while she was down like the coward he is. Grant, I ain't felt that much rage since they were taken. Just lost my mind on him, wanted him to pay for everything he had done to them." He rubbed a hand over his jaw, trying not to replay everything. "Chances are he's going to survive because we can't get rid of roaches like him."

Through the haze of his thoughts, he noticed the dried blood coating his hands. Bile crept up the back of his throat when he realized it was both Dacey's and the useless assholes. The urge to scrub his hands until they were raw overwhelmed him.

Grant drove in silence, letting the words sink in with each passing mile, contemplating who to call once the chaos of the night was over. "I have a few people in mind, but the hardest part is going to be getting their horses to our place. That demon Dacey rides can kill a man if he feels up to it and we don't need to add that on top of everything else that's going on. Do you think you're up to the task?"

"I'll fucking kill him before he kills me," Eddie assured him. As the lights of the hospital came into view, he swallowed thickly. "She's okay. She has to be." The ambulance that had taken her was pulling away, quiet when it passed the truck. The parking lot was almost empty; the only moving creature in it was a tubby raccoon waddling its way toward a line of bushes. Eddie watched it, envious of its oblivious life.

"Chances are she's in there screaming everything she can think of at those doctors, telling them how it's done if we wanna be honest." Grant joked half-heartedly. He killed the engine, sitting there looking up at the building. Most of the rooms were dark, but the occasional stretch of lights proved it wasn't abandoned. Shadows passed by them, some rushing, others taking their time.

Finally, Eddie tossed his door open. "Let's get this show on the road." He climbed out, heading for the emergency room doors. "Best bet is to start here, isn't it?"

Grant tossed the butt of his cigarette toward a trash can. "Pretty much. Worst they do is make us sit with the worst coffee on the planet while they talk in circles getting us nowhere."

"Sounds like you're speaking from experience," Eddie drawled as they walked in.

The smell of harsh cleaning products threatened to overwhelm them, clogging their noses. Harsh white walls and floors half blinded them, the fluorescent glow of the lights bouncing off them. Their monochrome color was broken by a blue stripe on one wall, while the other boasted a bright red. At the end of the hall, the stripes split off in different directions. There was no one around at first, just voices drifting to them beyond closed doors. Somewhere, a radio crackled out the play by play of a baseball game. Their boots echoed down the short hall, reverberating back to them.

"Me? Nah, must be thinking of my brother." Grant shot back with a faint smirk. He spotted the reception desk first, tapping Eddie on the shoulder as he nodded toward it. "There, come on."

They strode across the overly white floors to the desk, where an elderly woman was scribbling away on a sheet, not even bothering to look up at their approach. Stacks of papers surrounded her, battling for space with switchboards. On one wall, small numbered squares flared to life once in a while, turned off by a harried looking nurse. She would disappear down the hall, wandering into whatever room called for her. Another, younger nurse rushed past them, a tray covered in tubes of various sizes in her hands. Grant cleared his throat, trying to gain the receptionist's attention. "Excuse me, ma'am."

"Take a clipboard, fill out your problem, and a nurse will be with you shortly." She interrupted, not even bothered enough to look up. While she spoke, the clipboard clattered down on the counter. The men shared a look before Grant tried once more.

"No, we are here to see someone, she was–"

"If you're not family, you're not allowed in any room until a doctor has told you otherwise." She cut in once again without looking at them. "Please have a seat and wait with everyone else." A hand lifted just long enough to point down the hall where a sign announced the waiting room.

Eddie started to open his mouth in retaliation, cut short by Grant's hand on his shoulder. He gave a quick shake of his head. It wouldn't do either of them any favors to be thrown out before they knew what condition Dacey was in. Jaw locked, he allowed Grant to lead him to the nearly empty room. Antiseptic assaulted his nose with every step down the hallway, dragging up memories he wished would remain buried.

Blurred faces, muffled voices, tin canned machine sounds. Nausea washed over him, scalding the back of his throat. Doctors telling him he may never walk, let alone ride again. How lucky he had been. He had lived and recovered. Miles of IV lines, endless questions and tests. Scans that forced him to drink liquids so disgusting he wouldn't make it to the room before throwing up. Rodeo? How could he even ask them of that? It was a miracle his spine was whole, his hip not crushed into a thousand pieces. Rodeo wasn't something they could, or would, clear him for. They didn't even like the idea of him riding at the ranch.

The hallway tunneled, edges darkening. With a wicked sense of unwanted humor, his hip gave a sharp throb. Phantom pain? The sciatica they monitored yearly? Eddie gave himself a hard shake, forcing himself to calm down. Now wasn't the time to have a breakdown. Reaching the waiting room, he allowed Grant to go first, trailing after him.

Grant made a face as he took a seat in one of the uncomfortable, hard plastic chairs before he reached over to grab a magazine off the pile beside it. Eddie remained standing for a moment. "I'm gonna head to the bathroom real quick. Don't let anyone leave without me or tell you anything." He warned.

Grant gave a nod, tossing the magazine back to drum his fingers on his thighs. "With luck, it won't be a long wait. Doesn't seem to be too busy right now, but naturally, now that I've said something, they'll get slammed."

"Either way, I mean it." He left it at that to seek a bathroom that he could be alone in. It took a few tries before he located one in an empty room that was waiting for a patient he prayed would hold off until he was done. The moment the lock clicked into place, he slid down the door, face buried in his hands. His hat fell to the side as his fingers slid up to tangle in his hair and grip it while his breath came faster. Tears he had kept hidden from everyone fell as he muffled a self-loathing scream into his knees. His jaw ached from how tightly he clenched it to fight more of them as they clawed their way up his throat. She was in here because of him, could have died because of him having been so lax in his care.

Nightmarish thoughts of *what if* chased each other in endless loops, each worse than the one prior. Eddie tried to force them away, standing up in order to stagger to the sink and catch himself on the rim. His face was pale under tear-stained freckles, eyes ablaze with fury at himself and hatred for the boy that had caused it all to begin with. One fist clenched tightly before it connected with the mirror hard enough it shattered around the connection point. Blood welled up across the split knuckles, blending with the blood already dried there. He ignored it, his other hand rising to dig around in his breast pocket. Almost dropping the small baggie of powder, he fought the trembling in his entire body. An explosive string of curses burst out as fresh tears rained down after the rest. Eddie forced his hands to stop shaking long enough to gather the rest of the powder on his pinkie and snort it, making certain none was lost.

When he was sure he hadn't left any, he turned the hot water on. His hands clenched on the porcelain, tight enough he was surprised it hadn't shattered along with the mirror. It wasn't until steam began to rise that he deemed it hot enough to scrub hard at his face and hands. It burned, pain lacing up from the breaks in the skin, but he relished it.

Satisfied with his work, he stood up, ready to face Grant once more without a trace of his breakdown showing. Clean hands ran down the front of his shirt, smoothing out a few wrinkles to keep busy. The man staring back at him was impassive as ever, ready to tell the world where to go, how to get there, and when. Ignoring how the raw skin on his hands stung, he gave a final nod at the man he was growing more familiar with staring back at him.

Turning on a heel, he stalked across the now dirty tiles. Unlocking the door cautiously, he paused, afraid someone had heard him. When no one rushed forward to throw him out of the hospital, he stepped out. Leaving the door open, he hurried from the room back down the twisting halls to locate the waiting room he had abandoned Grant in. Hospital staff bustled past him, never looking more than once at him on their way to unknown destinations, forcing him to keep to the side of the hall. He never dropped his gaze or dipped his head to them while he walked.

Voices drifted to him as he turned a corner, and he caught Dacey's name. It took all of his willpower not to run the last length of the hall, shoving the staff out of the way in order to do so. Instead, he lengthened his stride, just shy of obviously trying to rush, reaching the doorway, appearing calm and collected. Grant spotted him first as he strode through, one hand rising to make Josie pause.

"What's going on?" Eddie asked, voice level, his gaze moving between the two.

Josie looked worse for wear under the bright lights, like she'd been dragged through a bush backwards. "She's fine. They didn't find any broken bones, just severe bruising on them, cuts and scrapes. No major internal damage. Doctor told me it's a miracle that nothing is worse with how she came in, so I was coming to get you guys to let you know. He also said you're welcome to see her." Her voice was hollow, eyes staring at them but seeing nothing. Licking her lips, she glanced toward her sister's room. "They aren't going to let her go just yet, they want to monitor her another hour to be sure she doesn't have any internal bleeding or anything they may have missed. She swears, in more ways than one, that she feels fine other than sore, but they still won't let her go. I warn you now, she's a little out of it on the pain medication that they gave her."

"Lead the way. I'm pretty sure if he doesn't see her, Eddie is going to bore a hole in the wall to get to her." Grant reached out to rub her back. "Can't say I'm not worried about her myself."

Turning, she led them down the opposite hallway Eddie had just come from. They heard Dacey before they even reached her room, her voice carrying. In no uncertain terms, she was informing the doctor he was not going to admit her overnight. The thought brought bile back up Eddie's throat, and he noticed Joise clench her fists. Standing to her full height, they walked into the room.

"I'm just saying it would be a good precaution is all."

The IV machines wailed in protest at the way Dacey waved her arms, pinching tubes and cutting off their flow. "I'm just telling you, if you try it, I'm gonna haul my ass out of here right now after I knock you on yours. I ain't fucking staying." She retaliated from her throne of pillows.

Josie moved to her side, perching on the edge of the bed to meet the doctor's eyes. "Are you seriously trying to keep her overnight? On what grounds? You told us the tests, x-rays and scans have all been fine aside from the bruised bones." She ground out.

"Yes, I…" He stuttered off as Eddie settled on the side opposite of Josie. He didn't say a word, just crossed his legs, his expression darkening while he settled in. Dacey reached for his hand, gripping it along with her sister's. The doctor swallowed, looking from Eddie's face to Josie before throwing his hands up in the air. "Fine! If she gets worse, she needs to come back as soon as possible. I'm going to release her with enough pain meds to be taken, as needed, for at least two weeks with no strenuous activity for four to six weeks if you want them to heal right. Otherwise, you're just going to suffer longer. Be sure to sleep sitting up at least partially in order to help control the pain for the first two to three nights. If you need more pain medicine, you will have to follow up with your primary doctor. Any questions?"

Dacey shook her head in time with Josie. Eddie dropped Dacey's hand to pat her upper leg before he stood. He joined Grant at the door, leaning on the frame. When he reached the older man, he noticed the way his lips quirked. "Something on your mind?" Eddie asked, voice low.

"I'm pretty sure if looks could kill, that doctor would have been on the floor." Grant mused, fighting a chuckle.

"Fucker was upsetting her and trying to keep her for no reason. Can you blame me?"

"Not in the least bit." Grant turned to address the girls, the doctor walking out the door shaking his head. Dacey stood up to hunt for her clothes so she could change out of the gown they had forced her into, a frown on her face. "Alright you two, I'm going to go and check to see if the others have found us or not. With luck, your beast didn't do anything to any of them while they were trying to get him settled."

An unreadable look was cast toward Dacey as he mentioned Cash. "If they're here, I'm going to send them ahead to our hotel to wait. No sense in everyone congregating in the waiting room. This way Dacey can tell us everything at once instead of person by person, agreed?" There was a collective nod. "Perfect. I'll see you out there." Before leaving the room, he rested one hand on Dacey's shoulder. "I'm glad you're okay." Dropping a kiss on her forehead, he hurried out.

Josie glanced at the clock as he left, stunned. After all that had happened, she could have sworn it was at least midnight with the way both her mind and body were dragging; instead, the hands read hardly past seven. Part of her questioned if it was busted or not with how early it still was. Dacey was making slow progress toward the bathroom, jaw locked with each step that jarred her aching body.

"Is it both sides, or just the one?" Eddie broke the silence hanging around them as the bathroom door snapped closed, never looking away from where she had disappeared.

"Her left is the worst. From almost her collarbone all the way down, the entire bone structure is bruised both externally and internally. I doubt this is much luckier, but her right side has just outer bruises, nothing internal." Josie replied, standing to pace as they waited for the nurse to discharge her sister. A rather loud string of colorful words drifted to them from the bathroom as Dacey cursed. She moved toward the ruckus, intent on offering help, but stopped short when the nurse made her way in.

"I'm going to need to go over these with you, and explain her pain medications." Her tone was brisk, slapping the file down on the abandoned nightstand. Josie stood frozen for a moment, trying to decide between helping her sister or listening to the nurse. She took a timid step toward the bathroom, stopping when Eddie blocked her path. Josie made a noise of protest at the action that was ignored when he rapped once on the wood. Not giving Dacey any time to answer, he slipped in.

Her back was to him, head bowed over the shirt, glaring at it, cursing under her breath. At the sound of the door closing, she lifted her head, allowing their eyes to meet in the mirror. “Can you lift your arms up very high?” Eddie questioned, walking over to her.

“Not really, just about halfway up.” Dacey lifted them up to demonstrate, nose wrinkling as pain shot up her sides, leaving her almost breathless.

“Alright, gonna show you a trick I learned to help when you get to this point. It’s called don’t be fuckin’ stupid and too proud to ask for help.” He drawled.

Dacey turned around to glare at him, tensing when he reached out. Holding the shirt up, he assessed the situation. The hospital gown hung limp over her frame, easy to slip off from the front. Getting her arms up high enough to allow her arms through her tank top was going to prove difficult.

Walking over, he held a hand out. “You’re gonna have to trust me on this. Otherwise, we’re gonna have bigger problems.”

“I’m fine, I trust you.” She assured him, eyes closing as her hands moved to grasp his biceps for support.

He studied her, brushing her hair away from her face. “Alright. Gonna start by getting this ugly potato sack off you.”

She giggled a little, stopping with a sharp inhale. The medicine seemed to be taking ages to kick in. Feeling the fabric slip down her arms, she couldn’t help but open her eyes. His face was unreadable, fingertips ghosting over her skin as he drug the gown off. She watched how hazel eyes darkened, his breathing becoming shallow. When he stepped back, she shot him a puzzled look, standing before him in nothing but her panties. A slow exhale escaped him, eyes roaming over her. Heat flooded her cheeks, and she swallowed, letting his arms go. “What now?” Her voice was hoarse, even to her own ears.

Clearing his throat, he kept working. "Maybe from now on you'll start wearing more button-downs instead of tank tops." The old, familiar tease eased some of the tension between them.

Opening her eyes, she tracked his fingers, working through the buttons on his shirt one by one. A blush crept up her cheeks, but she refused to look away as he worked each one through the hole, keeping it in place until the material slipped from his shoulders. Dacey felt her jaw drop.

"Close your mouth, that's how you catch flies." Smirking, he shed it, holding it up. "Don't go getting any ideas." Closing the distance between them once more, he fought the need to cup her breast and tease the hardened nipple with his thumb. His jeans grew uncomfortably tight, causing him to shift in place.

Dacey sucked a sharp breath through her teeth when old scars were laid bare for her. They mapped out his years of wrecks, twisting together with those of both his life on the ranch and his childhood. Blue eyes drank in the way they webbed across the tanned flesh like a broken road map laid in a sea of freckled stars.

One in particular caught her eye and she couldn't help but reach out to brush the tips of her fingers over it, earning a slight shudder from the warm flesh. It was thin, running the entire length of his chest from ribs up to his collarbone. It had been gifted to him by a broken board on the top of a pen, one he had unknowingly stabbed himself on. Tracing it once more, she thought back to the day he had earned it.

She was six years old again, laughing so hard she could hardly run as fast as her little legs could carry her away from the bunkhouse. One hand was planted firmly on her head, holding down her prize like it was the only thing in the world that mattered at that point. Behind her, the slam of the door echoed out over the ranch. "Dacey!" His voice earned a squeal as she tried to run faster. It was all in vain; he was older, and had longer legs than she did. Within seconds he was snatching her up as she half screamed, half laughed, flailing hard trying to make him drop her. "Damn it, you little monster, give that back." He warned her.

"No!" She managed to kick free, scrambling across the gravel toward the closest pen.

"Dacey! NO!" Eddie cried, fear sinking in as he realized where she had rolled. The heifers startled only a second, freezing with Dacey as she felt terror slam into her with the force of a train. One snorted hard, lowering her head with a warning bellow, recovered from her momentary fright, ready to charge the thing she had deemed a threat. Dacey could only stand there trembling, a whimper building up in her throat until strong hands grabbed her under the arms, hauling her up the fence so fast the world spun.

The scream that had bottled up in her throat tore free, but the impact she was expecting never came. Instead, she found herself landing on something soft that let out a string of explicit words so rapidly it was a wonder he kept them straight. "Next time pay attention! You could...you could.." Eddie stopped as Dacey rolled away from him and sat up. He panicked, spotting the blood that darkened the back of her shirt. Had he dragged her over a nail? A broken board? Before he could inspect further, she was scrambling closer to him.

"Eddie, you're bleeding!" She was crying from a mixture of fear and guilt, her little body landing in his lap.

He looked down just as the pain finally hit him through the haze of adrenaline and fear. The cut was fairly deep, and he marveled at it only a second before tiny hands were trying to press into it.

"I'm sorry." Dacey sobbed, trying her best to help him. "I didn't know Eddie, I didn't. Now look what I did." Her tears came harder as his blood covered her hands. As fast as his anger at her had shown up, it was gone. Rising to his feet, he gathered her to him, lifting her up to head toward the main house and the first aid kit he knew Grant kept fully stocked just for him.

"It's okay, little brat, I'll be okay." He pressed a kiss to the top of her warm head, doing his best to soothe her. "But now you have to help patch me up."

Chapter 20

Dark in My Imagination

Eddie raised a brow, clearing his throat to pull her back to the moment. "See something you like, Darlin'?" He taunted, taking her hand to guide the first sleeve on.

She scoffed, rolling her eyes with a shake of her head at his words. "I didn't realize this hospital visit came with a strip show," she countered, voice falsely sweet to mask the way she fought a cry.

"You didn't have to come to the hospital to make me strip, you know. If you wanted to get me naked, all you'd have to do is ask." A lopsided smirk was offered, his hands ghosting over her shoulders to assist her other arm into the sleeve.

"Jackass. What makes you think I would even want to see you naked?" She grumbled, delivering a slap to the hands that grazed over her collarbones when they brought the material together. "I can button this myself. I'm not a complete invalid."

He raised his hands, laughing. “Could have fooled me. The way you were eyeing me just now made me feel like you were going to pin me to that wall. You sure you don’t want me to keep going?”

“Bet you’d have liked that, wouldn’t you?” Finished with the buttons, she refused to meet his burning stare.

Eddie drank in the sight of her standing there in his shirt. The warm fabric hung almost to her knees, the short sleeves almost to her elbows. “You have no idea.” It was only a half tease at this point, as his mind wished for darker things. “Too bad you’re all banged up then, isn’t it? Can’t do a damn thing like this.” He reached out and flicked the tip of her nose. “Other than march your ass out to your sister before she beats this door down. How much do you want to bet she’s standing right outside, ready to knock me on my ass for coming in here? Then have the sheer audacity to walk out shirtless because at least some men on this planet have manners to be sure a lady is comfortable.”

Dacey managed a weak laugh, staring at her jeans folded on the counter.“First of all, you and I both know I ain’t a lady, so nice try. Second of all, walk with your head down just in case, ‘cause I ain’t stupid enough to bet against that idea.” Gripping the hem of his shirt in a white knuckle grip, she stared at the door a moment. “This whole month is gonna suck ass, isn’t it?” She gestured toward them in a silent plea for help.

He sighed, reaching out and lifting them up. “You have no idea. It just gets more frustrating as the days go on until you feel like saying fuck it all because you just want to try doing something you could do before. I don’t suggest it, though, because it’ll not only hurt like a real bitch, but it sets back healing.” Crouching down, he fought a tremble. It wasn't related to the powder, not this time. He knew it was due to how close he was to temptation.

Trying to keep herself distracted so she wouldn't bury her hands through his hair, she looked up. "Learn that the hard way, too?" Lifting her left leg, she was forced to brace herself on his shoulders. Feeling the way he eased the jeans up should have been considered a crime. Stepping into the right leg, her fingers dug into his shoulders.

His voice came out an octave deeper than normal. "Abso-fuckin'-lutely." The urge to run his hands up bare skin nearly brought him to his knees. With how hard she was holding him, it took all of his willpower not to lick a burning trail up. He wanted to taste her, devour her right there. Drawing them up her hips, he couldn't resist grabbing her ass. All he wanted was to set her down on the counter and have her.

A knock resounded through the small room. "Dacey! It shouldn't be taking this long." Josie snapped from the other side, rattling the, thankfully, locked handle.

Eddie let out a quiet, frustrated groan. "Couldn't have picked a worse time." He sighed, stepping away from her.

Dacey almost begged him to stay, to kiss her, touch her, do *something*. When he instead drew away, she clenched her fists on empty air, suddenly chilled by the distance. Letting out a careful breath, gathering what little courage she could muster, she made her way to open the door.

Josie had taken to pacing the room again from the bathroom to the bed and back. When she heard the door open, she wheeled on them. "Eddie! Who in the hell told you that you could just walk in on my sister like that?" She spat, turning from where she had paced toward the bed to face him. Realization dawned on her. "Why is she in your shirt?" Grinding her teeth, Josie stalked forward to look Dacey over as if Eddie had only added to her injuries instead of helping her dress.

"Josie, knock it off. I can't get mine on or off at the moment, so at least I'm not standing here like some sort of exhibitionist like he is." Dacey pointed out, stepping between them.

Rolling his eyes, Eddie sneered at her. "I ain't got anything to be ashamed of from here to the hotel. Unless you're jealous, she's in my shirt and you ain't?"

Josie seemed to puff up at the mere insinuation. "I'd rather be hit by a truck than be caught dead in your shirt." She hissed, gearing up to continue her tongue lashing of him.

"Can you two please just not? I'm exhausted enough as it is, without listening to you constantly bicker. When we get to the hotel, you can fight as much as you want then." Dacey interjected, wobbling toward the door on unsteady feet. The pain medicine was kicking in harder than she thought it would, causing the world to tilt.

Josie deflated, pulling away from him to snatch the folder of instructions and the bag of medicine from the tray. Stalking forward, Josie shook her head, grabbing Dacey's hand to help her down the hall to where she hoped Grant still waited.

Eddie's face was expressionless, watching them go, waiting only a few steps before he joined them. Taking her other arm, he helped guide Dacey down the hall. "When we get to the hotel room, I promise I will wait until you're asleep to start a screaming match."

The obscene gesture Josie aimed at him made a nurse pause, shooting the trio an offended look. Eddie shot her a wide smile, offering a wink with it that had Dacey fighting a matching grin of her own. Josie cleared her throat, hand moving to cover her own mouth, picking up the pace of their walk just a bit. When the woman marched into the room she had paused in front of, Josie caved. Her laughter broke through the tension that had sank into them, shattering it into a thousand pieces until Dacey was gripping her ribs, fighting her own weak breakdown.

Eddie kept most of his composure through it, though his fake smile evolving into one that was real, watching them in clear bemusement. It took them a moment to compose themselves, a fresh wave of giggles erupting whenever they would look at each other.

In time, Dacey began leaning heavily on him, wishing she hadn't given in, but knowing it had been worth it. The tiles of the floor seemed to shift under each step, wiggling like living beings under her feet. Stumbling, she relaxed into the warm arms wrapping around her. "The floor is moving." She mused aloud, earning a concerned look from Josie.

Waving it away, Eddie adjusted his hold on her. "The pain meds have kicked in, I see," He teased her. It was a feeling he didn't miss by any means. At least she wasn't throwing them up in the nearest trash can. He'd done that one a time or two. Josie glanced between them, unsure if she should say something or not. He caught the look. "At least she ain't talking about pink elephants on the ceiling." It earned a weak smile from her and a giggle from Dacey.

"Pink elephants." Dacey snorted under her breath, one hand rubbing her eyes. "Fuck, I'm tired. Is it always like this?"

"Not always, depends on what meds they gave you. Some can knock you out cold while others don't. Either way, be thankful they gave you the good stuff and not some knock off junk that don't work." He assured her. One hand rubbed her back, the other waved Josie ahead toward the neon light above the waiting room.

Chapter 21

Learn to Let Go

Hearing the commotion, Grant paused in his conversation with the Wheeler family. They had shown up only moments earlier, Riley slamming through the door so hard he thought the woman behind the desk would look up. She hadn't, just simply stated in no uncertain terms if the noise continued, she would throw them out, no question asked.

Ushering them into the waiting room, he motioned for them to sit down. "So far, I have nothing. Eddie and Josie are with her, but I figured I needed to wait for you. You guys don't know how much it means to us for y'all to show up."

Rider just nodded, tugging Riley down beside him when she moved to stand at the voices drifting to them. She pouted, but for once didn't make a comment, just shifted to sit on the very edge of her chair, ready to move.

Shooting him a grateful look, Grant made his way back out into the hallway. Spotting the trio meandering toward him, he shook his head. "I should have known you were the cause of this," He called. Eyebrows raising in surprise, he gestured from Dacey to Eddie. "I appreciate you helping her, and I know Josie does too, but we all know you're gonna regret this once Riley sees you." He pointed out, a slow smile creeping across his face. "Didn't think of that one, did you?" he teased, falling into step with them.

"Hell no, I didn't. You think there's a back door around here somewhere, so she doesn't see me like this?" He looked around, earning a snort from Josie. Dacey shook her head, grip tightening on his shirt as she did.

"Oh no, you set yourself up for this failure and I'm not about to let this opportunity get away." Grant laughed, waving off Eddie's one-finger salute. "I'll bet money she faints. Or swoons."

"Shut the hell up." Eddie cursed himself briefly, standing up straighter. "Do something nice for someone and end up screwing myself. Seems about right." He sighed, though the hand on Dacey's hip moved her close.

Grant noted the movement, clapping a hand on his shoulder. "Nah, she needed you, and we know you would do it all over again, so don't give me that crap."

A shrug was all he offered to the words as they reached the waiting room. The Wheeler family lunged to their feet, rushing forward. Josie stepped between them, Grant right beside her, hands raised.

The brothers shared a look between them before Rusty spoke up. "Damn Eddie, you trying to cause a couple of deaths here? Someone's granny is gonna see you and keel right on over if you keep strutting around looking like that." He teased.

"It ain't gonna be a granny if you keep talkin' that way." Eddie's smile did nothing to cover the thinly veiled threat.

The twins only laughed harder, Grant giving in and joining them. Josie snorted, crossing her arms as she shot a rather amused look at Dacey, who was trying not to laugh with them. She pressed at her ribs, a broken smile shining through.

Riley bristled at her brothers. "Maybe if you weren't jealous, you wouldn't be worried about that. Only thing that faints when it looks at you is the livestock." It only caused them to howl louder, finally capturing the woman at the reception desk's attention.

She marched over, a look more terrifying than a summer storm plastered on. "This is an emergency waiting room, not your local comedy club or adult club. If you are through here, I am going to have to ask you to leave before I call security." The woman snapped, pointing the pen at the twins.

They tried to calm themselves, but a shared look caused them to start all over, Rusty bent almost in half, leaning on Rider. Grant ushered them out, his laughter mingling in.

Josie turned to her sister, taking a half step toward her. Seeing Dacey leaning so heavily on Eddie made Josie want to rip them apart and scream at her to stay away from the man. Looking them over, she paused, noting the broken skin across his knuckles, the realization hitting her.

Despite their differences, and her deep-seated mistrust of him from their past, he had beaten her ex for Dacey. Dacey noticed her watching them, cocking her head a little in question. Josie waved her off, walking out after the others. For now, she would keep her comments to herself.

"You ready for this?" Eddie asked Dacey, shifting his hold on her.

"What difference would it make if I wasn't?" she asked, one hand lifting to rub at her eyes.

"None, come on." Guiding her to the parking lot, Eddie scanned the area, locating their group, returning the gesture Grant offered to gain their attention.

Grant allowed him to get Dacey settled against the seat first with a nod before he leaned against the hood. "First things first. Were you able to get the horses settled for the ladies?" He asked, looking at the Wheelers.

"Yes sir, we were. Cash didn't give us too much trouble, but I think he knew something was up, kept pacing the stall, but he should be fine." Rider replied. Sensing how Dacey sat up, ready to press him about the stallion, he beat her to the punch. "I promise you he's safe and sound, honey, don't you worry. We went ahead and put him in with Buckshot, though, in case someone tries something, he can be there to keep her safe. It was Riley's idea."

Josie beamed at Riley when her brother explained her choices. "Thank you. We could never replace those two, so it means a lot that you did that."

Dacey just gave a curt nod in thanks as she attempted to conceal her annoyance at the fact they had handled her horse without her around, instead trying to focus on why Rider had called her 'honey'.

Grant nodded, continuing. "Alright, we are going to head to the hotel for the night, and we will head home in the morning. Twins, you work on horses. I'll be settling sales fast as possible. Do not wait for each other, just head to the ranch. Eddie, you're gonna take Dacey. Josie, you'll be with me."

Josie frowned, crossing her arms, knowing it wouldn't do any good to argue with him then.

He pressed on, ignoring the look she shot him. "Tonight, I'll get a couple of pizzas delivered with beer and sodas. At the very least, I can feed you, but I'm willing to bet that no one is up for a sit-down restaurant." A collective agreement rippled through them. "I figured as much. Other than that, I believe we should head out so Dacey can tell us what happened."

At her name, Dacey made a small face, resting her head on the seat. "I don't have to wait; Seth found me, marched me at knifepoint to the trailers, and he kicked the shit out of me. That's it, all there was, the end, good night." When she attempted to cross her arms, pain seared up her ribs, causing her to fight a yelp. "Fuck me a runnin' that smarts."

Waving off their concerned faces, she closed her eyes until the flare-up passed. "It's just a bunch of bruised bones, so I'm on lockdown until this pathetic excuse of a mother hen," she waved at Josie, "lets me do anything again. Which, if she listened to the doctor, will be in four to six weeks, possibly. I'll read the paperwork once we get settled for the night."

"I've been in a similar situation, and I know how much it sucks. If you need anything at all, don't hesitate to ask. Since we're working there, I don't mind." Rider offered with a crooked smile.

Dacey flushed at his offer, looking past his shoulder to where Rusty and Riley were waiting for him. "Thanks, Rider; I'll keep that in mind."

"On that note, we need to get her back so I can help her get a shower." Josie cut in, shoving off of where she had leaned on the cab.

"Grant, our truck and trailer are still back in the lot since I rode with Dacey in the ambulance."

Grant studied the ragtag group assembled around him. "Eddie can ride with me. Riley, why don't you and Rusty take the back of my truck? Rider, take the ladies back to the hotel for me. We can worry about the truck and trailer tomorrow once we get everything else," He suggested.

"Works for me. Come on ladies, shall I escort you?" Rider joked, offering an arm out to each of them. Accepting it, Josie waited for Dacey to ease herself from the cab of Grant's truck. Pausing, she took shallow breaths, wishing the pain meds lasted longer than they had. Rusty frowned, taking a slight step toward her, but Rider beat him, letting Josie go to take her hands. "Take your time, ain't no hurry here." With slow, shuffling steps, they made it to the Wheeler's truck.

Opening the door, Rider helped her climb in, Josie on his heels. Dacey waved them both off, brow scrunched, jaw locked. They backed off, waiting for her to do what she needed to get comfortable.

Watching them cross the parking lot, Eddie climbed into Grant's truck, slamming the door shut. His nostrils flared, eyes narrowed to small slits, as he ground his jaw. Rolling the window down, he watched the way Rider helped Dacey, hand curling into a fist on the doorframe.

Grant helped Riley up into the bed of the truck, waiting until she and Rusty were settled. Satisfied, he climbed into the cab and started the engine. He cast a quick look toward Eddie. "Any particular reason you look like you want to ask me to hit someone with my truck?" he asked, reaching over to the lighter on the dash, pushing the tarnished knob in. A small thumbprint was worn into it, only visible from certain angles. Taking two cigarettes out of the pack tucked away in his shirt pocket, he let one dangle from between his lips, offering the other out.

"No reason at all. Just ready for this night to be over with so I can get a shower." Eddie lied, accepting the smoke, taking the lighter when Grant was done. His eyes flicked to the side mirror to watch the truck behind them for a few minutes. "So, who won the bet?"

Grant furrowed his brow. "Bet?"

"Riley didn't faint like you said she would," Eddie smirked, sitting up more to reach onto the dash for an abandoned, half-chewed pen. He toyed with it, rolling it back and forth as he mulled over his question. "She did look like she wanted to and was a pretty good shade of red by the time we left."

Laughter drifted across the cab. "Guess that means neither of us won, huh? Oh well, better luck next time, I guess." They drove in easy silence to the hotel, the radio on low crooning out country songs to the warm air that filled the cab, chasing away the smoke. Pulling into the crowded parking lot, Grant guided the truck into the spot before their rooms. Shutting the engine off, he leaned back on the worn leather seat, earning a soft creak. "Can I ask you something?"

"Shoot." Eddie flicked his butt out the window, watching the other truck pull in and park further down the lot. Rider was the first one out, rushing around the cab to open the door to allow Josie to climb down. Forcing his full attention to Grant, he waited.

The older man shifted once more, taking a slow breath in through his nose, and exhaling it through his mouth. "Would you mind taking a room with Dacey tonight? I know it's awkward, but Josie will be too much, don't you think? I'm pretty sure they could use some space and break from each other. Everyone needs that from those they're close with."

He mulled it over, looking down at the bags between them. "You sure this just ain't a reason to spend more time alone with Josie? Maybe knock some dust out of the chute?" The wicked laughter that accompanied his words was met with a shirt thrown into his face.

"Keep that up and you'll sleep in the bed of the truck again," Grant warned, grabbing the bags. "It's helping everyone across the board. If we don't separate them now, Josie is going to overwhelm Dacey by trying to help her. She means well, but out of all of us, you are the one who understands what she needs most right now. I'll handle the meltdown I know Josie is going to have." He assured Eddie as the younger man opened his mouth to state the obvious.

"Alright, it's your funeral buddy." Eddie grabbed a handful of the bags to help carry them to the door. Grant followed after him, unlocking their room, pausing as he heard Dacey's voice rise in volume.

"Josie! I'm not a complete cripple! I can get out of the truck myself." She snapped, slamming the door hard enough, most of the group winced.

"You look like you could fall over every time you move! How am I supposed to take it? If you were trying to pass a sobriety test, you'd fail." Josie shot back, hands planted on her hips.

The men exchanged a look before Grant broke away, walking over. "Ladies, can we not start the fighting already, please? I understand it's been a long day, and it seems like you're gonna force my hand on this for me. Josie, I don't care how much you don't like it, you're gonna sleep in my room tonight. Eddie will be with Dacey. And before you even start trying to tell me how wrong I am, stop and think. You need space and so does Dacey to keep another screaming match from happening in the middle of the night. While I don't know what's happened in the past, Eddie's been in her situation. Now, let's get clothes sorted out so you can take a nice, long, hot shower and just try to relax, please?"

Josie ground her teeth, looking between the three of them before she threw her hands up. "Fine! It's not like you're asking me." She snatched the bags away from Eddie, storming into the room Grant slept in.

Dacey shared an awkward glance with Grant. "I uh, thanks? I think?"

"She'll be fine. You both need this, trust me," Grant assured her. "Once I get the clothes for Dacey sorted out, I'll bring them over. Don't do anything too stupid." He warned.

Eddie scoffed. "Define 'too stupid' for me so I know what level you're meaning versus mine. Besides, I should be warning you of that." Eddie had to dodge a quick swipe aimed at his head. "I'm just saying practice safety." The laughter that broke out behind them grew louder as he was forced to rush into the room to avoid Grant dropping the bags to beat his ass. Dacey shot Grant a confused look as he rushed away.

"Don't worry about it. Just go ahead and get settled for the night. I'm gonna call in the food for everyone." He turned toward the Wheeler family. "Once I'm done with that call, I have a couple of others, but I can meet you at the pool." He pointed toward the dingy sign with half of the bulbs around it burned out. The concrete path was cracked in spots, weeds trying their best to poke through. "Go ahead, so we have enough chairs and tables for everyone. Though, I don't think there's anyone here stupid enough to think of swimming."

Riley wrinkled her nose, frowning. "I'd rather swim in a pond than a public pool. At least I have a good idea of what's in the water." Her brothers nodded their agreement. "Do you need us to get anything? We can run down to the corner store from here, grab ice and cups or something?"

Grant nodded. "Sounds good to me. While you're there, can you grab plates as well?"

"You got it! We'll meet you at the pool." Riley bounded back to the truck, Rusty not far behind her. Rider paused in front of Dacey, looking her over. Grant left them alone, choosing instead to face the wrath of Josie head-on.

"Are you sure you're comfortable being alone with him? If you want me to, I can stay."

"Eddie's a bigger help than I think anyone realizes. I promise I'll be okay. Now go on, I need to get cleaned up and sit down before the world throws me sideways again."

"Okay, okay, you win. I'll see you at the pool." Tipping his hat, he left. She watched them go, shifting her weight from one foot to the other until the door opened, and Eddie poked his head out.

"You gonna get your ass in here or you gonna sit out there like a puppy all night?" he asked, leaning on the frame. Offering a hand out to her, he cocked his head to the side.

Dacey accepted and felt it was warm, and rough with callous' from a hard life. His nails were blunt, chewed down, though they were clean. Looking up at him, she shook her head. "Shut up." Letting him lead her into the room, she paused for a moment and looked around. Taking cautious steps, she moved to the chair in front of the window where their Stetsons rested on the dirty cloth seat.

"I didn't think it would be this strange to be in a room alone with you after all this time." She admitted, toying with the dirty curtain fabric, making a face at the scratchy feel.

“Can’t say it bothers me. You’re still the same brat you always were, just grown up.” He sprawled halfway across the bed, feet crossed at the ankles. Reaching for the remote, he took a peek at her. “No reason to make it weird just because you’re no longer a kid and neither am I.”

Dacey stood frozen by the chair, looking around the room. A TV rested on the dresser to the right of the door, while on the left was the chair, a small wall heater next to it. The bed rested in the middle of the room close enough to the left wall that only walking space lay between them. On its right was the door for the tiny, cramped bathroom. She needed to take care not to knock her knees on the tub when she used the toilet. “Um, Eddie…” He gave a hum of attention as he flipped channels. “Where are you sleeping?” Without hesitation, he patted the bed with his free hand. “I don’t fucking think so!” she yelped, realization sinking in.

“What’s the matter? Am I not good enough for you? Gotta have that wet behind the ears, Wheeler boy?” He taunted, throwing the remote aside and sitting up. Dacey took in his shirtless figure as he rested his elbows on his knees, studying her.

A flush crept up her neck as she glared at him. “First of all, Rider is a good man, so let’s not even start. Second of all, you’re fucking kidding me, right? There’s no way I’m sleeping in a bed with you.”

“There’s the floor, feel free to use it.”

“Eddie!”

“It’s not that complicated, Darlin’. The bed or the floor, it’s your choice. I’ve made mine and you can best bet I ain’t sleeping on the damn floor.”

She wanted to throw her hands up, but instead turned her back on him. "I can always just take over the bed when you go to shower, you realize that, right?"

"You realize that I'll just shove your ass over to make room? You think you scare me?"

"I should be asking you that same question." She countered. Turning around, she peeked out the window to see if their noise had drawn unwanted attention. He rose from the bed, moving the few steps between them quietly to stand behind her. When she turned around, it took all of her self-control not to scream and hit him as he loomed over her.

"Darlin', I've warned you before, I should scare you. I should be the worst nightmare you find yourself waking from, still full of fear." One hand rose to grip her chin in a light hold, her eyes widening. He moved closer until the tips of their noses touched. "Those little boys in your past have nothing on the demon I can become when pushed."

His hand slid from her chin to the base of her skull, holding her in place as she swallowed when his breath warmed her ear.

He hardly spoke above a whisper. "You should learn to fear me, because I can make you beg on your knees without a word for so many things you never even knew were possible." A soft whimper escaped her, warmth building within her. Eddie drew back until their foreheads touched, hands trailing down her sides in feather-light touches. "Fear the things you don't understand before they show you why."

As her brain tried to wrap around what was going on, he was stepping away, leaving only cold air where he had stood. "Go get your shower while we wait for the food to get here." He commanded, settling back down on the edge of the bed to watch her. Dacey stood there a moment more, mouth working wordlessly, trying to piece together what had happened. “Now, Darlin’.”

“I don’t have any clothes yet.” She blurted. Eddie sat there staring at her for a split second, earning a mild squirm under the scrutiny.

“For fuck’s sake!” He moved from the bed to the door, jerking it open. Moving to Grant’s, he pounded on the solid wood until Josie yanked it open with a pissed off expression on her face.

“What?” she spat, crossing her arms over her chest.

“Your sister wants a shower and, last I knew, everything we got for her was brought in here. So, unless you want her walking around naked, you need to get her something,” Eddie deadpanned, unphased by the greeting he had received.

“Eddie!” Dacey cried, face turning the same brilliant scarlet Josie had.

“I don’t think so!” Josie snarled.

“Enough! Eddie, quit causing problems, damn it, and just get the clothes.” Grant ran a hand through his salt and pepper hair. Doing as he was told, Eddie dug through the bags clustered in the corner of the room by the bed. Finding everything he knew Dacey would need, he marched out, slamming the door behind him.

Chapter 22

Tiger by the Tail

Watching Eddie head back into the room he was sharing with her sister, Josie let out a broken half sob. "Why can't he just pretend to try with me? I get we have our differences, but he could at least make an attempt." She perched next to Grant on the threadbare comforter. "I'm just so tired, Grant. Tired of it all."

He rubbed her back, letting her rest her head on his shoulder. "I know, honey, I know. You've been through a lot for only twenty-four."

She sat up. "Yanked away from home at Dacey's age, forced to join a new school where I was completely hated, used as a housekeeper turned bargaining chip," she started ticking them off on her fingers, "abused by two men, hospitalized by the one that just put my sister in the same place, dad dies so we were pretty much kidnapped." By the end, Josie couldn't speak through her tears.

Grant held her, swaying them back and forth to comfort her the best he could. "I wish I could erase the past for both of you, I do. Every time

I look back, I think of everything I could have tried to do to keep you safe." He admitted, controlling his own tears. "Had they let me, I'd have laid my life down for both of you."

Josie pulled away to glare at him. "There was nothing you could have done! If I had stayed, Dacey would have been alone and none of us would have allowed that to happen. Both of you did everything you could, hell Eddie tried laying his life down when he went after the cop holding her. We never, ever, blamed either of you."

"He spent the night in jail for that. I swear they have a rewards system just for him with how many times he's been in there. 'Oh, you need better soap? Well, we see you've accumulated enough points, so here, have some.' I'll have to ask him." Grant joked. It broke the gloom cradled around them.

Josie cackled, flopping back on the bed at the very idea he had painted. "What's sad is now I would love to ask him that. Think he'd tell me the truth?"

"Higher chances he'd throw you in the pool without a second thought. Best not risk it. Although that doesn't mean that I can't ask him about it." The mischievous glint that sparked to life in Grant's eye made Josie pause.

"You're going to, aren't you?"

"Of course! He's more than earned my right to with how many times I've had to pick him up."

Another fit of giggles overcame her, easing the tight muscles along her shoulders. "You cannot ask him until I'm around. If you do, it'll be you going in the pool." She teased, sitting back up. "Thank you Grant, for everything. Everything that we've put you through since showing up can't be easy on you and yet you don't stop, you don't give up. I can't express how grateful I am to you."

He took her hands in his. "Josie, you and Dacey have always been my daughters. You mean the world to me just like Eddie does and if I didn't care for you, I would be no better than that moron you came from. There's no need to thank me for doing what needs done." Letting her go, he moved around on the bed until he was beside the phone. "Now, you go grab that shower while I order us pizza. Is there any kind in particular you like?"

"Dacey's big on ham and pineapple with extra cheese. I'm not picky, so whatever you and Eddie normally eat is good enough for me." Grabbing her clothes, she made her way toward the bathroom. "The only requirement is a bottle of Dr. Pepper for her or else you will never hear the end of it."

"Support the addiction, got it." Reading the small scrap of paper near the phone, he lifted it from its cradle to punch in a number to place their order. Once he was done Grant checked the closed door to the bathroom. Lifting the phone again, he dialed in a familiar number. It rang a few times before a woman's voice answered.

"Seiffert residence."

"Hey, Bailey, it's Grant."

"Grant! How are you? Everything okay?" Her tone became concerned. He could hear rustling in the background and a male talking to her.

"Not exactly. Is Dean around?"

"Yeah, hang on. Love, Grant needs to talk to you." There was a moment of rustling before a male voice came on the line.

"Bailes said you need me?" Dean was all business.

"I do, but it's a bit of a story. You got time for me, or do I need to call back in a bit?"

"Got all the time in the world for you right now." Grant could hear Dean shifting around, getting comfortable. Bailey's voice drifted to him, inaudible but unmistakably hers. "Bailes wants to know if you need her help as well?"

Grant mulled over the offer. "Actually, yeah. Can you have her call up Lucas and Connor for me? We're probably going to need them for this situation." He waited as the information was relayed.

"She said not a problem once we are off of here. I take it this is a pretty dangerous situation to need her brother's legal advice."

"Unfortunately, it is. Get comfortable." Grant launched into the story, tapping out random rhythms on the nightstand as he talked. At some point Josie made her way out of the bathroom, wringing her hair out in the towel. She listened in on the conversation just long enough to tug her boots on, waving at the door.

He nodded in response, watching her leave. By the time he was hanging up the phone with Dean, half an hour had passed, yet Grant was calmer than he had been in the last two days. The young sheriff had agreed to meet up with the family at Wildwood the next afternoon, kicking things into motion. With luck, one of his brother-in-laws would be there with him to offer their expertise, and Grant couldn't have been more thankful.

Hauling himself up, he wandered out, following the voices he could hear echoing around the parking lot. The Wheeler's had taken charge of the little gathering, shoving together a couple of tables. One held the food and drinks and a ripped open chip bags lay beside pizza boxes with the tops flipped open. A couple plastic trays held two types of cookies, one already missing half of its contents. It was questionable to have it all in such a state on the stained plastic of the tables, though it didn't seem to be bothering any of them. Underneath, tucked out of the way, was a cooler, hiding the beer and soda.

Risking a peek at the water, Grant edged away from it. The water was clear, but had a distinct discoloration the deeper it got until the bottom was blurred, almost invisible. Leaves floated across the surface, some used as tiny life rafts by various bugs, others more submerged. At the far end, faint green tinged the tiled steps, lead to a suspicious looking stain. Rejoining the group, he snagged a flimsy paper plate, adding another for fear of collapse under the weight of food.

A thin film of grease shone on top of the pizza, catching the glow of the lights surrounding them. Most of the group had taken chairs, though some of them looked on their literal last leg. The one Rusty had claimed listed so far to the left, Grant wondered if he hadn't lost a bet of some kind to have ended up where he was.

"You look worse for wear," Rider noted, popping the top off of a beer and holding it toward him. Crossing his legs at the ankles, he leaned back in the chair, stretched out almost cat like.

"I feel worse for wear. Thanks." Grant took it, settling down next to Riley as she chatted with Josie.

"You gonna eat anything else?" Rusty asked, frowning at the two slices on the other man's plate.

"In a minute I will." Taking a long pull from the bottle, he kicked his feet up on an empty chair across from him. "Eddie and Dacey still busy? Or did they not want to come play?"

Josie swallowed her bite. "I didn't stop to bother them, but I can go and get them."

Riley shook her head. “Nope, you sit your ass there and eat. This way, if Dacey’s asleep, you won’t feel guilty waking her up to feed her. If she isn’t, that’s just bonus points.”

“Are you sure? If anyone is going to incur Eddie’s wrath, it should be me.” While Josie was thankful for the help, she had to refrain from pointing out Riley more than likely had other motives.

“Positive.” She bound to her feet, snatching a chip off of Rusty’s plate as she passed.

He slapped her hand with a pointed look. “Get the hell out of here, you pest! You got your own plate.” He groused.

“Better when it’s stolen. I’ll be back.” Seeing herself out through the cheap wire gate, Riley took off toward the rooms. The group watched her a moment before turning back to each other. Josie toyed with her slice of pizza, picking at the toppings.

“Everything okay?” Grant asked, snagging a bag of chips for himself. Tucking it beside him, he chuckled at the fake hurt look Rusty shot him.

“Yeah! Sorry, just in my own little world. I probably should have gone with her, don’t you think? Dacey may need help that Eddie can’t give her.”

“Don’t even try it. You’re meant to be taking a break to keep your own sanity. They can handle this just fine without someone lurking over their shoulders.” Grant patted her knee. “Eat, relax, and let Riley handle this.”

Rider passed Josie a beer. “I think it’s good for my sister to be able to help, give her something to do other than get under our feet. Also gives her a slight sense of purpose she doesn’t get often at home. Mom runs our house like a dictator when it comes to what Riley can and can’t do, so this is a treat to make her own choices. Dacey is also a rare treat because anyone Riley's age has either left town for college or can't understand that she doesn't have a "normal life" in their eyes. Ranch work is hard, and demands a lot out of us, so for the chance to make a friend who gets what she's going through has her pretty excited."

"You mean excited not to have to deal with your stellar personality?" Rusty muttered into his plate.

Grant and Josie stifled chuckles when Rider made a rude gesture toward his twin in retaliation. "My point is, Riley isn't just trying to jump Eddie's bones. She's hopeful that Dacey will like her in return. You two can't seem to see eye to eye yet, but given time, I'm willing to bet you will. She grows on you even when you don't want her to." Rider took a sip of his beer, shrugging.

Raking a hand through her still damp hair, she winced when her fingers snagged a knot. "I guess? She just likes to shove her way into everything, thinking she has a right to tell me how my sister should and should not live. You can't blame me for not tolerating someone doing that. I know Dacey better than anyone. I don't need help caring for her." Josie countered.

"You may want to rephrase that, otherwise I'm liable to take offense." Grant warned her. "Everyone needs help in life, Josie, that's how the world works. It's why we separated you."

Humbled, Josie studied her plate instead of answering him. Rusty leaned over, resting a hand on her shoulder. "We are all guilty of it. Hell, I still catch myself grilling Riley over stupid shit, not realizing that's what I'm doing. Rider thinks he runs this show if you let him get going on one."

"Guilty." Rider raised his beer in salute, grinning.

"Don't beat yourself up over it, just do your best." Rusty sat back, taking a swallow of soda.

"I'm sorry, I am. It's not that I want to run her life or be an overbearing cow of a sister, I really don't. But she's been through so much for me, some days I feel guilty I wasn't there for her more. No matter what I was being put through, including times where I just shut down, she had my back." Taking a deep breath, Josie took a long drink of her beer, downing the rest of it. "It's like we switched roles and I'm embarrassed to admit that out loud. How can I claim to have her best interests at heart when I was a shell, just running on autopilot for over a year?" She blurted, tossing aside her plate, appetite lost.

The men sat in stunned silence, Grant breaking it when he cleared his throat. "You don't have to unpack that right now, but I expect you to later. As for Dacey, she made her own choices to do what she did. Yes, you are trying to make up for it, but have you asked her if she wants you to? Did she specifically tell you that you need to do all of this, or did you just assume?"

She sat there, jaw slack as his words hit home. Silence descended upon them in an uncomfortable wave while she processed. Rider passed another round of beers out, settling back in his chair with his plate on his lap. He knocked his boot against Rusty's, gaining his twin's attention. A tap back gave him the fortitude he needed. "Honey, you better come back to the present before I drink everything, and there's nothing for you to wallow in."

His words earned a startled, strangled sound from Josie. Looking up, she straightened her spine. "You're right, I can't do this right now." Grabbing her plate in one hand, the other stretched out toward Rider, wiggling her fingers. "Cough it up, you're not allowed to have them just for yourself."

"Can't argue with that." The beer he'd just opened was pressed into her palm, sweat dripping down the sides of it. "You earned it. But I bet you wish we had something stronger at this point."

"I do, but since this is all we have, I'll make do with it." Tipping the bottle, she drained half of it in one go.

"Maybe I need to get the stronger stuff," Rider offered, crossing his legs. "But by the way you're drinking those, I'm not sure it's a good idea. You trying to get drunk?"

"Don't hang that thought up just yet. We may need it if the night keeps going the way it does." Rusty commented, taking a bite of cookie.

Josie rolled her eyes. "No, I'm not trying to get drunk on purpose, but I will point out that even if I were, it shouldn't matter. I ain't been drunk in…" she thought back, trying to recall. "Well, never, but that doesn't mean I can't try tonight. And I like Bulleit more than Jack, keep that in mind."

"Just let me know when I need to go." Rider snatched the bag of chips closest to him, taking a handful. "Bulleit Bourbon is far superior to Jack, but we all know nothing beats a good cold glass of Woodford Reserve." They all held up their beers, muttering their agreements.

Settling back in her chair, Josie looked around. "I want to know when the others are gonna show up. Surely it don't take that long to get to the rooms and back." Josie stated. Taking a bite of pizza, she looked toward the gate like they would appear any second.

"You'd be surprised how well Eddie can drag his feet if he doesn't want to do something. I'm willing to bet Riley got there, and he's the one holding them up." Grant said. "Just give it some time, they'll be here."

She settled back to eat, leg bouncing just a little as she did.

Chapter 23

Low Rate Rendezvous

When Eddie stormed into their shared room, Dacey braced herself for his incoming tirade. None came, even though her sister had been shouting. He silently fumed, throwing the bag of clothing down on the comforter with more force than necessary. Lighting a cigarette, he sat against the headboard, reaching over to grab the remote. Catching her staring at him, he narrowed his eyes. "What?"

Dacey shook her head, grabbing an outfit. "Nothing, I just thought–"

"That's dangerous."

"Shut up! I just thought you were going to say something." She moved to the bags, digging through them in search of something to sleep in. With a snort, Eddie climbed off the bed, digging around in his suitcase for his last clean shirt, cigarette bouncing as he muttered under his breath to himself. Fishing underneath the jeans, he added boxers along with it. Tossing them in her lap when he passed, he resumed his position.

Gathering them up, she contained the blush that threatened to burn her cheeks. Instead, she hugged them to her chest, trying not to aggravate her injuries. The pain meds were wearing off, and a dull ache was blossoming on the left side, though her thoughts were getting clearer. “Do you need the bathroom? Or can I take a shower in peace?”

“It’s all yours.” He blew a slow stream of smoke out toward the water-stained ceiling, turning his attention to the television. Taking that as her sign to leave him alone, she slipped into the pathetic excuse for a bathroom.

As the latch clicked into place, realization slammed down on her like a ton of bricks. “Damn it!” She swore, throwing the material onto the tank of the toilet. The move pulled at her ribs, earning a hiss of pain, hands curling into fists. Resisting the urge to kick something as her vision swam, she backed against the door for support. Her world tilted, spinning so fast behind tightly closed lids it was all she could do not to scramble for purchase against warped wood under her palms.

The soft thud caught Eddie’s attention, spurring him to his feet. Pulling the door open without a second thought, he was forced to catch her when she staggered back into his bare chest. Her muffled cry had him scrambling to adjust his hold, still keeping her on her feet without gripping too tight.

“Dacey?” Concern colored his words as she turned in his grasp, resting her head against his chest, breathing shallow.

Letting the stars and colorful bursts clear from behind closed eyes, she licked her lips.“I’m fine, the meds wore off sooner than they told me they should.” She ground out, tears making silent tracks down her now red cheeks. Feeling warm skin under her palms, she took careful breaths, pleading with her heart to slow the now frantic tempo it chose to thunder in. Could he feel it? And why on earth was she reacting like she had never felt a man's chest before? While she hadn't been with a lot of guys, considering her past circumstances, she hadn't been a nun either. More than once, she had ended up in the bed of a truck with a half-naked farm hand. What was so different now?

His hands rubbed along her back, letting her gather herself. "Do you need my help?"

Dacey blanched, taking a small step back. "There isn't anything you can do," she lied.

Eddie snorted, one eyebrow rising. "That so? Your fairy godmother gonna wash your hair for you? What about your back?"

Trapped at the truth in his words, she longed to punch him in frustration. She shook her head, eyes going wide. "You are *not* getting naked in a shower with me!" Her voice was shrill, carrying through the thin walls.

"Now, come on, you ain't that stupid. I can wear my boxers, and if you keep bellowing like that, Josie is gonna hear you and come marching over to do it. So, I suggest you shut up before I make you shut up." He warned, crossing his arms. "I can sacrifice a pair of them for this and I'm more surprised you ain't griping that I'll see you naked, not the other way around."

Her jaw dropped, stunned speechless. Every protest against the idea died in her throat when he moved closer. When he took her hand, she allowed him to guide her into the bathroom, closing the door once more, praying he didn't feel her nervous tremors. When it clicked into place, Dacey became acutely aware of how cramped the space became with an extra body in it. Her back was against the door once more, she looked up, meeting his gaze.

"Well?" Eddie asked, leaning against the sink. His hands gripped the porcelain to both ground himself and to keep from stripping her himself. Moving to the tub, he perched on the edge of it, one leg itching to bounce.

Turning her back to him, she began unbuttoning her shirt, throat so dry she was sure he could hear each breath rasp out. Her fingertips worked each button out of their respective loop, fumbling more than once, all while being cursed. It wasn't like they were going to do anything but take a quick shower, and she did need the help.

"You gonna make it?" he asked, voice soft from where he sat, tugging his boots and socks off. A nod was offered, his shirt sliding down her shoulders to puddle on the stained, tiled floor. Eddie sucked in a sharp breath as her back came into full view once again. At the hospital, he had paid little attention to anything about her body other than to be gentle with it. Now his eyes drank in the sight before him, like a broken goddess had stumbled into the room with him. Small scars were scattered along sun-kissed skin with a larger jagged one, less than a quarter of an inch wide, running from her left side all the way up to her right shoulder blade.

Dacey shot him an annoyed look over her shoulder, gritting her teeth. "This was your idea. Why are you asking if I'm okay or not now?"

Desire twisted his thoughts while pure, primal need flooded his veins until all he could think about was bending her over the sink and fucking her until neither could remember their names.

"Good fuckin' night, Dacey; you just had to go and grow up the way you did." A puzzled look crossed her face at his words. She turned to face him, hands covering her bra like it would make a difference. Eyes trailing from her breasts down to jean clad curves and back, he reined himself in. "Sit down."

Something in his gaze made her obey, sitting on the edge of the tub without hesitation. He knelt down, slowly removing her boots for her. "Good girl." His voice was husky, fingertips leaving small trails of heat where they touched, making her want to cross her legs. Seeing him on the dingy floor in front of her made something deep within her stir to lift its head up with a feral growl, dark flames she had never felt before licking their way along her veins. Startled, she snapped her gaze away to stare at an ugly mildew spot on the wall, desperate for a distraction.

What was wrong with her? This was *Eddie,* of all people. The man before her pulling each sock off was the last person she needed to be feeling anything for. He had helped raise her, and while she couldn't help but admit she had a childhood crush on him, this was different, *they* were different. Eddie was a man now, and she had secrets that even he probably couldn't stomach.

He stood once more, head tilted to the side. "Something on your mind, Darlin'?" Dacey wasn't able to form a coherent thought, no matter how hard she studied him. "Think you can get those jeans off on your own?" His voice was little more than a whisper, fingers lacing together, drawing her to her feet. Once she was steady, he couldn't help but tease the warm skin just above the fabric.

"It's not hard to unbutton jeans, Cowboy." She drawled, slapping his hands away, hoping he didn't notice the higher octave her voice came out in.

"Watch your mouth before I make you learn why it's better to keep it closed." His warning chased shivers up her spine. She gripped the waistband of her jeans tighter, searching for the courage that seemed to have left. "I was trying to be considerate of you needing to bend at the waist to pull them off."

"I can do it. Once they get to my knees, I can kick them off." There was a roaring in her ears when his hands tried to ease her unrelenting grip. Coaxing her hold to ease up, he teased the small, metal button. He was standing nearly flush against her, forcing her to tilt her head up to meet his eyes. Her lips parted a little, breaths coming out in light pants, her heart skipping a beat when he slipped it free.

She found herself hypnotized by his eyes and the way they darkened at the move, a needy ache filling her when fingertips traced around her navel. They grazed the soft cotton of her panties, earning a sharp inhale from him. A low throated groan escaped him, giving in to press closer to her until their bodies were less than an inch apart. Feeling the way his body was responding to her through the fabric of his now painfully tight jeans, Dacey's breath hitched, mind stumbling over thoughts she couldn't sort out. They raced past so fast there was no way to comprehend any of them.

"It's more fun this way," he breathed against her ear.

Her eyes fell closed, hands moving up to his shoulders. What was the harm in giving in? Was there a reason?

A sudden knock echoed through the room, causing Eddie to jerk back into the sink with a loud curse. Dacey tried to keep from screaming, hand flying up to cover her mouth. Wrenching the door open, he stormed across the short expanse. Ripping the door open with a rather rude snarl, he smothered the tongue lashing when he noted who stood at the threshold. Riley took a hasty step back, eyes wide, hands held up to protect herself. "What?" He snapped, aware of how the bathroom door slammed shut behind him.

Riley peeked over her shoulder, curious. He blocked her view, forcing her full attention back to him. "I, um, Grant asked me to let you guys know the food is here," she blurted, trying to recover from the fear his greeting had caused.

Raking a hand through his auburn locks, a hard sigh escaped him. "Fuck. Fine. Hang on." Leaving the door open for her, he grabbed a shirt from his bag, yanking it on. Riley made her way in, looking like one wrong word would send her running for the hills. She cast a quick glance toward the room she knew Dacey to be in, shifting her weight from one foot to the other.

"Do you want me to wait for her?" She asked. "You can head out without me. I don't mind. I know she needs the help."

"I can leave her a note, she doesn't need or want help," he countered, gritting his teeth. His body was still thrumming with desire, lust clouding his mind to the point he wanted to throw Riley out to rejoin Dacey. Forcing himself under control, he searched for his boots, realizing too late they were still in the bathroom. Standing there, Eddie warred with himself if he should just walk in and grab them or not risk the high chances of not coming back out. "Damn it all."

"Something wrong?"

"Fuck yeah, but I can worry about it later." Turning to the door, an idea crossed his mind. Chances were high after everything that happened in the bathroom, he wouldn't care where those boots were by the end of the night if they picked up where they left off. "Are they waiting for us?"

"Nah, they're already out by the pool. That's why I asked if I should wait."

"Oh, of course." Eddie would bet his hat that Grant would ask about his boots. After all, who would risk walking barefoot to a hotel pool that wasn't inside?

"Um, Eddie?"

"What?" The word came out harsher than he meant it and he paused as she flinched.

"Did Dacey lie to me last night?" Brow furrowed, he stared at her, trying to piece together what she was referring to. When he didn't answer, she continued on. "I asked her outright if there was anything between you two and she told me there wasn't, pretty much laughed at the idea. But I'm wondering if it was a lie, considering you're barefoot and the only other place your boots can be is where she is."

Dacey had laughed at the idea of them being together? The confusion and lust were giving way to anger the longer she talked. He glanced at the door. "We ain't doing anything, she didn't lie. I was helping her get ready to shower and making sure she didn't pass out on us. Can't exactly climb into the shower in them, now can I?"

Riley brightened at his words. "So, I'm free to ask if we can hit the other bar in town tonight? I know it's been a rough day, but I think that's even more reason to get a drink. I'm also a pretty decent dancer." She grinned at him. "If it gets you to say yes, I'll even buy the first round."

Eddie found the idea of a bar rather appealing. His stash was out, even though he had been trying to limp it along with using less than he normally would. Pick a bar, throw a dart and chances were high it would hit who he needed to fix that issue. It wasn't like he wouldn't be back to babysit Dacey later in the night or finish what they started if he wanted to. "Sure, why not? Josie can watch her own sister if it means I get a couple of free beers." Smirking, he gestured out the door for Riley to lead the way. "She'll find us, eventually. Let's get a bite to eat and then see if I can't con Grant outta the truck keys."

"No need, Rider's letting me drive his so long as we drop them off at their rooms." She blushed a little as Eddie studied her.

"Are you trying to get lucky or something tonight?" His lip curved up just a little, causing her blush to darken.

"What if I said I was?" Her words caused him to stop dead in his tracks, dragging a slow look up her body. She refused to shift under the scrutiny, licking her lips. "There somethin' wrong with that? You already said that you're free and clear, so it ain't like you're gonna get in trouble for some fun. And let's be real, it's been a while since I've had the chance. You're attractive, and I have every right to."

Chapter 24

Girl Crush

Eddie couldn't help but laugh at the rushed explanation. "I ain't gonna judge someone for having a little fun. Lord knows I've had my share of it." He began walking once more toward the pool area. "Not unless your brothers have something to say about it. I've had enough knock-down-drag-outs this weekend to tide me over to at least the end of next month."

"They won't. If anything, it'll make Rider pretty happy to see he was wrong about you hooking up with Dacey. Frees up his chances to shoot his shot." She fell into step with him, rolling her eyes at the idea of her brother trying to be suave. "Anyway, we still can't wrap our heads around it all. Were you guys really apart for six years?"

Swallowing, he shoved down the memories that began pounding at the walls built up in his mind. "Longest years of my life, if I'm going to be honest. I watched her grow up until she was eleven, nearly twelve. What fucked me up more than anything is the sheer fact that they're back and yet I still keep thinking I'm gonna turn around and both of them will be gone." He admitted.

Riley bit her lip as she laid a cautious hand on his arm. "It seems like they're both happy to be back, though?"

He patted his shirt pocket in search of his cigarettes, realizing he had left them in the room on the dresser by the TV. Unsure of how to answer her, he continued walking, trying to sort something out. When the pool came into view, Riley broke away to have a quick, whispered conversation with Rider, one hand waving over as she did. Josie noted the pair were alone, sitting up in her chair where she had been relaxing.

"Where's Dacey?" Grant asked as Eddie reached the table of food.

"In the shower where she wanted to be. I tried to offer help, but she refused it." Eddie replied, snagging a beer. Twisting the top off, he flicked it across the pool, losing sight of it halfway.

Rusty nodded, offering his beer in salute. "Tried that, it's in the water now."

"Probably the cleanest thing in there."

The group laughed, save for Josie. "You didn't think that maybe you should have waited for her?" she hissed, eyes narrowing. "We gave you one simple thing to do and you can't even manage that?" Her voice began to climb, forcing Grant to rest a hand on her knee. Closing her eyes, she pinched the bridge of her nose, counting out loud from ten. When she reached one, she forced herself back into the chair. "Well?"

"She made it very clear every time I tried to do something for her, she didn't want me to. Which translates to her needing time alone, which she is allowed to have. What does it matter? I didn't leave her in a puddle on the floor, helpless to the world." Taking a drink, he lifted his chin to Grant, hand held out. The older man chuckled, digging his cigarettes out to pass them over. Dipping his head in thanks, he turned back to Josie. “She has clothes, she can walk, and knows where we are.” He was unphased as he spoke, taking a bite of pizza.

“Seriously?!” Josie’s voice hit a pitch that made most of the group flinch.

Eddie wasn’t phased. Lighting his smoke, he blew a trail at her. “Yes, seriously Joise. What do you want me to do, huh? Go hold her hand all night long? Carry her all over the place? She needs space, food, and sleep, all of which she will be getting. Dacey doesn’t need me looming over her like a stalker. Calm your tits.”

She bristled, shoving her chair back with an incoherent snarl. “I assumed you could do one single thing tonight and help her, hell I even gave you the benefit of the doubt! Yet here you are without her! This is a joke, right? You just saunter down here claiming she needs space when she can’t even dress herself?” She snarled, jabbing a finger in his chest.

Without a second thought, he slapped her hand down to her side, rising to loom up over her. “First of all, don’t fucking poke me like that again or I’ll…” He let the sentence die as Grant leveled him with a warning look over the beer bottle raised halfway to his lips. Eddie took a moment to reassess what to say.

When he did speak, his words were spit through clenched teeth. “You think you know better than me? The great Josie can read minds now? Like fuck you do. You weren’t in there when she was arguing with me every step of the way when it came down to helping her get ready to shower.” His breath began to come in short, quick bursts. “You weren’t there when the door was slammed closed, I was. Think before you get your damn panties in a twist up your ass! The food ain’t going to run off unless you take it." The bottle gave a warning squeal the tighter he gripped it, threatening to shatter. "It's not hard to fix a plate to bring back to the room when I go."

Reeling back as though slapped, twin spots of color blossomed in her cheeks. Scoffing, she geared up to snap back.

Before either of them could continue, Grant stood up, slamming his bottle down. "Both of you sit down now." Grant's voice left no room for argument. The twins exchanged wide-eyed looks. Riley shrunk down in her chair, trying to make herself as small as possible.

"You will not continue to disrespect each other in front of me unless you want me to duct tape your hands together like I did when you were little." Eddie snorted, walking to the edge of the pool, kicking in a piece of broken siding. Grant continued on, ignoring his little outburst. "Josie, he's got a point, remember? We already discussed this. Take a breath for me, sit down and get another drink." She didn't argue, just snatched the offered bottle from Rusty, downing half in one go.

Grant sighed, continuing on. "Eddie, you need to rethink how you're going to address her every time you two disagree, because I will not tolerate this any longer. Do you both understand me?" They nodded in unison, refusing to look at him or each other. Shaking his head, Grant settled back into his chair, lifting his beer up.

Rider climbed to his feet, eyes moving from Josie to Eddie. "I'll take her something to eat if you want? Make it easier on everyone since I'm a neutral party in this matter. No harm, no foul. I'll drop this off, stay if she wants to talk, or come back so Riley can take me to my room. I won't try to baby her, and I won't pressure her into letting me take care of her; she is free to make her own choices." He offered out, fishing around in the cooler for the two liter bottle of Dr. Pepper they'd bought for her. Swiping a paper towel over it to clean off the small bits of ice and water, he turned back to them.

Grant thought it over, eyes flicking from Eddie's bare feet to his face. "Yeah, go ahead. This way we at least know if she's asleep or not, she gets something to eat, and we can all take a step back." If looks could have killed, he'd have been dead in an instant. The pure fury aimed at him almost made him flash a taunting smile back.

Rider grinned, plating up a couple slices of pizza, stacking some cookies up beside them. Rusty offered out what was left of a bag of bar-b-que chips, tucking them in the crook of his brother's arm. Satisfied, he looked to Riley. "Can you wait for me? Just in case she doesn't want me to stay."

"She glanced at Rusty, who gave a nod. "Yeah, we can wait. But if you're not back in ten minutes, I am going to assume by default you stayed and leave, anyway."

Heaving a mock sigh, he looked to Grant."You mind giving me a ride back to our rooms if she does need me to hang out a bit, but not stay the whole night?"

"I don't see why not. Rusty, you want to hang out here with me and Josie a little longer? I ain't rushing back to the room if she's not." Grant offered.

"Nah, I wouldn't mind having Riley drop me off back at the room. I don't know how y'all are doing this. I wasn't even a part of the events and I'm exhausted." Rusty replied, rolling chip bags closed and combining what pizza was left into one box.

"Ain't no need to do that, Josie and I can get it all later. But if you want some of the food to take back with you, feel free. Don't forget, tomorrow just do what you have to do to get home, be at the ranch seven am sharp Monday morning." Grant crossed his legs, raising his beer. Josie ignored them both, playing with the ends of her hair like none of them existed.

The twins shared a high five, giddy at the rare opportunity they'd earned. Bidding everyone farewell, they trailed after Eddie and Riley. She shot him a wicked smile, bouncing ahead a few steps. "Looks like we gotta get your boots sooner than later, huh?"

He ground his teeth together, resisting the urge to shove her. Choosing to ignore her, he stalked down the path.

Rider jogged ahead of them, tapping at the door he knew Dacey was behind. Eddie shoved past him, pushing the door open without a second thought.

"Eddie!" Riley chided, slapping his upper arm. "That was uncalled for!" Turning to Dacey, she offered a slight grimace.

"Fuck, it was my room first." Ignoring Dacey, he stormed into the bathroom, grabbing his boots.

Rider moved to the side of the bed, doing his best not to stare at what Dacey wore. Setting the plate down, he made a grand show of producing her drink.

"What's going on?" Dacey asked, accepting it with a laugh. Cracking it open, she took a grateful swig, looking between him and his sister.

"Those two are going to the bar, I'm here to feed you and nurse you to health if you'd like." Rider answered, gesturing to the plate. "Just crack the whip and I'll do as bid."

"Oh." She was unsure of what else to say, watching Eddie finish pulling on his boots.

Standing, he grabbed the Stetson off the dresser, dropping it on his head. “Ready?” The question was aimed at Riley, hell bent to pretend the room was empty, save for her. If he didn’t, he knew he would give into the small voice whispering dangerous promises of broken bones. Who the hell had told the kid he had any right to be that close to Dacey?

She nodded, waving to her brother and Dacey.

“Have fun, and don’t forget, safety first!” Rider called after them with a broad grin. Riley stuck her tongue out, shutting the door to cut off anything further he could have said.

Dacey refused to watch them leave, choosing to pay more attention to her food. Her stomach churned a little at the thought of greasy pizza, but it gave an unpleasant roll the more she thought of Eddie and Riley alone together. Sighing, she climbed off the mattress, bringing the plate over to the desk. Setting it down, she toyed with the napkins, blotting off the shine.

“Something up?” Rider asked, genuine concern in his voice. Leaning over, he took the remote to mute the television.

“No, just not as hungry as I thought, I guess. I can eat it in a bit.” She offered him a weak smile that didn’t reach her eyes. “I don’t know if it’s the pain or the fact I’m just tired. It’s no reason to worry.”

He didn’t buy the lie for a second, but chose not to call her out on it. “Alright, but if that changes or you want something else, let me know.” He picked at a burn hole in the bedspread. Having dealt with Riley in situations like this, he knew to give it time. If she chose to talk to him, then he’d be there for her.

“Thanks again, Rider. You don’t have to stay if you don’t want to, I’m not very exciting at the moment.”

"Not a problem. If I wanted to be entertained tonight, I'd have stalked my sister on her date with Eddie. Since that's not what I was looking for, I asked to be here." She shot him a surprised look, wandering back to the bed. Shifting to the foot, he assisted her in curling up against the headboard. Clearing his throat, he faced her. "So, I promised you something last night."

"You did?" Dacey tried to think back on the conversations from the night before, coming up short as her tired brain refused to work.

"Yeah, if I won, I was gonna buy you a hat that actually fit you. I know that you've had a lot happen to you tonight, but um, here." He pulled the storm-gray Stetson off of his own head, setting it on hers. It fit her perfectly and made her question how it had fit him as well before she saw the marks of it digging in. "I had them measure Riley and then took a little off. Does it fit okay?"

At first, she found herself at a loss for words. Never, outside of Eddie, had anyone bought her a brand new hat. They were expensive, for one, and the fact that her father couldn't be bothered to buy them food, she knew better than to expect a hat. When Rider started to look worried, she flashed him a true smile. "It does. This is perfect." Reaching up, she took it off, turning it in her hands to inspect it. Soft, and supple, she felt her throat tighten up just a little. Fighting the sting that developed behind her eyes, her fingers ghosted over the black band, noting the tiny silver horse that raced over it. Its mane and tail streamed in the wind, head high.

"Can I be honest with you?" He asked, leg bouncing. Dacey shot him a quizzical look, hoping he couldn't see the shine of tears, but nodded for him to proceed. "I don't like Eddie, at least not yet. Now, I don't know him, but there's something about him that doesn't sit right with me." Running a hand through disheveled, dirty-blond locks, he pressed on. "Riley's an adult now and I can't tell her what she can and can't do, even when I feel like my advice would be for the best. He seems…off? I guess." Shifting in place as though the bed below him was suddenly on fire, he gave up holding back.

Moving up the bed, he plopped down beside her, head falling back to rest against the cracked, wooden headboard. "I'm not trying to pick a fight, nor am I trying to jump to conclusions higher than a bronc. Just, don't lie to me. Can I trust him with her?"

Dacey chewed her lower lip, debating on the best way to answer. One hand came to rest on his shoulder, soft as a butterfly. "I understand what you mean, and I wish that I could help you more than what I'm going to tell you." Moving to face him, she met his eyes. "Growing up, I swear he wasn't like this, not even close. He was a little withdrawn, sure, but whoever he's become now is a man that I'm having to learn about, just like everyone else." His face fell, and she hastened to keep going.

"He used to care, and was more protective than Josie was, but now I'm not sure what to think of him. All any of us can do is give him the chance. Please, because you're going to be working with him and she may end up dating him." The words made them both tense, Rider shaking his head. "In the end, if he hurts her, just be there to pick the pieces up. Help her learn the best thing to do is keep going forward." As she talked, she picked at a loose thread on the sheet. It unraveled a bit more, adding another frayed spot among the others.

Rider sighed, moving until he could stretch out properly. Lacing his hands behind his head, he stared at the ceiling, hoping it would have better answers than the ones he had just received. When none offered themselves up, he looked to her. "What if I don't trust him with you, either?"

Dacey froze at his words, looking up at him through her lashes. "Care to elaborate on that, Rider?" Her heart started to beat just a little faster, curiosity sinking deep into her bones.

"He looks at you like he wants to either kill you or eat you and doesn't know which one to do first. But then when it comes down to it, like tonight? He's gone. Real men don't just up and leave a woman who's hurt like he did." The tirade tapered off.

She laughed, patting his arm. "Let me assure you of one thing; Eddie is a man. But he's one that doesn't show it the way most people would expect." Getting a confused look, she moved to lay beside him, hands gesturing above them both. "You're a chocolate and candy type of date, right? Don't even try to deny it."

Rider's eyebrows rose, and he couldn't help but look away, offering a crooked smile.

"My point. Anyway, Eddie's already shown he'd rather have a smoky bar than dinner and a movie or bring a girl candy. But, on the other hand, he knocked out the man stalking us with no questions asked because he saw how Seth made me feel."

"I would have too, given the chance."

"I know, I know. Don't misunderstand me, I'm trying to explain. No one said I was very good at this." They shared a soft laugh. "Back at the hospital, I couldn't get my t-shirt on and he, quite literally, gave me the shirt off his back. He's always been that way, for as long as I remember." Part of her missed those days, when things were so much easier in life. Carefree days where she could spend hours at his side without ever saying anything.

"There were times he would yell at me for something I knew I shouldn't do," Rider shot her a look, "but once he was calmed down, instead of apologizing to me or anything of the sort he would hand me his soda or snack. Even if it was the only thing he'd had that day, he let me finish it." More than one almost full bottle of orange soda had been pressed into her tiny hands, or moon pies just opened. "He'd slap my hand for doing something dangerous, but then saddle my horse and lift me up. He's…well…he's always been complicated to understand."

Rider listened to her explanation, tapping the air with his toes. For a few minutes, the only sound was the TV low in the background announcing a movie Dacey had already seen that month at a different hotel. "You know him better than you seem to think you do. Even after he took off leaving you alone with me, you have his back." It annoyed him to an extent, but he understood why.

"Who you just described is a man that I guess I could, and probably should, trust with anyone in his care. But it chafes, ya know? Guy like him? That fuck-it-all attitude, doing whatever he wants without having to worry about what anyone thinks. Pisses me off a little, but it's probably more jealousy than anything."

A low, sad sigh escaped him. Rolling on to his side, he propped himself up on an elbow, looking at her. "I know I gotta to learn to deal with him, but there's still something about him that doesn't sit right with me."

"Riley will be fine, worry wort. If anything, she's safer with him at that bar than anyone else interested in taking her out." Dacey tried to assure him.

"Not about her, about you."

That made her frown a little. "Why would it matter?"

"Because, as a man myself, I can read his body language when I'm near you, and honey, that's a man staking claim on what he wants short of a hand on your ass." He deadpanned.

Dacey let out an incredulous laugh. "Chances are so high you're misunderstanding his body language it hurts." She held her aching ribs, trying to ease them from the laughter. "Besides, why would you feel the need to worry about it if you are right?"

Rider sat up and raked a hand through his hair, offering her a shrug but refusing to meet her gaze. Cocking her head to the side, she studied him, worried she had offended him. Scrambling to think of something to say to help break the sudden tension between them, she came up empty-handed. Nervous, she moved back against the headboard, brow furrowed.

"Fuck it." His voice broke through her thoughts, scattering them. Hauling himself to a sitting position, he placed a hand just over her left shoulder, bracing his weight. She froze, unsure of what to do.

Part of her mind was yelling something she couldn't understand, nor wanted to at that moment. A warm, calloused hand gently caught her chin, lifting it until their eyes locked. He moved closer, stopping mere centimeters away, giving her the chance to stop him.

When she did nothing, his lips met hers in a gentle kiss. Her mind went blank, body unresponsive until he began drawing away. Catching the front of his shirt, she tugged him back, returning it. What could it hurt? A few stolen kisses were nothing, even as her mind railed against the idea of his lips on hers. Unbidden memories of Eddie in the bathroom flashed across her mind like summer lightning; too quick to catch, but clear in their warnings. Dacey forced them back; why should she worry about Eddie when he was off with Riley, probably doing the same thing to her in search of his end goal?

Chapter 25

Rock My World

When Rider pulled away, she let him, keeping her eyes closed a moment longer. Taking a peek, she noted his blush, how he had moved to stand beside the foot of the bed. "I know that was forward of me, but I've wanted to do it since this morning. The original idea was going to ask you on a date, but with everything that happened, it didn't seem like a good idea." He admitted, rubbing the back of his neck.

"I don't mind things being out of order, sometimes it's just more fun that way," she countered. A light tap on the door broke their conversation, Rider holding a hand up to keep her in place. He checked through the curtains, relaxing at who was on the other side. Opening the door, he nodded to Josie and Grant.

"Just wanted to check in and let you know if you need us, we're heading to the gas station for some things. Once we're back, we'll just be relaxing in the room, so if you need us, knock." Grant explained, looking between them.

"Thanks, but I'm okay. Dacey, do you need anything?" Rider asked, stepping aside to let her talk.

"Josie knows what to get, thanks Grant." She waved them both off, settling back against the pillows. Could they see the blush she felt? Did they sense something was different? Josie was studying her, and Dacey hoped it was nothing.

"Alright, I'll knock when I leave the bag outside the door. You two have a good night and Rider, if you need to leave at any point, you just need to let me know." Grant reminded him.

"Yes, sir, I will." Rider's words received a nod, the two leaving them. He stepped back, closing the door, resting his forehead against it. Exhaling, he spoke more to the grimy wood than her. "Do you want me to lock it?"

She debated, wondering if he should or not. "Maybe not? I don't know if Eddie is coming back tonight."

"Don't count on it but, for your peace of mind, how about I lock it but stay up for a while to see if he does?" The offer was begrudging, but honest. Drawing the chain into place, he flipped the latch. "There. Safe as can be." Wandering back to the bed, he perched on the edge, not quite close to her but not so far it would make her question it.

"Thanks." Yawning, she drew back the comforter, slipping under it. "But be warned, you're sleeping on top of the covers and there's no chance in hell of you getting any." She teased, making a vain attempt at fluffing the flat pillows into better shape. By morning it wouldn't matter, they'd leave her neck sore and stiff.

Giving a mock salute, he helped her draw the comforter up to her chin, acting like he was about to tuck her in. "Yes, ma'am." He drawled, winking. "I'm gonna let everyone know you gave in, how begging you on my knees was what did the trick."

She shoved him with a laugh, regretting the move as pain laced up her ribs. Exhaling, she steadied herself on him until the spots left her vision. A ringing filled her ears, the world tilting at a dangerous angle. "Holy hell, those meds work, but I need to remember they don't fix me completely."

He nodded in reply, studying her. Satisfied she wasn't going to pass out on him, he got comfortable. Absentmindedly, his hand moved to her hair, running through the soft locks. She tensed, feeling the weight of his gaze. "What are you thinking?" The question wasn't much louder than the TV, forcing her attention to him.

"If you're ready for this slumber party. Because I thought there would be pillow fights and late night gossip. You know, fun stuff. Not just boring old movies we've both seen a thousand times in the past six months."

Her reply made him snort, fingertips brushing her temple. "Pillow fights are only allowed if we're in our underwear."

"I am, nice try." Her eyes drifted closed, enjoying the gentle touch.

"Well damn, you got me there. Does that mean I gotta strip?" A hopeful note colored his tone.

"You try starting a pillow fight and I'm going to throw you off this bed to sleep in the tub." She warned him.

He raised his hands in mock surrender. "Okay, okay. I promise to be on my absolute best behavior."

"Good." Dacey shifted around a little more, trying everything to find the perfect position so her ribs would let her sleep. "Alright, you can join the party, then."

Picking up the remote, he punched in a number, changing the station over to a comedy show.

“This okay?” He asked. A cool glow bathed the room, exaggerating the dark circle under one of her eyes. Rage crept over him, fists clenching where they rested on the bed. If Eddie hadn’t been the one to show Seth what it was like to have his ass beaten, Rider would have stepped up. Nothing was more pathetic in his eyes than a weak little boy who beat women.

“As long as it isn’t too loud, I don’t care.” She yawned. “I’m done. I need sleep. Are you sure you’re okay with sitting here watching this alone?”

He lifted a lock of hair, teasing her nose with it. “Wouldn’t be any different if I was in my room right now, I don’t sleep well in new places. Go ahead and get some rest; don’t worry about me.” He settled against the pillow better, crossing his legs at the ankles. “Night, honey.” What little self-control hanging on was doing its best; all he wanted to do was kiss her again.

Either she could read minds, or he was just poor at hiding his thoughts. Peeking up at him, she caught his wrist. “You want to kiss me again, don’t you.”

“How’d ya guess?”

“You’re burning a hole in my face, staring.”

“Can you blame me?”

“No reason to.”

“If I try, what’s gonna happen?” Even as he asked the question, his body was moving, sprawling out beside her.

“Won’t know until you try, right?”

Rolling, he straddled her, licking his lips. Leaning down until their foreheads rested together, he rubbed the tips of their noses. "Because if I start to kiss you now, I won't stop. I already knew that the second I kissed you the first time, didn't even need to ask what would happen." Cupping both of her cheeks, he studied her.

Stunned, Dacey lay there, not daring to breathe. Was this a dream? The smallest part of her wanted to let him, tell him it was fine, they were both adults who could do what they wanted. After all, it had been months since her last good romp.

Rider pressed a kiss to her jaw, nuzzling her neck. Just as she reached up, he moved off of her, settling back down against the headboard. "Much as I want to do this, we shouldn't. At least, not right now."

"Wait, what? Why not?" Her voice was low and throating, darkening the blush on her cheeks. Clearing her throat, she sat up, bracing against the thrum of pain lacing up and down her body.

Propping his head in his hand, he patted the pillow, encouraging her to lie back down. "For one, I'm not stupid. You're hurt, and now isn't the time to be testing the limits of what you can or can't handle."

She lay back at his prompting, worrying her lower lip. "Then why bring it up? Why start it?"

"Curiosity killed the cat."

"Satisfaction brought it back?"

He laughed, mussing up her hair. "Sometimes it does. Look, I'm not gonna lay here knowing I lied to you. I wanted to kiss you because I think I have a shot. But, the more the night goes on, the less I think that's true. I want to, don't get me wrong, but before we go jumping off in the deep end with no floaties, I want you to think about all of this."

Dacey quirked a brow at him. “Care to elaborate?”

“Not tonight. Get some rest, we can talk about it all later.” He assured her, carding his fingers through her hair. Giving the TV his full attention, he forced himself to ignore the way her gaze bore into the side of his face. “Night, honey.”

“Night, Rider.” She mumbled, eyes falling closed. Resuming his earlier task, a soft hum of approval greeted the action, spurring him on. It didn’t take long for her breathing to even out, body relaxing. Rider watched her, almost transfixed. When her guard was down, she looked happier, peaceful. Scrubbing a hand over his face, he let the canned laughter wash over him, forcing himself to focus on the TV instead of her every few minutes.

No matter how he looked at it, he couldn’t understand how he had ended up in the situation.. She and her sister had only shown up in their lives just over twenty-four hours ago, yet here he was making sure she wasn’t alone, kissing her even. Something magnetic kept drawing him to her, but he couldn’t put his finger on it outside of her determination. Despite everything that’d happened in that time, she’d stood up for herself more than once, returning each tease and flirt without a second thought.

It didn’t help that he liked to piss Eddie off, watching the other man get worked up. No matter what Dacey argued or claimed, Rider wasn’t stupid or blind. Eddie wanted her to himself come hell or high water, and nothing would stop him. Rider’s lip curled a little in annoyance at the thought. His chances may not have been very high, but he wasn’t about to just let her go without trying. That was the reason he had kissed her, wanted to keep kissing her. Who the hell did Eddie think he was? Sleeping with Riley all while making it clear to Rider he wanted Dacey?

Cautiously, afraid she would wake up or shatter in his hands, he touched her cheek. She was beautiful; he knew that didn't help his case either. Dacey muttered something in her sleep, turning her head away from his hand. He let her go, turning back to the show that had failed to lure his thoughts away. Sleep was what he needed, yet it was eluding him like smoke through his fingers. Just lying beside her was keeping him awake, overly aware of her being so close, yet untouchable. Rolling, he turned his back to her, leaving the TV on to serve as white noise in the background, so he could focus on anything other than her breathing behind him.

Chapter 26

Flatliner

After dropping Rusty off at his room, Riley headed across town to the second bar it housed. Eddie remained silent, watching the scenery pass while lost in thought. Parking, she tapped the steering wheel a little, mulling over her choices. "You still up for going in? You seem pretty pissed off."

"I'll be fine after a drink or four. Come on, thought you promised me you were a good dancer? Is this your way of backing out on me?" He challenged, climbing out. Not giving her a chance to answer the rhetorical question, he hustled to her door. Opening it, he helped her down, waiting until she was steady. Turning to the blazing neon lights, a wolfish grin spread over his face. "Ready for this?"

She linked their hands with a smile to drag him toward the door. "You're stuck with me for now, so don't even think about trying to trick me." Dodging people, Riley wove a path to the bar, feeling the pounding beat of the band envelop her.

He let her lead the way, nodding more than once to people he recognized from the rodeo. When they reached the bar, he leaned next to her. Surveying the crowded dance floor, his mind wandered. The last time he'd been on a date seemed more than a lifetime ago and, even now, he wasn't sure that's what he would have called it.

When the bubbly, raven-haired girl behind the bar took their order, he swatted Riley's money down despite her protests. "Look, I know you told me you'd buy the first round but, as a man, I'm not going to let that happen. Just accept the free drinks and don't bitch." He pointed out, accepting their beers with a nod of thanks.

"I'm not bitching. I'm just trying to keep my word." She countered, making a face at him and receiving a flick to her nose.

"No one said you didn't keep your word. You tried, I refused to let you." He took a step back, eyes searching for the person he needed. "I'm going to the bathroom, wait here for me." A nod of agreement was given while she took his drink, searching for a clear spot to sit down. A wicked thought crossed his mind, causing him to lean forward until his lips brushed her ear. "That's my girl."

Drawing back, he left her standing there, eyes wide, a blush darkening her cheeks. Walking closer to the wall in order not to run into anyone, Eddie resumed his search. It took longer than planned to locate the kind of man he needed but, when he saw his target, he was relieved. Their exchange was brief, however, neither of them wanted to risk getting caught by someone standing too close for comfort.

In the spur-of-the-moment, Eddie added on one more thing for later to share with Dacey, curiosity getting the better of him. Tucking the acquired goods deep into the pocket of his jeans, just the thought of her made him swallow. Closing his eyes, he fought the wave of lust crashing over him, almost bringing him to his knees. Forcing his emotions down, he wove his way back to Riley, who was waiting for him at the bar. A pang of guilt seared through the warmth the need had left behind, reminding him of a talk they needed to have.

She held the bottle out to him, cocking her head to the side. “You have something on your mind, don’t you?”

Her words caught him off guard. “Is it that obvious?” He hated it when someone could tell how he was feeling, as if he was exposed before the world.

“No, not to someone who isn’t looking or used to reading faces.” Patting the barstool she had saved for him, Riley rested her elbows on the sticky wood in front of them. “Spill it. No reason to be miserable all night.”

Joining her, he studied her for a minute. “If this makes you throw a fit or make a scene, I will make you regret it until your dying day.” He warned, voice low enough she was forced to lean closer to hear him.

“Like that’s something you need to worry about. Just spit it out.”

“I ain’t someone who’s looking for a relationship, period. If you think that you’re going to suddenly be my soulmate or something, this ain’t going to work.” Eddie did his best to make it clear to her, watching her face. When she laughed, he furrowed his brow. “Something amuses you about this?”

“Eddie, the more I think about things, the more I know I don’t want that either. Not a chance in hell, though I originally thought it would happen. Yes, you’re attractive, but other than that, I don’t think we would work together well. Our personalities alone would cause us to burn half the town down in fights.” Sipping her beer, she glanced over. “Does that mean that what we planned for tonight is off?”

"Not a chance in hell. I was promised a fun night and I plan on getting one." He played with the beer bottle. "Unless you're uncomfortable and feel like you have to. I'm not about that kind of fun and, speaking of fun, we need to discuss a couple of things."

Her brow scrunched in confusion. "What do you mean?"

"I like to be in complete control during sex. What I say, when I say it, goes without question. Yes, I've been trained in safety, before you even ask. Is that something you can get behind?" The label was becoming mere fragments along the scarred bar-top.

Riley caught his hand in hers. "No, I'm not uncomfortable with that. It sounds like this could be fun." Eddie relaxed, pulling away to face the bar. "Now, no more heavy stuff, okay? We are here to have a good time! Come on, let's dance." Leaping off the stool, she snagged his arm, hauling him out onto the dance floor, pressing close.

Eddie let his hands slide down her body, resting on her hips, guiding her from one song to the next. The next few hours drifted by in a blur of music, drinks, and small talk about their lives. He let her carry most of the conversation, adding his own on occasion. Any time it drifted toward dangerous territory, he would change the subject to something lighter. Riley caught on to his tactics, respecting his choices when possible. When they made their way to the bar for another round of drinks, she caught his wrist.

"I've got a pretty good buzz going, how about we get the hell out of here?" She asked, jerking her head toward the door. Eddie didn't need to be asked twice for him to make a quick exit, blood heating with each step.

Reaching the truck, he pinned her to the door, kissing her deeply. Returning it, her arms wrapped around his neck, rolling her hips against his. Breaking away to rest their foreheads together, he cupped her cheeks. "I'm not going to make it to the room to fuck you senseless, baby girl. How about we find a backroad?"

The sheer thrill his words sent through her earned a soft moan. "Sounds like a plan to me." Climbing into the cab, Riley expected him to stay on his side until they found a spot they deemed safe to use. When he slid across the seat next to her, she had no time to process what was going on before he slid a hand between her legs. She inhaled sharply when nimble fingers worked circles over her clit through the fabric of her jeans.

"Eyes on the road, can't have you crashing before we even get to the best part." He instructed, increasing the pressure with each pass. Riley gripped the steering wheel hard enough her knuckles turned white. "If you pull over or stop before I tell you to, then this ends." She forced herself to pay close attention despite the need building with every tortuous pass he made. All she wanted to do was press her thighs together in search of more contact. A soft, plaintive whine escaped the longer he worked on her. "Such a good girl, and you listen so well." A dead-end road sign caught his attention off to the right. "Turn here. Let's see how secluded this is."

Doing as instructed, Riley took the turn. For a moment she worried it was little more than a field road, but once they crossed over the curb it became graveled. The truck shook, adding to the pace Eddie stroked her with until she was struggling to continue driving.

"Stop."

She hit the brakes with a little more force than she meant to, earning a light chuckle.

Eddie pulled his hand away, sliding across the seat. His actions earned a loud noise of protest, with Riley unable to form coherent sentences. "Problems?" The smile he gave her could have finished her right there.

"Eddie, please." She begged, finally able to clench her legs.

"I ain't fuckin' you in the cab, hop on out now." He smirked, slipping out the passenger side. Without question, she scrambled out after him, eager for what he would do next. Dropping the tailgate, he patted it playfully for her. As she took a seat where instructed, Eddie leapt into the back, limber as a big cat. He grabbed the bag of gear her brothers kept tucked under the toolbox.

Watching him, her jaw dropped when he pulled a tie down out. Holding it up, he let her see it. "Are you okay with this? We don't have to."

She nodded. "Yes, I'm okay with it."

He hummed his approval, walking to the middle of the bed, and crouching beside the ball hitch. "Come here."

Scrambling over, Riley knelt opposite of him, the cold, hard steel between, watching him intently. "Arms out for me." Tucking the tie down between his teeth, he reached out, removing her shirt and bra in short order. "Damn, here I thought the bra was doing all the lifting." The tease broke some of the tension, and Riley realized when she laughed, she relaxed more.

"Be careful, if I turn too fast, I'll take your eye out." She countered, lighting up when he caved, joining in the laughter. "And here I thought you were gonna be cold and unfeeling during this."

Eddie took her wrists, knotting the rope around them so fast it stunned her. "Not always. Yeah, sex can be a serious thing, but you looked like you were going to pass out on me from a sudden fit of nerves." Checking to be sure it wasn't too tight, he tugged her forward. "That feel okay?"

"Yes." It was nearly a plea, causing Eddie to kiss her neck.

"Patience is a virtue." He breathed, nipping warm flesh. His hands ghosted from her wrist up to her shoulders, then down her sides. Just shy of touching her breasts, he noted the way she tried her best to press back against him. Reaching her hips, he slapped her ass hard enough that she rocked forward, held up only by his arm across her waist.

Trailing the same path back up, he cupped her breast, thumbs teasing her nipples until she dropped her head back against his shoulder with a soft moan. It strained her arms in front of her, the rope keeping her in place. Pinching one just shy of too hard, he twisted it until she cried out in pleasure. Moving around to the front of her, he eased her to her knees, making sure she didn't land too hard on the warm metal bed of the truck.

Leaning forward, he captured a nipple, flicking it with his tongue, grazing it with his teeth as a distraction until she was incoherent, and babbling in broken sentences. While his mouth worked, his hands wandered to the button on her jeans, thumbing it free while he shifted his attention to her other breast. Riley arched against him, seeking more contact, arms tugging at the restraint that prevented her from burying her hands in his hair.

Drawing back, he shoved the fabric down her hips to her knees. "Almost want to just fuck you in your panties. Pull them aside and have you that way. Then I'd make you wear them while you drip my cum," He taunted, brushing the soft cotton. When Riley tried to close the distance between them once again, he drew back. "Behave, or I'll stop."

He warned her, twisting her nipple again. “But this needy side of you is fuckin’ hot.” Hazel eyes trailed down in a slow assessment, taking in every inch of her they could.

The way he drank her in caused goosebumps to break out all over her body despite the warm air and need heating her to the point he bet she felt half mad with lust. It was clouded by confusion when he stood back up, but was overcome by understanding when he made his way back behind her.

Pressing against her back, he forced her to her knees and forearms, a hand pushing her shoulders closer to the truck bed until only her ass was in the air. “Now, this is a view I prefer.” His eyes trailed over her, drinking in the sight. “How about I reward you for being so eager and ready to please?”

“Please. Please, yes.” She begged.

One hand gripped her hip, the other drawing taunting lines from one sharp bone to the other. Licking his lips, his head cocked to the side, almost taunting. “Wonder if you taste as good as you look?” The words brought a darker flush to her cheeks. Not giving her a chance to think too long or hard on it, he slapped her ass, the pale skin turning a faint pink. It earns a squeal, and she instinctively shifts forward, hips dropping down.

“None of that.” The scolding is accompanied by a sudden, bite to the left cheek, earning a sharp inhale. Drawing her back up, his hands grip her hips harder. “If you move again, this ends.” She heeds the warning, the only movement from her, was the rapid rise and fall of her chest with each panting breath.

“That’s my clever girl.” Stroking her ass, he slaps the other cheek, leaving another handprint. Kneeling behind her, he eases her legs further apart, baring her to him. “Just soaked for me, needy little thing.” Leaning forward, he trails his tongue along her slit, dragging it the full length. Dipping in, he flicks it a little, twisting it the deeper he plunges it, before drawing back, sucking in as he does.

She gasps, head falling to rest on her arms, exposing more of herself to him. The urge to rock back was overwhelming, but she forced herself to keep still. When he drags his tongue over her clit, she gives in, pressing back into his face with a moan.

This time, he let her, repeating the motion harder with each pass. Drawing back, he bit the rounded curve of a cheek, earning a startled yelp, but she shoved back harder. A dark chuckle rose from him. “Like that, do you?” His fingers found her wet folds, teasing them while his lips closed around the small cluster of nerves to roll it with his tongue. Riley’s legs shook as he devoured her, fingers starting a slow, torturous rhythm, thrusting in and out of her as his mouth worked. Panting, she tried to work her hips in time with him, earning her a firm slap, skin darkening to a brilliant red.

When she stilled, panting, he resumed, picking up the pace, sucking on her clit hard with a curl of his fingers deep within her. She screamed, an orgasm tearing through her. Her legs gave out, forcing him to catch her from toppling sideways. While she calmed down, he stood up, pulling his wallet from his back pocket.

Revealing a condom, he tossed the leather to the side once it was in his hands. Unbuckling his jeans, he worked them down just far enough to free his throbbing cock, stroking himself a few times before rolling the rubber on. Lifting her back to her knees, he teased her a little, curling his fingers in her again. “Don’t think I’m done with you yet, baby girl. Next time you scream it’ll be my name, understand me?” Lining himself up with her entrance, he dragged his cock through the slick folds teasingly.

"Wish I could fuck that ass until you couldn't sit on a horse for a week, but I don't have anything with me to do that, so I guess I'll have to leave my memory a different way, huh?" Easing himself in until he was fully buried in her, his head dropped back, a groan working its way from his throat. "Damn, so fucking wet and ready. Taking me so perfect." Rolling his hips, he gave another thrust, rocking her up, forcing her arms to bear most of her weight. His words earned a hard shiver from her, a plaintive noise accompanying it.

Sliding one hand from the grip on her hip around, he started working circles in ever harder strokes to her clit. Her body moved with his, hands trying to grip the metal she was tied to, searching in vain for something to grip, her mind racing so fast that no thoughts stuck. He fit in her better than others she'd been with. Some had been so small it wasn't worth the attempt, while others had been overly large, making it borderline painful instead of pleasurable. Hips rolling in search of more friction, she gasped, silently pleading with him for more.

Eddie began to fuck her harder and faster, losing himself with each thrust. "Cum for me Riley, cum on my cock that's so deep in you. Let me feel you shatter on me." He commanded, slapping her clit with the hand that had been teasing it.

The world ceased to exist at the sharp sting that joined the pleasure, adding to it. His name was ripped from her throat, body tensed at the intense orgasm that tore through her. Her world went black, heartbeat echoing in her ears.

Feeling the way she clenched around him, Eddie thrust as deep as she could take him, his own release claiming him, unaware that he was groaning. Slumping over her, he caught himself, making sure she didn't bear his full weight, cheek resting on her back. She was limp against him, breathing becoming steadier.

Neither of them spoke, Riley letting him take the time needed for him to regain complete control of himself. Reaching forward, he removed the tie down from her arms, a smirk curling his lips at the marks on her wrists.

Riley slid down to lay on the warm metal for a moment with a grin clear on her face. "Holy shit." She breathed. A giggle escaped her when she faced him. "If that's just the tip of the iceberg I'd say I want this to keep going, but I know we can't." Sitting up, she started to collect her clothes, acutely aware of the warm, delicious aches that coursed throughout her body. Stretching, she glanced at him, watching as he tossed the condom over the side into the weeds.

Pulling his jeans back up, he buckled the worn, silver belt. "Maybe not tonight, but if you want it again later, we can." he dug out his cigarettes to light one.

Riley gave him a small, sad smile as she finished dressing. "You've been the best fuck I've had in a long time, but I don't think you were here at the moment." Her words earned a confused look. "I'm not mad, not offended, and this isn't me throwing a tantrum; it was a lot of fun, and I learned some new things about myself tonight. Just take a second and think. You were, let's say, caught up when it happened."

She wasn't sure how to explain the situation, having never found herself in it before. It didn't surprise her or offend her like she'd assumed it would. But hearing Dacey's name from him at the moment of his climax was more awkward than words could describe. "Think about it, but for now I'm exhausted and need to find my way to my room. Do you want to head to yours? Check on Dacey?"

"I guess? Are you sure you're okay?" He questioned, following her lead, climbing into the cab of the truck.

"I am. Stop working yourself up." She soothed him, one hand patting his leg. During the drive back to town, Riley could tell he was working over the details of their encounter, trying to find what she was talking about. Pulling into their hotel, she cut the engine and faced him. "Thank you for tonight, Eddie. I didn't know I could enjoy those things, and I'm planning on stealing some of them from you."

Her comment made him snort. "Steal them? Riles you earned them. But now I'm curious how *you* plan on using them."

Her devious smile almost made him feel sorry for asking. "Oh, don't worry, when I do, either she'll yell at you or I'll brag about how much I improved them." Eddie's face made her laugh, bounding from the truck.

"I'm sorry, *what* did you just say?!" He scrambled after her, determined to get answers. Riley waved him off, walking across the parking lot away from him. "Oh, come on now! Don't do that to me, that ain't fair!"

"Oh, it is! I can't say it'll be anytime soon that I get her willing enough to try, but believe me, you'll be the first to know." She assured him, rocking up on her tiptoes, planting a solid kiss on his cheek. "I may have to go to 'The School of Eddie' more often for lessons. Granted, they won't be physical, but if you can teach me more about what you did tonight, I will always pass along at least some details to you."

"Just some? And wait, you expect me to teach you anything without reaping any rewards? How the hell is that even an offer?" He didn't bother slapping her hand when she tapped his nose with a wink.

"If you don't teach me, I'll find a way to either learn myself or find someone who will, which could be a lot more dangerous." She dangled the tiny, mild threat in front of him. Eddie ground his teeth, forced to admit she was right.

"And just when do you think you're gonna have time to learn anything? In a few days, you'll be handling the work of two ranches while I keep ours up and running with your brothers. That doesn't count the time I'll be trapped playing nursemaid to Dacey."

"I'm going to be sure we make time for this. Now, are you ready to face the music of what's behind that door?" She rested a hand on his shoulder. "Because I am in way too good of a mood to break up a fight, so can you play nice with my brother? Please? Focus more on what I said to think about."

With that, she knocked on the door.

Chapter 27

Make My World Go Black

Rider was unsure how much time had crept by, the station playing an endless marathon of the show with no end in sight. Every time he dozed off, Dacey would shift a little closer or roll back onto her back to keep the pain in her ribs at bay, even in sleep. He was in another light doze when the knock came, causing him to sit straight up. Dazed, he staggered out of the bed toward the door when another sounded, louder than the first.

"Hold on, hold on, I'm coming." Checking through the peephole, he was surprised to see his sister and Eddie back. Glancing at the clock revealed it was later than he thought, the bright numbers blinding him with the fact it was a little after three in the morning. It took him a few seconds to fight the rusty chain, jerking it off in the end. Tugging the door open, he planted a hand on one hip, glaring at them, leaning on the frame, body blocking the room from view.

"Why are you back?" Voice low, rough with sleep, and thick with annoyance, he cocked his head to the side. "Thought you were going to stay in her room tonight?"

Riley brushed past him with a look that warned him to shut up while he was ahead. "Plans change, dear brother. Are you ready to go or not? I can't see you sharing a bed with this one here."

Her chin was lifted toward Eddie, where he remained by the door. His grip on the wood was white-knuckled, making Rider wonder if he would find indents later. Eddie bristled at the look he was given. "We had our fun, and she decided I didn't need to sleep over. Why the hell else would I be here if not for her decision?"

Rider faked a laugh. "That's great to know! Guess we're one step closer to being stepbrothers?" He snarked, crossing his arms.

An unidentifiable sound came from Riley as she stalked over to jab him in the chest. "Shut your trap before I shut it for you. Eddie already agreed he wasn't going to argue with you, and if he can handle that promise, you can too. I'm sure if any of us wake Dacey up, she'll kill us all, hurt or not, so do us all a favor and zip it. I love you, I do, but I do not need my brother acting like my choices are a crime." She placed her hands on her hips, staring him down. "You'd be a filthy hypocrite and you know it, so get your ass to that truck while you can walk of your own volition." Riley snarled.

His hands shot up, defending himself. "Okay, okay." One last glare was sent toward Eddie over the top of her head. Snatching his boots from their resting place beside the bed, he pulled them on, patting his pockets to be sure he had everything. "There, I'm ready to go."

"Good, march it." She pointed out the door, tapping her foot.

He did as instructed, but when he drew even with the other cowboy, he paused. “Neither of them deserves you, but I feel the need to inform you even though you’re a selfish asshole, she defended you to me.” With that, he walked out, climbing into the driver’s seat, slamming the door.

Riley sighed, shaking her head. “I’ll deal with him. You have a good night.”

“I plan on it. Good luck with him.”

“I won’t need it.” She marched out, joining Rider in the cab, handing the keys to him. Eddie waited until she was buckled in before closing the door, locking it, and drawing the chain. Turning, he had to refrain from jerking back when he was met with a bleary, cornflower-blue stare.

“Eddie?” Dacey’s voice was little more than a whisper, choked with sleep.

He moved over to her, settling on the edge of the bed to stroke a hand through her hair without thinking. “It’s me, Darlin’.” He whispered, continuing to play with soft locks.

“Why are you back? I thought you were staying with Riley?” She shifted in an attempt to prop herself up.

“Don’t you dare. Lay down. I was, but plans changed, and she brought me back.”

“Oh.”

“I’m going to grab a shower, okay? Do you need anything?” He still didn’t move, working a small braid where he was playing with.

“No.” Curiosity was eating her alive, mingled with a faint tinge of jealousy her sleep-addled brain couldn’t understand. “You slept with her, didn’t you?”

Eddie paused, meeting the stare burning into him. "If I did?"

"It's none of my business." She rolled away from him; the sudden space was cruel as any slap could have been. As he reached for her, Riley's voice drifted through his mind, her words slamming the truth into him harder than any bull. He'd said the wrong name. The very air rushed from his lungs as his hands clenched into fists on the sheets. Dacey sensed a shift in his mood and cautiously rolled over to face him. "Eddie?"

"I'm getting a shower." The man was in the bathroom before she could do more than sit up. Cranking on the hot water, he turned to face the mirror with a scowl. "You fucked it up good this time, didn't you? Can't ever do shit right, even when it counts." He spit at his reflection. Rage bubbled up, choking him until he wanted to punch the man staring back. Knowing it wouldn't do any good, he stripped down as steam filled the small space, fogging the glass to unrecognizable blurs. Self-loathing consumed him while he scrubbed at his skin until it was raw. No wonder Riley didn't want a thing to do with him again outside of learning. He'd fucked it all up.

A knock on the door was all the warning he got before Dacey stepped in. The curtain kept his body from view as he pulled it back to poke his head out. "Any particular reason you're here?"

"You didn't bring any clothes in, so I got some for you." Waving the boxers in her hand, she set them on the toilet lid. "Beats you coming out naked."

"Don't lie to yourself, you'd have liked that."

"Not a chance in hell." She turned, ready to head back out.

"Dacey?" The use of her name caught her off guard.

“Yeah?” Memories of earlier that night teased the edges of her mind.

“Thank you.” He ducked back behind the curtain. “How come it pissed you off that I slept with her?”

She paused, biting her lower lip. “I just don’t want things to become more complicated than they should be. You told me relationships aren’t your thing, yet you still fucked her.”

Turning his face into the spray, he counted down, searching for the right way to answer. “We already talked it over tonight. She’s well aware that I ain’t gonna suddenly want to woo her into marriage, and she made it clear this was a one-off.” Shutting the water off, he reached out to grab the towel. Checking to be sure Dacey wasn’t paying attention, he climbed out, grabbing the ragged, worn-out towel to wrap around his waist. “Does that help? Nothing is going to get complicated.” Pulling on the boxers, he touched her shoulder. “Come on, get in bed so we can sleep. Maybe if you ask nicely, I’ll show you what she learned tonight.”

“Keep dreaming.” Rolling her eyes, she forced herself to climb back into bed. Hissing through her teeth, she changed course, determined to get her pill bottles.

“What are you doing? Get in bed.”

“I need some painkillers, jackass. Mine have worn off.”

He walked past her to the desk where the pill bottle rested, reading each label in full. Making his selection, he shook two out, snagging the half-empty Dr. Pepper bottle for her to wash them down with. Satisfied with his mission, he snapped the lamp on the desk off, leaving only the one beside her to battle the dark with its pathetic, orange glow. Reaching the bed, he joined her under the covers, noting how she tensed up.

"Troubles, bubbles?" Offering the goods out, he waited.

"I never said you could sleep with me. Out, get out. You can sleep on top!"

"Not a chance in hell. This was my room before it was yours, and I made it clear that if you don't like where I sleep, you can sleep on the floor."

Dacey fell quiet, staring unseeing at the shadows dancing above her. They offered no solace, leaving her no choice but to accept the pills and drink. Taking them, she noted how he watched her, eyes darkening when she swallowed. Heat rose within her, devouring small thoughts like kindling.

When he snapped the lamp off, plunging them into full darkness, she forced herself to calm down and relax, steadying her breathing. He rolled, the springs of the mattress protesting the motion, settling in. Just as her eyes closed, they snapped back open to a warm hand resting lightly on her hip, a foot touching hers. Neither of them moved when she tensed up. Holding her breath, she waited to see what would happen. When he just drew in a deep breath, his body relaxing, she gave in, feeling calmer than she had all night. "Night, Eddie."

He gave a low hum, shifting around a little more on the mattress, moving closer to her until she was flush against him. "I have to know, what did he do to you?"

Dacey became tense once more, wondering what Eddie would do if she told him the truth. Chances were high that if she lied, the consequences would be much worse. "Just a kiss." She could feel Eddie become stiff as she spoke.

"One kiss?" The disbelief rolled off of him with those two simple words.

"Okay, so two, but it isn't like what the hell you were doing." She pointed out, her face so warm in the dark she would bet money he could see the glow.

He sat up and faced her unseeing. "He didn't do what I did because someone like him would probably run like a coward from the things I know and do."

"What makes you think that?" She rolled to face him. "Besides, what does it matter to you when you were off gallivanting around with his sister? It's okay for you to have sex, but if I kiss him, it's an issue? Why? Did you want to fuck me instead?"

Eddie wanted to pin her down and reclaim the lips that should have been his alone, to remind her of who should be in charge. Giving himself an adjustment, his mind tempted him with ideas of her begging for more with each slow thrust into her, teaching her exactly what he knew. Instead, he gripped the blanket, regaining control of himself. "I didn't say that, now did I?"

"Surprising. You think with your dick an awful lot." Her voice was so falsely sweet it was a wonder she didn't have cavities talking. It was enough for Eddie, and he rolled to straddle her carefully. An asshole, he was. Careless, he was not.

"I won't deny that, but it's got me in some pretty good places. Nothing is better than a woman wrapped around you, begging for more as you fuck her boneless. But I don't share, that's something that just never stuck with me."

Dacey glared up at him. "So, you can do whatever you want, but I'm not allowed? You think that's fair?"

"Do you even know what you want?" He leaned down closer to her. Just as his lips hovered above hers, she turned her head, biting her lower lip, trying to control the surge of emotions he could see spread across her face. "That's what I mean. You have no idea what you want and that's dangerous, that's how mistakes are made. Bet you didn't even like the kiss, did you?" she didn't respond, just continued to stare at him defiantly. "When I say he doesn't have the first clue of what I do or how to do it, I mean it. I don't go blind into anything unless it's a quick get-a-fix and-go. Otherwise, I make it a point to take my time so the one in my bed knows what they want and how to get it the right way." He rolled off her, turning his back to be done with the conversation.

Dacey lay there a few more moments before one hand reached out to touch his back. "You're right. I don't know what I want. But you have to stop and think; some of the ways you're trying to help me aren't always the easiest to understand. I'll make mistakes and learn from them, but I can't do that when you assume that I'm not able." She exhaled, trying to get comfortable on the scratchy sheets. "Just be there to pick the pieces up without judgment." She drew her hand away, a quiet sigh escaping her.

Eddie rolled to face her, watching her breathing even out. He reached out, tracing her face's curves and contours. His fingertips found her lips, following their outline with the barest pressure from the cupid's bow to the slightly fuller bottom one and back. They parted under his touch, her breath ghosting across his skin. With each pass, he added the slightest increase in pressure and was rewarded with her breathing increasing along with them.

"Do you want this?" His voice was faint, and Dacey questioned if her mind had made it up or if he had truly asked her. Her tongue flicked out, licking her bottom lip, catching his finger by mistake as she did so. Her voice was lost in her throat, unable to find its way to the surface as the featherlight touch on her lips increased in speed. No matter how she tried to form the words, they wouldn't obey her, and a soft moan escaped instead.

He crept closer. "Can you tell the difference now, Darlin'?" All he wanted was to capture her lips with his, but he held back to instead plant a gentle kiss on the tip of her nose followed by one on her forehead. "You'll learn the difference between a man and a boy like Rider in time. And learning is all the fun," he assured her, rolling away for the final time.

She fisted the sheet tightly in her hands. While he got comfortable, she dragged her voice out from whatever hole it had hidden in. "Does it always feel like this?"

"If the one you're with knows what they're doing, it can. It can also be so much more if you let it." She could hear the smile in his reply, and it took all her self-control not to snatch a pillow and clobber him to death with it before smothering herself. Her body was alight with pure, raw need. It begged her to do something, anything, but she laid there and let it build until her fingers twitched involuntarily. Inhaling to the count of six through her nose, she exhaled through her mouth until the count of four, calming herself down.

Eddie listened, painfully hard as he tried to follow along with her. They fell asleep at some point, lulled by the others' calm breathing. Like a gravitational pull, he rolled toward her, holding her close to him as their scents invaded the dreams of the other.

For the first time in years, they slept heavier than either would confess to when they awoke the next morning.

Chapter 28

Tiger in them tight fittin' jeans

Eddie was the first to wake, face buried in warm, silken locks that tickled his nose with each breath he took. They enveloped him in a pool of honeysuckle, so ingrained in her essence it lingered even with the cheap hotel shampoo attempting to smother it. Her body rested against his like she had been built to fill the gaps he wasn't aware were there until he held her in his arms. He carded a hand slowly through her hair as they lay there, drinking in the sight of her in the weak sunlight that managed to break through gaps in the curtains.

She began stirring, causing him to draw away, rolling out of bed and heading into the bathroom. The click of the door woke her, leaving her lying there trying to process why, even after only a few hours of sleep, she felt better than she had in a long time. Sitting up, her ribs reminded her that they didn't appreciate the movement, a sharp pain searing up them. It took a little work to sit on the edge of the bed, where she regained her bearings.

Slow, even breaths centered her as she became more aware of her surroundings. Realizing the bed was empty, save for a warm spot and herself, she looked around. Coming up empty-handed, she stood, freezing in place when he came out of the bathroom, heading straight for the dresser.

He didn't say a word, just sorted through the pill bottles, reading each label until he found the ones he wanted. She was out of soda, forcing him to stalk back into the bathroom to fill the bottle from the tap. Part of him debated on finding a way to boil it, knowing it couldn't be the best. Giving up, knowing she'd drunk worse by mistake, he brought it all out. Gathering everything needed for her, he tucked the medicine bottles into his bag for the trip home.

Walking back to where she waited, watching him work with a curious tilt to her head, he took her hand and poured the pills in, shoving the water bottle into the other. Making sure she took them all, he gave a nod of approval. Satisfied, he stretched languidly, popping his back while Dacey yawned, standing up to pad into the bathroom. She wasn't sure what to say, or if she even should comment on the night before. Voices floated to her from the front room, and she assumed he'd turned the TV on as she washed her face to wake up more.

Finishing up, she headed out to get clothes for the day only to pause as an unfamiliar bag rested on her worn one. "Grant stopped by with the rest of the stuff Josie picked out yesterday. She's still out, and he isn't in any big hurry to get moving either. So, no rush to get dressed and ready." Eddie explained, crossing his legs at the ankle. She rummaged through the clothes, eyes growing wide the longer she did. Most of them were items she never would have bought herself because of the cost alone. She was used to second-hand shops and stealing from cheap discount stores they passed through on the road, though it embarrassed her to admit they were that hard up.

"Oh, okay then." Selecting a short-sleeved pearl snap in mint green with no decorations, she added a pair of jeans. Satisfied with her choices, she paused, looking from them to the bathroom. Eddie waited a beat to see if she would ask for help or resume her stubborn streak.

When she refused to speak up, pretending it was all well in hand, he shook his head and reached out. "Do you need help getting them on? Or can you manage them on your own?" She could tell he was trying to help, and she studied the clothes, worrying her lower lip.

"If you wouldn't mind? I'll do what I can, but it would be nice to have you here if I can't." She admitted, fingers twisting in the fabric. It was a soft, light summer blend cotton, smelling faintly of the barn they had bought it in. Glancing between it and the one she wore, she gave in, holding her hands out with a sigh.

He eased it up over her head, cock twitching when her breasts came into view. Just a few inches separated him from them, and he almost leaned forward to catch one between his teeth. Instead, he shifted on the creaking mattress to adjust himself, picking up the bra on top of the pile. Guiding it up her arms, he kept an iron grip on his will; it was cracking, begging to pull her into his lap. Taking her hips, he spun her away from him, making her face the curtain-covered windows, gliding his hands up her back and hooking it.

He touched the scar there, feeling her stiffen while doing so. There were a thousand questions he wanted to ask, yet none came out. Instead, they worked to get the fresh shirt up over her shoulders where she could button it herself. Dacey was breathless by the time it was done. Standing, she paused before him. It was one thing to face away from him with nothing on her chest; it was another to find herself almost bare from the waist down, feeling his hands on her.

Sensing her hesitation, Eddie looked up from where he'd been getting the jeans ready. "Any particular reason you stopped?"

"How hard would it be for you to do this with your eyes closed?" She asked, half serious, half joking.

"More difficult than you think it'll be. How can I get your legs in without seeing where I'm putting them?"

She mulled over his words. "I can lift my legs so far without difficulty. Can we make that work?" Resting her hands on his shoulders, her left rose, demonstrating.

"I'm willing to try, but don't get your hopes up. I know it's awkward, but only because you're letting it be. If you weren't overthinking this, it wouldn't be a problem. Look, you're injured, we aren't here to do anything, we have no plans of doing anything anyway, and you gotta get dressed. It's all business, Darlin', let's not try to reinvent the wheel here." Eddie explained. His words made sense, they were there to work as a team, nothing more.

Weighing her options, she offered a nod. "You're right, I'm being silly." It was on repeat in her mind, forcing herself to ignore the blush scalding her neck and cheeks. This was Eddie, he wasn't going to look twice at her if they did anything. He'd already admitted as much about Riley; hit it and quit it.

She shivered when the boxers were slipped down, leaving her in just panties and her shirt. Under her grasp, his heart rate and breathing had kicked up, shoulders tense. He tapped her leg, reminding her she needed to step up and out so he could move the jeans in their place. She stared down at his bent form while they were drawn into place.

Trying to ease the uncomfortable moment, he spoke up. "I know what you're going through, for the most part. Broke my ribs once and no matter what, it hurt like a bitch. It gets better in time, but the first few days are gonna be the worst no matter what you do. Your body only heals so fast." Sliding them into place on her hips, he gripped the button, fighting with himself to slip it through its loop. Clearing his throat, he kept talking, thumbing it home. "While it does, don't be too proud to ask for help, even with things like this. It took me all day to ask Grant for anything and by that point I was far past any medicine helping me," he warned, coaxing her to sit on the edge of the bed. Moving past her, he grabbed the brush and ponytail holders she had tossed beside it the night before.

Once he began to brush her hair, she was taken back to easier times when she had been little.

"Will you sit your wiggling ass still for two seconds? I ain't gonna fight you all day, brat." Eddie warned, tapping her shoulder with the brush. Settling in with a huff, Dacey crossed her arms over her chest, kicking her feet while he worked the tangles out. "You know, if you'd learn to do this yourself, ya'd have more time in the mornings to do other things instead of hunting me down to help."

"Josie tried to teach me, but when I made a bunch of knots in her Barbie's hair, she yelled at me. Now I'm not allowed to use them." She whined with a pout.

He rolled his eyes. "Imagine that. Fine. Tonight, after the chores are done, I'll teach you. It'll be a lot harder on yourself than something else, but it'll be a step in the right direction." She started to turn around, earning another warning swat. A heavy sigh was given in response, and he knew she was rolling her eyes now. Resuming her position before him on the floor, she tried her best not to move. "There, get your coat and make sure your gloves are in it. I can't keep finding them all over the yard, understand? Next time I do, I'm gonna hide them." He helped her to her feet.

"No, you won't! If you hide them, I'll hide yours." She countered.

"More like steal them, you little thief. Can't have anything to myself without it growing legs and walking off." He tugged the end of a braid, smiling down at her. She stuck her tongue out at him, earning a laugh. "Go on now, you'll miss the bus."

He didn't have to tell her twice.

Josie burst in with the cool autumn breeze. "Are you ready yet? Pawpaw and Grant saddled the horses for us today! We can ride to the bus stop!" She was giddy, bouncing in place as she spoke. Dacey lit up, hugging Eddie quickly before racing out the door. Following her sister's lead, Josie hugged him as well, laughing when he flicked the end of her nose with a warning to learn something, not just mess around all day.

Pulling herself back to the present, she kept the smile on her face hidden. Even after he'd taught her, she had always sought him out to fix her braids when they were messed up. When it was just her and Josie, she refused to let her sister mess with her hair. The only time Josie was allowed was if Dacey needed a French braid for a run. The sudden urge to pull away overwhelmed her briefly at his touch, tears welling up as he softly ran the brush through her hair.

Eddie never pulled her hair by accident, unlike Josie, who would get too rough by mistake in her haste. He made it a point to take his time, to braid each pigtail with full attention. "There, you're done."

She sniffled, trying to keep from crying in front of him over something so simple as braiding her hair. Eddie kept quiet, pulling her back into his chest and resting a cheek on the top of her head. "I get it, Darlin', I do." He assured her, swaying them side to side, soft and slow.

They stayed that way for a little longer; everything unspoken, the dam within her breaking into rubble. The tears came hard and fast when it did. Eddie helped her turn around, holding her to him. She cried on his shoulder where she had so many times before over lesser things. These were tears from years of frustration, sorrow, and agony that words could never describe; hatred and rage mingled in at the life she had endured without the safety she once again had.

Eddie let her cry, holding her through it with soft, whispered assurances, one hand rubbing her back until the tears ran dry. Dacey was reduced to nothing more than the occasional hiccup that made her flinch. With one last shuddering breath, she drew away, scrubbing at her face with a weak laugh. "Well, that was embarrassing."

"Why should it be? Everyone cries once they've had enough."

"Oh, so you break down like that randomly?"

"Dacey, just because I have a dick doesn't mean I don't have feelings. You can't tell me you've forgotten times you helped me through a rough patch." He pointed out, standing up and heading to his bag. Digging around, he pulled out his clothes for the day and began to get dressed. "But if you tell anyone about this, not only will I deny it ever happened, but I'll make sure that you'll never be a tattle tits ever again."

A broken laugh escaped her, causing her to suck air in through her teeth. Even knowing that while he probably meant it, he wouldn't follow through any time soon. While he dressed, she eased past him to the dresser. She lifted the hat Rider had brought her and studied it. The thunder cloud grey would take her a while to get used to, nothing like the faded black of her old hat, nor the bright black of the new. Dropping it down on her brow, it fell snugly into place, leaving no gaps to cause worry. She found herself speechless, one hand toying with the brim, marveling at the fact someone she hardly knew had been so kind to her. Inhaling, Dacey looked up to meet the rather closed-off expression Eddie wore. "Problem, Cowboy?" She pressed, trying to calculate if it was his imagination on his nerves or her.

"So, even after our talk last night, you're gonna keep giving that boy hope? Or do you just feel pity he bought that for someone not interested?"

Dacey ground her teeth. "I see we are back to our regularly scheduled asshole. That was sure fast."

"Admit it, you wearing that hat's gonna make him think he has a chance with you. Think that's fair?"

She steadied herself, standing to her full height. "I said, and I quote myself, 'I will make my own mistakes, my own choices, but I can't do that when you assume that I'm not able to.' What part of that gave you any illusion I may turn him down? No one decides anything for me other than myself, so chew on that." Stomping to the door, she threw it open, bursting out into the bright sunshine.

Chapter 29

Flowers on the wall

In her haste to get out, she plowed into Grant, causing them both to stumble. Reaching out, he steadied her, looking her over. Realizing he must of seen her looking like she'd swallowed a lemon, she schooled her features into something less pinched and tight. Resting her hands on his forearms, a bright smile was offered his way. "Good morning!"

Grant was taken aback by both the bright greeting and Dacey already being up and moving. While Josie had slept through the chaos from the room connected to theirs, he'd heard it. One thing was certain, this weekend couldn't get over soon enough to give them all space and time to process. It clearly was getting on nerves, wearing them thin and causing lash-outs.

Offering his own gentle smile, he took her in from head to toe. "Good morning, Dacey. Are you doing okay? I was going to let you sleep in this morning while we got the plans in motion. I figured you remember them." The reminder was more of a firm order, earning a frown shot at the dirty walkway.

Dacey tilted her head to the side, hands moving to her hips. "I didn't forget, but there is something all of you forgot. Cash was fine last night because he could tell something was up. Bet you dollars to doughnuts that someone gets their shit rocked if they try again today." Her falsely sweet tone earned a rather unpleasant look.

Hearing them debating in the doorway, Josie climbed out of bed, scrubbing at her eyes to orient herself. Stumbling over, with her hair a wild tangle that floated in snarls around her, she shot them both an annoyed look. Wheeling on her sister, she ground her teeth together, speaking through them.

"Dacey, this isn't up for debate. You're going to keep your ass parked right here with…what the hell are you doing in there?" Josie seemed to puff up with indignation when Eddie wandered out of the room without even a pause. He stalked past the trio, hellbent on the restaurant and the awful coffee it offered.

She refused to be ignored and whirled on Dacey. Her little sister didn't so much as budge, watching Eddie pass by before looking back at Josie. "What the hell was he doing in there? I thought Rider was going to stay? And whose hat is that?" The words climbed in pitch as Josie carried on.

Dacey waited until she ran out of steam to be sure she wasn't going to be interrupted. "First of all, it's my hat, which one would think is obvious since it's on my head." Her tone was cold as she continued. "Second of all, most people would know that if someone came out of a room first thing in the morning, they slept there; which he did. It was his room anyway, before Grant yanked it out from under him, meaning he is, technically, free to come and go as he pleases. When he got back, Rider took off, since there's no room as it is without cramming another grown man in."

"Lose the attitude, Dacey! You will not talk to me like that, damn it!" Josie snapped, taking a step toward her.

"Or what, Josie? What will you do? Spank my ass like a child? Wash my mouth out with soap? I'm tired, tired of all of this!" Dacey threw her hands up, ending with a pained snarl as it pulled her ribs. "I can talk to you how I please when you continue to push me like this!" One hand pressed to the throb, the other jabbing a finger into the opposing chest.

"Ladies!" Grant stepped in. "I am tired of the fighting. Knock it off, please." He attempted to remain polite as he scolded them. Josie looked only mildly ashamed while Dacey ignored him, hands at her sides balled into fists, keeping her mouth closed. "This will be dropped, and we will go and get something to eat and then leave. Understood?" Even if they wanted to argue with him, his tone left no room.

"Fine." Dacey sighed, anger seeping away. "Are the Wheelers meeting us for breakfast?"

"Not today, they're going to meet us at the barns to help load up." Grant replied, gesturing for the sisters to lead the way toward the cafe. "Dacey, I know you hate this, but you really can't help." With practiced motions, he placed his hands in his pockets as he continued to walk. "Josie can handle Cash, I'm sure, and if he's too uncooperative, we can always run him down like we do the broncs. I promise nothing will happen to him without you there. Please stay in the truck and rest. The sooner we get done, the sooner we can get to the ranch and get you set up in a safe place to heal."

She chewed her lower lip, contemplating his suggestions. “Fine, but if I’m staying in the truck, I assume that means that, yet again, someone’s staying behind to watch after me like some kind of nursemaid. As if a truck doesn’t have locks.” Dacey just wanted to sleep until everything went away, not cater to someone’s questions or attempts to talk to her, nor did she want to sit in the heat of the day worried about her horse when she could help.

“You’re damn right you will have someone with you! It isn’t like Cole and Eva are going to let this go without retaliation now, and chances are high that they know what our truck looks like.” Josie pinched the bridge of her nose, knowing where this was leading. “Seth always covers bases, remember? You think those two lumberjacks won’t bust a window out? At this rate, I wouldn’t put it past them to rip a door off like King Kong.” Josie yanked on the door handle harder than she needed to.

Dacey knew she couldn’t slap her sister upside the back of her head, opting instead to scan the room for Eddie. He had chosen to sit at a window booth, looking out across the field of weeds that was housed on the other side of the hotel. Grant spotted him as well, nodding them both over to him as Josie licked her lips and rolled her eyes. “This isn’t over Dacey; you can’t keep running away. I don’t give a damn who stays with you today because no matter what I tell you, you’ll do what you want, anyway.”

“Because I can? What’s your point?” Dacey shot back, taking the seat beside Eddie.

Josie slipped in closer to the window, giving Grant more room to join her. A wicked glare was sent Dacey’s way. “My point is that for some reason, ever since we got here, you haven’t listened to a word I’ve said. You just go gallivanting off like nothing is going to happen and look at you!" She flung her arms in front of her, gesturing at Dacey, almost knocking Grant in the face. "Fresh out of the hospital and I swear you're determined to go back!"

"I am not!"

"Girls, if I have to remind you one more time that this is enough, I will not be as nice about it. Knock it off." Grant snapped, sitting back as the waitress arrived at their table. They fell quiet, staring down at the chipped Formica tabletop, thoroughly chastised.

Eddie snorted, shaking his head, looking at the waitress, one hand slipping beneath the table to squeeze Dacey's knee. She tensed under his touch before relaxing into it, pressing her leg harder into his. A wink was offered to the curious girl, who kept looking around the table, chewed pen poised over her battered notepad.

They were one of only three other tables in the room, and he knew she wasn't eager to stay in the tense atmosphere of theirs. Behind the stretch of counter, the cook was flipping a stack of pancakes. He sang along to the radio as he paused to turn what seemed to be half a tray of bacon. Eddie's attention returned to the waitress, "I'll take a coffee please, cream on the side." He ordered, hand leaving her knee to take her hat off and toss it beside his as he talked.

Dacey wanted to protest, but let it go when Josie looked at her after ordering tea instead of coffee.

"Milk and a coffee, please." She drummed her fingers on her thighs, waiting for their table to be alone once more. Satisfied they had a few moments, Dacey turned back to Grant. "Look, I am sorry about this. We don't argue this much, but you can't blame me, can you? Ever since this all fell apart like a house of cards, she has been insufferable. I get Seth is a threat, but he can't do a whole lot if he's still in the hospital, I'm assuming?"

"You're right, he can't, but Cole, Ben and Eva can," Josie interjected, unwrapping her silverware.

Grant leaned past Josie, pulling a small packet of grape jelly out of the holder to give his hands something to do. Spinning it on the tabletop, he hummed in thought. "Last night, I made a couple of calls. Rest assured, no one will do anything to the other without consequences. That goes for you as well," He aimed at Eddie, not missing the way the younger male tried to ignore him. "Eddie." Grant warned softly.

"I get it, I get it. No beating the piss out of the useless jerk, keep my hands to myself, yada yada." He waved the words away, watching as the coffee was set before him along with a small steel pitcher of cream. Once the drinks were passed out, Eddie ripped open the straw the waitress had placed down for Dacey's milk, blowing the wrapper at her with a smirk. She swatted his leg, holding her breath in a weak attempt to keep from jostling her ribs.

He chewed one end, looking back at Grant. "So, if she's in the truck while we load, which won't take long, why don't I just drive their truck back to the ranch? There's no sense in us sitting around waiting to get the bulls, checks and everything else. Gets her out of the heat, back to the bunkhouse, and settled." He suggested.

The tips of Josie's ears turned red at how easily Eddie ignored her, making all of the choices for Dacey. "Excuse you? You could at least ask me about driving my truck with my sister and horses in it!"

Dacey sat up, kicking Josie in the shin while pouring milk into her coffee without spilling a drop. Josie retaliated while pouring sugar into her mug, smirking when Dacey almost dropped her spoon.

"Ladies, if you're going to behave like children, I am going to have to take you to the parking lot and sort you out the same way," Grant warned. His tone darkened, he was growing tired of their constant back and forth. "Eddie has a point. Dacey can't just sit out in the truck; it would be best for him to take her back." Eddie shot Josie a smirk over the rim of his mug, enjoying how she looked like she had sucked the lemon wedge on her plate. "But once you get there, you need to work on getting everything ready for these guys to be home. You can't just sit with her and do nothing. The barn needs two stalls for their horses, the bulls need to go to the pond pasture so the gate needs to be set up and ready for them; are you sure you still want to take her?"

"Yeah, once I get there, after all that, I can take Jack and check on the heifers to see if any of them have dropped their calves yet. Willing to bet at least one has and you know the damn things like having them in the worst places out of spite."

"So, yet again, you're just going to dump her off as you see fit in order to do as you please? Grant should take her then and you can stay behind. At least then-"

"Josie, it's fine! I'm exhausted anyway! Please, stop speaking for me and let me make my own choice. Eddie taking me doesn't bother me if it means he can do something, and I get a nap." Dacey cut in, gripping her mug hard enough the spoon rattled

"I'm not sure the bunkhouse is fit for a nap anymore, but I figured you'd at least want to get your horses cared for. Once everything's settled down, we can start to clean it up. You, however, can't clean at all. If you need a nap, Eddie can take you into my house to show you where the guest room is." Grant interjected, trying to keep the peace before the sisters began another, louder argument if Josie's bright red face was anything to go by.

They glowered at one another in complete silence. Josie was the first to drop her gaze down to study the thin, almost invisible film of grease that, no matter the amount of cleaning, seemed to stick to everything in the restaurant. Dacey let her head rest against the back of the booth, staring up at the ceiling, stewing over Grant's orders.

"I can clean after I check for calves. The sooner we get them tagged, vaccinated, and switched from the south pasture to the bridge pasture, the better." Eddie insisted.

Grant shook his head. "That can be done later, after everything else, please. No one needs to clean anything at this very moment or tonight, other than changing the sheets and bedding." Standing, he stepped aside for their waitress to begin placing food orders for them. "I'll be right back. While something is fresh in my mind, I have got to make a phone call." Before anyone could say anything, he was turning to the waitress. "Hun, I'll take scrambled eggs with cheese, bacon, toast, and hash browns with gravy on the side, please." Satisfied she had his order, he walked out the door without a look back.

The waitress turned to the rest of the table, offering her bright smile against the dark cloud that seemed to hover over it. Dacey heaved a sigh before placing her order, Eddie and Josie following her lead. When the waitress made her way back toward the counter, they weren't sure how to break the silence that had been thrown on them. Even after she had returned to fill their coffees and left once more, they sat there without a word spoken. Eddie lit a cigarette, chewing the end out of habit, while Josie tapped a fingernail against the glass of her mug in a steady rhythm.

Dacey drummed her fingers against her knee once more, startled out of the quiet when Josie lifted her face to study Eddie.

"I don't know what about you has changed but I will say this, I don't like it. You've gone from the snake in the grass to the wolf at the barn door on a cold winter night. Whatever you have hidden away that you're not willing to share with us, has me concerned. I'm allowed to have this fear as her sister, so before either of you open your traps, let me continue." Pushing her cup aside, she chewed her lower lip, weighing her next words. "Whatever happens from here on out know I'm only playing fair because of her and Grant, not some long ago promise that you never kept your end of." Josie kept her voice steady, eyes never leaving his. "You may have Grant fooled, but the wool isn't over my eyes, Eddie."

His jaw ticked, and he reached over to the ashtray smashing the cigarette out. "You think whatever the hell you want to think, Josie, I won't waste my time trying to stop you. But I will say this to you; when it comes to my life, I suggest you keep the hell out of it." His eyes darkened as he continued. "Never once have you ever had a say in it, so why you think you do now's a mystery to me. When it comes to Dacey, she'll make her own choices and we have to honor them. Because if you try anything against her, your past'll haunt you just as much as mine." He warned.

Dacey wanted to cut in, but looking from one to the other, she knew anything she said would be ignored or shot down. There was an undercurrent left out of the conversation, save for vague hints, that left her more confused than anything. None of them heard the bell on the door ring, signaling Grant's return.

He made his way to the table, unaware of how tense they were as he sat down. “Whatever the hell happened in the time I was gone, better be dropped. I ain’t gonna try eating my breakfast in tension so thick I can slap it on my toast.” Grant warned them, reaching across the table to grab the saltshaker. All three heads turned to look at him with guilt in their eyes. “Is there any particular reason that every time you get near one another, it ends in a bunch of bickering? Nothing seems good enough for you to get along, no matter what the subject is. You squabble like your very lives depend on it, like you’re trying to have some kind of pissing match and I’m sick of it. No more. Do all of you understand me? One more argument and I’m going to have to resort to drastic measures that will only get worse the longer that you continue this.”

Their waitress sauntered over with a tray full of food, handing the plates out. Once everyone had settled down and began eating, Dacey spoke up. “They were arguing over me, because it seems they’ve both forgotten that I’m my own person. Both seem to be under the impression they know what’s better for me, no matter what the other says or what I want.” She quipped in a fake cheerful tone, reaching across the table to grab the saltshaker from Grant.

He frowned at her words, Josie staring down at her plate, trying to wish it into eating her instead. Eddie refused to pretend to feel ashamed, taking a bite of food and chewing it while he stared Grant down.

“I see. Well then, once you’re both back at the ranch, we are going to sit down and work this out. Eat.” The clear dismissal of the subject left them no real choice but to follow Grant’s command. They ate in silence, only breaking it to answer the waitress when she would occasionally check in on them. Once they finished, Grant led them to the door, where he waved them out, in order to pay. Eddie wasted no time opening it to herd the girls through to the truck.

"He isn't going to let this go, is he?" Josie sighed, lighting a cigarette.

Eddie lit one of his own with a shake of his head, blowing a thin trail of smoke toward the sky. "No. If someone hadn't run their mouth like a toddler, we wouldn't even be dealing with him."

Dacey flipped him off as she made her way toward their room. Josie laughed at her sister's antics, following her to help load their things up.

Eddie took a deeper drag, eyes closed to the bright sunshine. Grant made his way out the door to him. "Something wrong?" The older man questioned.

"Nothing you need to worry about. They're packing what's left right now, so I figure we might as well. Won't make sense coming back here today once we have all the livestock loaded up."

"I was throwing things in bags as I talked, so most of the room I was in is done now. Just throw them in the back for us, please." Grant suggested. They reached the rooms where the low voices of the women reached their ears. Dacey almost plowed into him as she emerged from the room with her bag in her hands, staggering back with a grimace at the sudden jostle. He glowered at her, reaching out and taking it away. "Do you think it's a good idea to be carrying this when you're meant to be resting?"

She took a tiny step back, biting her lip. "No Grant, I was trying to help."

Eddie took the bag from Grant, ducking into the room to grab the rest piled on the bed. Grant was always thorough with packing, so he had no doubt nothing would be missed. He headed out to put them in the front of the trailer, ignoring the pair beside the door. Dacey watched him go, clearly frustrated at the situation, and wishing for Josie to hurry up. When her sister emerged, Dacey narrowed her eyes at the smirk sent her way. Following Eddie's footsteps, Josie added everything left to the pile, Dacey watching them work. Eddie paused to softly touch her shoulder. "Get used to it, okay? Getting mad'll only make it worse." Guiding her to the cab, he helped her up.

Josie climbed into the back, opening the sliding window separating them with a tiny smile. "You'll be begging for time off once you get back to work, so enjoy it while you can."

Satisfied they were all loaded up, Grant ducked into both rooms, giving them both a once over, making sure nothing was left. Assured everything was cleaned out, he joined them in the cab, firing the engine up. "Let's go see how much we can fuck up today." He joked, earning a swat from Dacey.

The drive back to the barn revealed only a small handful of people milling around, most of them staff. Josie poked her head into the cab slightly. "They having cowboy Church later?" She asked.

"Earlier this morning for those that signed up. Were you wanting to go?" Grant peeked at her from the corner of his eye.

"No, just curious. Most of the time there are more people around is all." Part of her was relieved the crowd was small, knowing there was less of a chance for Seth's goons to hide. With a nod, she hopped down, moving to where Eddie had helped Dacey. "I'm heading in with Grant. Meet me at the horses once you have the trailer backed up." Passing him the keys, she held them for a moment. "Don't kill my truck or you won't see tomorrow." Leaving him with that warning, she jogged to catch up to Grant.

Chapter 30

Wrecked and Ruined

Dacey watched her go, turning toward their truck. "If you can even get it running, I'll eat my hat. That thing is so decrepit I'm surprised it hasn't fallen apart around us." She mused.

"What do you mean?"

"Remember those old cartoons I used to watch every Saturday? They'd be driving down the road and the next thing you know, the characters are riding just the seats and wheels?"

Eddie shot her a bemused look. "I do, considering it was always my TV you would take over."

"Then you have a good idea of what this thing is like. Held together by smoke, gum, and simple hope."

He snorted. "We'll have to fix that then, too. Just keep adding to the list, Darlin'. It's only money, after all." What he wasn't going to tell her was that, if memory served him correctly, Josie's old TransAm was still in the back of a barn under a tarp. The first chance he got, he was scraping the death trap, knowing when they needed to haul a trailer, his was available. If they really pitched a fit, either he or Grant would get them something safer.

"I never said a thing about you having to fix it! I was just explaining!"

Ignoring her, he unlocked the doors, flinging them open to let the heat trapped within rush out. "I'm well aware of that fact. Just worry about what we need to do now." Rolling the windows down, Eddie turned back to her. "Sooner you stop whining the sooner we get home, remember?"

"Yeah, yeah." She allowed him to help her in, poking through the cupholder in search of a missed stick of gum. When none offered themselves, she pouted. "Can we stop on the way back? Josie packed everything this morning, including my own stupid addiction."

"Doesn't bother me. We need drinks for the road, anyway. How come you never got hooked on this shitty habit?" Waving his pack of cigarettes at her, he put it back in his shirt pocket.

Dacey watched him. "I never cared for the taste. Yes, I'm well aware that makes no sense when I smoke pot now and then, but they're awful. Josie can't have any tastebuds left with those horrible strawberry ones she gets. They're so strong."

"Can't say that I ain't happy you don't. Chose the worst gum flavor instead, though." He teased, pulling up toward the loading chutes.

"We can't all be right." She let her head rest on the back of the seat, staring up at the roof. "You didn't get on my ass about the pot."

"Be a hypocrite then, now, wouldn't I? Nah, I'll leave that ass chewing for Josie to give you. Just make sure that when she does, I'm there to watch." Backing to where he was being guided, he put the truck in park. "Do not get out. These guys aren't going anywhere fast, okay? But no falling asleep until I'm back. Even with them around, we can't take chances."

"Deal."

Patting her leg once, he got out, wandering over to the gate. "I've got two horses for this trailer. One may need to be run down, we aren't sure of his mood yet."

One of the cowboys waiting to let him in nodded. "Wouldn't be the first today, won't be the last. Good luck with him."

"We'll need it." Wandering down the first alleyway, Eddie was forced to sidestep an over-excited pair of girls talking rapidly to each other, tugging their geldings along without a care. Whistling to himself, he was surprised to find Josie with Grant, talking to a man in official wear. Grant spotted him, waving him over.

"Eddie, Mr. VonBokel needs to speak with me about some of the bulls. Please take Josie down to the horses for me?"

Knowing it was a potential deal Grant was speaking about, Eddie didn't argue.

She wasted no time moving to his side, hauling him away when the men turned their backs to continue talking. "Never in my life would I be so happy to leave Grant. It was like they were speaking a completely different language!" She exclaimed the moment they were out of earshot.

Eddie nodded, pulling her out of the way as a small herd of calves ran toward their loading pen. "Yeah, it took me a while to learn what was what. For the first time in my life, I thought it would be the one thing Grant quit trying to teach me, he was so frustrated by the seventh sale I almost lost. It wasn't until I stopped stressing over it that everything clicked."

His words earned a small smile. Josie fell quiet, bracing herself for his reaction to her next question. "Dacey with the men at the load out?"

"You got it. Figured instead of risking her alone taking the quick route, I'd take a longer one to be sure she wasn't in trouble."

"Thank you. Now, I'll handle the horses if you can get everything else? Much as it would amuse me to see Cash bite your face off, Dacey would be more than a little upset at both of us if I did," Josie teased, earning a light shove toward the walls. She caught herself, keeping pace with him as the stall Cash and Buckshot were in came into sight. When they reached it, Josie let out a cry of dismay.

Strewn across the stall were bits of tack shredded into little more than thin strips of leather and cloth. Eddie couldn't help dropping a hand on her shoulder as she covered her mouth to muffle the frustrated cry that welled up. "Son of a bitch." The words hissed from between clenched teeth as he took in the sight. Buckshot was nibbling curiously at a particularly large piece of what had once been a saddle, while Cash bobbed his head in agitation, weaving anxiously in place.

Josie fought the tears that slipped down her cheeks, dashing them away with the back of her hand. She slipped into the stall, trying to keep her voice from breaking as she talked to them under her breath. Cash sidestepped her with a hard snort, spinning himself to point his hindquarters between her and anyone who wished to enter. Ignoring him, she leaned down, lifting a couple of pieces to study them closer. Eddie attempted to follow after her, jerking back when Cash kicked at him with a low throated wicker of warning.

It snapped Josie out of her daze, and she reached out to catch the stallion in a light grip. "I…just let me get him out first." Her mind was blank as she stood there holding Cash, staring at him with unseeing eyes, trying to process what was going on around her.

Eddie felt pity pull at him, hands falling to his sides, clenching into fists while his mind went into overdrive. Reaching out, he double checked she wasn't going to lose control of Cash. Scanning the area, he confirmed nothing was left to use, they'd have to make do. "Josie, take them and go. I'm gonna go look for the security, okay? Come on, let's start getting this ball rolling." His voice was soft, though it managed to gain her attention.

She nodded woodenly, looking from him back to the stall floor. He snagged the halter resting on Silver's wall, tossing it over for Cash's use. She caught it, slipping it on the stallion before he offered up the lead rope. Numb fingers fumbled it from his grasp, though he caught it and held it out again. Josie forced herself to take a deep breath, accepting it to use on Buckshot. Looping it around the mare's neck, she guided them from the stall, the bay stallion danced in place from nerves.

Cash swung his head back and forth, giving the smallest rear when she tugged the halter harder. Unable to keep the fight up, she dug a handful of lifesavers from her pocket to shove at him. Cash lipped them up eagerly, but planted his feet when he realized she was attempting to lead him from the stall.

"Come on, knuckle head, Dacey is in the truck already." She snapped, popping the halter once to gain his attention. Ears swiveled from their prior position, giving her his undivided attention. Whickering, he half ran her over in his attempts to get down the alleyway. "Damn it, Cash! Knock it off, you ding dong!" Jerking the halter, she forced him to look at her until all movement stilled. "There! About time." She took a step back, coaxing Buckshot out next.

"You let Dacey keep this Cujo?" Eddie questioned, narrowing his eyes in return at the look the horse gave him. Snorting, Cash stretched his neck out, attempting to get to Eddie. The man swatted his velvet muzzle, unfazed at the way the stallion didn't even flinch.

"Look, Cujo was a very good watchdog before he became rabid. Be thankful we are at least in that period before this dough dick begins foaming at the mouth." Josie sighed, frowning. "He keeps her safe when I'm not there and I dare you to even hint you're going to do something to him." She gave Cash a good pull to get him moving again. "You think Dacey is wrapped around your finger? Say something against this horse while I stand back laughing as she castrates you with a bendy straw." Josie offered Eddie a weak smirk as she spoke.

He knew she was trying her best to keep a level head. "That's a new one. You come up with the idea of a bendy straw, or did she?" He rubbed at Buckshot's warm nose when she approached him, searching for the treats her stall mate had been gifted. When none were offered, she snorted at him, blowing his hat to the ground. Picking it back up, he patted her neck. "Knock it off now, girl."

"Eddie I…" Josie fought tears once more, voice breaking.

"I know. Just go on." He motioned for her to head to the truck, turning to head in the opposite direction, searching for a security guard. She obeyed, both horses following her down the alley. Eddie didn't wait, instead he let long legs carry him across the barn. Reaching the office, he shoved past riders waiting to be paid, cries of protest following in his wake. Making it to the front of the line, both hands were slammed down on the countertop before the woman seated there. She rose halfway out of her chair to begin chastising him for his behavior, only to be cut off. "I need security, and I need them now." His tone left no room for argument. Something on his face made her sit back down, reaching for her phone.

"One moment please, I'll call them." Punching in a number, she waited a second for a voice to answer. "Yes, can you send Mr. Bradshaw to the front office for security assistance? Yes, I can do that. Alright, thank you." She hung up and looked up at Eddie. "Sir, if you would please wait just outside the door, Mr. Bradshaw will be here in a few minutes. He's coming from across the grounds."

Without another word, Eddie strode out, standing where he had been instructed, ignoring the people rushing past him, casting nervous glances his way. Bradshaw didn't make him wait long, cutting through the crowd with elongated strides. Eddie pushed off the wall to meet him halfway with a hand outstretched to offer a firm shake.

"I got a call from Cara that you needed some assistance?" Bradshaw asked, looking Eddie over.

"Just the messenger, I need you to come with me, please. Someone cut my friend's tack into ribbons."

Bradshaw frowned deeply at the statement. "Can you show me where this is?"

Eddie motioned for the other to follow, turning to head back to the scene. As they drew closer, he spotted Josie leading Grant, talking with her hands waving wildly. Bradshaw clapped a hand on Grant's back when the two men reached each other, offering a smile. "I know I told you I'd see you again, Sawyer, but this wasn't how I wanted to."

Grant gave a half-hearted laugh. "Not how I wanted to be meeting up either, but we're here." He turned to the last male in the group. "Eddie, go on and get Dacey home while we sort this out, please."

"Sounds like a plan. Be safe going home yourself." Eddie replied, nodding once to Bradshaw.

Josie turned to Eddie, stunning him with a hug. "Thank you. Just take care of her," she whispered. He nodded, shocked by the show of affection, before letting her go, turning on his heel to leave. She watched him go until she couldn't see him any longer. Behind her, Grant and Bradshaw inspected the stall, picking up and studying the pieces carefully. Bradshaw rocked back on his heels, looking up at her, a strip of leather from what had once been Dacey's bridle dangling from his hand.

"These are perfectly cut, almost surgically, so whatever did this was either a scalpel someone has or a damn good knife. Did they leave anything else behind? The trees?" Bradshaw asked, rising to his feet.

"No, neither of the trees are here nor the bits. Just this confetti of tack I can't afford to replace. We got here this morning to load everything up, and this…this is it; this is everything we could use to support ourselves." Her voice cracked as it all hit her hard. "We–we have–we have nothing left." Her breathing hitched, panic filling her, and she could feel herself begin to hyperventilate. The harder she tried to draw breath, the harder it became. It was like someone had clogged her lungs with mud, constricting her throat as they did so. "They–they took–they took everything." She struggled to breathe, trying to get enough air her head would stop swimming.

Grant rushed to her side, rubbing her back comfortingly while helping her down to the floor. "Easy Josie, take a second and listen to my voice." He soothed, his hand working steady circles. "We'll find who did this and hold them accountable. But you need to breathe for me. Can you do that?" Worry had him looking up at Bradshaw as she panted. "Go get a medic for me. She's going into shock, possibly an asthma attack." His tone was clipped, jaw clenched. Bradshaw spun on his heel, sprinting down the alleyway toward the area he knew help would be.

Grant turned his attention back to Josie as she started trembling under his hand. "Hey now, stay with me. Listen to me, Josie." He resisted the Green Beret in him, rising up to bark the order to gain her attention. Tear-filled eyes met his as she tried to speak, mouth forming words that never came out. "Just pay attention to the sound of my voice. Bradshaw's gone to get a medic; the sheer weight of this weekend got to you finally. You are going to be okay. This situation can be fixed, and we will take this step by step. Tilt your head up and back for me; let's get your throat more open. There you go." He walked her through the old steps, fear gripping him.

Josie just stared at him as the shaking grew harder. She couldn't stop trembling, head shaking in disbelief at the situation. Soft wheezes slipped from her mouth, rattling from her chest in tiny bursts. Lifting her up into a straight back position, he helped get her arms behind her head, lacing her fingers together. Grant was determined to open up her airways. When that didn't stop the attack, he lifted her up like a bride, heart breaking. She was so light, and he gripped her as if she would float away given the chance. Turning in the direction Bradshaw had gone, he began a quick, cautious jog to get her the help she needed sooner. People leaped to the side when they saw him coming, trying to get out of the way as fast as they could.

When the medic team came into sight, guided by Bradshaw, he picked his pace up to meet them. They took over without hesitation, getting Josie settled on the floor of the barn to begin their work. Grant paced behind them, trying his best to keep an eye on her, ready to step in the moment she needed him.

Bradshaw took pity on him, taking his arm and leading him over to the other side of the alleyway. "She's going to be fine, these guys know their stuff. If I didn't trust them, they wouldn't even be in this barn right now." He tried to assure Grant, offering a light pat on the back. "This is easy to treat at least, they won't send her off like her sister." Bradshaw waved away the look Grant sent him. "I know about last night, hell pretty much everyone does by now. Believe me, they have questions, but we all agree those can wait a day or two. Your phone call to Dean, who we both know called his brother-in-laws, also didn't leave anyone much room not to be running their mouths today. What do you want me to say once the hordes descend on me?"

Grant couldn't argue with him when the names were brought up. The girls had insisted nothing could be done against Seth and his cronies, but they didn't have the connections he did. "Tell the masses whatever you want; the truth, a lie, hell, I don't care. Those that want to run their mouths with bullshit don't deserve anything but to be straightened out. If they want the truth and believe you, that's even better for us to help build a case against this woman beater."

Bradshaw's face was unreadable at the mention of abuse, but Grant didn't miss the way his hands curled into tight fists at his sides. He nodded once in understanding, leaning against the wall to watch the medics work on Josie. She was slowly responding and Grant caught himself losing some of the tension that had gathered in his shoulders.

Her eyes sought his, panic filled until they locked together, and he watched as she calmed a little. “Do you have anything particular in mind for the one who did this to them?” Bradshaw asked, offering a nod to a young rider passing by them.

“Nothing I can get away with legally. I’m sure you understand?”

“Absolutely, I do. But I assure you, Grant, my men and I will look into who shredded their tack, although it seems like this lead won’t be too hard to find or follow. Pretty sloppy work, if you ask me.”

Grant ground his teeth together. “More like arrogant. Daddy’s money has always kept him safe back home, he assumes it means it’ll keep him safe here. Hopefully, I get to watch his face when he learns the hard way that isn’t how this is going to work.” A dark smile crossed Grant’s face so fast Bradshaw couldn’t guess if he had really seen it or not.

“On that note, I need to get the rest of my men gathered up and get to work. I’ll stop by this evening once we have everything where it needs to be. Need to get the girls’ statements on all of this as well.” Bradshaw tipped his hat.

“Tonight? You can’t wait until tomorrow?”

“Unfortunately, no. The sooner we get this done, the better. I know they’ve been through a lot the last forty-eight hours, but I can’t push this off. If I do, my boss will question if I was letting them get stories straight. The only saving grace they have right now is the fact they’re separate. Josie is obtaining medical attention and Dacey is under the influence of heavy painkillers.”

Annoyance flashed along Grant’s nerves as Bradshaw droned on at him, but he forced himself to smile. “You’ve forgotten Dean is already well aware of the situation at hand. He intends to visit the girls tomorrow, per my request, but if you wish to speak with them tonight about the current issue, then that's fine." Grant placed a hand on a stall wall, the other on his hip as he turned his face to Bradshaw. "But I assure you that he wouldn't care much if another day goes by," Grant reminded Bradshaw sharply.

He hated being short with the man he considered a friend, but his temper was fraying faster than it had since the war. A migraine was brewing at the base of his skull, the sharp ache creeping toward his temple.

Sighing, he rubbed his forehead for a moment. Reining it in, he reminded himself that picking more fights wouldn't do any good. "Sorry, Arthur, I'm just ready to be home and settled in. They've been through more than I can imagine, and the last two days haven't been easy on any of us. Feel free to swing by tonight and let me know what you've found, please."

"I understand, Grant. I know I was a little out of line trying to take control, it's just a habit at this point to take the lead and make sure things get done," Bradshaw offered.

Grant gave him a single nod as Josie was helped to her feet. It seemed like the medics were wrapping up their treatment, checking her over for lasting problems. He moved over to her, catching her wrist in a light hold when she tried waving away the medic speaking to her. "Is she good to go?" Grant asked, resting his hand on her shoulder.

"I think she should be okay. Just make sure she rests today as much as possible. Whatever sent her into an asthma attack can always cause a repeat if it isn't found." The man adjusted his stance, filling Grant in on what to do if it recurred. Beside him, Josie continued to shift from one foot to the other until the explanation was done, and they were left alone with Bradshaw. He made his way over to them at Grant's wave, looking Josie over quickly as he did so.

"Everything in order?" he asked as he drew level with them.

"Yeah. See you tonight?" Grant was already letting Josie walk toward the doors.

"See you tonight," Bradshaw affirmed, tipping his hat and walking away.

"It's going to be a long ass night." Grant sighed, moving to catch up with Josie.

Chapter 31

Something 'bout a truck

Whistling along with the radio, Eddie drummed his fingers against the worn leather of the steering wheel, unsure of what to say or even do as he glanced at Dacey. She had been oddly quiet as they drove, lost in her head, processing what he'd told her when he had gotten settled in the truck. The way her face paled still haunted him, and he ran over a mental list of saddles that sat unused in the barn. Most were in rough shape, waiting to be sent off for repair, whenever either of them remembered to. He sighed, shifting in place on the seat and digging a smoke from his shirt pocket, shoving the lighter in. Chewing the butt, he braved the main thought haunting him. "We can replace tack, Dacey. We couldn't replace the horses if anything happened to them." He hedged.

The look she shot him would have made a lesser man piss his pants, sitting up to the height her ribs would allow. "You can replace them, Eddie. Josie and I can't even afford to feed the horses and ourselves at the same time, let alone buy brand new tack. Even used, it's worth more than we have." She snapped.

He fought the urge to knock his head off of the steering wheel, refraining from retorting with something less than kind. "I'm going to suggest we drop the subject for now before we are trapped in a screaming match for four hours. Or I resort to throwing you out and leaving you to be picked up by whoever comes along so I can have a chance at sorting things out."

"Cowboy, you and I both know you wouldn't throw me out like this." Dacey sighed, trying to find a comfortable position, but doing as she was asked. Pulling her hat off, she dropped it between them, head falling back to stare at the roof.

"Take a nap, ain't gonna hurt anything for you to rest." He reached out and turned the radio up a little, feeling her study him. "Can I help you?" An eyebrow was raised as he glanced over at her.

"Not unless you can make the roads less like washboards. Someone can't comprehend how a roller works." Her words earned a startled laugh from him, and she couldn't help but grin.

"Sorry, Darlin', I know it sucks, but I can't do anything about them." Eddie rested his arm on the back of the seat, playing with her hair. "Just get some sleep. You're not missing anything we can't come back and see later if you really want to."

Dacey hummed softly in reply to his words, eyes already closed, focusing on the fingers that shifted from her hair down a cheek before they disappeared. Just as she started to drift off, Eddie hit the brakes, swearing loudly. A cry of pain left her lips, hands gripping the door handle as her own voice joined his. When the truck and trailer finally slid to a stop, both were breathing hard. "What the hell Eddie?"

He didn't reply, just leapt from the truck and rushed around to the front, disappearing when he knelt down. Dacey struggled with her seatbelt for a moment before getting it off and throwing her door open. "Eddie!" She held her ribs, moving to the trailer and checking on the horses. Cash was snorting, bobbing his head in displeasure as he kicked at the wall behind him. "Easy, easy, buddy." She soothed, digging around in her pocket to offer him a lifesaver.

He hoovered it down, ears still pinned, but the kicking stopped. Buckshot stood with her head high, ears pinned and eyes wide as she pawned the floor, sides heaving. "You're okay, I promise you're both fine." Her soft voice coaxed Buckshot to lower her head, nose poking out to be rubbed. "There you go, lovely, you're alright." Once she was sure the horses were safe, she made her way to the front of the truck, intent on yelling at Eddie in the middle of the road until the cops came. Those thoughts were chased from her head when she rounded the cab, skidding to a halt, mouth falling open. "Is…is that a puppy?" The pain in her ribs was forgotten when the bundle of dirty fur in Eddie's arms whined.

"No, it's a baby cow. What the hell does it look like?" Eddie shook his head, lifting the puppy higher to inspect it. "She's filthy, and I don't see or hear any others around here. I'm going to double check though, if you could hold her for me?"

He offered the wiggling mass toward Dacey, who quickly took her. "Hi baby, aren't you a lucky girl, huh? Getting mean old Eddie to stop for you like he did." She cradled the little body closer to her chest, trying to keep from wincing. "We're taking her home, right?"

Eddie gave one last look around before he sighed. Even if they had found a house nearby, or even another puppy, he knew it would be a losing battle against Dacey. "Yeah, get her in the truck. But she's your dog, I already have one, and she's enough trouble without adding another. I'm going to warn you now, Whistle and Ace aren't going to be the biggest fans of her at first and Josie is going to have a complete fit."

"You act like I have never had a pet before. Remember when you got me Missy?"

"Yeah, that was a mistake and a half, I assure you."

"No, it wasn't. She was a good girl, and very smart."

"She was a pain in my ass like her owner! I can't tell you how many times that damn dog would sneak into my bunkhouse and sleep in my bed after somehow getting completely soaked."

"She loved you. You just didn't like her brand of love." Dacey set the puppy in between them, climbing back into the cab. She wiggled, tail wagging a mile a minute as she tried to climb back up on Dacey. It earned a laugh and a quick head rub. "You need a bath so bad! What do we name you? Huh cutie?"

"Roadkill." Eddie supplied, starting back down the road.

Dacey shot him a dark look, stroking the messy fur. "Asshat. You cannot name a puppy something like that."

"Well, had I not been paying attention, she would have been."

"Eddie!"

"Okay, okay! Just think about it. No need to rush it and call her something stupid you'll hate later on."

Dacey rested her head back against the seat again, face turned toward him. "Where did you come up with Whistle?"

"She comes to it, and when she was about that age," he gestured to the puppy, "she made this stupid noise when she would run around the bunkhouse that sounded like a kettle whistle. So, it fit her pretty well."

She hummed at his words, tossing around a couple of names in her mind. “Queenie, Lady, Koda, Bambi. Alala”

“How the hell do you go from the typical Lady to fuckin’ Bambi?”

“She kind of looks like a deer.”

“I like Koda, but again, it isn’t like you gotta name her this very second. Try going back to sleep and think on it when you don’t look like the strain of tryin’ to find one is going to break your brain in half.”

“Okay, okay. Since you won’t give up ordering me around, I guess I can.”

Eddie kept his mouth closed, longing to tell her just how many ways he could order her around. He wanted to spank her for her insolence and the sass she continued to aim his way. He did none of it, just fished a toothpick out of the cupholder to chew on. Her eyes drifted closed, the puppy snuggling closer as she dozed off. Turning the radio up to whistle a bar or two of whatever song came on, he earned a curious look from warm brown eyes. Some he would whistle louder to see what she would do, while others he kept the same tone and pitch he always did. With each change, she would tilt her head one way, then the other, but she never left Dacey’s side where she had laid down.

“I wonder what kind of dog you are? Besides lucky, so don’t try to tell me the obvious.” He teased, lighting a cigarette. Her tail thumped quickly, whining at him. “You know I’m going to get you to come over here, can’t just lie by the fly catcher over there.” The last part earned him a pathetic, half assed swat, Dacey cracking one baleful eye open. He laughed, reaching over to run a hand down her cheek, only to be met with a light slap.

"Shaddup." She grumbled, turning her head toward the window. He caught the smile she was trying to hide, shaking his head before he dropped his hand to stroke the pup. "'M not even 'sleep."

"You're not even speakin' English there, Darlin', pretty sure that you're close to it. I'll leave you alone."

"Right." She yawned, crossing her arms.

"I will, I promise you." A warm, pink tongue licked his hand, the puppy butting her head further under, searching for more contact. He scrubbed at her a little longer before drawing back to hold the wheel, his hand resting on the door. She whined, tail thumping on the seat, shifting around in place. "Nope, you have to come over here if you want any more attention. I told you I'd get you over here one way or another." Eddie teased. Warm brown eyes watched his every move as a huff was aimed toward him, front paws tapping at the seat. A grin crossed his face when the small body moved an inch closer as she tapped at the seat again with a small bark. "Well, you're getting there, little bit, but not good enough."

She gave up, sitting up to start yapping at him, head whipping side to side, yelling at him in her own language. Dacey was the first to break, laughing at the annoyed shouting match that had started. "How on earth do you expect me to rest when you keep bickering like children?" She scolded, one hand pressing on her chest.

Eddie's laughter joined in, the man offering a slight rise of one shoulder. The puppy had stopped her tirade at him in favor of trying to crawl across Dacey's lap, seeking her attention. "Alright, alright. That mean, old Cowboy being awful to you? I know, he's always so rude to the ladies." Dacey soothed, rubbing her head.

"Hey now, I ain't always rude. Only when I have to be."

"So, from the moment you wake up to the time you go to bed?"

Eddie shook his head, faking hurt. "Go. Back. To. Sleep."

"You're so demanding and yet you keep waking me up."

"I'd like to point out I wasn't the one throwing a little temper tantrum at the fact I wasn't getting attention. That would be the fuzzy menace sprawled on your lap like she owns the place." Eddie countered.

She shook her head, trying to settle back into a more comfortable position. "How much longer till we're back at the ranch?"

For some reason, it stung a little she referred to it as the ranch instead of home. But just as quickly as the thought crossed his mind, he shoved it away; they had been gone six years, he needed to understand why it wasn't home anymore. He tapped the steering wheel, gauging where they were in comparison to time. "About another hour and a half. You have plenty of time to sleep." Dacey offered him a nod, facing him once more, watching him for a moment. He raised an eyebrow. "Something on your mind? I'm not an exhibit in a zoo."

"Just thinking, nothing you can do about it, though."

"Try me."

"Well, let's see," she drawled almost mockingly, "we have no tack, no money to buy more, I'm too broken up to get a job to save up for more, how do we afford food for the four, now five, of us. I can't clean shit, so Josie has to do it all alone in the bunkhouse if we stay." Each thing she listed was ticked off a finger.

"You're going to stay," Eddie interjected harshly. "Period, point blank, not another word on that, do you understand me? As for everything else, there ain't a single point in worrying about it right now because it's out of your hands. You need to just focus on getting better before you sit here panicking thinking about everything else," He scolded, the hand that gripped the steering wheel tightening.

Dacey clenched her jaw to keep from spouting back he had no right to tell her not to worry when he had everything he needed at any given point. Something must have shown on her face because Eddie glared at her so wickedly, she shrank back against the seat. Even the puppy whimpered. "Dacey Mae, I'm only going to warn you once, so listen carefully; throw your tiny pity party, then do me a favor and pull your head out of your ass. You're smarter than this, don't try to tell me you're not or I'll knock some sense back into you." His fingers splayed on the steering wheel in frustration. "The fact you had the audacity to try telling me to my face that you and your sister are going to be living in a filthy home starving is a downright insult to not only me, but to Grant. What the hell made you think even for a moment that either one of us would sit back watching you struggle to survive? I may be a jackass, but I ain't a heartless jackass."

She dropped her gaze from his, blinking away the tears that gathered so he wouldn't see them. Scrubbing a hand over her face and trying her best not to jar her ribs, she inhaled slowly. "What drives me insane is you always seem to be right one way or another when it comes to rational thinking for other people. You ain't got a lick of common sense for your own wellbeing." He flipped her off, but she plowed on. "You really don't. You can sit there snapping at me like an angry dog about how I'm being stupid, but yet, you never care for yourself."

"I ain't the one we need to worry about right now."

"How come? You think it's fair you can sit there telling me how my life's gonna go from now on, but when I offer help I'm ignored? It goes both ways." Dacey let her head drop back once more, eyes closed. "I can't keep doing this song and dance until the jukebox breaks; at least not right now."

He let the conversation die despite his need to quip back. Instead, he chose occasionally to glance over at her, looking for new details that had been missed since he first saw her. The freckles that dusted across her nose and cheeks were more prominent, highlighting a single thin, pale scar that traced a path from her left cheekbone down to her jaw. Eddie wondered if her dad or the piece of shit following them had caused it or if it had been a true accident.

Hazel eyes skimmed from the scar down to the hollow of her delicate throat, across her ample chest to the bare arm closest to him. His lips quirked up, she had always refused to wear regular shirts in the summer no matter how much she burned or how much Josie yelled at her. Even as a child, Dacey had worn tank tops in an effort to keep cool, although Eddie tried to remember a different reason she had given him. Freckles stood out against tanned skin, though there were far fewer on her than he himself had. The thought brought up a memory long lost. She couldn't have been more than ten at the time, all knees, elbows, and popsicle grins at him from beneath a hat much too large that she refused to give up.

"You have stories in your freckles." Dacey mused from where she sat cross-legged on his couch, inhaling her third slice of pizza.

Eddie paused on his way to the kitchen to grab himself another beer and a soda for her. "What the fuck do I have?"

"Stories, you know, like how stars do? If you follow them just right, you can even see what the stars draw. Remember? Pawpaw taught me how to find Orion and them?" She twisted her little body to look over

the back of the couch, keeping him in her sight. "The stars tell stories of what they make, he told some of them to me. So, that means you have stories in your freckles. You're lucky, I don't have hardly any. Pawpaw says if I don't start wearing something on my shoulders, I'll get more, so I keep trying, but nothing really helps. I think he lied."

Eddie didn't know what to say, stunned at her innocent observations. Wordlessly, he had carried the drinks back with only a shrug. "He didn't lie, I've just had a lot more years out in the sun than you."

She accepted the can with a tiny frown. "I guess."

The town coming into sight jerked him back to full attention. Dacey had finally fallen asleep where she sat, the puppy out like a light cuddled against her. Every wave offered by those on the streets was returned only half-heartedly, as he prayed no one would question the blonde beside him. Chances were, no one would. It wasn't a secret that he liked to spend most weekend nights at the bar searching for the right woman to take home, but something made him want to keep Dacey to himself a little longer without nosy neighbors trying to catch sight of her to confirm any suspicions.

They wouldn't be able to hide for long, reality wouldn't work in their favor like that, but Eddie could hope it would last for at least the next few weeks. They needed peace and quiet to settle in and sort things out between all of them. He dreaded the new fallout that was sure to come between him and Josie when she realized where he planned on putting Dacey while the bunkhouse was cleaned, stocked and made ready for their return.

He contemplated stopping at The Pit to grab something for later, but opted not to when he realized that if he stopped, Dacey would make herself get out. Chewing the butt of an unlit smoke that dangled from his lips, Eddie mulled over the options he had once they arrived back at the ranch. He could wake her up right away only to fight her tooth and nail to keep her from helping get the horses settled, or wait until they were at the ranch and already heading to his room. The last time Dacey had been in his room was the day they had buried her grandpa. Even Josie had been in with her braiding the fine locks back into a single plait. Josie had asked Eddie for help keeping Dacey calm as the two of them could during the visitation, and he had agreed at the time without a second thought.

Eddie gave himself a slight shake to force himself to pay better attention to his surroundings. Spotting the driveway, he turned down the long lane at last with a soft sigh of relief, ready to see the ranch after the weekend they had endured. Rounding a slight curve in the driveway, he spotted a truck he didn't recognize. When Ace and Whistle didn't rush to sound their warning at the strange truck he drove, the confusion in him grew into a blend of concern and rage so quick it almost choked him.

The man that leaned on the hood of the strange truck wasn't as complete a stranger as Eddie had assumed. He recognized him from the brawl they had found themselves in at the bar only a few days prior. All confusion faded in the face of the pure hatred that swelled in its place when the man shoved away from the truck to tuck his hands in his pockets and start walking idly toward them.

Chapter 32

Don't back up, don't back down

"Wake up, Darlin', we got unwanted company." Eddie tapped on her knee, earning a soft groan as she stirred. "Come on now, get with the current times."

Dacey sat up with an owlish blink, one hand pressed against her ribs. "What's going on?" She asked, voice thick with sleep.

"Nothing good." Eddie clutched the steering wheel so tight the top was slightly twisted. The puppy on her lap sat up on the seat, raising her hackles at the tension thick in the air, causing the hair along her spine to bristle up with a growl.

"Fuck me a running. What the hell is Ben doing here? How did he get here? Where are Cole and Layton, because they're never far from him?"

"No idea, but I know we need to think fast."

"Anyway you can turn around?" Dacey asked.

"Not with how they parked and they know it. The only way we can get out is back this big fucker back down the driveway clear to the road and that's tricky even without the need to hurry it up." He ground out, watching the men approaching the truck. "We're outnumbered without taking into consideration that you're mangled up."

"Thanks for that, Captain Obvious." She quipped. "What concerns me is where the moronic ringleader is. This group isn't smart enough to try planning something this elaborate on their own."

Eddie wasn't given a chance to answer as the cold steel of a barrel pressed against his temple. "Out. Now." Seth's voice left no room for argument as Eddie shut the truck off, easing his hands off the steering wheel to hold them up. The door was opened for him, Seth stepping back for him to climb out. Both eyes were blackened, and his bottom lip was stitched closed on the left side. His entire face was swollen, and she longed to make a comment about what playing with dangerous things had gotten him already.

Before he did, Eddie risked a glance at Dacey. "I swear to you, this'll be okay. Keep strong. I'm not letting anything more happen to you." His voice held a weight she hadn't heard before, helping slow her thundering heart. A nod was all she was able to offer in reply as Seth jerked Eddie out the rest of the way.

"Walk to the barn. Boys, get the little whore out for me, would you? She and I have a few things to discuss in the hayloft." Keeping the gun pressed to Eddie's back, Seth marched him toward the barn at a rapid pace.

Ben wrestled Dacey out, the young woman keeping a scream suppressed at the rough treatment of her ribs, vision going white as a fist landed in her stomach. Vaguely, she was aware of the puppy's howling, barking fit suddenly stopping with a short yelp. Bile scalded her throat at the thought one of the thugs had injured the innocent animal. Twisting in an attempt to escape along with desperation to check on the puppy, she was met with another blow to her jaw, causing her head to snap back. Tendrils of blinding pain laced from the point of impact over the entire cheek. A second blow jerked her head back in the opposite direction, ripping a cry from her.

"Move faster." He snapped, grabbing one braid to haul her after the others. Her scalp felt like fire was creeping across it everywhere he pulled, feeling a few strands ripped free. Half blinded by pain, she did her best to keep up, forced to jog to do so. Ben gave another hard jerk, yanking more hair out as he tossed her through the doors to the unforgiving floor. Eddie lay in a small pool of blood that oozed from a large gash across his temple where Seth had struck him hard with the butt of his pistol.

"Eddie?" Her voice was almost inaudible. "Eddie…Eddie!" By the end she was screaming his name, hands raking the straw strew stone to get to his side. A harsh kick delivered to her stomach rolled her to her back, breathless, vision bursting with black pinpoints. Mouth open in a silent scream, Dacey tried to drag a breath into aching lungs to no avail. Little by little, she was able to pull in the oxygen she needed, wheezing with each breath.

Voices that sounded like they were underwater floated over top of her, never clear enough to understand. The world spun so quickly it made her stomach lurch as Ben hauled her onto his shoulder effortlessly to follow Seth up the ladder into the hayloft. Dropping her onto a bale, he left, going back down to the main level without another word, clapping a hand on Seth's back when he passed. All Dacey could focus on was the sharp ache in her ribs, the bright sting on her scalp, anything to ignore Seth growing closer to.

Crouching down to study her, he rolled her onto her side, so she was facing him head on. “It’s such a shame you have the worst attitude between you and Josie. I would’ve had a harder time breaking you like I did her, though it would have been worth it.” He gave a mocking sigh, reaching out and forcing her to watch him. “But now I have plenty of time for me to break that spirit, don’t I you little bitch?” A hand connected with her face, leaving a bright red print.

Panic flooded her system, instincts screaming, pleading for her to do something, anything but lay there. Her subconscious whispered vague horrors; Eddie was dead, Seth was going to torture her to the point of insanity before killing her. Each one that followed only grew worse until she ground her teeth together, trying to spit in his face. Like hell she would go out like a lame horse stuck in the mud.

Seth sneered at her pitiful attempt, backhanding her hard enough her head jerked to the side. “None of that, you little bitch.” His tone was far too chipper, too happy. It made her stomach lurch. Still, he pressed on. “All the problems, questions, the sheer amount of trouble you’ve caused, all of it ends here, today. That pathetic washed-up Cowboy you were screaming for? Ben’s handling him, while Cole and Layton are just waiting for your whore of a sister.” She tried to roll over onto all fours, screaming in agony when he kicked her legs out from under her, causing her to land hard as rock.

“I’m sure you’re well aware I plan to drag her home to where she belongs. You see, people started getting nosy, wondering where my bride-to-be was after you disappeared with that little stunt. Do you have any idea how hard it was to explain, to lie?” He punched her, earning another sharp scream. Blood began rushing from her nose as it broke, painting her lips and chin a brilliant crimson in the low light of the hayloft.

He rocked back on his heels to admire his work. "I have to admit, it's rather satisfying to see you like this, it helps keeping your mouth shut." Seth pushed her over onto her back, rising to tower over her. "I had so many ideas about how to make you scream, how to make you bleed and pay for it all. But now that I have you here, none of them seem even close to what I really should do." His hands went to his buckle, loosening it.

Dacey coughed, dragging breath into burning lungs, the metallic taste of blood coating her tongue. Attempting to force herself into a sitting position, she clenched her fists so tight blood dripped from the tiny cuts her nails caused. It joined the drops from her nose, leaving speckles like morbid breadcrumbs along the old floorboards. If he was going to kill her, she wasn't about to die at his feet like a dog. Terror was choking her worse than the blood, heart pounding so loud in her ears she couldn't hear anything over the thunder of it.

When he stood up to slide the buckle free, she took her chance. Knowing what he planned to do, she fought the tremors that wracked her body. Fingertips of fear traced her spine, breaking goosebumps out all over. Horror began to war with anger. How dare he stand there like that? Looking down at her like she was little more than a bug he'd found to torment? Determination started to sink in, adrenaline flooding her veins until little remained but a single thought; get away.

Seth watched her use the bale closest for support, hauling herself to her feet, swaying in place as the room blurred before her eyes. He offered her a mockingly amused look, giving a fake clap of approval, looking her over from head to toe. "Going somewhere?" Stalking to her, Dacey felt a surge of fear spread back out through her veins the closer to her he got. Spinning on her heel, she attempted to make a dash for the hole in the floor and the slimmest chance at escape. He caught her easily, kicking her legs out from under her without a second thought, bringing her down in a crumpled heap. A soundless scream filled her throat on impact as one of her ribs broke under the stress of it all. She couldn't breathe, couldn't think, as stars blossomed behind her eyes.

"Such a beautiful sight." Seth crossed his arms as he watched her scramble to her knees, trying to suck in a breath. "Are you having troubles, little bitch? Want some help?" He strode over to her as she crawled away, still determined to make it to the ladder. "Here, maybe this will be what you need." His foot connected once more with her stomach, causing her to collapse into a crumpled heap, attempting to curl in on herself. Hatred reared its ugly head, baring fangs of pure, unfiltered loathing at the man above her. It was familiar, only one other time had it come on this strong and that scenario had ended in her favor. Now, she was positive that, while she wouldn't give up, it still wouldn't end her favor.

"Come on now, surely that smart mouth has something to…" The words were cut off as a hand grabbed him by the back of the neck, lifting him off his feet. Their tips were white with the force behind them, cutting off Seth's air supply. He did his best to free himself, hands closing around the tanned wrist behind them. It did no good, the man was unforgiving.

"That smart mouth's a bit busy at the moment. Maybe mine can help you." Eddie's voice was liquid steel as he threw Seth away from Dacey. He landed in a heap against a stack of hay, a few bales falling onto him.

"There we go, just where you belong." Striding across the short expanse of wooden floors, he loomed over the man, trying in vain to untangle himself from the bales. "Although I think I have a better place for you." Eddie dragged Seth to his feet by the front of his shirt until they were nose to nose. "Do me a favor, will you? Tell the Devil I'm coming for his throne when you see him."

Seth's eyes grew wide at the whispered words. He never got the chance to reply as Eddie lifted him high as he could before flinging him down with all the strength he could muster through the hole to the stone floor below. He watched emotionlessly as Seth hit, bounced once, and lay still. Ever so slowly, a pool of blood began to form under him, creeping ever closer to the random bales and other items that lined the aisle of the barn. Satisfied, Eddie turned to rush over to Dacey, sliding on his knees at the last foot or so.

"Hey, easy now, I'm here." He refused to let his own fear cloud his vision. If she died–no. He cut that train of thought off, helping her up onto her feet. One hand swiped away the blood trickling into his eyes from the wound on his head, determined to look her over. "Talk to me, Dacey, tell me what that useless waste of space did."

Dacey was breathing in short pants. Anything more hurt too much to continue attempting. "Broke my ribs, and my nose, I think." Her legs shook with each step like a newborn foals, and she cursed the entire way down. Eddie's jaw ached from how hard he was clenching it to keep from babbling hollow words that wouldn't help either of them. When they reached the bottom, he gave the body a swift, hard kick that rolled it face down. Dacey mustered a half-hearted one, spitting a glob of blood down with a look of pure loathing. "Finally, where you belong."

The sound of tires on gravel drew their attention to the barn doors. Eddie slipped an arm around her waist, keeping her steady as they made their way to see who had shown up. As Grant's truck pulled into view, realization seemed to slam into them both. Dacey shook away the support offered, sinking to the unforgiving gravel drive, head between her knees as she fought off a panic attack. "The others?" She whispered as Eddie joined her on the ground, hand rubbing circles so light on her back they were almost missed.

"Ace and Whistle smashed out the picture window of the house to get out. Ace is pretty cut up from it, but we have a vet we will call once we are done here. Whistle must have been second because she's okay, but Ben lost." Eddie let Dacey paint the rest of the picture.

"Cole and Layton?"

"Cole ran when I shot Layton with his gun. Coward that he was, wish I could have made a clean finish of this."

Dacey lifted her head to meet his eyes. "Thank you for this, I mean it."

"I told you, he wasn't going to win this. Now, listen well because we don't have time; he fell on his own, understand? You were going to run for it, he tripped you, couldn't stop, and down he went."

She nodded, looking towards the truck. "Got it." Pride at her unquestioning agreement filled him.

Chapter 33

Shatter Me

"Dacey!" Josie's scream split the air as she leapt from the truck before it stopped moving. "I saw Cole hauling ass away and I just, are you okay?" Josie was speaking so fast, Dacey's head spun.

Eddie held up a hand. "She needs medical attention, but she's going to live." The sight of a sheriff's office car pulling up made the man tense. "Who the hell is that?" If it were anyone but the sheriff, they were about to have more problems than relief.

"Some guy named Dean, I think? Who cares, what happened here?" Josie was hysterical as she lifted Dacey's face, looking it over.

Eddie rose to his feet, crossing the driveway in a few clipped strides, he met Grant halfway as he sprinted toward them, a tall blonde man hot on his heels. "Eddie! Josie said that the guy gunning it down the drive was–" He stopped dead, taking in the blood soaking the face before him. "Hell's fucking bells Eddie!"

"Dispatch, I'm going to need an ambulance out here, stat." Dean was speaking into his walkie-talkie as he surveyed Eddie, green eyes looking past to the two women in front of the barn. Ace and Whistle ran over, covered in just as much blood as the humans around them.

Eddie buried his hands in Whistle's warm sticky fur, closing his eyes to accept the wet kisses she covered him in. It helped to ground him and regain some of his bearings. "I don't need one, Dacey will, though. Fucker broke her nose and some ribs, she thinks." Eddie supplied, waving back towards the barn.

"Where's Seth?" Grant asked, a frown deepening the creases between his eyes.

"Fell out of the hayloft where he had her cornered. She was trying to run for it when he attempted to trip her, misjudged where he was going I guess, went right on through. The one not far from him had a gun on me, we got into a wrestling match over it and he was shot during it. Dogs tore the throat out of one who was watching the doors, but he had a gun hidden away, surprised they weren't shot." Eddie was rambling information, unaware of how hard he was shaking until Grant pressed a hand to his shoulder.

"Come on, come sit down before you fall down, you're pale as a ghost." Guiding him to the back of his truck, Grant dropped the tailgate for him. "Breathe for me, we can worry about all of this later when Dean asks after we get you both to the hospital."

"I don't want to go to the hospital for my issues! They're just gonna slap band-aids on them, and I can do that my damn self. We need to focus on Dacey." Eddie snapped, forcing the tremors down. Climbing to his feet, he accepted the shoulder offered to him, leaning on it until his legs grew steady.

Dean waved them back to the squad car where Josie had managed to coax Dacey. The younger blonde had a silver shock blanket wrapped around her shoulders, head bowed. Eddie could see the way her eyes saw nothing, and knew no matter what anyone said or did, she wasn't registering any of it. In the distance, the wail of sirens split the air, the racket startling birds into flight from the trees around them.

The young sheriff stood up from where he crouched, one hand resting on Josie's shoulder. "She won't tell me anything."

"Can't blame her, can you? Give her some time, get her statement at the hospital if it comes down to it," Grant assured him.

"Won't matter now, calvary has once again arrived." Eddie hooked a thumb over his shoulder at the ambulance, spraying gravel in its haste. Shoulders slumping, his feet dragged as they carried him to Dacey's side. Josie looked up at him, eyes brimming with unshed tears. When he held a hand out, she laced their fingers together, allowing him to pull her to her feet. "Come on, let's keep out of the way."

She nodded, lacing their fingers together tight enough, the tips of hers blanched white, causing the old, chipped pink polish to stand out. Her stomach churned, and her heart was pounding so hard it seemed to echo around in her mind. He pulled her close to him, hugging her for the first time since they reunited. Resting her head on his shoulder, they swayed together, doing their best to ignore the indistinguishable chatter behind them.

One rough voice broke through, shaking on each word. "Eddie? Please, I need you."

At the name, Josie flinched, hands fisting in the back of his shirt.

Eddie caught her chin, forcing her to meet his gaze. "I promise you, she will need you again soon. But for now, let her make her own choices."

Calming her breathing, she took a step back, letting him go. "If you put a toe out of line, Eddie, even she can't save you."

Her words were met with a snort and a condescending pat on the back. "Sure Princess, I'll keep that in mind." Pushing through the EMS, he moved to Dacey's side. Seeing her strapped down on the stretcher, neck brace in place, caused a wave of nausea to slam into him. "Listen to them and do as they say. If you don't, this is only going to take longer." Doing his best to ignore the way each breath rattled, he lifted her hand to kiss it.

"Come with me." She begged, reaching toward him.

He took a step toward her, only for his path to be blocked by one of the EMS. The man held up a hand, looking from where they were loading Dacey to Eddie, before his eyes flicked to Josie. "Are you family? We cannot allow anyone that is not family, in the ambulance."

"You better let him in with her or else I am going to have something to say about it later, Mack." Dean stepped in, jabbing a finger into his chest. "You know just as much as I do what these ladies mean to them. Get the fuck out of his way."

A weighted silence hung in the air for a beat before Mack stepped out of the way, motioning for Eddie to follow him. When the doors closed with a final slam, it took less than a minute for the driver to peel out. The group shielded themselves from the flying rocks, Dean cursing a bit when a few hit the patrol truck.

Watching it pull away, disappearing around the bend of the driveway, Grant cleared his throat. "Josie, we need to get loaded up, come on." Taking her by the elbow, he nodded to Dean. "Do you want to ride with us, or are you gonna take your truck?"

"I'll give you an escort, get you there quicker." Dean offered, pulling out the beat-up Walkie-Talkie. "Dispatch, doing an escort." A female voice replied, confirming they understood. "Let me know when y'all are ready."

Grant clapped his hands together. "Right. Josie, get that paddock over there opened for me. I only have two bulls left on the trailer, but we can't leave them. Dean, gonna need you to help me get them unloaded, guide me in, would you? But first, move Eddie's truck and trailer. Watch the horses, the bay is a beast. Back it over toward the chutes, nowhere special just out of the way with room to unload."

Josie snapped out of her daze, turning to face the men. "Got it." Without another word, she turned on her heel, rushing toward the barns.

Watching her go, Dean turned to Grant. "Keys in it? Or do you think they took them?"

"Chances are they're in it, but if they aren't, I got a spare in mine. Just let me know."

"Got it." Dean jogged to the truck, slowing when a loud whinny split the air. A second horse joined in, creating a call back from the herds hidden in various pastures. The horse that started it all called louder, kicking and pawing at the trailer. "I know, I know. I'm hurrying." He left the trailer, climbing in to crank the engine, when a pathetic whine startled him. A small, filthy puppy curled up on the floorboard lifted her head.

Blood streaked her fur from a cut across her muzzle, and she bared her tiny teeth at him when he reached out. "Easy baby, it's okay, I promise. Come on up here, that's a baby. Wanna help me move the trailer?" He coaxed, reaching out slower to stroke her head. She snarled at him when his fingers brushed over a lump on her head, backing further away until she ran into the door. “No, no. Stop that before you hurt yourself worse.” Dean tried to coax. A knock at the window caused him to jerk around with a strangled curse. “Damn it!”

Grant couldn’t fight the laugh that escaped him. “Sorry about that. Just wondering what’s going on? We need to hurry this up.”

“Not stalling on purpose, just having a couple of heart attacks in here. Figured Dacey could use the company. Anyway, that little ball of filth caused the first one.” One hand waved toward the puppy, now watching them, ears perked up.

“What the hell is that?” Stalking around the cab, he yanked the passenger side open. The pup scrambled not to fall out, tiny back legs kicking wildly to haul herself back in. “I got ya, I got ya.” Scooping her up, Grant looked her over, ignoring the way she snapped at his hands, wiggling around like his touch burned. “No idea where she came from, but she wasn’t with us this weekend. Bet this one belongs to Dacey, cause Whistle would eat her alive if Eddie tried to bring another dog in.”

“Whatever you say, just letting you know she ‘bout made me piss my pants. What do you want to do with her?”

“I’ll take her to the barn, there’s an empty stall I can stick her in for now.”

“Are you two gonna stand around yappin’ or are we gonna do this thing?” Josie shouted at them from where she stood with a gate open.

“Right, right. Sorry about that. Just pull up at this point along the front barn, but keep the door shut. Until I get Josie over there, you hear how he can be.” As though he heard, Cash planted a hoof so hard against the trailer wall it made Grant flinch. “I’m surprised they have a damn trailer at this point.” He grumbled, slamming the door with more force than necessary.

It took Dean a few tries before he got the set up close enough to the barn he could call it good. Leaving it, he hurried over to help Josie, guiding Grant into the pen. They worked quickly to get the bulls unloaded, splitting the work of checking water tanks, shutting gates and getting them settled.

When they finished, Josie shot Grant a thumbs up, following the trailer out with Dean. Watching him pull away to park, she glanced at the man walking with her. "Thank you for this."

He shot her a confused look. "For what? Being a good person?"

"For helping us, for not just questioning everything."

"Well, I know Grant, and you may not remember me, but I know you. You two were always amazing kids, and your Pawpaw was a huge part of how I got to where I am. He'd come back and whoop my ass if I let you hang."

"Still, don't you have to do your job instead of helping us?"

"I do, and I promise you that's next on my list. But when you're the boss, you can yell at yourself later." He assured her.

Grant met them halfway to the trailer where Cash was still throwing a tantrum. "Yell at yourself? Or have your wife chew you out so bad you sleep on the bar?" He teased, motioning for Dean to follow him around the side. Josie shot them a curious look, opening the door. "You know Bailey, she was in your year."

Josie took a minute to wrack her memory, coming up with a short, friendly, strawberry blonde. "Her parents own Crossroads Bar, right?"

"We bought it from them a couple years back, she runs it now while I do this," Dean replied with a small smile at the thought. "Anyway, what can I do now?"

"We got this. Go ahead and do what you need to in there." Grant lifted his chin toward the horse barn. "I'm gonna have to take these guys straight to the calving barn until we are given the all clear on that one."

"You got it, just holler if you need me." Tipping his Stetson, he left them to gather his equipment from the squad truck.

Josie turned to the trailer, unlatching the back door. "I'll hand you Buckshot, take her wherever you need to and I'll follow with Cash." Dropping the bar down, she eased up alongside her mare. Buckshot shifted her weight, whickering a low greeting, searching for a treat as she did. "Sorry girl, nothing right now. Come on, backup for me." Doing as she was told, Buckshot allowed herself to be backed off. Her head shot up as she cleared the door, calling back to the herd making their way up to fence lines.

Grant tugged it back toward him. "You can meet them later, we got bigger problems." Walking her toward the barn, he stopped halfway, watching Josie get dragged out by Cash. He danced on the end of the lead, head high, ignoring the woman yanking at him. "Come on, you got him." He muttered, taking half a step toward her.

The day's anger boiled over, a scream of her own splitting the air. "Cash! If you don't knock it the fuck off right now, I swear to you I'll fucking gut you myself!" Snapping the lead-line at his feet, she forced him in circles, making him focus on her. "Pull your worthless head out of your ass! Now is not the time!" Something in her tone, and the way she made him move his feet, gained his attention. Lowering his head, he slowed his race around her. "Thank you. Now, come on."

Satisfied, Grant turned away from them, coaxing Buckshot into the barn.

Chapter 34

Bandaids don't fix bullet holes

Of all the places Eddie would have placed bets on seeing again in one weekend, a hospital was not at the top of his list. The hard chair under him creaked with each shift of weight, protesting the constant movement. Its complaints blended with the inaudible voices drifting around him, forming an unending white noise. His hands were buried in his hair tight enough he wouldn't be surprised if chunks didn't wash out later and his teeth were ground together. One grueling hour they had kept him away from her; if they thought he'd last another, they were out of their minds.

People drifted past like he didn't even exist, from nurses and doctors down to the cleaning lady. They all just wandered off through the double doors without even a glance. When the admission doors slid open, Eddie glanced up, half expecting just another patient. Shooting to his feet, he snatched up the hat abandoned on the empty chair beside him. "Grant!" Rushing toward the trio walking in, he waved at the off hospital staff members streaming in and out.

"How is she?" Josie cut in, stepping between Eddie and Grant.

"No idea, they won't let me back there."

Grant frowned, moving past them both toward the reception desk. "Excuse me, ma'am, I need to know about a young woman you brought in earlier? Dacey Hempen?" His heart rate kicked up a beat every second he stood still. The assault of antiseptic was doing its best to bring him to his knees with old and new memories alike. Why was it always his kids? Why couldn't they be spared? Or at least learn to spare his blood pressure at this rate.

"Unless you're family, I can't tell you." The woman replied, never even looking up from the charts spread before her. Viciously, she slashed through a line on one, leaving a mark in a red so deep it resembled drying blood.

"That is my goddamn daughter!" Grant snapped, hands slamming down on the wooden top. "And if who I am to her is questioned one more time this weekend, I'll start kicking doors open myself!"

Her head snapped up, jaw hanging open. "Sir! I ask you to refrain from shouting and using physical threats! If you had told me that prior, I would have looked!" Standing, she shot him a dirty look. "Now, wait here while I get the doctor." Turning her back to the group, she strode off down the hall.

Looking around them, Dean gave a light cough. "Eddie, look man, I hate to do this, but I have to get your statement. I'll make it as quick as possible, because as soon we can get in her room, I have to talk to her alone and report back."

"For fuck's sake, fine. Where do you want to do this?"

"Outside, don't need half the county knowing more than they will by morning. Dispatch already told me reporters are sniffing around trying to get the story."

Grant turned his head, eyes narrowing. "Do I need to be concerned?"

Dean shook his head. "Not yet. Can't make any promises."

"Are we doing this or what?" Eddie snapped, stalking toward the exit.

Pinching the bridge of his nose, Dean clenched his eyes shut. Counting down from five, he followed Eddie out after a second round. Watching them step out, a weak, exhausted chuckle slipped from Grant. What was his life becoming?

Turning away, he reached out to Josie, taking her hand. She looked up, tears slipping down her pale cheeks. "Come on now, she's a tough cookie. After all we've been through this weekend you think this is what's gonna break her? Hell, bet if I tell her you even had a notion of that, she'd climb outta that bed to fight you."

His words earned a watery laugh. "I know, I know. I just…" she motioned toward the hall. "I don't even know. My mind can't stop, yet not a bit of what is going through it makes sense."

"Been there before. I promise it doesn't last, if that helps."

"Not even a little bit, but I appreciate you trying."

"Excuse me," the nurse made her way over to them. "You're allowed back in the room." Without waiting for them, she turned. Leaping to her feet, Josie rushed to follow, dragging Grant along. Not every room passed was occupied, but some of the ones that were chilled them in turn. While a few seemed harmless, more than one made bile scaled the backs of throats. A head splitting chorus of machines backed it all, some letting out whistles while others hummed uneven beats.

"Here she is. Don't expect a whole lot out of her, the doctor informed me they had to give her a mild sedative. That, combined with the painkillers she is on, she may not be conscious until tomorrow. As soon as the doctor is able, he will be in."

Neither Grant nor Josie were able to ask a question before the nurse strutted from the room, closing the door behind her. Josie sagged back against the warm chest behind her, hand covering her mouth to muffle a sob.

What little of her face that showed under the oxygen mask was pale under her tan, all framed in a wispy halo of tangled, blonde hair. Tubes and wires battled for dominance along her arms and the tip of one finger was hidden under a clamp made of plastic. Turning in his arms, Josie let loose a muffled wail, fresh tears soaking his shirt. He didn't say a word, just held her close, face buried in her hair. The scent of strawberries somewhat masked the nausea-inducing hospital smell, the soft locks catching his tears.

How long they stood that way no one could have said, but they broke apart when Eddie and Dean joined them. Dean tilted his head toward the hall, wordlessly asking Grant to join him. Letting Josie go, he gave her a gentle pat on the back. "I'll be right back." He assured her. She accepted the box of tissues Eddie held out, turning her back on the room to blow her nose.

"I got this. Do what you need to." Eddie muttered, rubbing the trembling back beside him. Grant could see the way a muscle ticked in his jaw, eyes red and brimming with unshed tears. He guided Josie toward the bed, snagging a chair on his way. Its legs scraped along the floor, making him grit his teeth harder, inhaling sharply through his nose.

"Sorry." She said.

No answer came, she sank down into the hard plastic with a sniffle.

Crossing the room to grab the next chair, he carried it to the opposite side of the bed. Dropping his hat on the side table, he settled in. Reaching out, mindful of everything, he took Dacey's limp hand in his own, feeling Josie's eyes boring a hole into the top of his head. Ignoring them, he studied Dacey's face. Faint streaks of blood still marred her skin, disappearing below the collar of the hospital gown. Searching the area around him, he spotted a small stack of washrags across the room. Hauling himself to his feet, he walked over to them, selecting the softest he could find. Wandering into the bathroom, he ran the water until it was warm and dipped the rag into it. He wrang it out, grabbing a hand towel to carry with him.

Josie cast him a curious look, taking in the handful of things he set on the side table. "I can't stand to see her like this," He explained, swiping at the spot by Dacey's mouth.

"I can help." Josie offered, rubbing at her eyes with a tissue to clean them up.

"Nah, just try to relax." Eddie wasn't about to admit if she took over, he would have another breakdown. Teeth clenched, he focused on cleaning Dacey up, each gentle swipe soothing his nerves. Acid burned the back of his throat, looking down at her this way, spurred on by a fresh wave of rage and hatred. If he could kill the bastard all over again, he would. But it wasn't only at Seth that they screamed at him. This was his fault, and his alone. After Saturday, how could he have just assumed everything would be fine? He had looked into her trusting eyes and sworn her a promise.

For what? Nothing.

Once more, Dacey was laying in a hospital bed, only this time she was far worse. What good was he doing? The rushing roar of blood in his ears drowned out the machines' chorus, giving way to a deafening, high-pitched ringing.

Dropping the rag down with the other things, he dried her off. Even with it being only in spots, the cleaning helped make her look better. He turned to Josie. "I need to go for a minute. You gonna be okay?" His voice was rough, scraping his aching throat.

"Go ahead. Grant should be back any minute." She assured him, never looking up from where she stroked her sister's hand. It was all he needed to hear before he was striding out of the room and down the hall.

Chapter 35

Just Breathe

Dacey knew if they didn't let her go home soon, she would go mad from the racket of monitors hooked up to her. Her eyes trailed up the IV cord from the crook of her left elbow to the bag of saline solution hanging from the stand, not even remembering when they had put it in. Looking away from the clear liquid to where Josie slept, head pillowed on Eddie's shoulder, Dacey felt a pang of guilt. Her sister looked hollow, dark shadows smudged under her eyes from stress and lack of sleep from spending two days in the hospital chairs, never leaving her side unless forced to.

From what little Dacey could see of his face, Eddie wasn't much better off. The pair had refused to take watching her in shifts, bickering quietly in the hallway over who would stay and who would go the day she had been admitted, from what Riley had told her. They had been overruled by Grant putting his foot down. They could both stay.

Shifting to find a more comfortable position on the hard mattress, she winced. Even with the medicine feeding directly into the drip line, she still felt the occasional sharp stab of pain. Breathing through it, she waited for it to pass. When it had, she opened her eyes once more to stare unseeing at the ceiling, almost wishing a nurse would come to check on her to break the loneliness sinking in. She knew neither Josie nor Eddie would mind if she woke them up, but Dacey didn't have the heart. She remembered all too well how uncomfortable the chairs were to sleep in when she had snagged rare moments waiting on Josie to recover. How the lights, no matter how dim, always cut through her eyelids like headlights aimed directly at them. She had done her best to make them leave ever since waking, assuring them that she would be fine, but her pleas had fallen on deaf ears.

A soft tap roused her from her sullen thoughts. "Come in." Dacey called out, keeping her voice low. Eddie stirred, lifting his head to blink dazedly. The door cracked open, and a nurse slipped in, glancing from the man now sitting up to where Dacey was huddled. She was a petite thing, glasses perched on gray hair cut short, framing a kind face.

"Just need to check your vitals, get a level on your pain, and a few other things." She explained.

"Alright." Dacey worked to sit up, accepting the warm, soft hands that were slightly dry from so much washing. When the woman was satisfied Dacey wouldn't fall back against the pillows once more, she picked up the clipboard housed at the foot of her bed, reading it over. From there, she made her way to the IV stand to check fluid rates and add in a small syringe of medicine. Every step was explained to Dacey, waiting to be sure they were understood before the next one was performed. Eddie monitored them both like a hawk, gaze trailing the nurse.

Josie stirred, almost falling off of her chair when she did. Eddie caught her instinctively, patting her back once he was sure she wouldn't make a second attempt at making friends with the floor.

She thanked him, turning to smile at Dacey just noticing she was awake. "You doing okay?" Josie asked, scooting her chair closer to the bed.

"As well as I can be. I'll be better when I'm out of here." Dacey groused.

"That should be later today! The doctor will be on the floor at eight a.m, making his usual rounds and then will come to talk to you. At least, to my understanding, that's the plan. For now, you need to focus on getting the rest you need." The nurse chimed in, tucking the scratchy blanket firmly back in place.

Dacey perked up at her words, offering Josie and Eddie a grin. "Perfect."

"Don't get overly excited, it ain't like you get to go home and just get to work. You're gonna wish you had stayed a little longer the moment the good stuff wears off." Eddie warned her.

"Like hell I will! None of us have slept more than a few hours since I got here." Dacey argued.

"So? We knew what we were signing up for, so don't even give me that crap," Josie said, arms crossed. "Don't sit there telling me that you want out of here for our comfort, because we could have gone to take a nap at any point at home. This is our choice, not yours."

"She's got you there. Now what's your next try?" Eddie asked with a small smirk.

Dacey offered them a rude gesture, eyes narrowed. The nurse smothered a laugh with a shake of her head, picking the clipboard up once more, filling it out with new information. “Alright, is there anything you need? Any of you, before I keep making my rounds?” She asked, looking up from the paper. Her question received three separate head shakes. “Okay then, I’m not far if you need me, but if you do and I am in a room, someone at the nurses’ station will be happy to help. Since I hopefully won’t see you tonight on my next shift, you take care of yourself.” She patted Dacey’s leg, offering the young woman a caring smile.

“I promise, Jennifer, and thank you for putting up with me. I know I haven’t been your best patient.” Dacey admitted. “I appreciate everything you’ve done.”

“Now you hush, you were better than a number of them, I can tell you that much.” With a wink, the nurse stepped back out into the hall.

Eddie waited for the click of the latch, standing up to stretch and pop his back. Josie joined him, taking a few steps around the room to get feeling back in her legs. “I’m going to go grab a smoke since I’m up anyway, Josie, you want to come?” He offered, patting his shirt pocket to be sure there was a pack.

“Yeah, I could use one. Maybe find a soda as well, if there’s a vending machine around.”

“Found one yesterday when Grant came to visit her down on the third floor just past the waiting room there. I can take you before we hit the patio.” He turned to Dacey, reaching out to push a piece of hair from her face. “Don’t do anything stupid while we are gone, okay? No getting up on your own, no trying to get something for yourself. If you need it, ask for it.”

“Since when have you been my boss?” Dacey asked, tilting her head.

Eddie tweaked the end of her nose, earning a face aimed his way. "Since you thought you'd be independent yesterday. We'll be back."

Josie stepped past him to press a kiss to her sister's forehead, offering a careful hug with it. "Love you, Dace. Please, just be sure to ask if you need help."

Dacey sighed, laying back as far as she could manage. "Fine, fine. But you better bring me a soda back, too." She pointed a finger at Eddie as she spoke.

"I'll think about it." Gesturing for Josie to lead the way, he trailed out behind her. "Do you want to take the elevator or the stairs down? I don't mind either of them, but I'm not going to make the decision for you."

She waved at a passing nurse, thinking over his offer. "Stairs work for me so we can walk off some of this god-awful food."

"Can't argue that." Locating the sign, he guided her to it, pushing it open. The sounds of it hitting the wall echoed around them, Eddie flinching at the sudden, loud noise.

Josie rubbed her ears, shaking her head. "Maybe this wasn't a good idea." She joked, grabbing the handrail.

"Could think of a million reasons To have a ringing in my ears, that wasn't one of them." They fell silent, paying closer attention than normal in their exhausted states. Josie paused on the final landing, holding the railing tightly. "You okay?" he asked, moving closer. Her cheeks were flushed, chest rising and falling rapidly as she struggled to draw in a breath. "Easy, easy now. Can you make it to the floor?"

She managed a tiny nod, allowing him to guide her to the bottom step. A soft wheeze escaped her throat the harder she tried to breathe. "Just take it easy okay, I'll be right back." Hauling the door open, he rushed inside, almost running over a janitor in his haste. Ignoring the indignant shouts following him, he kept his focus on finding the assistance needed. A nurse was leaving a room, pulling a small tray of items in her wake. Spotting him, she took a step back. "Wait! Wait, stop. My friend is having an asthma attack in the stairwell. She needs an inhaler, now." He called to her, gesturing toward where Josie was. The fear melted from the woman's features to be replaced with one of determination.

"Show me." She jogged to keep up with his long strides, flagging down a coworker for more help. Pulling the door open for them, Eddie did his best to keep out of their way, watching how they swooped in on her. Josie's breath was rattling by then, chest and stomach both pulling in as she fought to draw in air. It had been years since he had witnessed her struggling so badly, part of him wishing he could help her. Instead, he stepped away, letting the nurses carry her into the hallway, setting her down on a spare bed to the best of their ability. When she was sure the other nurse had the situation in hand, the one Eddie had flagged down first ran toward the medicine cart.

Josie's fingers scrambled against the sheet, seeking purchase to ground herself. Gathering his senses back from wherever they had run to, Eddie moved to her side. Reaching out, he took her hand, thumb rubbing over the back of it. "She's getting the inhaler. Just keep calm. You know panic doesn't help, sis." The old, unused name rolled off his tongue. It seemed to distract her a little, their eyes meeting briefly before the nurse was back. She had forgone the simple small piece used in favor of a large mask looking item she pressed over Josie's nose and mouth.

"Breathe deeply." She commanded, pressing the cartridge down. Josie tried, chest rising in search of the medicine. "Again." The nurse coaxed, dispatching a second round into the mask. This time, Josie was able to take a larger breath, lungs seeming to clear of the thick coating that clogged them. "Last time, sweetie, one more good breath for me." Her soothing words came with the final puff that was drawn much deeper than the previous ones. "There you go, that's good. Now you keep this here until you know you're not going to need it." She turned to the other woman. "Laura, stay here with her for me, please? I need to let the others know what's going on."

Laura offered a nod, eyes never leaving Josie as she closed her eyes to focus more on her breathing exercises. Eddie hadn't let her hand go through it all and, as her body relaxed, he felt a soft squeeze. Returning it to assure her he wouldn't leave, he risked rubbing small circles on her back. "There you go, sis, just calm down. You're gonna be fine now that these wonderful ladies have patched your ass up."

She opened her eyes, offering him a thin smile. "I'm pretty sure if I got any calmer, I'd be asleep." The adrenaline from fear mixing with the medicine started a light tremor in her limbs. They both noted it, Josie swallowing against her dry throat. "Can you go get us those sodas? That tastes beyond foul." Her voice was a thin rasp, making them both wince.

"Yeah, it's not too far down the hall from here. Just don't get any wild ideas to go on the warpath while I'm gone." Stepping away, he looked her over one more time to be sure she was going to make it.

Keeping out of the way of staff, he made his way down the hall, trying to follow his memories. Most of the floors looked the same, all sterile whites and mint greens that seemed endless. He did his best to follow signs pointing him toward the waiting room, only misreading one by mistake. By the time he reached the tiny, closet sized room that housed the vending machines, doctors and the day shift nurses had trickled in. They paid him little mind, only a few casting curious looks his way as he dropped quarters in the slots. He ignored them in turn, forcing himself to the task. Sodas in hand, he took a cursory glance over what little snacks remained behind fingerprinted plastic. Spotting a lone pack of Big Red gum, Eddie fished out the last nickel he had to feed the habit of his main charge.

"Are you finding everything okay?" A gentle voice caused him to look up, meeting the eyes of a petite redhead. She smiled at him, head cocked.

"Yeah, just stocking up on some things while we wait." He replied, waving a can.

"Do you need any help? My shift isn't for another half an hour. I got here early to chat with some of my patients, but it seems one left yesterday while I was off, and the other is still sleeping. I don't mind." She offered, nodding toward his full arms.

Eddie studied her for a second. "No, thanks though. We aren't even on this floor. I just found these wandering around and figured I might as well use them."

"I see. Well, you have a lovely day then, sir." She left it at that, turning on a heel to leave him be. Letting her get a decent head-start, he tucked the gum into the pocket with his wallet to keep from dropping it. Sure that he would be alone, he began the trek back to Josie. More staff were starting to fill the halls, the noise an unwanted contrast to the peaceful quiet of the night. He almost wished he had returned home the night before as a dull ache formed in the base of his skull, threatening to spread.

When he came into sight, Josie slid from the bed to unsteady legs. "Oh, thank God you're here. Everyone kept stopping to ask me if I was okay, what was wrong, and I wasn't sure what to do. There were so many questions from so many angles!"

"It's a hospital, that's what they do. As long as you were honest and didn't tell them some bullshit story, it'll be okay." He offered out a can of Dr. Pepper that was gratefully accepted. "Do you just want to head back to her room? I don't think smoking is going to be the smartest route for you."

"Ya' think?" Josie drawled, shaking her head. Taking a deep drink of cold, sticky liquid, she relished the way it soothed her throat. "Thanks for this, by the way. For all of it." The simple phrase seemed to belie more than just the soda she clutched.

"I may be a grade-A asshole, but you're still family at the end of all the differences. I'm not going to let you drown, even when you piss me off beyond belief." He offered an arm, noting how she shuffled a few steps. Josie hesitated a second, staring almost disbelievingly at the gesture. Giving in, she linked their arms, leaning on him just enough to assure them both she wouldn't land on the ground. Leading her toward the elevator, Eddie mulled over what to say. They were on thin ice that was ready to splinter beneath their feet at any second, the weak truce of her attack a thin shield from their normal fighting. Anything could shatter it. When the doors slid open with a happy ping, he helped her inside, keeping closer to the far wall to avoid the people still waiting for their floor. She yawned, head landing on his bicep, closing her eyes.

"This day just started and already I want it over." Her words were little more than a whisper to not offend anyone close enough to hear.

"I am right there with you." Getting off at their floor, he guided her to Dacey's room. She sat up at the sight of them, gearing up for what seemed to be a good scolding.

Spotting Josie, it died off. "Josie! What happened? Are you okay?" She struggled to the end of her bed, setting monitors off.

"Calm down, calm down! I'll be okay! Stop it before you hurt yourself all over again!" Josie raised her hands, motioning for Dacey to get back in the right spot. A nurse appeared out of nowhere, it seemed, eyes scanning the room to spot the problem.

"What's going on in here? Are you okay?" She moved to the screens, pushing keys to stop the incessant high-pitched beeps.

"I'm fine! These stupid things scream because the floor is the floor at this point." Dacey groused, wrinkling her nose.

"May I remind you they need to be this sensitive for valid reasons? You are not meant to be making rapid motions, nor are you to be yelling. What is the meaning of all this?"

Eddie moved between them, passing Dacey her soda. "We startled her. Went out for a walk and to get something to drink, her sister had an asthma attack and she's seeing the aftermath of it."

"Did you have to tell her like that?" Josie sighed, sinking onto the hard plastic chair once again.

"Better than lying, isn't it? Or beating around the bush?"

The nurse cleared her throat, gaining their attention. "May I do my job now, please?" she asked, foot tapping. Getting out of her way, Eddie joined Josie, still watching Dacey. The younger woman made a face at him before giving her undivided attention to her caregiver. "Well, it seems like whatever you did to set these off hasn't done any further damage or complications. Dr. Powell will be in around ten to look you over himself, so feel free to order breakfast and just sit tight. If you two need meal tickets, I can get them for you. Or are you going to be leaving to eat?"

"We're staying here, so they would be appreciated." Josie supplied.

"Then I'll get them to you as soon as I can. Go ahead and order, if they give you any issues on delivery, if I am not back, send them up to the station." Turning to Dacey, she crossed her arms. "And you, young lady, need to stop trying to stay longer."

"I promise nothing."

"Sounds about right. I'll be back later." She left, closing the door behind her.

As soon as she was gone, Dacey rounded on her sister. "You better start from the second you left and tell me every single detail until you got back here. Both of you. It's not right for you to be bossing me around and clucking over me like a worried mother hen, but then pretend nothing is going on with either of you. So, spill it, Josie."

Taking a deep breath, she did as Dacey asked, explaining everything so she would be in the loop. By the time she finished, her sister was red faced and holding her chest. "You mean to tell me that you're to the point you overexerted yourself because of me and yet you're both still here? Seriously? Josie, you can't take care of me if you're not taking care of yourself! That's not how this works!" Dacey snarled, voice breaking as she tried to keep herself controlled. "It's not that I don't appreciate you staying, but damn it, you both matter too! Why is this such a hard thing to understand?"

Josie let her rant, making sure she was done before speaking up. "I'm aware of that fact, but what you don't understand is that we aren't here just to be sure you're not dying on us. We're here because who knows what happens next? Seth is dead, Dacey, and all anyone knows is that you and Eddie were the only ones in the barn with him when it happened. You may have been cleared by the law around here, but that means nothing to his dad. His only son, the name of the family business, is gone. Don't you think he's going to retaliate? That family isn't known for just rolling over easily, you know that." She sighed, resigned to the fact this still wasn't over. "I'm not going to just leave my baby sister alone in a hospital of strangers with no idea what's going on. Now do you get it? I'll go through a hundred attacks before I go home to sleep properly."

Dacey could do nothing but sit wide eyed as it all sank in. "Fuck." She breathed, sinking in on herself. "I…I'm sorry." Her fingers twisted the blanket into unfamiliar shapes nervously. "With everything going on, I didn't think of it that way. None of it seemed to matter once he was gone other than I knew we were free of him."

"Yeah, well, I had that tunnel vision until Grant had a very unwanted visitor to the ranch yesterday. No, don't even ask right now, that's for when we get back, okay? Let's just get some food, settle down, and go from there." Josie took Dacey's hands. "We've gotten this far, it's only going to get better from here, okay? I promise you that." Kissing her forehead, Josie stepped back. "Now then, we need to have a serious talk since the cat's out of the bag." Drawing her chair up to the edge of the bed, she looked back at Eddie. "If you think now is a good time?"

"Beats getting to the ranch and finding out the hard way." His chair joined the cluster.

"Vanessa showed up yesterday with Ryan, of all people. Turns out, years ago, when Pawpaw died, she was the one who called our father. Never broke off contact with him even after we were off the property from my understanding. When he showed up to talk to Dean and Clint, she was his next stop. Guess they had some fond memories to share about life the past few years, then had the audacity to show up at the ranch unexpectedly and unwelcome together. Grant kept his calm, but Riley said it was a close call on it. Rider had to be escorted off to the main house. Guess, he didn't care much for what Ryan was saying about us. We can ask him ourselves later."

Dacey looked up, closing her eyes. "Can you stop fucking with us at any time? Just, please? Whoever the hell is listening and shoving us off cliffs needs to know I want a break." She pleaded, dropping her head back down to look at them. "How are you handling this?" The question was aimed at Eddie, who rocked his chair up on the back legs.

He shrugged. "How the hell do you expect? Crying in my bunkhouse or something? She can't touch the ranch, not legally anymore. Not only is it mine for that very reason, but Grant's lawyers also sealed up every loophole, loose end, and everything in between so tight a mouse's ass is looser."

Josie never dropped her gaze from his, expression unreadable. He shot her a warning look of his own, so slight that Dacey never noticed either of them. She shuffled to the edge of the bed, swinging her legs over to kick her feet. "Now what? We just head back in and keep swinging? Why is he here, anyway? I thought they sent the body home?"

"They did. He's here to argue about the final ruling, which is why Dean was there again, too. He's demanding that the investigation be reopened, but what he doesn't realize is that we can turn it against him. He doesn't have a leg to stand on." Josie assured her. "All I ask is that you keep away from him so we don't have a fight on our hands."

"I can keep my hands to myself."

"Like hell! You throw hands like a beast when you're mad," Josie retorted.

"Not unless they've earned it. Eddie always taught me not to throw the first punch, but be damned sure I'm throwing the last one."

The man smirked with a nod. "You're right, I did. But just this once, I'm going to agree with her as much as I don't want to. We don't want him to get anything on us at any point. If you clock him a good one, he can nail you with assault."

"Fine, fine. I swear I won't touch him. What about Vanessa? Who gets that warning?" Dacey asked, shifting the IV line out of the way.

"That would be me." Josie's reply earned an incredulous look.

"You? Josie, I've never seen you fight a day in your life." Dacey deadpanned.

"She's why we were shipped off. She's why we are even in this place. Trust me, I may not be the strongest person in the room, but I'll rip her hair out to throw it like confetti." Josie assured her.

"Why don't we burn that bridge when we get there?" Eddie reminded them. "Not a lot either of you can do in the shapes you're in."

"Shut up." Dacey's words did little to hide the smile she offered him. "You'd be surprised what I can do being broken like I am."

"Promises, promises." He quipped, earning a pillow to the face. The nervous energy that had been sinking in around them broke, giving way to weak laughter. "Now then, who's hungry?"

Chapter 36

Bring it on Home

When the trio finally stepped out of the sliding glass doors to the parking lot hours later, Josie wanted to sing. "Sunshine! Fresh air!" She allowed herself a quick twirl, arms thrown wide.

"Check yourself before you wreck yourself." Eddie cautioned. Fishing the keys from his pocket, he spun them around his finger. "If you are the reason we go back in, I'm going to drive off without you claiming you were never even here to begin with."

"I doubt that." Still, she calmed. Dacey linked their hands for the first time in so long Josie almost stopped. Playing it off, she stopped beside Eddie's truck. "I'm glad you're okay."

"Don't be thankful yet. We have no idea when this will be done." Pushing the latch just right, Dacey opened the finicky door. "Either way, I have no doubt this will be one hell of a fight to the top." When the engine fired up, Dacey turned the radio on, scanning every station she could find. Everyone passed with hardly a pause in her search.

"What are you looking for?" Eddie asked, tired of getting only a few clips of music.

"While you guys were asleep earlier last night, the nurses had the radio on a rock station and I could hear it. There's a song I am dying to find now, but I don't know what station." She explained, giving up to sit back.

He sighed and, to their surprise, began turning the dial to a station he knew well. "Can't say I have a clue what song it was, but this will be your best bet."

"Why am I shocked that you listen to this?" Dacey questioned.

"Because you automatically assumed that I only listen to country. Never stopped to think maybe I get tired of the same songs, Darlin'?"

Dacey flicked his wrist, earning a pinch to the end of her nose. Josie tried to keep composed, one hand covering her mouth as the two dissolved into a light-hearted slap fight. It ended quickly, Eddie resting his arm on the back of the seat, tapping along to the beat on Josie's shoulder. She caught his hand with hers, tossing it away, amusement plain on her face. "You are a pure child when you want to be."

He flipped her off, lips curved up at the edges. Their banter wasn't able to go any further when Dacey excitedly tapped his leg to gain attention. "This one! It's this one!" She turned the volume up, disappointed she couldn't sing along. Eddie did join in the vocals, though he kept his voice low enough Josie couldn't hear him. The song filled the cab, invading their senses until it sank into their very bones. When the next song came on right after with no breaks, they continued the session, Eddie singing slightly louder as Josie beat the dashboard in her best attempt at drums. Dacey could only tap her feet, using her legs to keep time to prevent jarring herself, but she gave it her all.

When their hometown came into sight, Eddie turned the radio down, lighting a cigarette. “Ya'll sure you're ready for this?” He mused, arm falling into place behind Dacey once more.

“Ready as we can ever be. What else can we do? I'm never going to run away again if I have anything to say about the situation. That shit was more than rough.” Dacey replied, chewing the inside of her lip. Josie nodded her agreement, knuckles stark where they clenched her jeans.

“Running isn't an option, not now that Grant and I have you home. With the Wheeler monsters helping us, you two couldn't be safer than if you lived underground in a secret bunker.”

“I mean, if you're offering to build one for us, I won't say no.”

“You're a wreck.” Eddie sighed, pinching the bridge of his nose.

“Like you didn't make me this way?” Dacey taunted, batting her eyelashes at him.

“Oh, I know I had help, ain't no way living with that thing in the passenger seat didn't have a hand in this.” He countered.

“Hey, now, I am innocent.” Joise argued, the ghost of a grin creeping in.

“If you're innocent, I'll just give you both the ranch and move along.”

Dacey offered a return wave to the passing truck. “It'll be mine one day anyway. I've always said that.”

Eddie reached out, taking her wrist in a gentle hold to keep from startling her. Lifting her hand up, he turned it around. “Funny, I don't see a ring there saying it will be.” He let it fall, smothering the urge to put one on it. She had grown up without him into a beautiful mess, one that he would be more than happy to bed and try breaking his walls down for. Never, since he was a young buck himself, had marriage ever crossed his mind. Yet here she was now, crashing into his life and demolishing the bachelor life he had settled in comfortably. What scared him the most was the fact he wasn't opposed to it. He wanted her, craved her more than any drug before her.

"Nor will there ever be a ring on that hand. She's always going to be my baby sister, so no growing up." Josie said, laughing as Dacey turned to her.

"I have to grow up sometime."

"No, you don't, Peter Pan. Just like I'm always staying in Never Never Land."

Eddie snorted, shaking his head. Turning down their driveway, he suddenly hit the brakes, arm moving to hold Dacey in place as he did, cursing the whole time. Dacey, meanwhile, was holding her breath to contain the string of vulgar words that flooded her brain at the pain.

"What the hell?" Josie snapped, lifting her hat out of her eyes. Eddie couldn't speak, anger rising within him so fast his vision clouded, ears ringing so loudly he didn't register her words. Throat dry, chest heaving, he battled the tremors that threatened to overcome him, hands instinctively clenching into fists around the steering wheel tight enough the leather squealed ever so faintly. Dacey smothered her own irritation, hand landing on his leg in a weak attempt to calm him. Josie looked as though she was going to be sick, her face an odd shade of pale green as she stared out the windshield.

There, standing in the driveway with her arms crossed midway through a shouting match with Grant and Dean, stood Vanessa with Ryan.

Acknowledgments:

To J.C Fuller: No matter how I try to write it, thank you doesn't cut it. I owe you so much for all you have helped me learn with this novel. From dealing with my poor writing, offering the best advice I could have ever had, all the way to putting up with me disappearing to do side quests on my own story so nothing was done on the main portion when it needed it. You both have helped me grow more than I could have thought possible. From my very soul, thank you. Thank you to the moon in the sky, the stars beyond, and very core of our world.

To Misty Walker: your stories helped me see that the "twisted" way I write is perfectly okay and CAN be done. There's no reason to hide what I like just to make others feel better about themselves or comfortable. To just write the story however however, it plays out in my head! ! And thank you so so, so much for putting up with me driving you banana sandwich since I found you on TikTok. You have become one of my favorite authors and your worlds help me have to have an escape when mine gets too hard on me. Thank you, a thousand times over to the Moon and stars above. You deserve to grace the shelves of bookstores across the globe with your work, and I will forever fight to make this a reality.

To Emily: Yet another TikTok friend who has been with me pretty much from the moment I chose to begin writing this story again. You've been a HUGE cheerleader, a wonderful friend, and an insanely creative assistant. I can't thank you enough for what you have done for this story, but just know that there are many areas here that are for you alone. You have more than earned them.

To my family and friends who have been with me this entire time; you are true rockstars. I know it's taken YEARS for me to write even ONE of the novels in my head head, but through it, none of you gave up on me. You have continued to do everything in your power to keep me going and remind me that this is something I've always been able to do. I love you all,all so deeply. John, Mom, and the rest, here it finally is. <3 The first of many to come. This never would have happened without any of you behind me,me. I truly owe it all to you

To Rae: You have been the best friend I could have ever asked for, dealing with so much from me over the years that I probably could pay off the therapy I cost you with how much I owe you. You've always pushed me to be my best, listened to me be a petulant child, and through it all kept the fire lit under my ass. With you, in my corner, I have never felt alone or lost no matter how upset I got with this story or wanted to give up on it. Even though you have more talent in your pinkie finger than I ever will, I'll forever be grateful.

To Kennedy Sutton: You're one of the most beautiful, kind souls I've been lucky enough to meet. When you saw a fellow indie author struggling, you went above and beyond for me. Picking me up off the floor, joking with me, and so much more I can't even begin to say. Ever since we started talking more, my life has become far brighter, you true Pirate Queen.

To Kirsha Fox: When you took a chance on interviewing me, it meant the world to me. And as soon as you saw someone in need, you stepped up like a true baddie. Between you and Kennedy I have laughed a lot, been picked up and dusted off, and given the best virtual hugs. Thank you, so so much.

To Rachel: Surprise! I told you this would be in my novella, but I knew all along it would be here! You have been one of the most helpful people when I start throwing random ideas at you, from art to booth set ups, you've given me honest feedback. Plus, having you in the background when I'm in the big sads always brightens my day!

To Natalie: Just like Rachel, you have put up with some truly insane ideas I've thrown your way. But you always made sure that even when I was being ridiculous (See 90% of our talks) you were beyond helpful. And, just like Rachel, I couldn't have gotten through some of my most depressive moments without your works.

Finally, to Misti. My emotional support Dino Nuggie. The woman who has gone above and beyond for not only this book, but for me. Words really don't do justice for how grateful I am that we met and became friends. You're a bad bitch, and we both know it. I could wax poetic about you for days (you've seen me do it) so I'm gonna keep this just short and sweet or we will both cry like toddlers. <3

About The Author

Ivy is a small town, country girl who devotes herself to being an amazing mother and loving wife while simultaneously running a business, writing novels, and working a full-time job. When she's not writing, she enjoys taking care of her horses and spending as much time making memories with her family as she can. Writing is her passion, and someday, she hopes to be a household name. If you'd like to stay up to date with Ivy and her books you can follow her below on her socials.